SCHEMES IN THE MONTH OF
March

Bilingual Press/Editorial Bilingüe

Address:

Editorial
Bilingual Press
Department of Foreign Languages
York College, CUNY
Jamaica, New York 11451
212-969-4047/4035

Business
Bilingual Press
552 Riverside Drive Suite 1-B
New York, New York 10027
212-866-4595

EMILIO DÍAZ VALCÁRCEL

SCHEMES IN THE MONTH OF
March

□ ■ □ ■ □

Translated by Nancy A. Sebastiani

Bilingual Press/Editorial Bilingüe
NEW YORK

ISBN: 0-916950-06-9
Printed simultaneously in a softcover edition. ISBN: 0-916950-05-0

Library of Congress Catalog Card Number: 76-45296

Printed in the United States of America

The editors wish to express their appreciation to Jerome S.
Bernstein, Tomás López Ramírez, and Xaé Reyes for their
revision of this translation.

Cover design by Richard S. Haymes

Photo by Guy Paizy

To the Puerto Rican revolutionaries

I ought to take care of a few things while I am alive.

VLADIMIR MAYAKOVSKY

. . . how alike are the groans of love to those of the dying.

MALCOLM LOWRY

There is such a thing as an excess of reality, an abundance that one can no longer tolerate.

WITOLD GOMBROWICZ

Did you say three, four in the morning? I'm really not sure because during those moments I don't listen to you, I can't listen to you. Did you throw in a curse? When you squeezed your lids together to imprison the sleep that threatened to escape like a predator into the underbrush, did you remember, in that intense fraction of a minute, our meeting in the overcrowded bus that afternoon, our chance meeting? Perhaps you thought about the old man in white with the dreadful black thread on his lapel, about your ancient aunt with her rusty hymen, about the warm afternoons when we would stroll through a park almost in ruins, under a row of oak trees, methodically scolding one another, or the refreshing outings to the beach, the nights when I would gather up my few coins and count them and recount them in order to dine out like an upper cruster at a particular restaurant in the old quarter of town. During that minute, overwhelming in its precision, you saw me set fire to a manuscript no one would publish, for which no reader would pay one red cent, you saw me tear my hair screaming disaster, that word disaster, my persistent best word. All you had to do was hear my lamentations to relate my "case" to a muddled reading of Freud, adopting the attitude of one who has been through it all? Perhaps just to save me, you undertook this adventure in which we immersed ourselves as in a labyrinth at whose end we could surmise a luminous exit, the transition to a fuller life, while the ships, engulfed in flames, were sinking in the harbor.

Driven by a dark sense of decorum, I never spoke to you of my nights at the boarding house, of my daily nightmares as I lay flattened on a small iron cot while the students played cards, ate, eagerly answered the telephone, turned to their homework amidst these familiar surroundings, impressing an exacted image onto the air, firm in their attitudes and intentions, so necessary among the trees, on the sidewalks, in their classrooms, clutching knives and napkins without worrying about an overturned glass, a grain of rice on a tie, without making excuses for partaking in the banquet and being alive and calling themselves by their own names. And I would spend many long hours trying to read the same paragraph, paralyzed with fear, coughing up phlegm, covering myself from head to toe with my blanket to keep the bees, which when I was at my worst filled the

1

room with their maddening drone, from landing on me and turning me into a dark, tortured hive, into a blob of wax, into the miserable recollection of a man.

It would have been stupid to tell you about the letters from my relatives and the brief menacing communiqués from Mancio which I'd throw into the basket as soon as I had opened the envelope. I had to encourage you, tell you that everything was coming along beautifully; on this side of the planet it would certainly be possible to widen our horizons, to forget the stifling atmosphere of our homeland from which, under my auspices, you had begun to suffer so intolerably. From here I could imagine you lost in a crowd that became more alien to us each day, humiliated through and through by fallacy, deceit, living intense emotions during the harrassed freedom marches, mingling with ardent throngs that attempted to rekindle hope in us. In my broken-down cot, so many miles away, was I really thinking about these things? But one morning in June I saw you come down the steps of the airplane, blackened by the sun, surrounded by a cloud of white swallows that flew all around, then lit on the shoulders of the customs officers, on the lights, filling the vast waiting rooms of the airport with their wings and screeches, crashing into the glass panels and falling back stone dead, their tiny legs tucked up on their breasts. Then life caught its breath; my phantoms were heard without great aspirations, the sweating and the scoldings began anew, but your slender body found its place in the bed, the household air became accustomed to your presence, your sleep was brusquely interrupted, not always for a game of love but because of the fear (then you would protest and angrily implore me to let you sleep). And that night, like so many others, you were cross, mumbling about the hour, but I was already crouching near the bed, exploring a small area of torment; I put my socks inside my shoes, aligned the soles and heels next to each other and left the toes pointing directly toward the wall, I jumped into bed and lay on my back breathing evenly; now I was sure I was breathing beautifully as I walked along a foamy mirage, a forest of silence in which there suddenly appeared a prow without anchors, a monstruous blade that split my dream into two halves. Startled once again, completely awake, I staggered over your grunting form, groping for the window. Slightly opened, an icy wind came through it. I closed it, profoundly alarmed by such an inconceivable oversight, because if the lash of the March wind caught me (it's true, Yolanda), it would be enough to break every bone in my body. Would you have laughed if I had told you? Would you have bitten your lips, incapable of hitting upon the right word to describe my obsessions? In moments during which sleep already had overcome me, how many times would I find myself in the middle of an avenue with cars zooming by at top speed? How often would I feel that a tremendous mass hurled from the heights was crashing down on my head? But it wasn't only in my room, fiercely locked by four bolts, that I suffered the harrassment of nightmares. Not only at home, nor in the street, nor in the open countryside. It would happen even in places where I had found a sensation most nearly resembling peace. For example, in a concert hall. If the orchestra struck, let's say, a weak prelude where it would have been totally possible to count the breaths of the girl seated three rows in front of us, you would move away a little, Yoli, and would scrutinize me with heavy irony and ill-concealed curiosity, waiting for the moment of the explosion. But naturally, no one was going to explode, not I, nor the first violinist, nor the man bored to death behind the kettledrum, probably thinking about how extraordinarily simple it would be to unleash a formidable blow on the tense skin in the middle of the delightful flow of violins. Plunged into the most sinister of silences, I was biting my nails, waiting for the second trombonist, irritated by the metallic belching the tuba was expelling on the back of his neck, to leap up, overtaken by a terrible tantrum. Upon violently lowering the baton, the conductor might lose his balance and fall crashing to the ground. And the gong, wasn't it about to come off its frame to fall like an inconceivable platter designed for the world of giants? The last patient and inhibited trumpet, in a painful fit of rage, would begin a screeching jazz bray, the harpist would cross her beautiful legs to make the cellos go off-key, the triangle would tinkle happily announcing frothy vanilla ice-cream. But of all the scandalous possibilities the orchestra offered, the most plausible seemed that of the mallet falling on the rotund bass kettledrum: then pandemonium would take over: the air become so dense that we had to loosen our ties, open the doors wide, immediately injecting fresh, sparkling oxygen into the battered atmosphere, the walls would begin a hurried erosion, the tremendous chandelier could explode onto the middle of the orchestra floor; from the cracks in the floor, from the walls and the ceiling, waves of symphonic rats would surge forth. But lacking such a moving event I tightened my grip on the arms of the seat—under your ironic look of triumph, Yoli—and counted one two three one two three trying to rid my head of the recently born idea of seeing myself overcome by a violent coughing spell just when an asthmatic flute, in the general throbbing silence, was fastidiously tripping along uncounted measures, alone and finally heard, backtracking and retracing its predictable path. The cough was forming and gaining

3

consistency, round and shining like a pearl in the shell of my brain, turning and jumping at my throat, determined to break through freely before the disapproval of the well-to-do and the usher and the liveried doorman. But it could be that it wouldn't leap out, but rather slip out awkwardly in a tight hoarseness, a sad, muzzled roar; my throat would sound like a bassoon being blown by a fool. Then I would sweat profusely, prepared for the most minute breath of fresh air to provoke a long string of sneezes. I always feared that, a man of the tropics transplanted to a climate that would welcome a splendid morning and bid it farewell wrapped in a haze that clung to one's bones; following a resplendent sky it would wickedly raise a gloomy flag as wide as the celestial valley (black fighting bulls charging on high—their hooves thundering, spewing out a nitid slime). In the morning would there be frost on the roofs, a white frozen flowering on the sidewalks, ships of frozen flakes on the potholes? During those days of unsure qualities, it was inevitable that I should dream of a green plot of land, a typical scarlet blush of flamboyants, a bright sun that tortured plants and animals for twelve full months. A river of wandering consistency flowed beneath the silvered arch of the bridge and I walked among the cane fields, dizzied by the fragance of the sweetness inside, by the vapors of the sizzling earth; in the shadow of a *bucayo* tree I breathed deeply and then walked into a small perfumed forest, coming upon some rails on whose crossties lay pieces of sugar cane endowed with the magic of attracting armies of ants. These memories assaulted me on the subway, in our room, at a little table on Callao, in the concert hall of the Royal Theater, in the narrow back streets of old Madrid so similar to those of the ancient capital of my own homeland. Vulnerable to the sun, I would allow myself to be taken in by the flashing memories, fascinated and wordless. And you waved a hand before my eyes, "Wake up, wake up." I didn't tell you of the procession of lights and shadows that paraded through my head, fearful of your possible nostalgia, that you might insist on returning, not to the quietly lit path nor to the overwhelming cane fields, but rather to the harshness of the falsely Mediterranean city, to our Nebraska Heights development, to the thousands of tail pipes blowing their dirty fumes into the scorched streets, to the huge, arbitrary buildings full of foreign accents. In the unstable Castilian winter afternoons it was possible to reconstruct our island, sparkling beneath the sun, invent her anew in the Caribbean, walk among the luxuriant foliage and stop near the train tracks waiting waiting waiting for what my God waiting enraptured simply enraptured.

* * *

4

Loíza, P.R.

My dear children Eddy and Yolanda:

I pray to God that when you receive this you're all well, we're well thank God though your father Sebastián complains of pains in his back and working all day in the store and the other night he didn't even let me close my eyes complaining of the pain in his back and he said that I didn't take care of him anymore that I didn't have a thought or a care except for you my son in Madrid and that he could die without my ever taking care of him like a human being and that I wouldn't even take one flower to his grave that's what he said and he was bothering me so much my children that I sat up and told him four clear pure truths and he should remember that if he complained he couldn't urinate it wasn't my fault because of his running around when he was young and he made me suffer enough my God I don't even want to remember it Ramona Eusebia Julia who he took away from the mayor himself and all those from San Juan that I never saw because I was buried in this town no one visits and one time his breathing cramped up and he had sick blood and we had to rush him to Digno the druggist may God rest his soul and Digno said that he had an ugly thing your father Sebastián and he inserted something like a little closed umbrella into him and they opened it up inside and then they pulled it out to scrape away the sin and filth, I told Sebastián not to forget that my son the many times I had to prepare baths of medicinal plants for him so he could sit and loosen up inside I mean the filth which was all he got out of running around with Ramona and Julia who drove her husband crazy and Eusebia. But it was only that night since then your father Sebastián isn't at all like he used to be when for any little thing he would say shit on Sebastopol which is certainly the name of a foreign saint and Digno the druggist may God rest his soul said it was something due to watered down or tired blood or from the glands that's what he said but I'm sure that what was wrong with your father Sebastián was that he had his head full of bad things but he had an appetite and he himself would go to the slaughter house in person and talk with Ismael the Watch and pick out some tripe which is the best remedy for everything and he was in such shape that not even a bull could match the way he looked he was all ruddy and with bright eyes but already the rot was working on

5

him inside I'm telling you that you couldn't even tell from the outside because of those degenerated married women and all and Eusebia with seven children from different husbands and maybe the Lord our God couldn't put up with it any more and told Sebastián your father here this is for you and I was so scared because the father of your father Don Segundo had suffered a disease and his stomach filled up with tadpoles and he turned green and got mean and he would spend his time reading the newspaper and cursing all night and one morning dawned with him stiff in his chair because a little maggot had crawled up and bitten into his heart and he ended up like a ramrod in his chair. What came to my mind scared me but your father Sebastián my son made such a change that no one recognized him and that was when he had his fiftieth birthday in June maybe you remember it son but Yoli doesn't since she didn't know you then and in the middle of the town plaza with everybody there because it was during the fiesta for our patron saint he kneeled in front of me and cried and said that I was a saint and was skinny as a slat from suffering because of the bad life he had been giving me crying and everybody looking at us and everyone crying even the mayor himself crying there next to us imagine my son what a spectacle but with people who love each other truly that's the way it is and the priest himself who hated your father because he was a mason came and raised his hand and blessed us without our asking for it and for free because we looked like two little angels there talking with everyone and telling about our sorrows in public and they dedicated a song to us on the microphone and we even danced all alone and everyone was looking at us, ay my children the things you do when you're all upset and Sebastián said over the microphone he wouldn't run around with women any more and to forgive him if he'd offended so many people in his past life and from then on you already know how he worked like an ox! And then we went home and Sebastián has never again gone running around and some time ago after you went to Spain he began going to mass every Sunday and he hasn't missed once and we both go to mass both of us every Sunday and the new priest asked if he wanted to sing in the choir on Sundays at the mass and he said yes and now things are really fine my children and friends tell him maybe he missed his calling and your father should have been a radio singer because who knows if he might not have been like Daniel Santos himself who sings midnight virgin and I don't know what else I wasn't there, but your father laughs and says for them not to joke that his thing is selling ham and bacon and just because they praise him not to think that he's going to forget to charge for the bills that they owe him, and then they talk about the old days and

Sebastián your father laughs a lot and says that's youth. Well my son I don't want to bother you any more around here everything is the same old story nothing ever happens though on Sunday at about three in the morning at a dance that they had at the country club a man pumped six bullets into his wife and they say it was out of jealousy and then he tried to kill himself but he didn't have any bullets left in his revolver by then, your father Sebastián sends you his regards and says not to be a bum and you Yolanda you should write to him too you're also our daughter and it's been a month since we received a letter from you and we worry my children and you Yolanda see what you can do because your father-in-law Sebastián says to see what you can do because we don't have any grandchildren see what you can do many hugs and kisses and love and regards and keep on being good and don't stay over in that part of the world too long I'm talking just to talk because Eddy is a full grown man and intelligent and knows what he does see what you can do we look forward to your answer don't be lazy see what you can do.

Hugs and kisses and love from

Mamá and also Sebastián

P.S. Since I know you like it Eddy and you also Yolanda I sent you a little jar of olive oil. Since it's cold over there and you have snow tell me son if you can't get tomatoes to see what I can do to send you tomatoes since you like salads so much.

7

Tegucigalpa, Honduras

Dear Mr. Leiseca:

I consider it opportune to clarify the fact that if we took the initiative of publishing your story "Muddled Intrigues" without consulting with you, it was motivated by an unspoken, unwaning interest that we, the men who compose the editorial staff of this magazine, have in making known the names of young and unknown writers.

Great continental writers have seen fit to publish their distinguished works in our magazine (among them I can proudly point out Aníbal Cebollero, Julio Alicante, Antonio L'Intriga and others of no lesser importance). Because of this, we cannot but be surprised by the fact that you, being totally unknown, are opposed to appearing amongst such a prestigious list.

We understand that due to your inexperience, and in the fire of your ardent youth, you might have felt inexorably compelled to write us in such a violent manner, to the extreme of calling us "exploiters of the intellectual workers," but we are certain that with time you will appreciate our having concerned ourselves with your first manuscript in such a generous manner.

It is evident that, due to the difficult economic situation our publication is going through (resulting from the latest coup d'etat and the war with El Salvador), it will be impossible for us to economically remunerate you for your work by paying royalties, as you demand.

Your faithful servant,
Romualdo Serafín Popote
Director
The Cotton Flute

8

Dear Yoli:

Forgive me for having taken so long to answer you; it's not that
I've forgotten you but I've been very busy with the office and with
grandfather who, as you know, is at an age where they become
children again, and we have to watch over him as if he were a baby.
He's going on no less than his 98th birthday which doesn't amuse me
at all because he goes on himself and everything. Father had hired a
lady to take care of him, but the clever old goat started courting her,
as old as he is, and took her hand and recited some poem about
daisies and clouds, I don't know if he got it out of his head or whether
it is a song from his childhood. The lady's name was Panchita, but he
called her Andreíta, always telling her Andreíta this Andreíta that
and you simply had to see how the lecherous old man was almost
melting with honey. Apparently this so-called Andrea was something
else indeed, judging from what he says when he talks to himself; I'm
convinced that people used to be greater hypocrites than now, with
their skirts down to their ankles, but who knows if a few more yards
of material are going to control all the other business (sex, etc.).
Well, Panchita couldn't put up with the old man any more and she left
and Panchita's husband said he was going to wring grandfather's
neck like a chicken's and then father intervened and we almost had
one hell of a fight on our hands. I don't know why the other children
don't take care of the old man even if just for a while and it always has
to be father who carries the burden. That's the way the world turns.
He always acted so badly towards father while he doted on his other
children and now father is the only one who has known how to
behave like a truly self-sacrificing son and all. And on top of that, he
never loses his temper.

Last week Chiqui had a nervous breakdown and we had to rush
her to the doctor. I'm almost ashamed to tell you but I was a lot to
blame. It so happened that I went to the beauty parlor to give my
spirits a lift because Jimmy had guard duty at the base that weekend
and I went to get my hair fixed because of that. Well, here's what
happened: you know how in those places you can find out about
everything, and there was a very outspoken girl and in her
conversation she brought up a certain Justino Figueroa, and without

9

even realizing it, I kept pumping her for information. And she told me that Justino was the television repairman and his wife was a friend of hers and they had just had another baby, number four I believe, and she gave me the whole scoop, as they say. After that I was wracking my brains to figure out how to tell Chiqui that her beloved Justino, the little twerp, had a wife and four children. Well I decided that the poor thing should not keep on buying blankets and sheets and pillowcases for her wedding (she was already thinking about what the wedding "favors" should be and whether they should toast with French champagne) and one day I told her, and, trembling, she called him on the phone and he admitted that it was true and said that he was very sorry but he was just about to confess the whole truth and that his love for her was true love and not one tainted with life's pettiness. Chiqui locked herself up and spent days without eating a bite and on the eighth day when we knocked down the door she was kneeling and reciting my hands are flowering roses, which was the poem she recited when we graduated from eighth grade, I don't know if you remember it. The poor thing has been under observation ever since with sedatives and all. That's why I'm checking into Jimmy's life so he won't take me for a fool, but luckily his mother and his sister Dorothy are very open and they tell me the truth, that Jimmy was about to get married once, but he realized it wasn't what he wanted and he started working for the Coast Guard. Dorothy invited me to spend next summer in a little town in Delaware, where they are from, but we'll see what happens. When Jimmy has guard duty I can't find anything to do and I'm very lonely and sad at night.

Nena, I have to tell you something that happened last week and everyone knows about although they've tried to keep it a secret. And the whole affair is more complicated than it appears because several of the best families are involved. It's about Julie Ferrara's wedding who as you know was Queen at the Casino. There were guests who came from Mexico, Venezuela, the United States and they say even from Europe. The bride's gown was made by Dior, a dream, Nena! Don Macedonio Ferrara picked out the most beautiful chapel in the city, and do you know what he did? He installed air conditioning so that Julie wouldn't sweat during the ceremony, and they put a carpet on the floor that even if you worked a hundred years you still wouldn't be able to pay for, more beautiful than what you see in the movies. Over a million dollars spent on the wedding, Yoli! Champagne, caviar, wedding favors with letters in real gold, and an opera singer hired in Italy to sing the wedding march. Well, they went to spend their honeymoon in Acapulco. And what happened? Well, the husband, a doctor from San Juan, turned out to be a wife, I mean he was a pansy or something like that. The story has come out into the open because there was a swimming championship in that place that a lot of Puerto Ricans had gone to. It seems that the first night the doctor threw himself out a window and almost broke his neck, screaming that he was such and such and what could he do about it and where was his friend, that he had betrayed his friend and his conscience was bothering him and Jimmy laughed on hearing the story and said what a sissy and dumb little faggot (excuse me) for losing Julie who is strictly peaches and cream, that's what Jimmy said being from Delaware, imagine. Jimmy says that what men like that need is a good thrashing on the ass, you know how funny Jimmy is. He's from Delaware and people from Delaware are like that.

Have you been keeping up with your treatment, Yoli? In New York a woman had quintuplets due to that hormone treatment, and in Sweden they broke the record, I think there were seven at once, what an outrage and then they talk about overpopulation. If I'm not mistaken I think you told me you were expecting, right? I hope so, it would do Eddy good, and don't forget that I would like to be the godmother. Will it be a little Spanish girl or a little Spanish boy? Olé!

Well Yoli, sorry for all the chatter and until I hear from you, love from your friend who always remembers you,

Wanda

Regards to Eddy.

San Juan, P.R.

Mr. Eduardo Leiseca:

Given the impossibility of my obtaining the fees you owe me in return for the last four psychotherapy sessions that we conducted during the month of July of 1969, and in view of the fact that you have left the country, I am obliged to submit this bothersome matter to my lawyer and to a collection agency.

There is still time for you to pay me the amount due (100 dollars, if I may permit myself to remind you). A money order or check, preferably from American Express, which has branches all over the world, would suffice for me to reverse the procedure initiated by my lawyer.

I hope that you, who presume to be an intellectual, will understand once and for all that psychiatry is a science and not simple witchcraft as you told me during one of our sessions, that a psychiatrist is a doctor like any other, only it is not like pulling a tooth.

Awaiting your immediate reply, I remain,

Dr. Winston Olmo, Psychiatrist

Buenos Aires, Argentina

Dear Mr. Leiseca:

In answer to your kind letter of last June it is with pleasure that we request that you send us, as soon as possible, the manuscript of your *Unexpected Nights* so that our panel of readers might examine it rigorously in the light of our editorial budget.

However, it is our wish to notify you that the genre you cultivate, the short story, has a very limited market in the book world.

If your manuscript is accepted, we will see in which of our collections it might be included.

With nothing more for now, I remain,

Your faithful servant,
Orpheus Triano Rapputti
Director
Free Pampa, Inc.

P.S. Please forgive the tardiness in answering, which was due to the reorganization of our company.

* * *

She arrived slowly tired and called from the door hi melodious hi
how have you spent the day and I showed her my manuscripts and
answered that I had worked a lot awaiting her absolution and she
asked me if I had eaten and yes I lied because in those days I had lost
my appetite everything was sordid the planet would shrug its
shoulders before the vaguely human ants and she came in taking off
her coat almost frozen and might have said for example at noon I
wanted to go to the hairdresser but I didn't have time and asked if I
thought that long hair looked good on her and I said yes then I won't
go to the hairdresser she ended up saying and began to undress in
the inviting twilight of the room in a delicious provocative sex appeal
dance slowly dropping her skirt raising one thigh and then the other
lifting her arms and taking off her blouse and me looking at her from
the unmade bed in two impossibly suggestive angles of the mirror
with the dim exactly appropriate lighting and the distant rumble of
cars and the muffled pulsating of mysterious atavistic castanets
engendered in the depth of the blood and the temperature of the first
days of March defeated by the silent strength of the radiators and I
sat up wrapped in a cowhide and shoved her happily savagely onto
the floor or the bed playing laughing without one unnecessary word
only with the language of hands of the five petaled flowers and my
cheek traveled over her legs like a blind prow my mouth reaching up
murmuring without words murmuring silence with the beats of
drums and found a happy haven surrounded by sparse darkish
vegetation and went to where her mouth was waiting for me we fused
in one long sigh sustained in a gulp of tormented air in a blushing
spiral in a second's endless epilepsy and the world was abolished
germinally propitiously in theory and there were no bombs nor tears
nor empty stomachs nor a fragrant colonized island but rather a
stellar shudder a planetary glow a river of thick warm sap and all the
birds in all the trees would sing in the four corners of the earth and
the celestial bodies rushed through the fully sonorous vacuum like
Van Gogh's "Starry Night" tears of sparkling silver on a vibrantly
blue background.

but I knew something didn't come to an end that the tiny rain
travelers died ignominiously that the doors to the future were closed
that pollen asphyxiated in the bottom of the corolla that nothingness

had established itself precisely at the root of life and only silence would prevail and blood wouldn't prolong its voices in a bud our names wouldn't transcend death and the invisible headstone was right in place a paralyzed microcosm inhibiting long-awaited germination

naturally this didn't happen every day I mean that type of amorous reception usually I would welcome her saying words like winch strap switchboard pulley chassis because everything depended on the translations that I might have finished during the day and she would undress and somewhere else I might crawl around checking out plugs the bare wires in the electrical installations any possible inexplicable oversight a razor blade in a shoe for example

I shuddered at the sight of the long knife she brandished with obvious relentless cruelty licking her lips with satisfaction while slowly piercing the meat for the next meal twisting the knife around with evident assassin's pleasure

oh her arrival collected into one bundle into one pulsating fist my most long-standing obsessions strutting in the kitchen in the living room in the bedroom strangely asking me about my health while I one two three one two three one two three was caught in an inexorably mathematical net and had to beat my head against the wall in order to crack that abstract prison which immobilized me from within

you need help she would tell me and it sounded like the classic stereotyped you need help with which an american wife recommends to her american husband an american psychiatrist you desperately need an analyst honey

but anyone who wasn't a fool could understand that this type of help wouldn't do anything but disturb me more starting with my beloved suffering tormented pocket as in the case of doctor Winston Olmo twenty-five smackeroos per visit would hurt my largely economically determined emotional health old Karl would have said so nodding with his frankly less than courteous beard

nevertheless for a long time I had nursed my inseparable compulsions which fit me as closely as a sportscoat a jacket designed by the best Carnaby Street tailor thanks to which we met that afternoon on the crowded five-thirty bus she looking pensively through the window with her pocketbook on her lap and I standing uncomfortably in front of an old-fashioned gentleman with a grave congested apoplectic face whose hand trembled and who blew into my face a bittersour stench of rotten tobacco and tartar and old dried saliva from the corners of his mouth but that didn't matter because I was accustomed to all sorts of disagreeable odors since childhood in my father's store penetrating cod and blind lard and the boisterous anal sighs of my father while he sold sugar such a sweet white substance or sold five cents worth of cigarettes to a snotty-nosed kid or aromatic coffee or transparent or cloudy golden rum

what was truly serious was that the man dressed in a magnificent anachronistic inadvertently camp white linen suit and a flat surprisingly camp old straw hat wore on his lapel with criminal incongruity a visible loud fiery black thread shaped like an S so striking and scandalous and fascinating that I was immediately obliged to turn my face mortally injured if you wish and move ahead furiously squeezing against the passengers excuse me look where you're going don't push and I stopped behind the conductor forcing myself to expel from my brain that incandescent thread that root of misfortune but in the exaggeratedly large rear view mirror appeared the hateful old man spraying his abominable breath on any human being within his reach

the adorably childish recourse of closing my eyes of burying my head in the sand of covering the rear view mirror with a rag had no effect for it turns out that with eyes closed with my head anchored in the sand with all mirrors swathed I can see three times as well I see much more the details light up surprisingly behind my eyelids of alarming transparency so I began humming a song I travel the tropical path etcetera but its outdatedness fiercely reminded me of the Methuselenic persistence of the linen suit ironed to delirium the clouded eyes the wrinkled chin reddened by a razor blade and full of little purple veins and my God the black crevice in the white frozen plain in which I was forever submerged losing my breath my God with my shoes and my hands on the black volcanic opening with pulsations and buttons in the crater filled with crackling flames I was sinking helplessly with my mustache and my Bulova watch with my young hair loose on the back of my neck in a familiar mane with my eyes opened wide watching the walls of horror the seams of the earth and I was enveloped by the hope that the old man would get off at the next stop

but in fact it wouldn't have been an effective remedy because the crevice was a bleeding wound not on the blinding lapel but in some vague spot in my awareness and I leaned toward the window searching for distraction and relief and I saw the faces of the passers-by the girls' asses the black grey brown white red skins and it so happened that the sidewalks were covered with black scars and the sun opened a resplendent crack in the sky and the few clouds began dissolving revealing glowing volcanic mouths which spewed forth torrents of fire the walls separated in the corners of the gaping mouths dark tree trunks in the foliage the darkly asphalted highway everything reminded me of the intolerable aperture

so I decided to attack the nightmare frontally cast it off like a malignant vine and I went directly to the old man who sat stiffly erect and I must have had the face of a person addicted to artificial paradises for after contemplating me for a violently brief lapse of time he averted his gaze with undisguised displeasure and I asked what time do you have sir and he didn't hear well and I said what time is it please sir if it's no trouble my Bulova has stopped and he said furiously ga ga ga brandishing that intolerable thread mute on top of everything else and I was going to say trembling furiously you have a thread there sir you have a horrible grease stain please be kind enough to quickly clean up that unbecoming blemish sir would you have the mercy and throw that damned thread on your lapel far away from here but at that instant the gentleman as if determined to drown me in my madness turned uncomfortably wooden-like and exposed the back of his neck to my eyes committing me to his red dried skin furrowed by deep channels territory crossed by mechanically regular chasms over which flowed sparse tufts of copper painted cotton

it would have been feasible at that moment to strike up a faltering dialogue with the passively sweet young lady gazing at me from her seat fondling a little book smiling and lovely confronting my inevitable sweat ironically injected into my shadow but frankly speaking if I didn't go ahead and resolve within myself my most urgent controversy that night I would be assaulted by strange surrealist nightmares like the Statue of Liberty rolling up her tunic and urinating shamelessly into the Atlantic or worms coming out of my shoes and the soup I must say that actually they were men who due to a certain daily posture had acquired a repugnant worm-like state or an insufferable cloud of blue-eyed flies would emerge from my pockets nothing strange in the persistence of these images all perfectly assembled in a magnificent eisensteinian montage captured by the marvelous eye of the arreiflex of the subconscious mind and one time I had even decided to discontinue my visits to doctor Winston Olmo because given the characteristics of my internal revelations I deemed it preferable to re-read Breton for example or trace in coarse Dalí reproductions the hermetic key to this world that anarchically manifested itself inside me without allowing me to breathe without my express consent I should say reproducing in my brain in open contradiction to the sensible almost bourgeois man who lives relentlessly within me

17

for the time being I hadn't found an efficient way to avert the asphyxiating spell of the black thread on the white lapel and the worst took place when I recognized in the old man that strange mannerism of passengers on a bus or a plane or a train of shifting and squaring their shoulders and clearing their throats and adjusting their hats with an air of importance when the time comes to leave the bus or plane or train and thus I knew he would get off at the next stop

the bus had already started its fateful deceleration and I knew that once out of my reach the problem would remain hideously unresolved and I would be shipwrecked among innumerable miseries one two three perhaps for weeks one two three and I would finally feel compelled by a maddening internal demand native to certain spirits to wander soulstruck throughout that region with the hope of meeting up with the old man and at last moved by a fierce urge explain to him sir that thread had turned into a long chain wrapped around my body and the key to the manacles was in your wrinkled pensioner's hands sir make sure that the threadchain doesn't exist that you threw it hatefully into the garbage can that you burned it happily pyromaniac that your snowy lapel is of perfect immaculate whiteness excuse the inconvenience it's a matter of life or death sir

finally to avoid such cumbersome annoyances it seemed reasonable to attempt the only possible step

the only correct step

the one I dreamed was accurate

the only correctaccurateinevitable step

and the moment the bus was slowly stopping I expanded my chest and tensed my muscles getting my nerve up and in the slight shudder the bus underwent when it came to a full stop I pretended to rudely lose my balance and to the amazement of a good number of passengers I directed a ferociously disproportionate butt to the bleeding lapel like a Miura bull charging a cape

ga ga ga said the old man without air sealed in an empty atmosphere clearly pale saying ga ga ga I don't know whether it was because of his muteness or on account of that notably serious absence of oxygen I begged his pardon I am truly sorry I lost my balance seeing with authentic panic how the thread remained on the lapel in the shape of a C that is to say a tighter design like a claw a gaping mouth an enormous ear a tremendous ear listening to everything and I said to the gentleman of unfortunate contained breath of sad exhalation of breathing held in suspense due to strongly external causes that I sir was ashamed of losing my balance so negligently and in a fury I placed my claw on the impertinent C and pulled downwards compulsively with every intention of tearing it apart if necessary until I felt the warm thread deliciously twisted up in my ignominious hands

everyone looked at me with mixed enigmatic wonder and unrestrained resentment while my soul became crystallized in a sweaty contented peace with the notes of a viola as an exacting background and the young lady with the book watched me smiling approvingly metaphysically and watched in the same way the strangled snake in my hands she knew it all she knew everything she didn't miss anything

sir whom I would gleefully strangle with the thread

what hideously established neck would hang from such a rope

aside from those bothersome images three necessary gossips fanned the old man with furious sweetness and he looked at me from his sealed world from his improvised oxygen-proof test tube exhausted in a quickly emptied seat with his greatly deteriorated lungs lined in goat skin

I rested my cool forehead on my warm hands overcome by vertigo and immensely happy immensely and the girl with the book told me you're pale and I said that's my color miss or something even more absurd for example it's that it's December although even babies knew it was mid-August and everyone was indicating in muffled voices that there was no relation between the gentle halt of the bus and my violent loss of balance what a frankly brazen imbalance they practically wanted to lynch me and the girl said

let me touch your hands they are numb come rest lean back smile but I know you're not at all well it's true your loss of balance was exaggerated it seems to me that first you lost a secret equilibrium you don't hear me I understand all your attention is on yourself and that thread what are you planning on doing with such a lovely trophy you probably collect unmentionable things pieces of yarn dusty petals worn heels burned matches tacks plane fuselages refrigerator doors broom handles ant cadavers I'm happy to introduce myself my name is Yolanda almost a gerund you know that mania for saddling us with obscure entries in the compendium of Christian names but what a name Eddy Leiseca it makes me think of prohibition in the roaring 20s Bonnie and Clyde it was my aunt's idea let's see how your hands are still numb but the thread is as hot as a coal it was your way of solving your problem with dignity only you must recognize it's only a partial momentary solution I'm daring to read your mind as if it were a photo-novelette which by the way I love

and then while my sweet compatriots conspired against me in

19

the bus looking for a fitting form of justice the girl showed me the little book about Freud and shortly thereafter began a discourse amidst the grunts of the traveling populace and somehow linked my youthful stumble to the geriatric recipient and said it was the old traditional rejection felt toward the ancestral father that's what she said saying that at the beginning of humanity we had joyously assassinated our original father thus we are all murderers and we still eat his flesh and drink his blood so that his virility his enviable power his qualities might be vested in us and after having said this she looked out the window as if she hadn't said anything and even mentioned modestly that the sidewalks should be widened and daisies and forget-me-nots and acacias planted and surely the pig was the totem animal of all Puerto Ricans and it wasn't difficult for me to arrive at the conclusion that in some way our father was a pig if that animal was elected to represent him and if in our parties we drink and dance tribal rituals and we vomit and fall in an atavistic trance and howl and devour enormous quantities of pork during the most significant feasts the truth was that throughout those obscure subconscious ceremonies we aspire to have communicated to us and transferred to our souls and our bodies all the essentially porcine qualities of our nebulous island progenitor

but I rejected that conclusion as antipoetic and humiliating and unpatriotic and said it was only one of many interpretations of man and his appearance on the scene and I said darkly homo faber and she said with clear calculation that the essential problem lay in the question of the father Prometheus Oedipus Christ and at this point she asked me if I'd ever received holy communion at mass and I should think carefully what the ceremony was about sir think it over carefully Eddy bread and wine body and blood no need to go into it further

I answered that in this country it's too hot to go into such things and all that about man's behavior being conditioned by what's it called yes the libido sounded like I don't know overexplanation maybe it seems to me that it's too hot I said and she answered that it depended on the school of psychology that one might want to follow that they should widen the bridge to Condado that Adler the ingrate had dared to refute his teacher Freud that they should improve the public transportation system and that Jung was also another story with his heterodox theories that the coasts of our country were just one long marvelous beach that it was necessary to read psychology books if we wanted to understand our more profound motivations and that if a tire on the bus were to blow out we would be lost because the next one would take a good half hour to come by of course the young lady was unaware of how grateful I was for that encounter which saved my worthless porcine-descended life from the lynching the censorious passengers were no doubt preparing perhaps they would have stopped the bus and inserted the exhaust pipe up to my tonsils with the motor running at least six hours so that there would be no doubt that any odious antisocial individual could be executed in the time-honored Auschwitz fashion

and then I remember we got off at an unexpected unknown stop under the absurd pretense that it was exactly the hour for a cup of coffee and if one doesn't drink coffee at the hour prescribed by custom one will certainly end up with an intolerable headache and dense clouds of flies swarmed around our cups but we didn't notice because we were engrossed in already overly sincere chatter and she swallowed sips of coffee like a fine little hen and without becoming upset with an admirable scientific precision she cursed her aunt whom she quickly qualified as having an ego being eaten away by obsessive-compulsive tendencies such as examining her underwear when she arrived after eleven p.m. to see if any questionable experience might have taken place and I laughed uproariously amused when she described the old woman snooping in her panties poor old maid obsessed by the idea that some day she might stumble on a starchy scab a dried stain of fragant fish in order to then oh supreme happiness be able to die in joyful peace because she had finally been able to close in on the source of life itself the mythical unknown mysterious celebrated source of existence oh magnificent anonymous upright fountain thy will be done

and she had the admirable boldness of telling me how her devout aunt collected photographs of old long-gone actors villains and heroes of the silent movies Valentino crushed beneath her pillow and her mania of secretly applying make-up and unbelievable amounts of rouge before going to bed where she would fall onanistically spread out hugging her pillow on her desolate honeymoon what a marvelous aunt with her dreaming fingers what a magnificent piece of loneliness how tenderly perverted how delicately pornographic

perhaps because the young lady lived with these ghosts she captivated me she received clear and unequivocally my signal like a dummy's lightning rod she accepted me alternating her reading of Freud with photo-novelettes already slightly contaminated by my nightmares by my oneiric despair

it's so sad to realize that now we quarrel meticulously things can take a bad turn and we no longer walk barefooted along the beach nor drink carloads of beer with intricate friends of anarchic tendencies and long mustachios and fleas and take her back home and die laughing listening to how her aunt would scold her and then we knew once again that the definitive ceremony of solitude was beginning the old nose enmeshed in the silk of her underwear that I had kissed endlessly kissed endlessly kissed endlessly unknowingly trying on one of Sigmund's obscure theories but kissing exhaustively endlessly her vibrant body which smelled like a melodious fruit already mine.

* * *

TO ALL RESIDENTS OF THE LERIDA ESTATES

Dear Neighbors:

How goes it with you all? At peace in your homes with your families? We hope so, and that you will continue to be so with the unselfish assistance of all for the good of all. You should have no reason for complaint about the building in which you presently reside except, perhaps, for an occasional insignificant trifle of no major consequence.

The Tenants' Council has held its monthly meeting and has decided to present the following points for your consideration:

1.   Some users are in the habit of carelessly leaving the doors of the Escudero elevator open, thereby making its use impossible. Think of the families who live on higher floors (thirteenth, sixteenth and so forth) and of what would happen if said elevator were stuck during an emergency. We ask all residents not to forget to shut the doors properly to avoid the inconvenience of having to call the super all the time, as he is also a human being and deserves consideration.

2.   Some people throw their cigarette butts (filtered and un-filtered) and cigar ends in the elevator, the lobby and the corridor, producing an undesirable odor at best, and an unpleasant appearance. The superintendent, Don Juan Manuel, has complained about this matter many times.

3.   Garbage cans should be lined with paper or cardboard so that scraps such as green or white beans, pieces of Spanish omelette, oyster shells, sardines, Galician-style pickled octopus, tripe, shrimps, sausages, slices of veal in its own juice or simply grilled, olives, Manchego or Cabrales cheese, Wonder bread or crumbs don't soil the receptacle and liquids don't wet the floor. In all of Madrid it is difficult to find such an efficient and capable superintendent.

4.   Don't forget, as it so often happens unintentionally, to pay the super his modest monthly gratuity for garbage collection.

5.   We are pleased to inform you that, as of April, all the occupants of the building will be benefited by the protection of a new night watchman in the neighborhood whose name is Don José María López. Can you guess where he is from? Where his home is? Asturias, naturally. From Cangas del Narcea, to be more exact. We ask you not to.forget to be courteous with our new friend, and if ever you forget your front-door key, don't shout for him. Remember our typically national tradition of calling by clapping softly, which won't

23

disturb the deserved rest of the other tenants nor of Don Juan Manuel, the superintendent.

6. The superintendent informs us that certain residents of the building have a habit of entering the hallway and the Escudero elevator without having properly wiped off the soles of their shoes, slippers, sandals and so forth, thus soiling the floor he cleans daily with such loving care and civic pride.

7. The boys who sell bread and milk and yogurt at the entrance every day complain that certain tenants unintentionally forget to pay their bills. You may leave the amount due with the super, who will be happy to pay for you.

8. Don't leave curtains, blankets, socks and other sorts of bed linen and personal clothing drying on the clotheslines at improper times of day. Some tenants have complained to Don Juan Manuel that the water dripping from such articles has ruined many a good stew.

9. Residents have complained that on certain floors of the building, radios, victrolas, televisions and very loud conversations are heard well into the night, preventing them from getting their so-well-deserved nighttime rest. We request that those alluded to abstain from such undesirable practices. All of us like the zarzuela, the flamenco rumba, Peret and so forth, but it's not the same listening to them played softly as hearing them blaring deafeningly. We have the same to say to those who violently slam doors, drag their heels on the floor, drop spitoons, washbowls, chairs, records, books or turn on the water heater full force during early morning hours.

10. We ask all tenants to refrain from throwing empty tins of bean and bacon soup from Asturias and the coastal area, sardines in olive oil, turkey stuffed with truffles and chicken in giblet gravy, empty bottles of red, white or claret, Rioja or Valdepeñas wine, as well as Coca-Cola, Kas, Revoltosa, Casera or Schweppes bottles around the garbage area. Last week Don Juan Manuel's little niece, who came all the way from La Mancha to visit her beloved uncle, cut her finger on an anchovy can.

11. For the second time, we are forced to warn *two of the bachelor tenants* of the Lérida Estates that they must discontinue certain practices which are incompatible with Christian morals and which openly offend families with children, as well as those without them. Last week a highly deplorable incident occurred. Don Juan Manuel was humbly collecting the garbage cans on Friday morning, when he happened to look to the side and see that one of the doors was open and that the two aforementioned tenants were in full view,

dressed in their birthday suits, with a girl, who looked to be Swedish, in the same state and condition, all three evidently lit-up from too much DYC whiskey, as Don Juan Manuel noticed four bottles of this genuinely Spanish whiskey in the entranceway. Shockingly, the two said residents and the young woman offered our superintendent a drink, calling it a toast to friendship and solidarity and other things that one hears among students, but seized by understandable indignation, he reprimanded them right then and there and lectured to them about Christian ethics and morality and about Eternal Spain. It is lamentable that such acts of sensual vandalism should take place in a residence where honorable people, jealous of their moral code, reside. We repeat it is lamentable, much too lamentable, ladies and gentlemen!!!

12. We remind all residents that in his small cubicle at the entrance to the building, Don Juan Manuel has a list of telephone numbers you might need unexpectedly at some time or other, such as those of plumbers, practitioners (fifteen pesetas per injection), surgeons, obstetricians, chiropodists, veterinarians, tailors, television, radio, refrigerator, automatic and non-automatic washing machine repairmen, midwives, private investigators, pianists, translators and interpreters for the heavy tourist season, professors of Arabic, ancient Greek, Latin and Quechua, maids for everything, photographers, Seat auto mechanics (600, 800 and so forth), banderilleros and rejoneadors, sauna, judo and karate experts, flamenco dance instructors, lessons in Caló and hairdressers, identification card negotiators, attire and preparations for First Communion, scapulary, embroidered shawl and mantilla factories, souvenirs from Toledo, Avila, Granada and La Coruña, regular taxis and limousines, Spanish airlines, boarding houses and bars for lonely husbands whose wives are away, tickets for the San Fermín fair, the works of J.M. Pemán, Gironella and Alfonso Paso.

13. Avoid allowing children to run in and out of the main entrance all day long, disturbing Don Juan Manuel in his labors such as scouring the floor with Vim, washing the windows, polishing the brass on the Escudero elevator, shaking out the rug, replacing the burned-out light bulbs, washing the walls and ceiling, making the elevator come down (or go up, or whatever) when it's stuck, carefully questioning strange-looking people who enter the building in order to protect us (from them, from the strange-looking people who enter), distributing the mail in the proper boxes, stretching out the clotheslines, setting traps for the rats, cockroaches and other loathsome insects, helping ladies carry their groceries, memorizing the racing results, helping children, blind men and old ladies cross

the avenue, notifying applicants of vacant apartments, making sure that the heat begins at exactly 10:00 in the morning on the first of December until 9:00 in the evening, and ends the last day of January, directing telegraph messengers, affably reprimanding those tenants who behave improperly (as in the celebrated case of paragraph number eleven), advising heads of families on their financial problems, and—why not?—tasting a sip of good, red wine every now and then with some lonely, unhappy husband, and so forth. We must remember that our good-natured Don Juan Manuel is a true man from La Mancha (just like The One that every good Spaniard knows well) and that it is important to consider him part of the UNITED AND EXTENDED FAMILY OF THE LERIDA ESTATES.

Sincerely,
The Tenants' Council of Lérida Estates

Dear Yolanda and Eddy:

Thank you for answering my letter so promptly, Yolanda, and for your recommendations on where to look for work. Friends like you simply can't be found in an office any more, but one must resign oneself.

Of the six offices you mention, Mr. Iglesias' looks the most promising for me. They need two secretaries and a messenger (to take mail to the post office and things like that), and Mr. Iglesias gave me a shorthand test and was very happy with it. It seems like a dream, Yolanda, because I didn't have any hope of getting a job so easily, and much less with *our own* people. Of course I went with the single-star flag pinned to my lapel, and when Mr. Iglesias saw it he smiled at me right away and said we must wear it not only there (on the lapel), but also inside, in the heart, and that he shares those same hopes for independence, but only through law and order and religion.

You can't imagine how happy I am. And all because you thought of giving me this marvelous address. I believe good times are on the way for me. I've already met my future coworkers, all very congenial and courteous and friendly people. And they aren't at all like the people where I worked before, which was a real hornets' nest, where they all spent their time accusing one another if they were late or missed work or drank at the office, and they all kept bottles of rum in their desk drawers. That's all over now, I have faith in the future, and my sister even asked me if I was crazy because I spent an afternoon dancing alone in the living room like a nut. I think Saint Jude of Thadeus heard me this time. I'm overflowing with happiness because I know that this time I'll fit into the office, because Mr. Iglesias selects his employees from among *the best!* And those who aren't like that to begin with, end up that way, if you can believe it.

A little bird told me some news about you. You must be really happy about becoming a mother! I truly love children and you've seen my album full of photographs of my nieces and nephews. I'm already saving several pages for when you send me his picture, because being your son (or daughter, but one always hopes that the first will be a boy, an unjustifiable prejudice) it will be as though he were one of my nephews, right?

Okay, I'll let you know how things turn out. The political situation is really getting bad here. Is Eduardo writing a lot? Several days ago they mentioned him in the San Juan Bookstore because they thought he'd published a book or something like that. But later they realized that it wasn't him.

When the baby is born, I'll send him a little bracelet with a jet bead in it to protect him against the evil eye (don't laugh, I know it's superstitious, but it's important to keep up our old traditions these days).

Regards and love from
Graciela

I can also send him a scapular with his saint on it.

False friend:

I should be writing to Yolanda, who at least bothered to send us a postcard last Christmas, and not to you. But, what can you do? I still consider you my friend (true friendship isn't a type of personal colonialism, as you once had the gall to tell me).

I assume you haven't forgotten Ambrosio, the policeman on San Justo Street. Early this morning, at around four a.m., he knocked at my door. I opened it. There he was, a complete wreck; I invited him in because there was nothing else to do and he sat down in an armchair, moaning, with his head in his hands, a real sight to behold. You can probably imagine what was wrong: that afternoon he had given a ticket to a gentleman who parked his car on the sidewalk, which is against the law, and later, during the night, remorse overcame our friend so badly he couldn't sleep. I explained to him that he was only performing his duty as a traffic policeman, but he just kept on moaning. It's useless, he'll have to give up being a cop; this is the way he's spent the entire ten years he's been on the job: he reports someone for breaking the law and then spends two or three sleepless nights repenting and crying. And the worst of it is that he got in trouble with his superiors because he's gone in for decorating his regulation revolver and his night stick. He's taken the bullets out of the pistol and painted flowers on the barrel and on the butt. But that isn't all; one day when they had target practice, Ambrosio's gun shot out a stream of water, and you can imagine the commotion that caused. There's even more: on his birthday a strange lady showed up and gave him a precious little kitten. Naturally, Ambrosio wanted to know who the woman was and what he'd done to deserve such a nice present, but she disappeared, saying it was in return for having kept her husband out of jail. The kitten was very beautiful, but right off it started giving him headaches: it destroyed the furniture, attacked the kids, devoured massive quantities of meat. After two weeks Ambrosio realized that he'd been given a darling baby tiger. Another time, he was given tiny little goldfish that turned out to be piranhas, as well as a box of candy filled with dynamite. And all that in spite of the fact that he isn't a bad guy and has even gone to the extreme of paying fines for people he

29

himself has ticketed. Now he says he's going to leave the police force and become a crooner, which has always been his great dream. He says that Daniel Santos' style suits him well and that in school he won a prize for imitating it.

Some very strange things go on in this neighborhood. But the prize for eccentricity easily goes to the Molinari family, who live in a big old mansion not very far from here. That family once had money but lost it all. They still keep enormous portraits of their ancestors, dusty portraits like those you see in a Hitchcock movie. Well, the grandfather got sick once, no one knows from what, and whenever any of the neighbors asked about his health they were told that he was very well, thank you, that Grandfather had never been sick, etc. But the guy died. This is the sort of macabre story that should suit your delicate taste. The fellow died sitting in an armchair, looking through the blinds, and everyone kept passing by, saying how are you to him and if he'd gotten better and how good it was to see him, and we're so happy to see you've recovered so quickly, Alejandro. No one thought it strange that the guy never answered their greetings because he had always been very haughty, conscious of his lineage and his bourgeois social position. The upshot was that when the family finally realized what had happened, the old guy had already been dead for hours and they couldn't straighten out his legs or arms to put him in a coffin, and since they didn't want to open themselves to ridicule and publicly admit that he'd died without their knowing it, instead of renting a hearse, they put him on a bus to the cemetery. Some very interesting things happened on the bus, because a few of the women who got on after them thought it only right that some gentleman give them his seat, and resentfully eyed the elegant old fellow, freshly shaven, strong and good looking, his mustache turned up at the ends, powdered and stern, visibly lost in thought, with his expensive new hat and his linen suit which was also new, a gentleman who, in spite of his distinguished and almost aristocratic demeanor, wasn't aware of the most elementary social graces, namely getting up and giving a lady his seat. They even went so far as to begin insulting and heckling him. Whereupon, naturally, the struggle between the classes came to the fore: the peasant and the bourgeois confronting one another as always. The people were enraged that he didn't even condescend to look at them; they found this the epitome of indifference, his continuing to look ahead, acutely conscious of his social position, in spite of their insults. It was just as bad at the cemetery. They left Don Alejandro Molinari-Sagasta seated on a bench, sandwiched between two relatives, his hands on his thighs, as he watched two workers dig a grave not far away. The nosy types drew near to ask him who had died, but the distinguished old gentleman maintained his composure, not lowering himself to address the illiterate rabble; the relatives turned the meddlers away, telling them that they should be kind enough not to bother Don Alejandro, who was managing to remain very quiet and contained. Then, the grave diggers refused to take that formidable and glorious-looking specimen of humanity by the arms to plant him in the ground, but in the end they looked to the heavens and realized that it was beginning to drizzle and decided that it would be a shame to keep the gentleman sitting on his bench in the rain, even though his family held an umbrella over his head. So they sat him at the bottom of the grave on a little slab, flowers strewn around his magnificent, brand new Italian shoes, and respectfully covered him with a piece of canvas so he wouldn't soil his suit.

Do you remember Apolinar Morcibes, the cook at Sunny Borinquen? He's still in the same boat, in love with Betty, the American girl who lives on the corner of Cruz and San Sebastián streets. Every day at six Betty walks her puppy in front of the bar where we are inevitably drinking and, as always, bends over, pretending to pick up something; since she still wears her dresses short, we avidly follow this lovely spectacle, as you can well imagine. There are ladies with dogs all over, but this one's hardly someone out of Chekhov. Yesterday, after this maneuver, which is fully intended to excite our passionate tropical blood, Apolinar jumped up, showing us the handle of the knife he wears in his belt, and said that she "has to be mine or I'll kill her." Some of us took it as a joke, but I know Apolinar is dangerous and very strong and you remember that he used to work in a foundry where he made threads in the steel pipes with his teeth. Some afternoons he sits around drinking and listening to records, magnificently Argentinian tangos like the one that talks about "props in her cleavage" among other things and which is another example of how the Spanish tongue has developed in Argentina. Apolinar got drunk one night and knocked on Betty's door; she opened it wearing just a pair of earrings and begged him to leave and stop bothering her; her husband got up too and said oh, it's Apolinar again and went back to bed. Confronted with the vision of a naked Eve, the antigovernmental eye of Apolinar Morcibes rolled and flashed (Fano's words). From then on, Apolinar has gone to the dogs, he's drunk all the time, stooped over, the soup is always spoiled, he no longer slices raw meat, he assassinates it, he cries into the bean pot, but all this with one practical result: the consumption of salt in the kitchen has lessened considerably.

That's how things stand. I hope our fiery native Don Juan isn't going to stick his foot in it again.

Greetings from
Akiro

P.S. Regards to the self-sacrificing Yolanda.

Dear Yoli:

Just by chance I ran into Wanda at the supermarket on Loíza Street. She was buying low-cal foods for her diet, because the truth of the matter is that if she keeps on the way she's going she'll soon weigh a ton. We reminisced about the old days in high school, it had been so long since we had seen each other! As you know, I married Luis right after graduation and we went to live all over the island, you might say, because Luis is a police corporal and they send him wherever they need him. Luis says that the higher-ups have it in for him and that's why they won't leave him in one place for more than two years. Our oldest child, little Luisín, is the image of his father, even in his mannerisms (he raises his eyebrows and spits to one side without laughing and everything), a carbon copy, in other words. Unfortunately, poor little Esther has my face (the poor thing), and Luis says that it would have been worse if I'd passed it on to Luisín (my face). Well, I've finally been able to get an Avon product that has helped me quite a bit and has whitened my skin. Even though I'm aware that acne is more an emotional condition than anything else. Talking about Luisín, I forgot to mention that Wanda told me you're going to have a baby. Eddy must be really delighted. I'm happy about Eddy, too, because Wanda told me he's gotten much better. Since Luis is a police corporal he can't drink, but if they allowed it, that would be another story. Of all the delinquents he runs into on the streets, the ones he can sympathize with most are the alcoholics.

I'm knitting some little shirts for the baby, in a neutral color just in case, which I'll send you soon. With Luis out all day, I get pretty bored and all I do is knit. Luis thinks that in time we'll be able to set ourselves up in a store and he can quit the police. Honey, you can't imagine the problems he's had. One day he gave a man a ticket for speeding, they struggled and almost came to blows over it and everything. Then in court the man said that Luis had asked him for money and the awful thing was that during the scuffle, of all the bad luck, this man really had slipped a five dollar bill in his pocket and then the man brought up the business about the bribe as if Luis were willing to ruin his reputation over five dollars. Luckily, everything turned out all right, but many a night I would hide away and cry, I swear to you Yoli that I cried and cried till I almost went crazy and my eyes stung and I thought my heart would break from so much suffering. Do you remember how in school everything seemed pink and pretty and sweet-smelling and we believed the world was beautiful and rose-colored? And all that even though I had so many complexes because of my skin. But life isn't a bed of roses like they told us. I miscarried my first baby, and Luisín was a Caeserean and I almost died from it. But the worst is behind us. Do you remember when Luis was courting me? My God, I don't know why I want to remember that! My parents locked me in my room and screamed at me every day asking if I was still in love "with that nigger." Tears have taught me that all that stuff about there not being any racial prejudice here is a lie, we're all just a bunch of hypocrites and then we deny it. Do you remember when Aunt Monse insulted Luis on Loíza Street telling him he was a Negro? Luis had the bright idea of telling her that she didn't exactly look like she'd descended from the Vikings who are white as snow and that in this country everybody has his little tinge and a grandmother locked up in the kitchen so no one could see her color. And sometimes when he gives some bad citizen a ticket they yell at him dirty nigger, can you believe it? I remember you were always on my side, Yoli, because you've always been a modern, open-minded girl and you proved it by marrying Eddy in spite of everything they said about him.

Do you know where Josefina is? They told me she married a marvelous guy and went to New York and that she's really well off. Who would have thought it! Now we've all gone our separate ways and the old gang has broken up, as they say. If only we could get together some time like in the old days. Teresa lives in Mayagüez and has a boutique near the college. Do you remember Tony, Carmelo the plumber's son? Well, he had an accident at work and they had to amputate a leg and the insurance company paid him twenty thousand dollars and Luis says it's worth it for that.

Well, Yoli, don't play deaf now and forget to write me. As soon as I get the addresses of the rest of the girls I'll send them to you in case you need anything from here. I'm at your service as always. Give Eddy a friendly hello from me and tell him to keep it up.

Amanda

P.S. Now that you're in Spain, don't miss the chance to visit the Casa de la Troya by Palacio Valdés that we studied about in school, it must be a museum or something by now. Freddy, who knows a lot about these things, will naturally be happy to take you there.

THE NIGHTWATCHMAN FOR THE

SHOPS AND RESIDENTS

of Number 144 Romasáns Street

has received from Mr. Eduardo Leiseca

the sum of thirty (30) pesetas

for services rendered

during the current month.

Madrid, March 1, 1970.

                        The Nightwatchman

Received 30 pesetas.

Buenos Aires, Argentina

Dear Mr. Leiseca:

We have sent you the manuscript of your "The Endless Nights" by surface mail.

The staff of readers of our publishing company decided that in dealing with stories which focus on the problems of your compatriots in New York—a topic to which the readers of the southern continent are not sensitive—it is preferable that their publication take place in a country whose sociopolitical and economic situation resembles, more or less, that of your own country. For example, why not in Mexico, whose emigrants to the United States (migrant workers, wetbacks, as they are contemptuously called) are treated in almost the same way as those from your country?

Another point that the readers made is the fact that four of the central characters are eunuchs. This, naturally, seems a bit excessive in a book of five stories.

We do want you to send us your next manuscript without delay, inasmuch as the readers have detected a certain vein of violent lyricism in your work which, properly channelled, could bear most favorable fruits in the future.

Your faithful servant,
Bernardo Facundo Thompson
Free Pampa Publishing Co., Inc.

Dear Son:

You should have at least answered your mother's letter which she wrote you with so much effort. I say with so much effort because you know that she never got past the 5th grade and when she writes her name Ramona she puts Ramonona, it's always going to be like that and there's nothing to be done about it because of that business about old dogs learning new tricks. Don't be lazy and go ahead and write. You mustn't believe that stuff about her not sleeping because I complain all night of a pain in my back. It's just the opposite. And it's not a pain that's bothering her, it's fear that burglars are going to get in, as if we had something worth stealing. Your mother's like that, since she's a little ignorant the poor thing sees demons hiding behind doors. And now she cries over anything and I think you and she are a lot alike, I mean when you were a little boy you used to cry for no reason and were afraid of the dark and the time you read that booklet about volcanos you spent a whole week without shutting an eye because you got the idea that a volcano was going to grow out of the hill behind the house, remember? And later when there were those earthquakes I don't remember where, you weren't able to sleep either because you thought the sea was going to flood the country; as they say, he who inherits doesn't steal. And besides that, now she's on a soap opera kick and knows the names of all the actors and the poor thing even wrote a letter to a contest where an actor sends an autographed picture to the winner. But first she had to send in four Coca Cola caps. The actor plays the part of a count or something like that in the serial, which is called "Intrigue in the Appenines," and the count falls in love with a poor girl who's lost a shoe and the girl has a stepmother. And the tears are so plentiful you could collect them in buckets, what with the drought we've had this year. So at nine o'clock instead of letting me watch the news she nestles down in front of the television set and the sobbing begins. To top it all, she says that this count is just like you, so refined and good-hearted and all. The poor thing spends her whole life thinking about you and you're so ungrateful that you never even write her. And I've already told you that you mustn't believe this business about me complaining of pain all the time, she only said that so she could tell you about my running around when I was young, which was just an occasional affair like any other man would have, and all that about them giving me a treatment to rid me of sins wasn't like that at all; it didn't happen to me but to her brother Pipe when he was very young and hanging around with one of those tricks from Marina Street in San Juan. And now your mother jumbles everything up and says it was me, but don't believe her when it comes to such business, that's just the way she is these days.

They've built a Pentecostal Church next to the house, one of those so-called hallelujah churches. I believe that everyone is free to have his own religion, but not many people agree and I had a terrible time when I joined the Brothers of Silence masonic lodge, and the priest almost had me kicked out of town and a lot of people didn't even speak to me any more. The priest would get up in the pulpit and say that certain businessmen and all were walking hand-in-hand with the devil—imagine me hand-in-hand with that character! What happened was that I was one of the few people in town who could read and I even had sixty-two books and I developed some very definite ideas about the great French free-thinkers. As I say, they opened the Pentecostal temple, which is all right, but the bad thing is that they have their meetings till late at night, playing tambourines and maracas and singing a hymn that goes "Send us fire, Lord, send us fire," and aside from the racket they make I don't like that refrain at all because it seems wrong to ask so insistently for a punishment as terrible as that and asking for a return of bonfires like what happened to that French girl Joan of Arc, which the great French free-thinkers fought so hard against. But the strangest thing about that church is that the hallelujahs make public confessions of their sins and you can just imagine what sort of sins—that they used to come home drunk late at night and beat their wives, that they had lost everything playing dice, and one woman claimed brazenly, trembling all over as if in a divine trance, that she would go out to work to help her husband and would meet her lover instead and the husband was there too saying yes, sir, she's telling the truth and that now they had both repented since they had found the Lord's way. And Rogelio, Cheo the garbage man's boy, who's never left the village and who everyone used to swear was an idiot began to speak in public and was changing tongues the way you change shirts; like I say, it's the strangest thing, but it's true! He speaks English and then turns around and speaks French, this guy who's nothing but a peon, I swear to you I would have bet my life that he was an idiot at the very least, he speaks and sounds like a kwa kwa falufé. Put that one in your pipe, you who says there's nothing to write about here.

Last week a gentleman who said his name was Olmo Winston or something like that came by here and told me he was a friend of yours and that he'd written you and you hadn't answered and that you shouldn't be such a false friend, that's what he told me to tell you. And I told him that you didn't even write to your poor mother, and he laughed and said you should at least write him a little note just so he'd know you're alive. I won't tell you to write because I know you're as stubborn as a mule. That's up to you and your strange friends. He was the first to congratulate me because I'm going to be a grand-father. Why have you kept it so quiet?

Since your mother only writes you to complain about me, although I'm the one who has the right to complain, I'm going to give you some news about this town you hate so much, although I don't know why. You remember the new mayor? Well, he hasn't turned out so badly, you have to give people a chance to prove what they're worth. Anyway, he started by fixing up the plaza that had begun to look like a pigsty, and he planted mango trees because he said they're not only pretty, they produce fruit as well and that way he could kill two birds with one stone because he's a practical man, he improved the sanitation services, hired a character to write the town history, fired a health inspector without hesitation for taking money from the owners of the dairy in exchange for letting them water down the milk, built a road in the Pozos Dulces neighborhood and even helped Crazy Tony's wife give birth when there wasn't a doctor or midwife around. He's always spending time with the farmers, trying to solve their problems and he even reduced his own salary without anyone asking him to, and he put up posters that said all citizens had equal rights whether black or white or rich or poor or pro-statehood or pro-independence, he's like that, and I'd say he's read those great French free-thinkers too and he won't wear a tie even if they hogtie him. Anyway, you know how gossipy and ungrateful people are. Well, it was announced that the governor was going to visit the town and the mayor got everything ready with flags and all and ordered that the streets be cleaned and gave money from his own pocket to those who live on the main street, where the governor was supposed to pass, to paint their houses. Well, the governor arrived and the mayor spoke on the P.A. system, wearing a jacket but no tie, but that's nothing, the bad thing is that he asked the people, there were thousands and thousands, to stand facing the governor with their asses towards the houses. Well right away a committee of all the parties was formed to vote against him because he'd been so vulgar and inconsiderate in talking about asses. Four

39

assemblymen have resigned and now a campaign is under way because they say that such a man can never represent a town as refined as this one. So his number is up for the next election.

Your mother didn't want to tell you about Eusebio Morales because she says it's a sin. I don't know if you remember him, he's the father of Tingo Morales, who went to elementary school with you and who plays the accordion. Well, last week Eusebio keeled over and died, the doctor came and checked him and said okay he's dead, bury him, but it turned out that Eusebio has a daughter in Chicago and the family sent for her, but since it was going to take at least two days for her to get here they stuck Eusebio in the refrigerator vault in Río Piedras. The daughter arrived the next day and went to Río Piedras in tears and asked to see her father Eusebio Morales and they pulled out a drawer and showed him to her, and the daughter was crying a lot, as you can imagine, when Eusebio opened one bleary eye like he always has, they say that he moved a hand too but that's no longer important, and the daughter got such a bad case of the shakes they had to give her sedatives. It turned out that Eusebio was alive and had had a serious attack. The doctor who declared him dead went on vacation and nobody knows where he is and now they're going to sue him for damages. Since then, Eusebio Morales wanders around town selling his lottery tickets as if nothing had happened, bundled up to his ears no matter how hot it is and he made them take the refrigerator out of his house, and he insults the boys who try to sell him ice cream. Now they call him Tamarind Snow-Cone. His son Tingo, who as you know has a real ear for music, composed a bolero in his honor that speaks of cold winter nights and such things.

And what are you going to do? Do you plan to stay over there the rest of your life? Think carefully about what you're doing, study medicine or something useful while I'm still young enough to help you out. That book you wrote is okay, but now that you're going to be a father you have to think about getting into something serious and setting your head straight, because the family is going to keep growing. And if you stay over there much longer don't forget to teach the child English, since over there, naturally, they only teach Spanish and it isn't like over here.

Tell Yoli she should take good care of herself now that she's going to be a mother and she shouldn't be frightened, giving birth is as natural as eating a peanut. And if your mother writes any more of those exaggerated things about me, don't pay any attention, she just has a screw loose. Behave yourself and act honorably. Regards from your mother and Vinicia who always asks about you and remembers when she used to hold you on her lap.

Papá

P.S. Do you want me to send you any books by the great French free-thinkers?

He felt that she was laughing secretly and happily resigned to his usual inner violence while she assumed a magnificent knowing face, a sage in the middle of chaos, telling him that if only he would go out, that he should take his pale body, the result of his obstinate, self-imposed imprisonment, out for a walk, not stay at home. This said flicking the dust from the armchair with the fine hand of an imported secretary. She said:

"But you spend your life inside these four walls. You're going to end up making yourself sick. Why don't you take the bus and go to the Retiro? Or to the Casa de Campo? Or to an experimental art movie? I think they're showing something by Bergman, baby."

"Leave the prison of this apartment to stick myself in Bergman's prison? Are they showing *The Silence*? I saw it in New York. The Nazis appear in the first scene. But only in the first. After that they disappear and if I'm not mistaken, some little Spanish dwarfs emerge. Two different approaches to the grotesque."

"As far as I know the sun has never killed anyone."

"What sun?"

"Give me a cigarette."

He took a dirty white Chesterfield from his crushed pack and she looked at it, smoothing it out between her fingers, picking little bits of tobacco off her fingers. He brought the flame towards her and she moved back a little, ducking her head, her lips shaped unnaturally, pressing the end of the little white chimney, two little flames flashing brightly in the depths of her clear eyes, for he noticed that they were clearer than ever today, even caught by the pale red of the two tiny flames which moved like autumn leaves in the slow, interminably brief dance of the two tiny flames. Even the fingers, his fingers, thin and yellow at their tips like fine-quality asparagus in the nearby grocery store, the tobacco-stained ends of his fingers pointed out (not very nobly) that instant of contagion, that blazing essence, that brilliant determination that moved like golden tresses down her frankly stylized neck (something out of Modigliani? he thought darkly, crudely, laughing maliciously simply because he was capable of remembering at that moment the European name of a painter who in America, certainly, wouldn't have been worth the match that winked, darkening, consummately consumed), but he didn't know what was happening to him. He shook the asparagus, infinitely afraid that they would spring away in flames.

"If you already saw it, take a look in the newspaper. There must be something that would interest you, baby."

She said this wrapped in a transparent veil of smoke.

"Translations" he said, "Who will finish them then? Aunt. Ant. It's enough to make you die laughing."

"So? Why did you come to this country?"

"You can't deny that it's cold. If it weren't for the heating. I would have seen *Nazarín*, but it's too far away."

"Is it going to kill you?"

"I get sick very easily. You shouldn't have wiped the dust off your hand. *Viridiana* was good. But there's one I can't remember, oh yes, *Los Olvidados*, it's unbearable. Its meaning was twisted. It was bad from the start. From its conception. I saw it at the Thalia on 96th Street, right? The audience rebelled. The whole business was incredible. Even in spite of the little prologue he added attempting to justify his idiocy. They claim the movie's inspired. Don't believe a word of it."

"The sun has vitamin D. You could use some."

"What sun? The sun here is devitaminized. Haven't you seen decaffeinated coffee? Beerless beer? Wineless wine? I'd rather take pills. Honey, you can bet your life on *Viridiana*, but not on *Los Olvidados*."

"Don't argue so much. It's not good for you."

"The myth. It isn't right. He himself couldn't accept it. I believe he's a demythifier, don't you think so?"

She drew a heavy line of kohl beneath her eyelid in order to make herself appear more exotic, who doubts it (not he), and then she rubbed deodorant under her armpits, raising her arms delicately, like a woman drowning in slow motion. He tilted his head back and the slightly bitter liquid (he'd left the bottle uncapped and some foamy gnomes had gotten into it) slid down his throat, got to his stomach, and made a little pool. He pictured it: a little wine-colored puddle (Valdepeñas, in fact) bubbling away. It was easy to imagine, he thought, because he could feel it.

"And nonetheless," she said pensively scratching her chin, "it's so. Don't you agree?"

"Sure."

"You finally agree with me. You deserve a kiss. Mwa."

"If you're telling the truth, I see no reason why I should contradict you."

"Very reasonable. Work a little and then go out, okay?"

"And the translations?"

"I don't want to start an argument."

"It's already started. *Juliet of the Spirits* is great. That is, it's right on target. You've taken my last cigarette."

"Wouldn't it be better if you looked for work elsewhere? In an office, for example?"

"Aunt. Ant. You don't laugh because you have no sense of humor. Neither do I. No."

She walked around, lowering and raising the pistons of her arms because she needed to emphasize something, she still didn't know what, perhaps to highlight every word with the two accents of her arms. The wine ran down the other throat.

"People aren't going to eat you."

"I know that. I know I'm going out, I'm sure they're not going to eat me, but what will they think? That's where the dilemma lies."

"You remind me of a bad joke, baby. Put down the bottle. Let's try and find out why you're afraid to go out."

He held the bottle tightly against his chest, hit the parquet floors with his bare feet, shouted in a low voice:

"I don't need to go out."

"If at least they paid you well. Well, I'm going to be late. Come on, get yourself together. Go take a walk. I forgot to tell you that the phone bill is overdue. It has to be paid and I can't leave the office even for a minute."

"Unforgettable ITT. It seems to me that they're more considerate of their clients here."

"It's simply because it's Europe."

"Europe? That remains to be seen. Baby, I didn't know I was going to be a father. It seems a little unfair that half of humanity found out before I did."

"Wanda's letter?"

"All of them."

"That was last year, don't you remember? That idiot answers me now. She would believe that a woman can be pregnant for more than a year."

"Personally, I don't like those people."

"Personally, you don't like anyone. Period."

"You're impossible to talk with."

"What does that have to do with anything?"

"The same as with *Los Olvidados*, for example. And then rubbing that cream under your arms as if nothing had happened and taking my last cigarette."

"So I'll go myself. I'll take a minute and pay it."

"But just imagine. Be reasonable. How long since she last wrote you?"

"I haven't kept track."

"Well, I have. Twelve months."

"And when someone writes you, you don't even bother to open the envelope."

And those words made him look at her with a violence she never could have imagined. Was that the state of affairs? How was it possible that she? Was she able to hurt him to such an extent, to offend him to his very marrow? Even her? She of all people? And as though nothing were happening, without paying any attention to the eyes that were opening in the walls, to the claws that were coming out of the floor, to the hands that hung from the ceiling. Hundreds of thousands of flies were swarming around, forming a halo around her, and he was afraid to speak like a normal person. Because he knew, he wasn't unaware, he thought that knowing about the flies (that they were waiting for him to open his mouth so they could enter it and carry him over the roofs of Madrid) he shouldn't do it. When he met her, had he presented as great a problem for her as now, suddenly? She couldn't hear it, naturally, because she was spraying herself with perfume. Several fingers crept up her ankles, her calves, along her thighs, and she acted as if nothing. How can you calmly trust a woman! he thought passionately. But he couldn't scream, he couldn't. She gravely pointed a palm-frond pistol at him. It was the worst threat ever suffered by her or by him. She shot bullet words birdshot projectile words:

"There's Mancio's letter." *Está la carta de Mancio.*

God, getting rid of everything, digging in his flesh to extract those mortal fragments which had sharply perforated his arms, his breast all as ripe as ever and always, raggedly ripping away a nipple (can it have been written already?) oh, God forbid. The *á* went the farthest, grazing his most legitimate femur, perhaps encouraged by the gross abandon of speed of the accent stuck to its back like a flea truly impossible to unstick due to the very tempo of the word, the very nature of the verb, and then the *r* nailed like a splinter, no one, nothing doubted it was a splinter, and it tore off little fringes of red meat with its sharp edges just like the two *t*'s and the *s*'s, and the heavy capital letter, extracted like a rusted anchor after five centuries in the depths of the Caribbean. Furiously he glared at her, approaching between the hands that now hung down to her head, watching her pierce her feet with the claws that rose like a field of perfectly vertical cattails. He shouted, lowering his voice to a murmur:

"Yes, lucky me, lucky me. If I were to make a chair you'd praise me. Well, I'm going to make it. Without legs. Without a back. And then I'll remove the seat."

"See you this evening. Bye."

That's the way it was. He could make a note of it, noting it down in his notebook.

* * *

DIALOGUES IN NEBRASKA HEIGHTS, P.R.

1

"Good morning."

"Hello, good morning."

"How's your Ford?"

"Its transmission is slightly under the weather. I hope it's nothing serious. Besides that, we had an accident and it had to have eleven stitches in its bumper. And your Volkswagen, how's it doing?"

"Oh, a little sluggish. I think it might be the heat. It's always been inhibited, timid, it must be self-conscious about its size. Did you know that Antonio's Chevrolet has been indisposed all weekend?"

"Poor thing. I'll have to take a minute to go visit it. What's wrong?"

"The carburator!"

"My God!"

"Infirmities always begin at that age. Thank God I don't have anything serious to complain about."

"Bob Rivera's Rambler has a little something wrong with its radiator."

"Contagious?"

"I don't know. It's probably the dust."

"I hope it doesn't mean an epidemic. It's been days since I've heard your electric pruner. Don't tell me that. . ."

"Oh, it's just a dental problem. Cavities."

"That's exactly what's wrong with my shaver. The same thing happened to Cristeto."

"He must be disconsolate."

2

"My automatic washer threw up when I put the clothes in."

"You're kidding."

"Apparently the detergent disagreed with it."

"You think it's indigestion?"

"Allergy."

"Oh. You'll have to take it to a specialist."

"Who'll charge me an arm and a leg."

"I've been having some problems too."

"What's wrong?"

"My television."

"Something serious?"

"It's gone blind."

"Oh, no! Cataracts, or something worse?"

"It has an unbearable glare in its eye and when it talks it shouts."

"It could have something to do with the retina, or something like that."

"No. It must be something emotional, one of those complexes they talk about. Millicent is worried too."

"Don't think I'm nosy, but I'm dying to know what you're talking about."

"Her vacuum cleaner!"

"Holy cow!"

"It has trouble breathing."

"It could be something bronchial."

"It's very tired; it seems a lot like asthma. I hope it's not contagious and going to infect us all."

"God will protect us. Did you hear about María's tragedy?"

"No, I haven't heard."

"Her stereo's gone hoarse, it's constantly complaining and making rasping noises. She thinks it's acute laryngitis. It probably needs a good rest."

"Poor thing, it used to sing so nicely. Are we being punished for something in Nebraska Heights?"

"A real penance, my dear."

"Because I'd hardly touched the iron when it got red."

"It must have something to do with its heat resistance."

"How true, not all of us have the same resistance."

"Did you know about Julia's refrigerator? It caught a cold. It's been teary and sniffling for the last two days. And such cold sweats, my God!"

"Oh, and Carmita's blender."

"Yes?"

"It seems that she gave it too much food and the poor thing went into convulsions and its digestion became paralyzed. It had to be uncovered immediately and forced to throw up everything inside it."

"Imagine. Teresa told me that the other day she put her pressure cooker on the stove and carelessly left a saucer over the escape valve. What a mistake that was! You know how delicate they are, you can't lay a finger on them when they're on the flame. It exploded with a tremendous noise. Since then it has refused to work at all."

"Angélica had problems with her air conditioner. Its breath was hot and smelled bad, what they call halitosis. A fever of 107 degrees. I hope to God this run of bad luck won't continue."

"IhavefaithinGodourFathercreatorofheavenandearththatitwill beso."

3

"Cauliflower's problems are insurmountable."

"She isn't a long distance runner. But she's priceless in short races."

"And on wet tracks."

"The wetter the better. Each one has its own quirks."

"Of course. Cauliflower's just like her mother. Right down to the star on her forehead."

"But Cauliflower's mother has never been in this country."

"I've seen her in photographs."

"That surprises me. Would you like another highball?"

"Yes. Why does it surprise you?"

"Beautiful Lady died giving birth to Cauliflower. That's three years ago. I didn't think they'd keep her picture as though she'd been important."

"Well, I saw it. A very pretty mare."

"Her reputation comes from her father, Royal Badge."

"Royal Badge Cauliflower's father?"

"Why are you so surprised? Everybody knows that."

"Lies. She was a decent mare. Cauliflower's father is a Panamanian of impeccable breeding: Colonel."

"He's the putative father. But it had been over a year since Colonel serviced her. Cauliflower's clear eyes are the same as Royal Badge's. The eyes of an American colt. How's the highball? Strong?"

"Just the way I like it. Lies, lies. They have no respect for the memory of the dead."

"Sometimes I don't sleep thinking of the good old days of Kolito."

"Father or son?"

"Well, as they say, like father like son."

"What, are there rumors about paternity in this case too?"

"Not rumors. It's known that Kolito Jr. isn't the old man's son but his nephew."

"Wait a minute, why can't he be his son?"

"For the simple reason that Kolito Sr. was impotent. He sublimated his impotence by becoming the best runner of his time."

"So, you think you know everything."

"I read a lot."

"Sure, you have time to read. I, on the other hand, keep the books for forty-five businesses. . ."

"Cheap excuses. Anyone who has an interest in reading can find the time at night or early in the morning. One has to make time to cultivate oneself."

"Are you suggesting I'm uncultured?"

"No. Only that you lack discipline. In order to acquire culture you have to be disciplined. Well, would you like to come with me to the race track this afternoon?"

"Why do you keep on joking about my ignorance?"

"Don't take it like that. The race track's a school. Shall we have another highball?"

"Yes, I want to tell you that. . ."

"Speak up."

"I hate to praise people. Especially when they're right in front of me. I admire you, you know? You're really a very learned man. Count on me for the race track."

"Wonderful. Shall I add more ice?"

*   *   *

In the mornings, among the busy crowds that scurried to catch the subway, a bus, a taxi—a limousine, in a moment of panic, against the better judgment of the pocketbook—hurried crowds at eight in the morning. A fixed number of hours within the walls of an office, a cafeteria, a hospital. Dear Ant. Aunt for ant. The English storekeeper in Torremolinos. Franks smeared with mustard, that baby's crap, inspired while frying an egg, sweetly philosophic amidst the smoke of fried onions. That made him ponder existentialist philosophies. Das Man. Gulp. Who said an ant is an ant is an ant? An aunt is an aunt is an aunt? Phonetically disastrous. In one instance there's an a that's not an a. But in the other, contrary to all predictions, there's an a that's not an a. Pol mol and pal mal, depending on which side of the Atlantic the speaker is standing. When would I decide to read it? It was a temptation that haunted me day and night. Throw myself on the desk, tear open the envelope, read it? Mancio's small, almost illegible handwriting, tight and stubborn and hardheaded, pregnant with unpronounced, unheard curses. Oh, that faithfulness, like barbed wire inside a pillow. Long-esteemed, hated being. Oh, but he was fascinated by music. For example, the majestic chords of a gigantic door opening on its rusty hinges, the desperate chord of a child's sob, the basso profundo of a bomb exploding in a crowd, the harmonious laugh of a hyena, the ethereal symphonic murmur of a packed hospital collapsing, the delicate chords of a zinc plate being cut with a saw. In the afternoons he would take his favorite viper for a walk on a golden chain, while in the hallways of his house crawled noisy rattlesnakes, greenish lizards with abrupt spines, a boa constrictor would stand guard over his sleep, occupying the other half of the bed. His fishbowl was divided into two parts: on one side were eels, capable of electrocuting a bull with a single charge; on the other, one could observe the swarming dance of duly starved piranhas. Outside, on the terrace, grew an abundance of thistles, nettles, aromatic herbs, carnivorous plants, little bushes from which you could extract a pure, deliciously fatal sap. Surrounded by this vegetation, overgrown with weeds, Mancio would spend his time caressing dizzying surfaces: crushed glass, sandpaper, coagulated blood; and his chest would swell pleasurably at the smell of decaying carcasses (hence his *Malodorous Cantos*?).

Covered by a scab of violence, he was, nevertheless, as tender as a newly sprouted head of lettuce. But his handwriting, there, tight, relentlessly pulsating beneath a pile of papers that only served to rekindle his cold fire, his frozen inferno, his strictly logical system of tortures. There and everywhere: in the bathroom, in the oven, in the bedlinens, in my study; and he had contaminated the mailbox with an unnameable virus: now all my letters arrived trembling with disease, happily infected. They all bore the same profoundly dark, clouded, almond-shaped eyes; the high wide cheekbones reminiscent of engravings of Indians exterminated four centuries ago; large, salient ears touched by a rare transparency; a powerful, straight nose that could have been aquiline had not a few drops of African blood frustrated it by widening its base; dark straight hair without lustre; skin the color of antique copper that appeared greenish-gold some mornings; his tortured skin filled with secret wasps, his green veins obstructed, his sweet pancreatic process turned bitter, sir. Hesitating never or later? Neither one nor the other, for example. I would have to explain him that if they wasn't part of our ways of being, neither I of the same ways. But they won't understand my explanations. He, all logic, would laugh at my madness, fully my rights. Oh clever Mancio Flintstone.

It might develop thus:

"How's your book coming along, dimwit?"

"Well, I."

"Yes, yes. Well you. Are you working on it?"

"Yes."

"Listen, you've been working on this thing for a number of years now."

"Four years and ten months."

"Apparently you're not making any headway. If you would spend less time with the bottle, if you'd decide to work, there might be some hope for you. I say there *might* be. Nothing is certain until you prove it. And another thing is this business about the clouds. If the clouds this or the other thing. Come on, we're halfway through the 20th century. You have to learn about your language first, my boy. Those anglicisms are going to kill you."

"But you. Certainly a lot of anglicisms, Manson. Spanglish."

It was impossible to argue with him because he would jump up saying you had to tie yourself to the leg of the table and work furiously without allowing yourself a moment of weakness or indecision and he would calmly note that Tolstoy wrote *War and Peace* I believe nineteen times and that *there* was a genius and that folks such as ourselves with so little creative stature were obliged to bust our guts if we wanted to make the most modest of contributions, at least at the level of our deviant colonial country, that's what he would say smoking right down to the butt and burning his finger with visible irritation, and they weren't really writers those scribblers who rationalized idiotically in order not to write saying if so and so had produced such a masterpiece the best thing to do was shut up, because following that line of thought Dostoyevsky would not have even written one letter tormented by the ghost of Cervantes, and Faulkner, that great Southern Yankee, would have devoted himself to raising cotton for a buck if the ghost of the Russian had obsessed him, and you could even take a more distant approach, beginning with the Greeks and ending up with the most recent writer discovered by some lowly editor and if you wanted to color things differently, yet still within the realm of art, you had to consider that Picasso shouldn't have defiled a single canvas after recognizing that in Altamira it had already been done, and all the cave painting, etc., that we can't be sure has been surpassed. A person writes because he needs to write and in spite of those stunning gentlemen who are up to their ears in the mythology of the consumer, he would say, gentlemen who had to be carefully read and studied, but not with the vile aim of shooting them down, for everyone was compelled to add his own bit without thinking about fucking editorial demands, about those furious book salesmen, humbly and silently each of us contributing his own grain of sand, his most personal self, painfully in a vast majority of cases, ignored but persistent as he said Lezama had been: cloistered in chaos among tattered books writing writing patiently every day while the names of great writers exploded like fireworks over his embarrassing studio, a library rat, a fat ghost enslaved by strange mental structures, a flashing magician who suddenly pulled a fascinating product from his hat, a strange, overly subtle fascinating product, a marvelously nonsensical and crazy and intricate work, Mancio said cursing, but he had achieved it thanks to many years of work, work, work. That's what he always said and that literature is a tree and everyone should contribute a little leaf, he'd say. And lately he had contributed two good-sized leaves of 600 pages each. I had written a letter to him during the summer and he answered with a book without a word attached to it, impolitely lacking an inscription. I wrote him again and he answered me with another volume, as silent as the stone his heart was made from. Five years spent on the first. Five years on the second. Meritorious ant. I didn't write him again. And after many long months he chose to send me that dangerous letter, sealed forever, that inexorable germ, that atrocious source of panic, that seed of madness. Drunk, barefooted, unshaven, with my shirt open to my groin, I must have presented a depressing spectacle.

"I write him and write him and look how he answers me! A novel per letter. Does that seem right to you? I write him as a friend. I tell him about life in this country, give him some news, tell him about the bookstores and the Book Fair and look what he does!"

"During the bullfight season we'll have to see El Viti, honey. He's fantastic, he never laughs and he acts like a madman. Someone ought to study why a man goes into that profession, aside from economic reasons. The crowing machismo of the Hispanic race? If that were the case there would be a bullfighter for every ten people in Puerto Rico."

"And now, after so many months, that letter. Doesn't it seem strange to you? I wonder what he has on his mind?"

"And the worst is that for every good bullfighter you have to see a lot of bad ones. El Cordobés, for example, is he worth it? They say that he's too careful, now that he has his millions he isn't going to risk his hide for anything. Paco Camino is up there with the great matadors. There are good ones, there are still some good ones left. People complain that the Fiesta Brava is just a masquerade nowadays. They miss the times of El Gallo and Joselito and Manuel Torre and Manolete."

"Manuel Torre was a magnificent *cantaor*, don't stick him in with a bunch of bulls! Have you ever seen such gall? I write him, I tell him things about this country that he's never visited, that he doesn't know and I do, and look how he answers. First with *El Mirador* and then with *Estación de brujas*. He answers me with 1200 pages and a letter whose content I have no idea of."

"Calm down. Soon we'll be able to see the first bullfights of the season. I hope El Niño de la Capea has matured a little, he's very young. Did you know he comes from Salamanca? Just like Francisco García Lorca."

"He lives in Río Piedras, but he mailed the letter in San Juan. Is he trying to confuse me? I tell him about this country as a friend. I tell him that I went to Toledo and that it's a marvelous city, and also to Avila and that the estuaries and the scenery of Galicia remind me of The Island, that he shouldn't be fooled by the flamenco rumba, that I've seen thousands of bookstores and there are hundreds of publishing companies, that I went to the Arco de Cuchilleros and all that, and that old Madrid looks like old San Juan which really pleased me because I could see certain roots, you know, a very definite origin, that many women look like my aunts which is really something: I mean we didn't just come from air, there's an origin aside from the African contribution, you know what I mean. And much more, a minute description of the festival of La Paloma and the abundant wine and that the Rastro is a swarm of people where you can buy anything from a needle without a point to huge furniture and probably even a jet engine I told him to see if he'd laugh. And you know the rest: one thousand two hundred pages, his little leaf for the tree of literature, and an incredible letter because of the threat that's in it. As if he wanted to say that I'm just an amateur in the arena he's starring in."

"An amateur? There are gobs of them. They go into the pastures at night and riddle the beasts, magnificent fighting bulls completely ruined. They dream of glory."

"It would suffice for me to light a match to it, right? But its ashes would continue to haunt me. It's a curse."

"I'm going out for onions."

Yoli was washing the pot, lighting the oven, she worked concretely, visibly, and the results of that laborious submission would be apparent in a quarter of an hour. She never vacillated, she never asked herself any questions, she simply knew that if she threw pieces of meat, potatoes, and spices in a pot, she'd end up with a stew. Mancio Flintstone would arrange words in a mold, season them to taste, a touch of salt and pepper, stir and check the concoction with endless patience, and five years later would release the cake from the mold. It might be a little burned from too hot an oven, or an erroneous calculation of spices might make it slightly insipid, and then there was no turning back, right? The dinner guests would taste it and grimace; or perhaps displaying the courtesy that the situation called for they would say that it was fine, tasty, truly a delicate treat. And did Mancio really give a damn about the opinion of the dinner guests? He didn't follow the recipes of the great chefs, he did his own thing without making excuses to the sophisticated palates of great international cuisine. But most likely not one single guest would make any comment, the cake would turn out to be invisible and therein Mancio's basic virtue would be confirmed: to gather his ingredients patiently, silently in the great vacuum of crushing indifference rampant in his country in order to produce in five years, with an unpredictable personal recipe—his cake. Silent, angry, filled with lightning in the midst of his dinner guests' closed obscurity, incorrigible braggart, hateful prosecutor, Mancio would walk his gentle viper among his scandalized countrymen. Chewing on my fingernails there was the letter. But worse yet. To the "Señor" he had added a "Don." An impulse of his black humor?

"You won't know until you read it," Yoli repeated softly. "You won't know. Open it and read it."

"Because it is inconceivable that a fellow countryman would use that formula. Señor is fine, that's what you always put. But 'Don' on top of it is a distasteful joke, he's pulling my leg."

"You have the vice of creating problems for yourself, Eddy. Maybe the key is in the letter. What difference does Señor Don make anyway? It's a correct form of address."

"Maybe I let a 'vosotros' slip out in my last letter," I reasoned, submerged in my favorite depression. "That probably sounded treacherously Castilian to him. And that is his ironic, bloody answer."

"I thought Manuel Torre was a bullfighter from Cataluña," Yoli said, uncovering the pot.

Seven black butterflies flew over her head.

* * *

Akiro was telling me the story of his dog, Medal. He was a proletarian canine, sans pedigree, but with surprisingly human intuitions. Medal could tell the difference between a bottle of white rum and a bottle of dark rum, he would growl when he heard Stockhausen played or a conversation in English, and he would jump happily when he heard a poem by Rimbaud. If he arrived late, Medal would give three soft knocks, duly spaced out, on the door; other times he would push it, come in and stop in the living room, bowing his head repeatedly in front of each of the persons present in a well-mannered greeting. These demonstrations of intelligence caused Akiro to surmise that in a billion years Medal's descendants would invent the first ax.

*   *   *

Somewhere behind the clothes hung out in hopes of catching the shy March sun, through half-closed windows, a canary chirped. In summer one might clearly hear not only its magnificent trill, but also the harsh intonation of Nordic words. He had seen the blonde legs on the high inside balconies. Strong legs, calisthenically trained, thin hardened bodies leaning over the chasm of the inner patio beneath the rectangular sky. In summer or when winter was drawing to a close, he would see them hanging their clothes out on the lines. They could awaken Don Juan-like adventures on a cheerful fjord, among birches that had never seen the sun (survivors of the endless night), among delicate Bergmanesque wild strawberries, showing from the dizzy heights whatever was showable, including the blonde vegetation of postulant Viking girls. All this and him from below, on his balcony, from which hung his Fruit of the Loom shorts, bourgeois Arrow shirts and the inevitable handkerchiefs. And if they turned toward him from their pedestals of frozen heights they weren't surprised by that face upturned imploringly like someone searching for justice, that clear justice which consists of giving to each according to his needs. From the knees up, to the waist and a little further on, to the truly northern pink nipples which had probably pointed like perfectly aimed pistols up the streets of Stockholm, Oslo and maybe Uppsala (because secret earthquakes have been registered there, witnessed by a cold system of seismological measurements). Sooner or later their willowy bodies would end up on the southern beaches, Marbella was waiting for them, happily impatient, the lights of Torremolinos would play on their darkened, naked legs. Alicante, Benidorm, Sant Feliu de Guíxols. In their bikinis made out of strips of cellophane they would lie on the Mediterranean sands to worship that wayward god who barely shone on the northern coasts for a few weeks with decisive, inconsequential fury (if that is possible). And that German or whatever girl lying a short distance from her beach umbrella, and he looked at her insistently and she rolled over on the deplorable sands of Torremolinos, waiting for his approach, flashing something akin to a slight Teutonic smile, with luxurious high-rise buildings behind her, built in the center of escapism, but Yolanda, coming out of a feigned sleep, turned over and faced her, and the girl looked away and was lost forever. That's the only language there was. Lower a gaze, look away, close your eyes, turn away, a vocabulary generated by two blind and mute bodies that come together reaching the melting point if possible in a concrete androgenic theory, put into realistic practice. The girl's hair had fallen across her face, not golden nor honey-colored but rather a dark, not too pretty color, a Valkyrie in slight disgrace but joyfully attractive. At night they would walk alone along the streets of Torremolinos with no consciousness of their mass-produced bodies, blonde and smiling, ignoring the Celtiberian storm they provoked in their wake. Scandinavian workers on vacation from their offices and their matrimonial beds dreaming of vague romantic Mediterranean adventures (because it is suspected that the olive trees and vineyards in this area nourish a particularly erotic blood). Actually he laughed, commenting on his impressions to the ever-vigilant Yolanda, untiring policewoman. What would happen if such an abundance of delights were to blossom on the northern coast of their own country with such intensity? Oh, the island would sink to one side. Our fiery Casanovas would probably abandon their jobs and homes and suddenly establish themselves where scorched sands offered such lush catches, because a horizontal woman excites a Third World male to the point of making him lose his coordinates. The northern coast submerged and the southern one emerging from the sea with algae and marine grasses and spongy rocks dripping water while the fragrant incandescent motto of Underdeveloped Man floated in the air: it may kill me but I'm going to enjoy it. But those girls wouldn't travel to the Caribbean. They paraded their naked rumps along the Gran Vía, going in and out of boutiques with dark, hairy types, into discotheques with loud screeching breathing, attracted like flies to honey, dreaming vaguely of operatic Carmens and Don Josés, their not-so-cold brains crackling like fiery castanets (like Yoli, with her fiery thoughts), sprawled out in the sun on the benches of the Plaza Callao, scattered in fake rags along the Cuatro Caminos and Serrano avenues from which the Yankees of Torrejón Air Base had slowly begun their retreat to the despair of numerous Chinese tailors, installed in the perfectly transparent Madrid air where one could clearly distinguish night from day (recalling in contrast the chilling tundra). There they were, occupying everything, inspiring dreadful comedies of a most appalling taste. They were there in summer, in winter, their bodies hanging over the wrought-iron balconies of the inner patio, hanging out their scanty clothing, perfectly practical, logically functional. Yoli would make no comment about the girls who so generously and uncaringly showed honorable husbands, peeking through curtains, the fundamental reasons for their success. Yoli didn't even make a remark when she caught him craning his neck uncomfortably upwards surveying the gentle Nordic hills, but she did ask him what he was doing in that position and he said he was looking at the brilliant summer sky and she told him that from there all you could see were the walls of the building; it would be better, she said, for him to go to the balcony where he could see not only the summer sky, but also the interesting rooftops of old Madrid.

The canary was still singing exquisitely.

* * *

Dear ant. Aunt and ant. Halfway through the paragraph I get up, run to the kitchen and check to make sure all the gas knobs are turned off. I return to the work table and close the door with two heavy latches. In spite of all my security measures, an invisible mass could break down the door. I continue suffering the agonizing journey that begins at the drafted pages, moves to the dictionary and returns to the tip of my pencil. An unknown mass could break it down. At some point the words that have been haunting me for the past few days rise to the surface: "We've come to settle accounts with you." Calm in the fierce determination they bring to bear. *The most exciting night of the year, honey.* The door could be torn down by a formidable unknown mass, *she said*, but what had I done? If the gas knobs had been turned off (Yolanda took precious care of that, prompted by my nagging), on my last trip to the kitchen I had probably turned them on unconsciously, automatically, thinking I was turning them off. Enigmatic self-destructive behavior. Weren't these things happening too often or at least with alarming frequency? People who fear high places, fear jumping off, hence vertigo, the implacable dialectics, the red flag, the wire fence, the light that flicks on, the alarm siren. I go up to the 98th floor of the Empire State Building and look down: human ants, toy cars, a little street I could block out with my hand, a fascinating attractive serpentine: it beckons me with a thousand barely audible voices, embrace me, just one tiny step, a ridiculously small effort and you'll have me, seraphic music, something by Corelli, perhaps the sleepy trumpets of some Vivaldi, nothing serious, you don't worry about whether it's good, bad, liberating, enslaving, it's simply an act without a history or a future, as if it came from nothing, a purely incommunicable act, divested of theories. It presents itself there for a split second and then windows and ledges and rooftops rush up to your eyes, meteorically they rise rising toward infinity and the air is hard and violently rasps the skin on your face (especially if you travel head first, which is usually the case, I know from my dreams); the wind produces an insensitive erosion of the face, your limbs turn cold, your heart goes on a temporary strike, a silently waiting dramatic tempo, the streets draw nearer at indescribable speed there it is. Ergo the ring, the red light, the siren coiled in the air, the smoke from a nearby fire asphixiates, provokes vertigo. I turn away from the railing on the 98th floor with cold hands and my heart on a string. The train tracks vibrate violently in the tunnel, the throngs of people, poorly dressed and sweating, wait for the subway to come by. In the midst of this anonymous mass a man waits without knowing what for, perhaps he smokes quietly while the echoes of the trains come closer, roaring more loudly; perhaps he has been chatting at the office about his upcoming vacation, about the imperative need for a change of scenery, he would talk it over with his wife; in two weeks it would be his youngest son's birthday (Lovey he would occasionally call him on relaxed afternoons); on Sunday they'd all bury themselves in a family movie, and the deep roar of metal in motion draws nearer through the tunnel just like any other day at any other time, the prow of the engine slicing the darkness, violent untamable chest, and the man glances at the rails thinking he's run out of cigarettes, at the ground stained by those ugly lubricant abstractions, black some places, brown, grey, the tracks take on a silvery shine from the wear of the wheels between stations; the man takes another look at the old earth humiliated by the absence of sun, he discovers a piece of newspaper that discusses the rise in the stock market, wars, triumphant young ladies, astronauts on the moon, bargains at a shoe store, spring was never more beautiful, next to him a distracted woman laughs uproariously, an oldster stoops over his cane, the metal prow is there fast as light and the anonymous man merely possesses the slightly oversized skeleton, nails, teeth and a vague dream of growing an outrageous mustache in order to scare his nephews and children, tiny invisible among the huge multitude that crowds the platform, grow a beard to irritate the boss, the morning paper rolled up in his pocket to show his wife (who has become excessively fat in the last year), but the red lights don't go on, there are no alarms, no vertigo; only flesh, a thin layer of flesh on the bones which are too wide for his height, and the crowd steps back because it doesn't want to see, a whirlpool of arms and legs on this side of the platform because his blood is red like that of the rest of us, it's red and has a morbidly fascinating shine, a fascinating odiously loud red, a liquid dark flame on the tracks.

On my second trip to the kitchen I confirm that the gas knobs are in fact turned off. When the handles on the stove and the water heater are in a vertical position it means there won't be a dangerous gas leak. Besides I had drawn arrows on the wall pointing vertically, exactly perpendicular to the floor, and written with wide, very visible black letters:

OFF   OFF   OFF

And I had drawn horizontal arrows marked:

ON   ON   ON

DANGER!!!

Respected families, known by everyone, living at number such and such on such and such street, who walked their doggies in the evening and carried identification, ate, urinated, and went to sleep, who turned on the news with great curiosity and were pleased when the Royal Madrid soccer team won, families who vacationed in summer and hibernated in winter, made of flesh and blood like you and me, who dreamed of buying a little apartment in Aluche with their life savings, the same ones who almost won at off-track betting last week, who are swallowed up in the Sunday crowds at the bullfights at Ventas or Carabanchel, I'm telling you that families like yours and mine would turn up dead some rosy morning in the month of April for example, the grandfather in his chair with the newspaper still in his hands, the mother in front of the television set which is hot from being on all night, the screen crossed by fluctuating bright lines that buzz in the silence, the children apparently asleep next to their toys—a little car without wheels, a doll that opens its eyes—everything was spelled out in the afternoon paper. After two days of uncomfortable silence the neighbor had decided—along with the super—to break down the door of the two philosophy students' apartment; one had the book in his hand, the other a bottle of wine, the radio was on and spoke in low tones of the temperature expected for that night, scattered clouds, relative humidity, the forecast for tomorrow: sunny with a few scattered showers in the Cantabrian region; the news might be discovered in some corner of the morning paper, perhaps next to a Cortefiel ad.

Yoli, how then can I appease my panic? Fear that the door would be broken down by a dark presence. Have you understood why the young Argentinian professor keeled over next to me? He was eating his half-raw steak—he said it helped him get over his hangover—when I suddenly saw a surprised look on his face I'll never forget; he got up, tried to cough, we slapped his back, stuck our fingers down his throat, he turned red, purple, ran around hitting his head against the walls, went through a glass door (but that blood didn't matter), and when we put him into a friend's car, while we were waiting for the traffic to clear up, sounding the horn like crazy, his head fell to one side, his arms and legs went limp. A friend I can't remember caught a glimpse of something, a piece of meat anchored deep in his throat. Now do you understand why I've never eaten meat again? You know why, but I'm not sure you understand fully what I've felt since then. Do you understand why when I see you eat even a crust of bread and you cough I jump up and hit you on the back? And the time a friend was killed in a holdup when they cut his main artery with a straight razor? By then you no longer laughed when you saw me show up with my neck protected by one of those high collars that are used for cervical fractures. I used it for three months, Yoli, and if it hadn't been for the fact that we had already shared a bed innumerable times you would have left me and all my apparently exaggerated obsessions, lost as I've always been in a meticulous labyrinth of terrifying premonitions.

So, while I work on the translations, I keep the door tightly locked with two big latches. Nevertheless, an invisible mass could violently break it down. The music of a few calm words, spoken without rancor, without indifference, poured out by an impersonal will, reverberates obstinately. "We've come to settle matters with you. We can't wait any longer. There is neither pleasure nor hate in this mission. It's our duty to talk to you. You're there. We can see you perfectly. It's useless to act scared, to laugh, jump, cry or beg. It's time to put things in their place. Hate, rancor, happiness, we are unaware of the meaning of those words. We know that your gesture has a name. But that name doesn't interest us. We know there's such a thing as a scream, but we ignore its significance. We only perceive a sound. Are you urinating, sweating, defecating in your clothes? Glands. You're totally free to feel however you like. You're there. We have searched for you since you were an infant, year after year, tirelessly. You weren't aware of that. But perhaps you had a certain intuition. We followed determined, unmistakable clues, certain signs that were undeniably yours, we recognized your number. Finally we found you. Duty, fate, mission accomplished. Now let's begin. Let's settle things once and for all. It's the mission we've been entrusted with." Yes, but who, when, where?

Aunt and ant.

*   *   *

MARTIN HEIDEGGER[1]

In dealing with the problem of being and its methodology one would have to consider Dasein as a basic element within the ineffable politics of Being for the purpose of death. Constitutionally and constitutively Man is, therefore, a Being for death.[2] Is there a way to confront the problem of God? Naturally. We are not unaware that a Being is not necessarily (nor even precisely) God. Now then, from all this one can deduce that thought, as such, has, we repeat only when treated as such, the obligation, if it can be called that, to find the means to return to that which is creatively transcendent, which is the same as the initial creative idea (i.e., all that which is transcendental), or in other words, a return to God, not even precariously found in the Being.

JEAN-PAUL

We present the thoughts of this great existential philosopher in the form of an outline which, naturally, only aspires to give an over-all idea of the problematics which managed to shake even the innermost being of Juliette Greco. In spite of this, there is one question which must be systematized. What is nausea?[3] Better yet, we should ask ourselves what basis the intermediate viscosity between non-Being and the crushing solidity of Being-in-itself has in reality. Can the solution to such overwhelming problematics be found? The answer is affirmative if the following affirmation is affirmed.[4] Man (perhaps Heidegger's Das Man?) is nothing more than a project. However, the answer is negative if we happily take Man to be a naked[5] deficiency. Now then, based on the preceding it is not even difficult and much less impossible to cautiously approach the concrete affirmation that Man, as a Being-unto-himself-for-Death, has no escape (*Scapatorium*), that is to say, the apparent causality of

---

[1] In German in the original version.
[2] Underlined in the Quechua version.
[3] Deleted in the Finnish version.
[4] Untranslatable semantic pun.
[5] In the Vatican's version: "uncovered."

a paradoxical tension of nothingness in the star-studded universe of existence, we repeat, only as an ambivalent eterodoxical[6] project. In spite of this, the idea of God is, fortunately, abundantly problematic. This being so, we must start from the premise that the ultimate reality of Man is that he goes astray as such in his effort to create a God (*Gottenskraffterlosen*). Hence we must adopt the following inevitable corollary: Man is, perhaps to the misfortune of mankind, a useless passion.[7]

NIETZSCHE[8]

Observe the genius of this democratic philosopher in his own words: "I have written my books with my very own blood." Is it possible for Man to look at himself and see his own absurdity? We firmly suspect so. Nevertheless, and in spite of the foregoing, there is one door yet open (*Oppenddooresein*), one avenue of escape: a direct and uninterrupted voyage to the "refreshing edge of madness."[9] However, we can perceive a sort of systematization and a clear determination of the problematics which are very much opposed to the very essence of philosophy as a highly hierarchical and polyvalent discipline. If preferred, opposed to the tight structural group which we have now discovered to be integrally constitutive of cybernetics (a fully justifiable reason to initiate an extended study bearing in mind the demands that such proposals represent without rushing into the common vice of schools which in one way or another show the rigidity of their dogmatism and the faddish notoriety of their unlimited utopianism, in other words: the impossibility of generic

[6] Sic.

[7] At this point it would be interesting to establish in my dear Jean-Paul the existing dialectical relationship between his blood type (we aren't aware if the Rh factor had any part in his character formation) and his frankly astrological condition. To be more precise: what was his ascendant at the moment of birth? Where was the Fourth House? Where was the Fifth? Through a rigorous and, of course, exhaustive study, would it be possible to establish with blazing clarity that our illustrious friend was born outside the sign which, according to astral forces, corresponded to him? Perhaps an accident of his progenetrix (while driving the family Citröen) in a state of gestation, in other words, while she was expecting? A somewhat fatalist notion of the conception of a Venusian dominance. In any case, in these pages we exhort our astrologist and structuralist friends to undertake the realization of this very necessary project.

[8] Friedrich, of course.

[9] Himmler, Heinrich, *Die Und Spragen nix ober ish Telefunkenberlach Shupstragensitulrithmanners die Herr Friedrich Nietzsche*. Third Reich Press, Munich, 1938.

66

abstraction without previously performing disciplined and highly specialized studies within each pannick particularity). For example: theories which, like the one on relativity, create, or better yet engender,[10] pseudo-philosophic activities which could lead to facts that pull at contemporary history such as the systematic arrival of Man on the Moon. Is religion, therefore, a purely biological product?

KIERKEGAARD[11]

Last, but not by any means the least important on the list of existentialist philosophers (at some other time we'll speak of Abbagnano)[12] we have this great Swedish thinker,[13] who at a certain point even stated, in a fit of extremism quite rare among Swedes, Norwegians, Finns, et al., that there was nothing malignantly awry in that parents, under non-explicit but certainly implicit demands from the Supreme Being or Creator, sacrificed their children if this act were authentically religious. This illustrious thinker opposed the most tenacious individualism (*Eggothismenspraggerish*) to any theory with the simplifying tendency toward massification. In other words: "you against me," as it were: "unavoidable cause of irritation" (*Die Grrr*). His Biblical example in which the good Abraham decides to "liquidate" his own son[14] as an altruistic offering to the Creator is well known. Neither the Larousse Dictionary nor No. 100,487 of the Reader's Digest indicates whether he died a rich or a poor man.[15]

*　*　*

[10] Underlined in the Ukrainian version.

[11] Although with typical British reserve the author of this study doesn't so indicate, it is suspected that he refers to Soren (Translator's Note).

[12] In Italian the consonant group gn is pronounced ny. Ex. Ana Magnani, Maro Del Pegnis.

[13] According to recent investigations it has been confirmed that our author wasn't Swedish, but Norwegian.

[14] In the Roman version of Pius XII, "deliciously offer."

[15] This statement has provoked angry polemics among exegetes. Who died rich or poor, Abraham, his son, or Soren? Some brand the final statement as confusing, unresolved, symbolic and dangerously tainted with a socializing nuance, while the majority of philosophers categorize it as a simply brilliant comment (Translator's Note).

Al Tohelj, Abdul, *The Camel, Metaphysical Being*. Cairo, 1950.

Assim, Joao, *Nos artes da placer TNT os Butoes da generais fascistas*. Recife, 1964.

Beckett, Gustavo Adolfo, *Rimas y leyendas*. Despeñaperros, 1951.

Cu Pi, O, *Taiwan, Our Motherland*. Washington, 1960.

Chimilco, Alejo, *Loss of the X Phoneme in Xlantixloxlo*. Mexico, 1948.

Dell Chitti, Beniamino, *Tutto el neorealismo e sua inmortalita e demostratta en la prostituzione della madonna Pronunciatta Liberace*. Milano, 1953.

Depressedi, Mario, *Prima de la canzionetta populare digli Abruchi en cuesto titulare, "Il doce infarto dell mio Cardio"*. Rome, 1935.

Doltus, Mikos, *Alexandrine Verse in Greece Today*. Athens, 1970.

Fuqueiros, Colonel Amilcar Cafe, *Os metodos practicos da tortura, meo catalogo*. Ediçoes da Ministerio da Defensa, Brazilia, 1969.

Gonorrechea, Dr. José María, *Venereal Diseases and Folklore*. Donostiarra Publications, San Sebastián, 1925.

Khoria, Charles, *Free Enterprise, A Solution to the Problems of the Third World*. OAS Editorial, 1964.

Kordio, Benjamin, *How to Pleasantly Surprise Your Friends at Club Meetings*. Carnegie Press, 1956.

Lopescu, Georgiu, *Smelt Fishing in Rumania*. Bucharest, 1970.

Lopian, Josefa, *Woman, That Non-entity*. Inner Life Publications, 1968.

Lumpit, Paul, *Spiritual Salvation Through LSD*. San Francisco, Cal., 1966.

Lunfardi, Sarmiento. *The Voice of Stupidity in Current Argentinian Literature*. Buenos Aires, 1970.

Mhedari, Alexandro, *The Bedouin and Hendecasyllabic Verse*. Cairo, 1945.

Misantropoulous, Nikos, *Socrates and the Progressive Government of the Colonels*. Praxis Rifrafittis Press, Athens, 1970.

O'Neill, Salicio, *Diseases of the Jejunum*. Lima, 1940.

Pies, Aristides, *Three Reasons to Blow Up the World*. Charenton Publishers, 1960.

Porcine, Colonel Pierre, *Nous scruerons l'indépendance aux petits pays africains*. Ed. Lacrappe, Paris, 1953.

Prick, John, *Weak is the Meat.* (Translated: *Débil es la carne.* Buenos Aires, 1952).

Qui Det, Li, *Representative Democracy in Formosa.* Changing World Press, Washington, 1965.

Ratta, Stampano, *Per una revoluzione internatta e una reformatta interiore de la Cosa Nostra.* Edizione Bonny e Clyde, Sicilia, 1967.

Ravioli, Giacomo, *Pizza, spagetti, lasagna, popolo e struttura di podere en la primma Roma de Caligula.* Milano, 1963.

Risupa, Gertrudis, *Cuba, Free in Exile.* Off Key Press, Miami, 1968.

Shtew, Ira, *The Culinary Art of Guinea.* Oporto, 1932.

Soto, P.J., *Usmail.* (Translation into the Spanish in preparation).

Täzzal, Kôr, *How to Attain a Zen-Tao Revolution.* Port au Prince, 1965.

Thata, Miprös, *The Dubcek Policy and Difficulties of the Urinary Tract.* Prague, 1969.

Trom Bon, Nguyen, *Tan shen nan bang Kao bang Diem bang Ky bang.* Saigon, 1968.

Trafficantti, Giusseppe, *La mia desideratta del bootlegger acordato en la sesione portuaria di nostra coloniatta en Manhattan.* Edizione Salvatore Giuliano, New Jersey, 1960.

Von Sprouts, Herr Brussels, *Esh schichiste der strassen volks nix Wagen und Henrichbollen und Guntergrassen.* Munchen, 1967.

Wealthy, John, *Is Macondo a Marketable Territory?* Texas, 1970.

* * *

On the telephone one tends to resort to needlessly grave tones of voice. But sometimes I would suddenly forget my Castilian residency and say hello; then annoyed I would correct myself, *dígame, hola,* wrong number sir. Strange adventure. The telephone was becoming the only means I had left to communicate with others. There was no need to display the profile of a supernumerary being. Nevertheless, I often remembered impossible conversations, tormented dialogues that drove away all desire to attempt them once again. Paralyzingly. Maybe it wasn't such a big thing after all.

"Coach service," the man growled.

"Is this the Felix Coach Transport Company?"

"Isn't that what I just said?"

"The Felix?"

"Listen, if you dialed our number don't expect to get the all-night drugstore or the Carabanchel bullring."

I said humbly:

"Yes, sir, the bullring. I mean excuse me, I'd like to know what time the *guaguas,* the buses leave for Vigo."

"Coaches."

"Yes, that's what I meant."

"Vigo, you say?"

"Yes, sir, Vigo."

"With *v* as in Valencia?"

"Exactly."

And he growled out the schedule quickly. And then the fare.

"Pardon me," I said with what Yoli calmly calls an innate Puerto Rican guilt complex. "Could you repeat the schedule?"

"Eh? What's that?"

"Would you be kind enough to repeat the schedule to me, sir?"

"The schedule? Now listen, listen!"

"I'm listening, sir."

"How many times am I going to have to tell you!"

"I didn't hear you well, sir."

"If you'd at least write down the information, but how can *you* be expected to write anything down!"

"I'm writing, sir, but the schedule slipped by."

"The schedule slipped by? 'Chrissake! If you'd write it down."

"I have been writing, sir. How do you know I'm not marking all this down in my notebook?"

"Notebook! Will you lay off me, for the love of God!"

"Listen, sir, I just arrived in this country. I don't know the customs and you know. . .I'm a tourist."

There was silence on the other end. Finally, restrained, the voice said:

"Okay, okay, if that's the case. . .Did you say to Pontevedra?"

"Vigo."

"It's all the same. The same coach. Vigo is a pretty city. Of course a little steep and they say it's been raining a lot. I recognize your accent. You're an American. There are a lot of Galicians in America, eh? They call all Spaniards Galicians over there. They say that when the Americans got to the Moon they discovered a Galician family had already been settled there for some time, ha, ha, ha. You'll have to make a stop at Ribadavia, you won't believe your eyes, you've never seen a more beautiful place. Of course there aren't the riches of your countries over there, with their skyscrapers and tremendous progress, you see? but the Galician streams, ah! you won't find those anywhere else in the world, not even in Europe. My wife is from Cangas, a village across the bay from Vigo. Everything is very pretty, very typical, you know what I mean, but there's nothing like Madrid, nothing, nothing at all, they say from Madrid straight to Heaven, you know what I mean. My wife wants us to go live in Cangas, she inherited a little plot of land there and you can make a good living on the docks or at the transportation company office, but me leave Madrid after 30 years? If I leave here it's to go to Barcelona, you know? it's a great city. Vigo, Vigo. A city which has seen many Spaniards leave for that land of yours. You know there's a lot of typical Spanish adventurism, right? but Galicia is a poor land, you know what I mean. Almost the total population of one of its villages moved to Caracas. They all live over there in one neighborhood, they've set up grocery stores, butcher shops, taxis. A lot of them say that when they've filled their pockets they'll return, but don't believe it; their children and their grandchildren were born there, some return, you know, it's true. They're the eternal *indianos*, the nabobs. Sometimes the community throws a welcoming party for them and maybe the *indiano* provides the folding green for some charitable project or something, you know what I mean. Some of them become famous over there, wealthy men, mayors and things like that, but they are always thinking of their *tierriña*. But just imagine, sir, to tear a six-year-old kid away from his games in his own land and take him to foreign worlds which may be very hospitable and all but foreign, you know what I mean, won't he die of nostalgia thinking of his forest, his streams that look like the Lord's own mirrors? You see, it's sad, isn't it? And many want to return because they long for their homeland, but not all of them have the money, you know what I mean, and they die without ever seeing their mountains or their home towns again. You'll never find a wine like Ribeiro in Chile or Argentina, sir. They do have Galician meat pies, the emigrants took the recipe and it seems they make some over there that are fairly similar to ours, right? Although over there they're very rich and Castile, for example, is harsh and arid and dry, but you already know about the ties that bind us, so to speak. Of course if you people preferred to live cut off on your own, then so be it! You had every right, although that's not always the best solution, do you know what I mean? You've probably heard about the Basques, that can't be allowed. After all, they're just a small group, you know. Of course America is another story. Are you Cuban, Venezuelan?"

"From Puerto Rico."

There was silence at the other end. I seemed to perceive a slight irritation through the earpiece, as if I had put my finger on an old wound, as if the name of my country reminded him of tremendous frustrations, interrupted dreams, humiliating substitutions, lost ties.

"Ah," the voice said, too softly, almost in a whisper. "Pretty country, no? As far as I can tell, you keep good company."

"What do you mean?"

"The Americans. North Americans, you know what I mean. A friend married a young man who came to study medicine. She says she's really happy there. Her husband says he owes everything to the Americans. Even the life his father gave him, everything, everything."

"There are a lot who feel that way," I said, profoundly fatigued. "He's not the only one. It's not just that one imbecile. But there are many of us who are opposed to colonialism."

And while I was at it I made an impassioned declaration of love for our traditions and language and idiosyncracies of reputedly Hispanic origin and added without conviction (actually lying drastically) that we were a people who held high the standard of Celtiberian-hewn nobility, that's what I said, a transported, Hispanicized colonial. And I begged my improvised listener, with an abundance of adjectives and fifty-cent words, to have confidence in us, we were not yet lost, for centuries we had fought alone, we needed the support of other peoples, that for now it would be worthwhile for every beloved Spaniard to know that the struggle still raged on, that we weren't surrendering, I said, but that since we "belonged" to the number one power on this globe, that the fine international press took great pains to silence our struggle.

"You know what I mean," I concluded.

But he merely said:

"The coach leaves at three o'clock."

"Baby?"

"Yes."

"Are you there?"

"That's the big question."

"Why? You're not answering me, now I understand." I heard the brush of her hand over the mouthpiece; she was probably providing Mayte with some free information about me. "Baby, I saw a little book that might interest us."

"Does it interest you or not?"

"In the stand across from the office."

"What's it about?"

"It costs a hundred pesetas. It's a paperback. It's called *Psychoanalysis and Marxism*. Do you like the title?"

"The author, please."

"Oh, that's not important."

"Of course, I forgot."

"It's divided into two parts. Before I forget, baby, take out the package of chick peas that's in the cupboard and pour it into a pot of water. Then put it on the stove for at least an hour and a half, okay? I want to fix a stew."

"An hour and a half?"

"Yes."

"Over a high flame?"

"Medium. I'll read the first half and you read the second which deals with Marxism and all that stuff. That business about surplus value is a real killer, isn't it? Don't fill it to the top, Eddy, when it boils it overflows."

"Do you remember the publisher?"

"If you want, use the saucepan instead of a pot. No, I don't remember it. Did you leave a bottle of beer in the freezer last night? I think you did. Take it out. It's probably frozen, as you can well imagine."

"If the saucepan is dirty, I'm not going to wash it."

"It's clean. I wash all the dishes before leaving for the office. On the cover there's a man on a couch, must be the psychoanalysis bit. Now I don't know about the Marxism, there's no symbol for it. There are only two copies left. Do you know if there's any ham left in the cupboard?"

"I don't know."

The hand pressed on the mouthpiece once again. She was probably talking to Mayte, telling her: "It's him, I always like to call him at this hour; he's spoiled." She said:

"Well then, find out, *maño.*

She would surprise me with terms like *cachondo, maño, chaval,* words she'd picked up during trips on the subway, the bus, in office meetings, at the cafeteria, from a zarzuela or at the hairdresser's.

"I'm busy," I answered. "Do you really have something to tell me?"

"If there isn't any garlic, go get some at the grocer's. I'm going to fix a nice stew *a la madrileña.* What are you doing?"

"Probably wasting my time."

"Good Lord, honey. I'm not trying to pick on you. You writers never waste time. Do you remember Azorín? When he was working in his garden, sweating like a pig, he would say he was resting, and when he'd sit on his terrace letting the hours go by without raising a finger, he'd say he was working."

"That was Baroja."

"What?"

"You said an hour and a half over a medium flame."

"It was Azorín. I studied that as a senior. Are you working on something of yours or on translations?"

"Translations."

"You're going to have to do something else. English isn't your forte. Seventy pesetas a page. They're real exploiters, don't you think? You ought to spend your time on your manuscript, we can live on what I make. Don't feel bad about what I'm saying, *majo.*" I grimaced at the Castilian word violated by a *j* from the Antilles. "Down deep you hate that language."

"I don't hate any language. Why should I?"

"You know very well. The language of the master. True or not?"

I had the impression I was being interviewed for Mayte's benefit, a girl from Burgos at heart, and I asked myself if she might not be listening on a second phone. Yoli was capable of acting like the spoiled brat who insists on showing all her friends a picture of her boyfriend.

"I don't hate any language," I repeated. "The language of what master? I don't have any master."

There was silence and the hand, given away by the brushing noise, muffled the phone again.

"I have a lot to do, Yolanda!"

"You seem tense, baby, she answered and then kept silent for a moment while she was probably informing Mayte, surely born next to the Cid's headstone: "My husband has very delicate feelings; one time he wrote a short play in one act, something about the war called *Tet-Barabúm,* but people couldn't understand it because they weren't up to his revolutionary and renewing intellect; as a creative artist it's natural that he be hyperesthetic, that's why he answers me with a certain crudeness common to exceptional talents." She said: "Let me tell you that there are some excellent doctors in Madrid. You yourself have spoken to me about Marañón. He's dead, but there are others."

"Enough!"

"Baby, you surprise me! Enough, like in a Pérez Galdós play. Don't forget about the chick peas and the garlic. Don't fill the saucepan too much. It's just for them to soften up. But pay attention, an hour and a half. Don't turn the stove off right away because there can't be a gas leak as long as it's lit since the flame burns it."

"I know that very well!"

"Are you sure?" she let out a little giggle. "Well, even if you do know. I doesn't make any difference."

That way of saying "difference" bothered me, almost without opening her mouth, enclosing the two e's in a cavern so it sounded darkly like "difforonce." Just like she'd say "See you lator, baby." It's the way they spoke here; nothing escaped her, she recorded everything, like virgin film.

"Yolanda, I have things to do."

"Shall I buy the little book? It only costs 100 *calas.*"

"Pesetas. Cut out that *calas* stuff, it's vulgar."

Yolanda laughed again. She liked for me to scold her, she found me enchanting when I was serious, a man of true character like Kirk Douglas. She said:

"Then I'll buy it."

"Buy it, buy it," I answered in a strangely pompous voice; I had the odd certainty that I was speaking before a television camera, that Yolanda, Mayte, the boss, the messenger, the custodian, the bellboy, the customers, stretched out in their chairs, were placidly following the show and glancing sympathetically at my wife, who, filled with pride, smiled condescendingly and whispered, "That's him, unmistakably." I added: "And don't ever mention a doctor to me again. You think I'm hopeless?"

Everyone in the room would applaud the appropriateness of my response; totally submissive to her husband, with complete abnegation, just as anyone might expect from a womanly woman, Yolanda would be angry at the astute way I had of shutting her up. In those cases which became public property she loved to lose, for me to defeat her. Nevertheless, in the absence of witnesses she'd usually become stubborn, she didn't want to give in, and if I managed to show her that truth was on my side, she got angry and spent hours treating me to the most varied collection of quips related to the topic of the dispute, without ever losing hope of finally convincing me or at least calling it a draw. She said:

"A few hours spent chatting with an analyst wouldn't hurt you. It's incredible that such a well-informed young man as yourself should maintain this almost superstitious belief about psychiatry. Nowadays you go to a psychiatrist like to any other doctor, times have changed. What's more, I'd almost say people who never visit an analyst aren't to be trusted. Because with all the things going on in this world of ours, it's only logical for a person to suffer some kind of imbalance, unless he's completely insensitive. Do you remember the little book I gave you for your last birthday? *Be Glad You Are Neurotic*. Of course you don't have to go that far. Afterwards I realized it's a conformist book. Be glad you're neurotic and just sit back? There are neuroses and neuroses. When the neurosis goes beyond a person's control, it's time to go see an analyst. Do you see my point? Maybe a little neurosis doesn't hurt. After all, it's a matter of degree. They say it's the motor of creativity. What's more, we couldn't live without it. It's creative energy, but, as I say, if the neurosis is overpowering. . .Baby, are you there?"

"That's where I fit in, isn't it?"

"What?"

"This morning I saw my last drop of neurosis. The cup ran over. It was terrible. It flooded the house, I had to stand on the table to avoid drowning."

"Make fun of me. You'll have plenty of time to think over what I'm saying. After you've left the pot of chick peas on the stove for an hour and a half, turn it off, lock the apartment and go out for some fresh air. Go to Arganzuela, la Paloma, the Plaza Mayor. You need a change of scenery. Let the translations go for today. They're going to kill you. Intellectual work is exhausting, you need some rest. Will you do it? Will you go out for a walk? It's good for you, Eddy. And while you're out you can get the garlic."

Was it a provocation, a ruse? Did she want to motivate me to compose a florid paragraph for her about the rights of man to work and to realize his full potential or something like that? An exciting little speech that would move the audience? I said flatly, without pride, conscious that I was ruining the barely begun audition:

"Yes, whatever you say, since you insist."

I was able to sense an embarrassed relaxation in the tension, a winding down, touching earth.

"Don't take it like that. The San Francisco church is a jewel and it's close to the house. Don't you think we're lucky? Don't look at the negative side of things. There's a positive side too, you just have to want to find it. Don't get discouraged and remember, tipping the bottle is no solution. Go out for a walk. Lucky us, we live in the most typical part of the city, authentic old Madrid. That's where *La verbena de la Paloma* was inspired and all that about Pichi being 'that heart-breaking stud.' "

"Please!" I yelled harshly. "Enough folklore and local color!"

"What's the matter with you? It's typical."

"To hell with typical," I said, definitely destroying the program; I could almost hear the chairs being dragged back to their original positions before the show; once more in my obscure little life I admitted that people who had been willing to listen to me were turning their backs, sorry they had bet even one meager cent on me. I added with outraged misanthropy: "And don't start chattering about 'flamenco rumbas' to my very few friends when we're talking about *The Girl With the Combs*! No more mystifications! The best thing for you to do is shut your trap. You're not supposed to know everything!"

Someone in the room would probably get up and say "geeez. . ." and change channels; it was better to listen to music, watch a football game or listen to horrifying news about all the numerous wars. Yolanda screeched in my ear.

"Wait a minute, just one minute. You can't talk to me like that! I'm not your slave, I'm a free woman, lib-er-a-ted. My financial contribution to this home is as great as yours or more."

She was telling the truth, and she had no reason to complain. She could be satisfied with her work among people, that she could mix her typing with a few comforting chatty moments: she could always talk about a movie or a novel, get rid of loneliness, that enemy which lay in constant ambush. I tried to calm her down:

"Buy it. The book. And don't worry about the chick peas or the garlic. *I'll go out for it.*"

"Well, be careful how you talk to me next time."

"I don't know what the devil 'surplus value' means either. Few people do, honest."

"Try to control your self-destructive impulses. That you project by attacking me."

"Yes, yes, of course. You're me."

"That's right. Baby, listen to me carefully. Don't hide your head in the sand. That's not a solution. Mayte told me that since you don't see a priest for confession, a doctor would be the best thing. Wipe that look off your face, I can see it from here. The second alternative isn't so bad. Are you listening to me? There's a very good doctor who isn't at all expensive. He published a book and all. I think he's a Jungian, but that doesn't matter."

"You spoke to me about a book that interests you, right? Well buy it. For a change this time I'll read your part and you read mine."

"Me? Marxism? That business about dialectics is a bomb, baby. No one can stomach it."

"Then don't read it. I would be immensely happy reading your photo-novelettes."

"Are you kidding?"

"I'm serious. Immensely happy."

"You're kidding. It's cheap reading, that's true, but sometimes you sound a little bourgeois."

I said without conviction:

"No, no, I like them. They talk about knights and princesses. I love them. They're a real relief."

"It's weird hearing you talk like this. It's escapist literature; they run from reality, they're cowards. But you have to read it to become familiar with that particular aspect of the world we live in, you know what I mean?"

"You mean to tell me," I answered with a certain amount of surprise, "that your reading photo-novelettes responds to a sort of personal research, a secret investigation, the sociology of soap-opera literature?"

"A little of everything," she answered obscurely. "Those stories and situations and characters have been so innocently blown out of proportion that somehow they grow on you. They're refreshing, as you say, for their naiveté."

"I see."

"Do you think I'm going to leave the office where I work all day, go home to face more work. . .and then during my few free moments crawl into bed with *Crime and Punishment* or the *Karamazous*? If you do, you're pie-eyed. What's the guy's name? The one who takes a hatchet to the female moneylender? Well, it doesn't matter. Do you remember that novel you gave me, it was a monstruous thing, Argentinian or Chilean, I don't recall which, and it has a section on the blind? The author should have seen an analyst. Fine, to please you and be up to date, I silently took in some 300 pages and all, but when I came to the part about the servant couple locked in an elevator, without any hope of getting out alive, do you remember that part? and then the husband begins justifying to himself his intention of eating his wife by accusing her of I don't know what guilty deed, adultery or something like that, in order to carry out his cannibalistic act, as I say, I don't even want to think about it, I threw the book away, hid it in a lost corner of the library because I was frankly horrified, my God! I would ache all over when I got home from the office and you would ask me what was wrong and I didn't want to tell you, but the truth is I didn't use the elevator for two months, I had to go up and down every day, up twice and down twice, the fourteen floors of the building on foot. Photo-novelettes have never given me any kind of ache anywhere."

I let out an uproarious, very exaggerated laugh.

"So that's what it was!" I said half triumphantly. "Two months! And not a word to me, the invisible man! The drawing on the wall, the big zero!"

"Be reasonable, Eddy. I couldn't tell you. I was trying to cure your manias; how could I help you if it turned out I had a worse obsession than yours?"

"Boy, that tops them all!"

"But that's over. I overcame it, I'm totally cured and in excellent condition to help you."

"Don't get any bright ideas, I don't need that kind of help."

"Oh, of course, you don't need it. No, you don't need it. It's always like that. That's evident. They're just interviews, Eddy. Did we come to this country for you to spend your life inside four walls? We could have stayed in Nebraska Heights for that."

"Don't mention that name or I'll hang up!"

"You see? You're tense. We were bored, but it wasn't all that bad."

"We were bored and a lot more! Do you remember that enormous guy, over six feet five inches tall, who weighed about a ton? Do you remember how he'd come out on the balcony with a little four-inch American flag? It seemed grotesque. If he was such a Yankee, and considering his size, he should have shown up with an outsized flag, something that would smack of 'heroic,' but it's not even that, it's the smallness, the smallness of character, the pettiness. Do you think I want Cristeto Aguayo for a neighbor? And that bunch of foreigners? You end up being chauvinistic."

"I know you're going to mention the foreigner's paradise. But don't you realize it's just a phrase? A cliché, you can't judge the situation of a country armed with a few stereotypes. I know it was hard to be looking for work and have four foreigners decide they couldn't use you, but. . ."

"Don't remind me! Four worms!"

"That's it. Worms. I hope our stay here will cool you off a little. That's one of the reasons I agreed to come here with you, vows aside. Baby, calm down, it's high time. What's past is past."

"Would my fellow countrymen stick their necks out for me? Do they care that I'm unemployed and that a bunch of schmucks are snatching up the few jobs that are left? They're incapable of feeling anything for their own kind. They don't know the difference. The logical, normal, natural thing is to first attend to needs at home, then other things. There not even that most basic rule of self-defense exists."

"Calm down, calm down. I hope that you'll manage to regain some composure in the not too distant future; perspective. . . whatever. Because some day we'll have to go back. Things change, they're not static."

I kept silent because Yoli's last words had surprised me.

"Yes, yes," I said disheartedly. "But what about now? I'm not going back to that pack of consumers! Don't you realize that something has broken there, the internal cohesion that a country needs to not be just a simple crowd? Between chatter and gossip and speeches and poems about flamboyant trees and folklore we've let the country be taken away from us! We haven't realized that in our case our folklore has greased the wheels of imperialism. The only thing that matters is selling land, soil, subsoil, air, sea, squeezing the juice from the country without any other consideration, filling pockets with dollars and more dollars. An eternal banquet with photographers and music and publicity, an endless feast at which everyone steals the next person's bit and puts cyanide in his neighbor's Coke. We don't have a country, we lost it, but we don't want to accept that simple, objective, easily proven fact. Let them empty the pantry, *let them eat everything and get it over with*, even the crumbs! Lumpen, bourgeoisie, oligarchy, foreigners and natives shake hands ideologically."

Yolanda was silent; I listened to her heavy breathing. Finally she said:

"Baby, are you there? What can I say? It's our country, our homeland or whatever you want to call it. But I think. . .you've regressed a lot. Of course, you're upset; lay off the bottle, Eddy. Not so long ago you were telling me we had lost our country, but we had to get it back by fire because there was no other way. And now you talk like this. We were born there, grew up there, our dead are buried there. You're born in a place and time, not out of thin air, as is the pretense of many that you yourself have attacked. What you say worries me. That verse 'let them eat it all and get it over with' is okay for what it is, a verse. Vallejo? You talked to me about him. He said that but he fought. You forget that our fight is more intense than ever, Eddy, and with all our ammunition. It's beautiful mysticism, baby, a reason to live, we're fighting hard. A lot of Yankee property has been destroyed, young men refuse to be drafted into the enemy's army. You make me very sad. What you just told me worries me. You react very emotionally, your nerves are devouring you. Calm down, take a walk. Talk to people, they aren't going to eat you; these are good people, believe me, very pleasant."

I waited a moment before answering, breathing deeply.

"Okay. I'll go for a walk. Don't worry. I'm not drinking, how could I work if I were? I still have quite a lot to do."

"But you will go out, won't you? You promised me. Cheer up, for God's sake."

"I'll go when I'm finished. Don't worry."

"Weren't you going to talk with the barber, Eddy? He knows a lot about the city and the war. You could get a good story from that."

"I won't write another word. I'm rejected everywhere. They don't want what I write, it's no good. That's the truth."

"Come on, that's part of your profession. Your time will come. Cervantes also. . ."

"Shut up!"

"Boy, today you're really. . ."

"I'm sorry."

"Baby, guess what? Mayte saw your picture and thought you were good-looking."

But how then? How? Yolanda, Yochaste, Yocanda. I said: "Listen Yoli. . ."

"You look like a gypsy bullfighter. Everyone at the office wants to meet you."

"It's ridiculous for you to go around recommending me like a great two-legged movie."

"But it's them. I only showed your picture. They all want to meet you. You know what else Mayte told me? she said: 'A dark bullfighter, a gypsy lord and olé.' "

With that I couldn't take it any longer and I'm sorry, Yoli, I hung up and I hope your eardrums didn't burst. What was going on in your head? Freud plus photo-novellettes plus some little sociology book and a history of Spain bought in Puerto Rico. Was Mayte making fun of your candor? Did she want to sell you the pigmentation, the epidermal product, as if you were some English tourist dazzled by the Malaga sun and olé, some Swedish girl stretched out flacidly on the torrid sands of Benidorm? Was this all that could be recognized in a country whose history could be breathed like the smoke along its narrow streets? One morning, confronted with my refusal to submit myself to folklore, you had surprised me with your answer: "But have you looked carefully at the monument to Cervantes in the Plaza de España? Quijote, perhaps the noblest product of Hispanic culture, essence of universality, of the Hispanic soul, etc., a monumental work, unique, without limitations, and right there, on the base of the monument, there is a bas-relief of a crowd of Madrilenian dandies and their ladies and shepherds and I think even bullfighters. Don't you realize, baby? That's Spain. The highest and most universal expression next to popular, even vulgar local color. You're surprised that I stick my nose into every *verbena* on earth? That's Spain, too. You laugh, but locked up in your study you're not going to see anything of anything." Partially disarmed I reminded you then of when Archibald, who wrote poems about our fellow countrymen in New York, had invited me to an evening at his home on Park Avenue. For two hours we discussed everything that was open to discussion: the Puerto Ricans in the City and Truman Capote and the escapist writers in the New Yorker and the liberating madness of John Cage and the New Left and Chomsky and Eldridge Cleaver and Central Park and liverwurst sandwiches and kosher wine and Yom Kippur and the Hamburgers at 96th Street and Broadway and he said that when a junky missed his fix he had a monkey on his back. That night we were all agreeing that a radical change in structure was more than desirable, imperative, when Archibald raised his hands in the middle of his small living room and said:

"Ladies and gentlemen, actually I invited you tonight because I have a very pleasant surprise for you."

Everyone said in unison what surprise do you have for us dear Archibald and Archibald looked at me deeply with his clear Bethlehem steel eyes and said you'll see and smiled handsomely and disappeared behind a screen decorated with pop op art nouveau and we waited and were all happy because Archibald, who had studied anthropology at Yale, always had very enjoyable surprises for his guests and always managed to be the center of attention, and Daisy said our host must have taken an intensive course at Dale Carnegie, how to win friends or how to be successful among friends or lend me a minute of your life and I'll make you a millionaire, an interesting guy who had gotten itchy to go into the Amazon and study the social behavior of a tribe threatened with extinction, he said to sort out the structure of their language which was curiously related to the Indo-

European ones, he explained in a long peroration that had us on the edge of our chairs because it was so interesting, so *cru et cuit*, he said that lately he was inclined towards ethnology as such and it was a case of undeniable dialectic interdisciplinary interrelation in full praxis and what could you expect from such an individual but understanding and solidarity when we spoke of the daily viacrusis undergone by my compatriots in this megalopolitan Babel. And Archibald reappeared from behind the screen with a brightly colored box, placed it on a Louis XIV table, bowed ceremoniously to approving smiles, opened it and took out,—remember, Yolanda, I told you about it, my eyes filled with angry tears?—he took out a set of bongo drums with two very tight skins and came toward me amidst the general expectation and said to me:

"Play."

I said what and he said smiling but firmly play, play it, you understand English, so you know what I mean, play. He wasn't talking with his usual fluency, but rather in broken English, without conjunctions and in the present, the same way factory managers speak to their Puerto Rican workers.

"Play, okay? Be good. You play, we listen. You Puerto Rican, you play bongos for us, okay? You play, we listen. Come on. Play, baby, play. We no time. Expecting you, understand?"

And he went further and began patting my back paternalistically. The others began clapping in rhythm: "Play, baby, play."

I couldn't get over my shock and said no, my face red with embarrassment.

"Play, baby, play. You play, we listen."

"I don't know how to play the bongos," I said, politely enough, "I don't play any instrument except for a record player or a radio."

No one laughed. Instead they seemed disappointed by that indecent, humiliated joke entrusted with the secret mission of pleasing them.

Archibald shook his head because it was the first time in his tidy life that something had gone wrong, for the first time he had been contradicted, however timidly.

"Play," he said. "Hey, amigo, play. Understand? We listen, you play. You no Puerto Rican? No? Yes? Then play."

Then I got up and kicked the bongos furiously, I broke the skins with my kicks, I kicked so hard that it hit a vase bought in Chinatown, smashing it to smithereens, and Archibald came toward me with his hands outstretched, but I was full of fire, and he sat on his heels as if he were having a stroke and held his head between his delicate little hands, deep into Zen or Laotze, so before leaving I directed a few kicks at the furniture, searched for my raincoat, cast an enraged look at the group, which had begun to talk about LSD without looking at Archibald, who was now on his back crying, swallowing tears and mucus. I left and slammed the door, aiming a fresh barrage of kicks and punches at it and went down the sooty stairs, indelible soot ground for years into the city, strewn with chimneys and exhaust pipes, and I stood cursing away in the cold street, and you remember, Yolanda, I got home swallowing my angry tears disaster, disaster, and that's why I warn you: don't make Archibald's mistake, a country isn't made of sounds nor the heat it produces unpremeditatedly nor the nuances that don't even cross borders, you have interrupted my hateful work and I shall have to dare to go out on those streets you so highly recommend, what the hell, if you were a doctor, you'd pretend to cure cancer with a visit to the caves of Sacromonte, ciao, go back to your typewriter and drink your Colombian coffee every hour with Mayte and talk non-stop about your phenomenal husband, at least try to believe it since you talk about it so much, ciao, enough, Freudian *maja*, I'll see you tonight, I mean this afternoon, Goyesque *manola*.

* * *

Akiro maintained that it was marvelous to be a father because only in that state was it possible to live certain surrealistic experiences during an otherwise atrocious, ordinary life contaminated by commercialism. For example to find Mother's fork lodged carefully inside your left shoe, your toothbrush in the noodle soup, a double pointed pencil in a beer bottle, chocolate candy in your pipe, a color picture of a smiling dinosaur inside your shaving kit.

Only children, submerged in the "pleasure principle," have the ability, according to Akiro, to make the innumerable possibilities of wonderment calmly materialize.

Dear Mr. Leiseca:

You may find it strange to receive the missive of a total stranger, who in this specific case turns out to be the undersigned. I am a native of the romantic little village of Ciales, cradle of illustrious poets, tucked away poetically in the midst of the Puerto Rican sierra. So I feel as much a part of this land as the breadfruit trees, the kingbirds and the black coffee.

I am an algebra teacher in the town of Ciales and I founded a Club which I named "The Sons of Ciales." Our aim is to make known our Cialian poets, as well as others. We've already had our first recital and we invited the great poet Corretjer. His poetry is very good although a bit strong for some people's taste, and a friend told me his poems are confected from the authentic life-blood of the earth.

But quite legitimately you are probably asking yourself how I came up with your address in the Mother Country. It wasn't easy, as the people I asked who knew you all kept a sepulchral silence. No one wanted to tell me and one person went so far as to assert that he had never heard your name. Well, it was no less than Don Mancio, a friend of yours for many years, Mancio, that famous novelist of ours who years back abandoned the little patch of land cultivated by his father and now lives in the maremagnum of our capital city, who finally agreed to provide me with your address in the Old World. Don Mancio read some of my poems and he says I must work on them day and night and yet not forget algebra which is so necessary. I met him at an exhibit of the works of the great Puerto Rican painter, Lorenzo Homar, with whom I assume you're familiar. Don Mancio was quite serious and I was very shy and didn't know what to do with my hands because he looks at you so deeply and mercilessly. He is quite a character and for a moment when he forgot that my name is Nicanor Ríos he called me Dimwit. It seems he's always in a bad mood. When I told him I was planning on going to Madrid he replied that it was a good idea to leave the "garbage" of one's own country although only for a short time. And he was very happy to give me your address in Madrid because I reminded him of that phrase in one of your first

stories, Don Eduardo, which goes, if I remember correctly, something like "the breeze blew tempestuously in the night," as you
can see I learned it by heart. Don Mancio told me it was a typical
expression of yours.

That night I showed him some poems I had penned in my
classroom while my students were taking an exam on equations.
I very respectfully take the liberty of forwarding them to you to
see what you think of them:

My Beautiful Isle with tamarinds strewn
Her nights illumined by the Moon
Her cultivated fields all abloom
And her shores tepidly bathed in spume.

What do you think? That's when Don Mancio hurried to give
me your address without my even asking for it, and he told me to
write you and go visit you as soon as I made my way to Madrid, as
you and I wrote in such a similar way that we seemed like literary
twins. I clearly felt very flattered because you're one of the most
promising young men of our island's literature. As such I would
now like to inform you that I took the liberty of publishing one
of your stories in the high school review, the one that talks of the
tempestuous breeze in the night.

Later on that same evening during which I had the privilege of
meeting such an important person, we went to a bar and Don
Mancio had an argument with Akiro, the painter who studied in
Mexico. Because he said the painter spent his life in bars talking
about painting but he didn't produce. And our novelist said to him,
"And what the hell (pardon me) are you doing besides ruining
yourself with rum? Start painting and forget all that idle chatter
about art." The artist did nothing but laugh, he would say forget it
Mancio and laugh stroking his enormous mustache. Then Don
Mancio said that there was a phenomenon taking place in our
country that went against all logic: in spite of the abundance of
cr. . . (excrement), it was being very well subsidized and we were
getting up to our necks in cr. . . but it was still very well paid for.
Then I went up to him and told him he was one writer who wrote
the way he talked, and I had read his marvelous novel *Season of
Witches* and had been fascinated. And what do you think he did?
He turned his back on me and began cursing and asked for a
double rum saying that bad times had to be survived in any way
possible, that's just what he said, cursing all the while. My God
what a temperamental artist! It was an unforgettable evening,
although when the gathering was really getting good (I didn't miss
one word of what those artists were saying because I had so much

to learn), when everything was at its greatest brilliance, Don Mancio got up from his chair and started scolding a thin, half-deaf gentleman they call The Playwright, and told him to cut out the pseudo-patriotic theme in his work and not write so much about love for celestial virgins and Indians who had disappeared four centuries ago and to cut out writing such subjective and un-documented essays, that's just what he said. He said he'd had enough chatter (a word he repeats on pages 18, 62, 134 and 572 of his novel) and the best thing for all of us to do was to hightail it back to our homes to work, as time marches onward and you can't live twice. But the crowning moment was when the waiter, a very serious and respectable looking old gentleman, came up to him, bowed and said "Good night." And Mancio turned to him and said "Why?" And he went over to some American girl who was waiting for him at another table. I laughed a lot because the waiter just stood there dumbfounded, and then Akiro said Don Mancio was more irritating than a tar enema. Following the advice of our novelist, I began working that very night, first correcting my students' exams and then on a poem entitled "Mad Bohemian Night." I'm not sending it because I'm still working on it for you to see in Madrid.

Well, Don Eduardo, I hope you're in good health as well as your wife, Doña Yolanda, and that your soon-to-be-born child will inherit your talents (yours, Don Eduardo).

Your faithful servant and admirer,
Nicanor Ríos

P.S. I don't know when it will be possible for me to drink from the pristine fountains of the Mother Country, as I have not yet purchased my plane ticket. I heard there is an airline called Iveria which flies to that country quite frequently; it that true?

Dear Friend:

I have meditated at length on the letter I sent you previously. Doubtless my impatience and, shall we say, ill humor could be read between the lines. That was no doubt motivated by the frustration one feels upon trying to contact someone and receiving no answer. This proves that I, too, as a human being, am able to react with a certain amount of violence, if only of the verbal sort. Confronted with your obstinate silence, my very normal reaction was to be expected. Nevertheless, I wish to inform you that, although I hope the amount you owe me will be paid promptly and by the amicable means available to two human beings, I will not hesitate to resort to legal means if the former does not yield positive results. Please don't take this as a threat, my intentions are far from utilizing such "tactics."

It might interest you to know that a few days back I had to testify in court in my role of expert in the field of Psychiatry. Don't think it was easy for me. To begin with, the accused had grown up in an atmosphere of total hostility. With the mother dead, the father remained in charge of the three daughters, of which the accused is the youngest, being only 17 years old. The father has a small plot of land on which he cultivates fruit trees with the help of a young neighbor. As was proven beyond a doubt during the trial, the father cohabits maritally with the two oldest daughters, threatening to kill them if they resist; the oldest daughter has a child who is to all appearances abnormal (a family trait brought to light by the incestuous relationship). As for the second daughter, it came out that the father forced her to get illegal abortions three times. It's truly a hair-raising story and I thought you might be interested in it as a writer (although you insist on doubting your own capabilities, as you demonstrated to me during our sessions). But aside from that, I think the trial will last over two months, so I'll be wrapped up in this sticky (but, in the name of Justice, necessary) affair all that time.

Well, the matter came to a head when the youngest daughter fell in love with her father's assistant (do you follow me?). The father was obstinately opposed and tried to force the girl to enter into the same carnal relations he had with the other sisters. But the girl resisted, hitting him on the head with a pipe, fracturing his skull and killing him on the spot. Therefore, the girl is being accused of second-degree homicide. Her lawyer is trying to prove that the girl is lacking her mental faculties, so they have called me in to investigate the case and give my professional verdict.

Now are you convinced that my work is not as easy as you said on a certain occasion? Do you remember your words, Leiseca my friend? Of course I don't always have to run back and forth to court. But what's your opinion of clinical work? What do you think of having to hear, for ten hours a day, including lunch, the terrible confessions of my patients, their problems, which to someone unfamiliar with this line of work would seem incredible? Pederasts who refuse to recognize their condition, paranoids who suspect that you're a police informer, catatonics, delusions of grandeur, inferiority complexes, onanism, exhibitionism, coprophagy, etc. Can just anyone do my work? You must get that out of your head. It's a science which is gaining in prestige day by day.

Allow me to remind you that I'm in a receptive mood. I won't resort to any legal action if you agree to pay the bill in question. I'm agreeable to waiting a reasonable period of time, say three months. You can send a money order or a special check from American Express or some other reliable company.

My regards to your wife.

Dr. Winston Olmo

México, D.F.

Dear Mr. Leiseca:

We have read carefully and with great interest the manuscript of your book *Unbearable Nights,* which you sent us for our editorial consideration some time ago.

We regret to inform you that, due to the long list of books awaiting publication, your book could perhaps come to light towards the fall of 1975. Would you be willing to wait five years for us to put your book into print?

Of course, even so we cannot assure you of any commitment for publication.

Affectionately,
Porfirio Valverde Ch.
Editor
Ediciones Xltetlantlinotloltl

Dear Friend:

Vera and Morena and Mancio sometimes ask about you. I have nothing to tell them. I've heard nothing about what has become of you for over a year. Mancio told me you hadn't even acknowledged receipt of the books he sent you, which all else aside, have been remarkably well-received by the students, although the critics (how can those underdeveloped minds be so called?) haven't seen fit to open their traps.

Last Friday there was a cooperative exhibit at the Galería Campeche. I hung a couple of paintings there and had to control myself to avoid giving those little scholarly critics, who embroil everything in theory, a good punch in the nose. In addition there was someone from our political organization who confronted me because my painting had marked bourgeois tendencies. He suggested I should "imbibe the sap of the People," what do you think of that? Well, what he's looking for is the most daring socialist realism, and I reminded him of Diego Rivera's experience in the Soviet Union, do you remember those paintings of plump, smiling exhilarated workers who made you think of cover slogans: "I'm fulfilled since reading Lenin," etc.? Well that night half the world came by and I must confess I took a beating. Because the university students began the noisy mock serenade of electronic music. Well, I agree with "certain" modern music, Stravinsky and Schoenberg and a few other "modernists" don't bother me. But I'm against extravagance: pianists have taken to pounding on the keyboard cover, violinists go bats using their bows on the ribs of their instruments and sawing away viciously at the strings, musicians in the middle of an orchestra crawling around among the chairs to see what damn thing they might hit; crap, pure regression. Somehow they call that noise an "open work" and then sit back complacently. I have had many discussions, all, in fact, fairly confusing ones, and sometimes merely the word "melting-pot" enrages me as if it brought to mind the bitterest of recollections. I can quote from memory the words they tossed out that night: "You must understand that the musical instruments used today are inadequate for us to express ourselves according to the demands of our times. Almost all of them were invented centuries ago by men who were very different from us, men with other concerns and other perspectives and who responded to different emotional impulses. We have to destroy that unjust order imposed by tradition, that tyranny of corpses which stifles our most legitimate expression; before completely discarding them, we are searching for secrets within those inherited instruments that their creators were not able to reveal to us. An endless search which won't terminate at that nor will it ever end because art cannot stagnate without decaying. Let our new ideas flow; restiveness, investigation, and experimentation are inseparable elements of art. Make way for new structures, my friend!" Well, I agree up to a certain point, but why do they feel so victimized, why are they always on the verge of proclaiming themselves martyrs? Every artist comes up against a variety of challenges, there's nothing new in that, but these beshitted anarchists think of themselves as the Christs of "new music." Every artist has to interpret the world with whatever instruments he has at his disposal, to work with imagination within the limitations that he'll naturally come up against, work with imagination but without ruining his tools. A piano is a piano, not a bongo drum. The keys aren't sufficient for a tortured musician to express himself? That's all part of the vocation. In any case, those keys could be used in truly original compositions, daring harmonious combinations, to squeeze out of them all possible sounds. You can't go any further? Then invent another piano or change the strings or whatever but don't climb all over it impiously and scratch the paint, all of which is very antiesthetic. What happens in many cases is that all these guys are incapable of creating a single melodious line, however brief, and with the frustration this signifies, given the opportunity, they're likely to blow up the most inoffensive tuba. As far as violins and cellos are concerned, they've gone crazy, sadistically destroying their frames. But don't think I oppose the true development of art. Don't even let that cross your mind. I recognize the advance of science, man has already put his dirty paws on the moon, cybernetics, information theory, computers, etc., and I know that science and its advances will influence art, it's only logical, but that doesn't mean that a composer, for example, has to turn into a sound engineer. I can see your face now: you're furious and probably calling me a troglodyte, a reactionary, a zhdanovite, an illiterate, etc.; you can shove all those epithets. I'm going to continue, even if you explode. Vulgar noises, whatever they are, properly organized, are tremendously interesting in the same way that those sculptures made out of junk—headlights, fenders, old machines, etc.—are interesting. As an experiment and child's play they're okay, but from there to categorizing them as true art, there's quite a stretch.

I don't recall what all we talked about that night. It didn't occur to that damned Mancio to back me up at all. He said that what we really needed to do was go home to work and to hell with spending our lives in bars. Someone said that the obsessive phenomenon of some of the more notable painters in the room of minutely portraying the faces and landscapes of the country was nothing more than a magical attempt to retain what is in danger of disappearing (traditions etc.) in Yankee hands. Fear of perishing as a people? To the degree with which you reproduce your subject with greater exactitude and fidelity, the more it belongs to you, fewer are the chances of its escaping from you? From the cavemen on nothing has changed in that respect. Of course it was promptly alleged that the only way to truly represent our time is through the forms, and structures, and findings that have come from its very bowels, using its secret, intimate language, its own waves, the possibilities generated by the incredible potential of mass communication media and a return to science, etc. Well, I didn't have much to say to those gentlemen, there are no concrete problems for them, no here and now, for them it's the same to create art in this country, or in the Soviet Union, or in the United States of Cochinchina: everything is up in the air, universalism without roots, with their backs turned on everyday reality, and it's well-known where those theories come from, who the beneficiaries of such an escapist attitude are! Well, I got it off my chest. I told them that they pretended to forget the revelatory mission of art as a political instrument: threatened with disappearing as a people, they go around covering expensive canvases with experimental splotches, giving play to their precious little souls and making the brain labor on frivolous machinations which are, let me tell you, pure, unadulterated crap for a market of snobs and bourgeois; let the whole country as such be absorbed and stripped of its land, let it then live in fenceless concentration camps enclosed by the walls of prejudice, let them turn us into fucked over hybrids like certain worthless journalists incapable of thinking in English or Spanish because they think and write Spanglish, let our four centuries of history go up in smoke, let us die as a nation, make us disappear from the map, let them commit that atrocious genocide as long as they can continue putting thumbtacks on a board so that on top of everything else they can assault us with precious literary epigrams like "Circular Space with Hematomas" and musicians can play with their electronic toys, turn their backs to the audience, to the people (even if you do call me a demagogue again); in other words: let the masses be kneaded daily, manipulated by the nest of businessmen, merchant whore mongers who will take charge of filling and programming their scarce free moments with conformist music and jingles and things go better with Coke, and give us your sweat and yours is the kingdom of Heaven; an entire host of words carefully selected like the components of a chosen poison, the bastards. That's what they're proposing, when you really think about it, or are at least fostering with their ignorance, their childish, mama's-baby, petit bourgeois naiveté; oh, they're only interested in taking care of the complicated coordinates of creativity with the meticulous care with which a Latin American virgin is handled, those things are for the chosen, "spiritual aristocrats," may they all rot in hell along with their fucking mothers.

How did the gathering end? A blond boy began screaming at me, enraged by my vulgarity: "Apocalyptic! My God, what an apocalyptic man!" Well, at least I was able to amuse myself for a while.

Ciao. Regards to the self-sacrificing Yolanda, I don't know how the devil she keeps on putting up with you.

A fond embrace from
Akiro

P.S. The great Diego Rivera always carried a revolver. Once someone asked him why he wore it and he answered it was "to orient the critics." That old guy really had balls.

READING *EL MUNDO*

WARDROBE OF MISS PUERTO RICO
SYMBOLIZES SEA, SUN AND GREEN PLAINS

Her wardrobe is made up of daytime outfits designed by Fernando Pena and by Manet, things like French purses, shoes from La Favorita, a Reinhold solid gold watch, Chanel fragrances, a set of red luggage from Sears, and enough stockings to last at least one full year. Miss Puerto Rico left yesterday, Friday, at three thirty p.m. by Eastern Airlines after having taken part in the Chrysler parade.

135,000 PEOPLE LIVING IN SHANTIES

At the present time there is no possibility of securing the necessary funds to pay for sufficient concrete buildings.

PRESIDENT OF UNIVERSITY OF PUERTO RICO SAYS
GIVE IN TO ANARCHIST PRESSURES

"A thirty-day suspension was the only punishment decreed for the troublemakers who attempted to keep the student body from entering the cafeteria." On the other hand, Edison Misla Aldarondo, the assemblyman from San Juan, went on to allege that the poor students and the ones on scholarship with little access to economic resources had to go hungry because Díaz González ordered the closing of the cafeteria, giving in, as has happened in other instances, to the pressure of the anarchists. "Díaz González," continued the PNP Youth leader, "thus puts into effect the wishes of his administration to strangle Slater International, Inc., which manages the University cafeteria. The People shall judge."

SCANDALOUS BOOK ABOUT JACKIE ATTACKED

ANOTHER DRAFT EVADER BROUGHT TO TRIAL

Judge Hiram R. Cancio asked for explanatory memoranda regarding the defense motion which alleged that the Selective Service Law is discriminatory in Puerto Rico in light of the fact that young Puerto Ricans who do not speak English take the exams in Spanish, whereas in the State of California, young men without a fluent command of English are deferred with a 1-Y classification.

MAINTAINS LEADERSHIP OF P.P.D.
IS PRO-INDEPENDENCE

Angel Viera Martínez, president of the House of Representatives, stated that "the leadership of the Popular Party is pro-independence but it refuses to show its true colors."

FIFTEEN WOMEN ARRESTED IN ROUNDUP

It was reported by the Vice Squad that the majority of those arrested are Puerto Rican.

EDITORIAL

The Fourth of July should be a day to express loyalty to our American citizenship, reflect upon the serious problems of the nation, and decide how we, the Puerto Ricans, can help the country solve those problems.

CLEARER AND MORE BEAUTIFUL SKIN
IN JUST FOURTEEN DAYS

By applying BEAUTY DAWN facial cream, with its special formula, every night. Don't let a dark or splotchy complexion stand in the way of romance or keep you from enjoying happiness.

AROUND *LA FORTALEZA*
by E. Combas Guerra

As far as we know, except for those taking vows of poverty, men study and struggle in order to licitly attain the greatest possible monetary accumulations, so as to be able to enjoy life as peacefully as possible. . .

The university campus in Río Piedras has become a refuge and a stronghold for separatist and anti-American sentiments in Puerto Rico.

Occasionally, several of its professors, paid with funds coming from the University itself, take trips through neighboring countries (including Cuba), giving lectures and supporting the impression that the inhabitants of this island are under the boot of the American military and that we have no freedom of any kind here and that the independence movement is very strong, but is smothered by what they call "Yankee Imperialism."

The following information was printed for distribution by the Office of the Dean of Students of the Río Piedras campus of the University of Puerto Rico:

"Exchange Office. Trip to Cuernavaca, Mexico." (The inclusion of "exchange" means that another group is also being prepared by Ivan Illich there in Cuernavaca to come to Puerto Rico, United States territory.)

The official announcement continues, saying:

"Seminar: The Cuban Revolution. Cuba as the answer to the liberation of the Third World from imperialism."

It is certainly evident that this is a propaganda mission in favor of Communist Cuba. . .It would be interesting to know the reaction of the honorable members of the Board of Higher Education to this and other communistic and anti-American activities of the Office of the Dean of Students.

ENGLISH IN THE COURTS

A panel of three judges ruled against the petition attacking the use of the English language in the San Juan Federal Court. Federal judges Hiram Cancio, Frank Coffin, and Sylvester Ryan also ruled against a petition regarding the constitutionality of criminal proceedings brought before that district court and the allegations that conscientious objectors to the Selective Service Law for other than religious reasons are discriminated against.

The decision of the three-judge panel was handed down at the request of the Legal Aid Institute of Puerto Rico in the case of Florencio Merced Rosa, who is awaiting trial for refusing induction into the United States Armed Forces.

CLAIM LAW 80 THREATENS FREE ENTERPRISE SYSTEM

VIETNAM HERO HONORED

Last Monday residents of the Vista Hermosa housing project in Río Piedras honored Félix Cosme, Puerto Rican hero, who was decorated four times during his service in the Vietnam war.

Mrs. Carmen Rivera de Cosme, mother of the honored guest, stated emotionally that she had been through a great deal worrying about her son, but that she feels very proud of him. Félix Cosme was involved in many battles and was wounded once, although he himself confesses that he didn't realize it and kept firing at the enemy. For his deeds he received the Purple Heart, two Bronze Stars, and the Army Commendation Medal. *218549*

VOTING FOR THE PRESIDENT
by Alex W. Maldonado

Tomorrow's Commonwealth State must be one that serves the needs of a Puerto Rico which is fully integrated into the United States. And one of those needs may very well be the right to vote in the Presidential elections. Córdova Díaz's argument is a very powerful one: it is the President who sends soldiers to fight, some to die. Puerto Rico, which participates in national defense, should also participate in the election of the person who directs that defense. And also, integration doesn't mean assimilation. The culture of a people is not the result of its political life; quite the contrary. Political identity is a product of culture. Presidential candidates eat beans in the Bronx, pizza in Brooklyn, wear feathers on their heads in Oklahoma and dance "à go-go" in San Francisco. In Puerto Rico they'll eat peas and rice, put straw hats on their heads, and begin every speech with the words: "My dear friends. . ."

SEVEN BOMBS FOUND IN STORES

Four of the devices were found in the Metropolitan Shopping Center. The three others were found in the Lerners Shop at Stop 18. Various American-owned firms in the Metropolitan area were immediately notified.

JURY FINDS OBJECTOR TO MILITARY DUTY GUILTY

Members of the jury appeared tired and upset as they filed into the courtroom to announce their verdict. After reading the decision, counselor Kennedy asked the judge to poll the jury to verify that the verdict was unanimous. Each member of the jury answered "guilty."

When the trial was over, the members of the jury were escorted to various cars by Federal Marshals and members of the Puerto Rican Police. There was some fear for their safety. Almost a hundred young people, most of them students, milled around the accused, Feliciano, at the courthouse.

Earlier in the day Judge Cancio denied three motions for dismissal entered by the defense. When instructing the jury, Judge Cancio said the Selective Service Law is legal in Puerto Rico.

Some 96 young men who have refused to serve are awaiting trial.

ANNOUNCE GRITO DE LARES
WILL BE CELEBRATED

Sixty-five Exchange Clubs of the Island will take part in a "Truth Caravan" which will go to Lares. At a luncheon which took place last Friday, it was explained that the "Truth Caravan" came into being to support a democratic way of life in Puerto Rico, to cultivate appreciation for American citizenship, and to make known to the world the true image of the Puerto Rican.

LAWYERS WILL TAKE OBJECTIONS TO MILITARY
SERVICE TO NIXON AND U.N.

EXCHANGE WON'T GO TO LARES

The Exchange Clubs of Puerto Rico decided to cancel the activities scheduled for the celebration of the Grito de Lares, but they clarified that their decision was in no way motivated by the threats that several pro-independence groups had directed at the ceremony.

* * *

But it wasn't the fiery season. When the taxi drivers, their shirts open, sleeves rolled up, breathing hard, commented about the year's incredible heat. I wasn't immersed in that atrocious month that begins July 15th and melts the sidewalks until the 15th of August. Then it was impossible. The empty city, the packed southern and northern beaches, the Sierra teeming with summer decisions. Ah, then it was impossible to simply stroll around. Because there was no breeze except for a suffocating, exhaustingly hot one, and the sun was a decisive disk from six in the morning until nine at night, blind in its determination to drive your lungs, armpits, even your hair to desperation. Stroll? She said. Stroll on air and yet anchored in the prosaic breathing of the insufferable pavement. And without a single lucid thought because it just wasn't possible. Everyone knew it: the boy dragging along the purchases from the grocer's dreaming vaguely of a dunk in Alicante (which he had never seen), the aunt in charge of the children while her sister (blessed a thousand times over) splashed in Somonte in her new bathing suit, the taxi driver who showed off a few new foreign words each year, the night watchman for the neighborhood and the shops clutched night after endless night by phantasmagorias of female forms, the secretary waiting impatiently (no longer even answering the telephone, making countless mistakes on the typewriter), holding on, it was said, impatiently for the moment of her summer escape. But we're not there. March is the blurred heart of cold. Ah, if I could. People are people, complaining about the heat, complaining about the cold. And that man, bent over, huddled under his overcoat and an umbrella. But it's not going to rain. The difference lies between Schweppes and Schweppes. Stupidly looking for that difference the first few days. Not a thing. Reading slowly, one s, a ch, one w, two p's an e and an s. Nothing. So read it over again. And again. They're clever, propaganda salesmen. They make you read it ten times. They hope the word will become engraved on your brain. Hidden Persuaders, Inc., she said. Is it German? Das Schweppenstein, better yet Frau Gretta Schweppenstein. Herr Leisekenstein. Mister Drylaw. Girls can't drink cognac on T.V. They can touch the glass, invite a friend with a seductive smile, but drink it, never.

Oh, it's immoral. Women to their labor, she said. And that Soberano ad, the girl who swings around so her blond hair spills across her forehead and she smiles with her beautiful Iberian face, almost Slavic in its semi-square oval shape (if that's possible). Because Soberano is a man's drink. The little gong. A quick montage, enough. Consumus. Could that complicated, odd word be German? The factory? Where does it figure that Germans and Celtiberians? In other words, they're fond of each other. Admiration. Love at first sight. Goths or vice-Goths? Ortega. They've been telling you that since ninth grade. In Leipzig, right? Due to such austerity, isn't that so? Could it be true that there's a hippy in every Spaniard? Individualism. Thou shalt love one another even though you be Spanish, that caricature in *El Triunfo*. León Felipe, go ahead and have your tantrum, pull at your noble beard from deep within your grave. Scold, growl, and delightfully love unto death. Is that business about the ax true? The ax that divides. They called them Reds for the gunshots, for the blood that covered the earth. But not I, eh, I was on this side, geographically, I was recruited; hell, I didn't care one way or the other at first; of course later. . .Listen, can you imagine the resistance of this beseiged city? Fire rained down from an acrid sky, you were just a boy, you probably don't remember, you probably weren't even born. You're not from around here, although you'd never know it, honest. Telefunken planes every day, machine gun fire, *rrr rrrr rrrr* like that. Here, it hit him here. Laid him out. Sirens were sirens, you know? The line was down around there, where Carabanchel is, yes sir. The Manzanares, that quiet, carefully channeled river, was stained. Red veins. Boom. It was our business, you know? A brotherly argument. Oh, my God, but how I wish. Burgos to the north and Valencia to the east. This old, dying city in the middle of the sky. The Manzanares was furious, like a mirror bitten by lightning, like a quiet puddle awakened by a blast. would you like a beer Schweppes, Skol? Another? A San Miguel, also produced in the Philippines, or an Aguila Imperial? They're cold, which isn't at all good for you in this weather. You could choose a Soberano, a 103, any other brandy. They're a man's drink. So you're from over there, no secrets, right? You weren't born yet or were just a little boy. Yes, that was in Guadalajara. The most beautiful night of the year, he said. Oh, come with me to La Mancha, I'll show you how to tell a story by telling it to you. No man from La Mancha will ever let you down, you'll see. No, no, I'll pay for that. Let's try and have you eat something, my good man. Grilled, in garlic sauce. We eat a lot, eh? It's true. We know how to live, I don't give a hoot. Just relax. They tell me it's a very pretty country, very pretty. Let's see, why did you get the urge to leave it, if I may ask? Hmmmm. Since December it's been like a refrigerator. It gets into your bones. But you insist they be good and cold? Dress warmly, it's not too cold, but the temperature could drop at any moment. It's a despicable climate, the Sierra blows and goes right through you. You were all warmed up from over there when you came. Us, forty years here, our bones are made of paper. A little breeze blows us over. It should be the opposite, no? Oh, New York, of course. Cold too. But probably not like here. Cold cold all the time? In winter, of course. No fluctuation. Summer is summer, hard, you know. Well, you will. Allow me to introduce my friend here. The gentleman drinks a lot of beers in quick succession. You should dress more warmly, this weather is treacherous and hits hard. America, America, don't they like us much over there? I would really like to go. But at this stage, you understand. Grandchildren, so there you are. Go on, they kicked you out of Germany for God knows what reason. Marks, well, marks, like any other currency. Yes, people there don't throw trash on the floor, everything is the picture of cleanliness. Well, what are you trying to tell me? You could die in the street, hearts of stone, they're like that. Not here. It's another matter, you know? Of course, of course, difficult, but no one, not on the streets. White, black, yellow, it doesn't matter. We're just like that. What are you going to do? It's a poor country, arid land, but we manage. Go out for a walk with your wife at 2:00 a.m. No one says a word, no one bothers you. Paris, Rome, Berlin, that New York, they're nothing but jungles. Savages. They'll slit your throat in broad daylight for a coin. You know what I mean? You're leaving already? Yes, it's about that time. Well, okay, at your service, goodbye, good afternoon. Goodbye good afternoon. Not at all, I'll pay for it. Cheers. God bless you. But my God, this guise, me an intruder, Aguila Imperial the most expensive. His mask how charming. Hmmm. My throat again, it must be the cigarettes. And that cold breeze; you can feel it penetrating through your nose, it freezes your pipes and becomes a balloon in your lungs, refreshing. Crystal in a gaseous state. The Gate of Toledo. Wasn't Pepe Bonaparte responsible for the first stone? Imagine a four-engine fuselage on that monument, the ends torn off, an enormous aluminum tube covered with ivy, a perplexed face at one of the windows; thousands of gnomes scurrying down a ladder. Was it a nightmare? It's as if I were seeing it now. I didn't dream it. I saw it. The shootings of May 2nd. He was ahead of his time, a man who could paint like that in his day. Lucidly Goya, but what a character. And then the Mexican, what's his name. He took a long drink at that fountain. A squadron with guns aimed at his face, bayonets on heroic chests, it deals with overcrowding, cramming together. Orozco, no? I make mistakes with astonishing ease. But yes, this time I'm right. Anything is possible, for example Urtain boxing with himself in an optician's window. Strong, old Basque stonemason, but nevertheless sentimental, tender as a wild daisy. He had to win destructively losing it totally. Let's applaud the unavoidable champion. Queen Elizabeth selling watches without hands at the Rastro, Falla playing the bongos at Pasapoga, Paco Camino fighting a huge Miura bull at La Paloma church, Gabriel Miró crying happily while reading *The Sound and the Fury*, Federico García Lorca doing the accounting for the Plaza Hotel, Yáñez Pinzón drowning in a kiddie pool, Juan de la Cierva overcome by vertigo on a second-story balcony, Miguel Fleta singing inside a deep-sea diver's suit, Cisneros playing soccer, María Cristina fighting a buffalo, the Giralda is equal to the sum of Santander province and the Ebro river, infinite unpublished possibilities. Yes, another one please. Good and cold. And the girl. I love them in those wide pants, their hair loose over their shoulders. The first bell-bottoms were worn by the Chinese, wide pants over their shoes. Inscrutable race, 10,000 kilometers, a million enemy soldiers hounding them, planes bombing them, they're marvelous. Ninety percent of them died. Yenan. Amazing. Let me sing for you. I must finish reading that biography, it has taken me too long, difficulty concentrating. Mao. One wife strangled, the second one died of exhaustion, the third one a movie actress. He saw the first two die, he fought and had time to write poems. It's marvelous to be alive and recognize it. It's worth not ignoring this. Ay, if I. Bah. For every wing, every feather, every beak, every melodious bird there are thousands of millions of ants. So no, don't even think about it, honey. The most exciting afternoon of the year, she said. *La gaseosa debe ser Revoltosa*. Also zarzuela. Oh, we were shabbily treated in that thing called *The Last Romantic*, I think I read it in a magazine. The matter was treated as if it were completely trivial. The part about the tongue-twister spoken by a parrot and one of my fellow countrymen. That phonetic stuff ridiculed. Well, so what? Do they expect us to say thoup and thuch thtuff? People say *guagua* in the Canary Islands too. 170 million Spanish-speaking people in Spanish America, you understand? Put it on the scale, dammit, and see which way it tilts! But the girl, with her hair down her back. She's a student, that's for sure. No wedding band, so she's single. A wedding band. What she'd give for one! On a day like this, embracing under a blanket. Is her name Puri, Mayte Maricarmen, Pilar? Maybe Paloma. Coo for me. Mmm. She knows I'm looking at her. They aren't offended when you look at them. On the contrary, they like it and don't try to hide the fact. Let's buy a little apartment in Aluche, dear, and have ten darling little Catholic babies. Unless Ogino stands in the way. Ogino tomorrow yes. He shells shrimp in nothing flat and bites them with his sharp teeth that are going to be swallowed by the earth. Are the teeth going to swallow earth or is the earth going to swallow the teeth? Shells, toothpicks, napkins all over the floor. The waiter says something funny to her. She laughs, answers. A dialogue is always established, completely naturally. A blessing. Ay, if only I. Nothing. I arrive, say hello, deepening my voice. But then silence. People keep arriving, me in my corner, without so much as indicating I even have a mouth, then it seems everyone is looking at me, my ears buzz, I spill the glass of beer. Stupidity. Awkwardly. And then I might engage in a dialogue of a second's duration, I could make a superhuman effort and say that I drink beer precisely at the hour others drink coffee. It's understood that I'm deprecating myself in public, self-criticism of the I which is intrusively dysfunctional. The waiter answers uh. He leaves. He must think what a stupid jerk, allowing himself to go to pot like that. And no one even asked him to do it. Then mute. I'm a mute who trembles, thirsting for normal conversation. Falling into the cliché of bad movies: it looks like rain, it's cold today. Then silence while I order beer, more beer, please, with a dry, rasping, off-key voice, either too strong or too weak. My silent, scared presence ends up irritating them. Our glances stumble across each other uncomfortably. It's impossible, impossible now, I'm lost. Although at times, with an acquaintance, there might be a quick exchange of chit-chat, tense chit-chat, with strange words on my part. Nevertheless, I could with the girl. Act like a brazen Romeo. But everyone would begin looking at me. Insatiable curiosity. They never forget a face, they talk about things. Two months after arriving in this place, everyone already knew my name, what I did, who my wife was, where she worked. They don't forget a single detail. "That particular day, which was Monday, at three fifteen you came and asked for an Aguila Imperial, but then you drank a San Miguel, and your wife, who was dressed in grey, had a stuffy nose." On the subway, faces turn toward my mustache, my gypsy coloring, without the slightest dissimulation. "I haven't seen your wife for two days, she isn't sick, is she?" Because she was looking at me so insistently, an old lady almost broke her neck coming down some stairs. Bashfully I'm withdrawing. Is it a big town? They say Barcelona. The mania of calling it the most "European" of Spanish cities. Cosmopolitan, yes. But give me a corner of Galicia and I would be eternally grateful. Something mystical, I don't know. Rubbing elbows, what a weird guy. The girl said goodbye, she has said goodbye see you lator. The fool just stands there like a stupid tower with his beer. They don't understand how anyone can drink so much, one after another, without breathing. Especially at this hour. Everyone working and that guy over there drinking as if it were the normal thing to do. What a way to waste time, what a useless guy, probably a hood from North Africa. An exile waiting for his free food handout while we kill ourselves moonlighting. God only knows why they kicked him out of his own country. Is he a son of a somebody? No, sir, I don't play the lottery. And the blind men on corners. They work, tickets. At first it seemed there were too many. But here everyone is out on the streets. Those cafés on the Gran Vía, with withered old men who have to be helped up the stairs. Militantly Madrilenian. Hours and hours telling the same old story with a little coffee cup filled with cigarette butts. Everyone is relaxed. The waiters don't get upset if you occupy a table for long periods of time without ordering anything. In my country they kick us out. Okay, either spend your dough or get out. My fellow countrymen come as tourists and are amazed, how is it possible, they say. Take a Spanish boy, make him work like a donkey, make the business boom. Because they're workers. Over there people don't work any more, we're very comfortable, sir, but look here, how great, responsible, right? That old man with his American Legion-in-Manila cap drank ten Cuba Libres in nothing flat to the amazement of the waiters. Talking non-stop about his participation in the Monte Cassino campaign, poor stupid clown, then he got extremely tiresome and had to be asked to leave, they weren't going to serve him anything else, with his broken Spanish ruined by thirty years in the slums of New York. And the big, fat, atrociously dressed woman paying for a cup of coffee with a hundred dollar bill, and the skinny girl with the copper tinted hair pronouncing her z's carefully and flirting with anyone in uniform: the bellboy, the doorman, perhaps confusing them with generals, much too amiable on this side of the Atlantic, rigorously Boricua. They were all over the place in summer, they invaded the Gran Vía, the little tables on the Callao terraces, speaking loudly like all of us speak over there, stumbling over display cases, pulling the doors they were supposed to push, with their green passports written in English stored in some corner of their subconscious, increasingly contradictory, shamelessly lost. Spitefully furious, I once fell down on a bench painfully dying of laughter at the pathetic parade of a tour group made up of my countrymen, while Yolanda cried openly, she cried out of immense anger and despair, crying silently over what that parade of people would never understand, that bewildered flock, that multiple error. But not now. Because it's not the fiery season. Next summer we'll go there to spy on them, shoddy, with loud ties, perfectly sunburned, tropically noisy, begging forgiveness for living, blandly superfluous. I promise not to laugh tearfully, I promise to understand courteously: 1898, public and private schools modeled after the North, all that. Let's understand this in a fatherly fashion. She was right: things evolve dialectically. Let's help the contradictions become sharper, let's make everything problematic. The explosion. Yes, but. You go to the sea, my friend and find it dry, she said. 10,000 kilometers without tasting a Schweppes. After that lesson anything is possible. Four cats, three million, seven hundred million. No that's too much, isn't it? How many have you drunk? Oh, but it's a good idea to get away from your cubicle, the hamburger vendor in Torremolinos. Tamanaco. Strange name. Venezuelan Indians, the name of a river? Let's see. The owner looks Latin American. The waitresses aren't bad. Last year, during the August holidays, that little old lady fanning herself, carefully powdered, lamenting the changes brought on by time. My son, Madrid is no longer Madrid. All that crazy music, we're terrible, you know? The organ grinder turning the crank, the crowds, the olés and Hail to the Virgin, the wine flowed with that happy naturalness of the Jarama. Yoli very much moved and impossible, talking of buying a Spanish fringed shawl, incorrigible, drinking a glass of red wine because one must drink red wine at such affairs. Yes, cold. Any kind, once it's cold, all beers are beer. No, I'm not Venezuelan, Puerto Rican. Yes, exactly. San Juan, the capital. Very pretty, of course. Warm all year. Yes, yes. No, always the same weather. I don't know yet, it depends on what develops. Ah, Maricarmen, I thought so. No, it's okay. Nancy, Margaret, Julie, you know. So you don't have a day off until next week. That's a shame, I know a little place. Of course, not this modern dancing. Nice and cozy. But last year Yoli had protested when I suddenly said let's go. But why? Simply because a man had tossed away a cigarette butt that had miraculously landed upright, a tiny smoking torch? The other people laughed, applauded, drank some wine and exhorted him to repeat his prowess, but the young man didn't even attempt it. I stood up, grabbed Yoli by the hand and said let's go; I was beginning to sweat. Let's go, for the love of God, let's go, because there is the mysterious equivalent of the thread on the lapel, of the aggressive crevice. I had to explain to her that my mother had told me the story of Ricardo Molina, a brilliant university student from her village who, when he was just about to get his law degree, had accomplished, unpremeditatedly, the feat I had just witnessed. On that occasion also there was applause, perhaps a shot of rum, a round of beers, Ricardo tried to repeat the feat, he attempted it four, five times, until his friends got bored and suggested he give up. Ricardo said he'd only give up once he had done it, so he spent the next quarter of a century trying to have his cigarette butt land upright. Of course he quit his studies, fell into terrible poverty, and one fine day he had to be locked up in an insane asylum where, deprived of cigarettes, he threw himself on the floor; jumping up he would land firmly in his feet, achieving, amidst great laughter, the fulfillment of his obsession, of becoming a butt of a man, a human butt. For that reason, fearful that I'd get the bright idea of daring Fate and tossing my cigarette "just this once," I ran out and threw my pack of cigarettes into the garbage can. If it ever occurs to me to run that terrible risk, I'll get rid of my cigarettes and swear off smoking forever. At least I will have taken a step in my own defense. Grumbling, Yolanda ended up shrugging her shoulders. Not even remembering it. The butt. No. So you don't have a day off until next week, Mari, what a shame, yes, another cold one. You're right, I should dress more warmly. I didn't think the temperature would go down. This hoarseness. Mmmm, sneezes. It's getting started. A little cold and you keel over, as if struck by lightning. Idiot, you could have foreseen the temperature change. You haven't learned a thing. And the cold beer, will it do you any good? It'll do you in, that's what. And more cigarettes on top of that. My throat is burning. I don't want to think about two weeks spent shaking under the covers, fever, coughing, headaches, covered with all kinds of balms. Maybe a cognac, a man's drink, would be good for you. Something hot. Mix a dozen beers with Soberano, a man's drink? You drunk, you're going to end up in the gutter. Why didn't you drink wine, that ancient Mediterranean blood, the most democratic of drinks, historically consecrated? Maybe gin with Schweppes tonic, the difference is between Schweppes and Schweppes. Shall we try a Guinness dark? If it's Guinness, it's got to be dark. Dog's Head Ale. Oh, there's also Japanese beer, *choto mate,* Dutch, but no, Czechoslovakian, Hungarian, gulp. What I'd give to drink a beer made in Ulan Bator, for example, the city of a thousand traffic lights. It's true, isn't it? A city where yaks and old broken down camels, as well as an occasional buffalo, amble around with the right of way, lost in thought. They say it was a Polish joke. Poland had a surplus of traffic lights and sold them to Mongolia, which was delighted with the toy that lit up and went off, that winked in three colors. Maybe the Abominable Snowman stopped in shock when confronted with the reddened surprise of a traffic light. Do they drink Soviet beer? No, spasiva. Mmm. Enough, Dimwit, Drylaw, speak easy. Shameful! Drinking like a camel after crossing the Sahara while poor Yoli kills herself inside the four walls of an office. Despicable. They're looking at me, aren't they? Not at me? Is it noticeable that I've been drinking? Get control of my steps, if I can. Hmmm. . . One always wavers a little. Hello, hi, I was doing some business, yes, it's always good to go out for a walk and take advantage of an opportunity to run some errands outside the study. Yes, of course, evidently, it has cooled off considerably, of course, the wind from the Sierra, yes, it goes right through you, brrr. It sure does blow. Yes, good, see you lator, brrr. Freezing wind, My God when will winter be over, six long months. I hope the heating system is working properly. It's destroying my marrow, and they sing about the sun so much, Spain is different. Where is the sun? Oh, on vacation or pub-hopping. My chin hurts on my chest, my fists in my pockets, hunched over, you can touch your navel with your nose. Brrr. Intolerable. Mmm. There are bubbles of thick clouds over the highest rooftops. But it won't rain, it won't snow. Frugal, stingy sky, on an austerity program. It accumulates flocks of clouds of solidified ashes, it shows them threatening rudely, but it remains merely a threat, without deciding to stampede. I miss the admirable lash of a lightning bolt traveling across the sky's dorso, thunder pealing richly sonorous in an extraordinary toccata of fabulous kettledrums. I miss the fullness which causes the earth to tremble slightly, that echoes within your breast like the plucking of contrabasses from outer space, the grave snorting of a tuba I haven't heard for two years. Of course lightning here seems like worms that promptly disappear drowned among thick layers of menacing clouds. During moments like these, it's easy to think about the other clouds, the other lightning, the other thunder, the other cosmogonic manifestations. *Over there* the sky becomes overcast too, as is only natural. Tension is every-where, like in a suspense drama: in the dark shadow covering the groves of trees, in the sweating faces turned toward the heavens as if imploring the advent of birth, in the air clogged with unbreathable matter. But there is the certainty that an orifice will open up in that heavy bladder, torrents of refreshing rain spill over the heated geography; bolts of lightning cross the sky with luminous violence, like fiery serpents, shocking in their frequency and duration, admirable in their ability to impose day upon night. The claps of thunder burst forth like cauliflowers, take on form, become rounded, running along the loudest resonator, racing around within the confines of the circular mountain chains, braying, maddened by their own deep voices. But this Madrid sky, charged, scowlingly quiet, impassive, withstands that charge without wincing, without taking it to its final consequences, mature Afro-European sky, cultured atmosphere, civilized dome. Brrr. There goes the girl of just a moment ago, her hair over her shoulders, those wide-bottomed pants snug around her buttocks, gulp. Can she notice how unsteady I am? I won't say a word to her because I probably won't be able to control my voice, a bellow something out of chime. Hey, good-looking, I'd like to be a cold rasping in your chest, ugh! Antiesthetic. Goodby, precious; she would laugh at that nonexistent *c*, that numerous *s*, selfconsciousness, she said. The most exciting afternoon. Go on, send that tongue to the depths of hell, Archibald said. We suffer from acute pseudobilingualitis, muy nice. Oh, that wind penetrating my lungs, an icy hand, I'll never get out of this alive. Mmm. Go to the Guadalquivir and you'll see it's gone dry. The Loíza is dry, the Portugués is dry, the Yagüez River is dry. My God, protect us, they're squeezing us dry. They come to the doors talking about soccer. They look at me. What are they saying? Pretty spectacle. A Seat auto goes by with an open sun roof through which a giraffe extends its long neck. Once again the mutilated fuselage of the plane on top of the Gate of Toledo. I can't see the face with the staring eyes, opened wide; yes, there it is, looking with a surprised expression toward Carabanchel, perhaps toward the sluggish waters of the river. The aluminum shines like great stains under the ivy. But the ladders and the gnomes have disappeared. I walk along dodging the hands surfacing from the cracks in the sidewalk, they try to grab me, they move, turn, rush at me, closing into fists as if they had grabbed me. From the streets, from the buildings, from the telegraph posts, from the sky there surges a tide of hands. In the Lérida Estates, the doormen are gathered among the hands reaching for their knees like agitated grass. They look at me. They whisper. Don Juan Manuel changes his expression, he doesn't hide his displeasure. What could they be saying, My God! What a spectacle. The rat from the fourth floor left its hiding place. That's what they're saying. Drunk at two in the afternoon. Sponger. Wife exploiter. I stumble and laugh, drooling. Excuse me, sir. Excuse my wavering presence, gentlemen. It's not the fiery season.

It's always a marvelous experience to go into one of those old buildings in Argüelles, La Latina, La Arganzuela, and be confronted with a small square glass showcase displaying a little sign behind the wire mesh: "Elevator. Only for going up." Aren't these the most logical and authentic lifts in the world? (To go down in them would be like committing suicide by pressing a vanilla ice-cream cone to your forehead.)

But I have heard that a very complicated new invention is being worked on—technicians are spending many sleepless nights in order to finish it—by which one will be able to go down. Among many possible names, "Lowervator" is being considered.

*　*　*

SAVINGS BANK

┌─ ACCOUNT TITLE ─┐

Eduardo Leiseca
....

....

Account No. ...38349...

WITHDRAWAL

Ptas. ...500... Cts. ....

Received from the Spanish Credit Bank the amount of
...five hundred... pesetas, which constitutes a withdrawal from the Savings Account held by the aforementioned, there remaining after this transaction a balance of ...2300... Ptas. and ...40... Cts.

Date ...March 5..., 19 ...70...

APPROVED

Shens

Bank Officer

Signature of the account holder,

E. Leiseca

Address: ...144 Romasáns...

No. 132885

114

Nevertheless, it had been clearly demonstrated. When you got out of bed you nurtured the vain hope that I would jump up, stand up fully awake like all other husbands in the building normally do and you grumbled because I would turn my back on you, purring sleepily ay leave me alone. An acute feeling of guilt almost made your wish come true, a little more, two words and that's all, but I dozed until ten in the morning and then started in on the trans. Nevertheless, it had been clearly demonstrated. The trans. encouraged me to go out and buy cigarettes for example and be able to hold my head more or less high and greet the doormen crushing their kidneys mercilessly while scrubbing the floor with tenacity and a rag, the dark coal deliverymen, the road repairmen who struck me with their tasks as solid as hammers, all those who worked fourteen hours in fifteen minutes. They all chased me ferociously, fanning me with their sweaty shirts. But it had been clearly demonstrated that what was most important in the last analysis was for me to keep on hammering at my fantasies from which neuroses flowed luxuriantly and in such a way that you began acquiring slowly but surely an attitude of irreversible aggressiveness and I slowly and calmly and crushed into the floor and eaten away by the most coarse contradictions because the pants are worn as everyone knows by the man of the house but you bring home the bread, economically speaking, nevertheless it had been clearly demonstrated that had I devoted myself to the national pastime, moonlighting with difficulty a piece of fiction, a character and I wouldn't be able to lovingly embrace the cause of my most esteemed delirium. In any case it wasn't easy to announce to you at six in the afternoon that today I worked from ten to five because you might look at me questioningly, you might think coldly that manufacturing those eccentric characters could in no way represent work, let the Almighty come and see for himself, while you from eight-thirty to five banging away at the typewriter approximately like I was, but your version brought money, *dinero*, you know. On the other hand it was clearly demonstrated that when I didn't feed the feeble creatures of my imagination I would sink into the most depressing of worlds and drown in wine and beer and cigarettes and how gratefully I would have taken on the cylindrical company of a marihuana cigarette or something truly serious like morph. or the white goddess Joan of Arc was a heroine, increasing our expenses considerably, leaning over the crevice, my God, putting the word life disadvantagously in the balance with the words extinction death final erasure 50 new. For how long would Yoli continue accepting my flights, that rising to brush the clouds and the damp return to earth, to fraudulently called reality, toward the concrete which I'll be damned if I really find so amusing? Listen to me I won't ask you to put up with reading my stories stay with Sigmund but listen to me: maybe one of my books will catch on and then. Oh if only I could believe it myself oh. I would sit tied to the work table for many long years and with the most sincere intention I would create that elusive work which turns you around and tortures you and doesn't quite come to you totally ay gulp if only I could. Or perhaps it would be better to set aside the books, the frowning dictionaries, the dreams of a writer, and immerse myself in cotton soaked in the dreams of certain Yolandian readings: magazines that tell of kings and actresses and international playboys and notable weddings of notable families and illustrated with the splendor of jewels, what a relief for you my candid, blushing and humble soul, what an adorable evasion of the little apartment with its overdue rent!

But naturally I'm not like the daring and wise and humanitarian writers that Hollywood presents on its screens, men who knock down walls and extraterrestrial giants with their fists, climb dangerous towers, scale dizzying peaks in order to save the son of the ambassador from an incredible death, and who still have more than enough time to play Chopin on a grand piano. Oh, better to die automatically!

E. Leiseca

Dear Friend:

Perhaps my name doesn't ring a bell and it may seem strange that I write to you; it's just that I need some information and I don't know anyone else to write in Madrid. You and I were in Basic Spanish class together with Mr. Gutiérrez, but then you went on with secretarial courses and I became a librarian. At times I've seen you around Río Piedras with you husband, whom I know by sight, and I'm not sure if not also from the university.

Wanda Rivera gave me your address one day when I ran into her at the supermarket. She was buying dietetic products (for herself) and we were very happy to see one another. It was a surprise and a stroke of luck for me to find out you live in Spain with your husband.

Maybe you remember I got married before finishing at the university and had three children, the oldest is now eight years old. Afterwards I had to get a divorce, two years ago, and I remarried a boy from Corozal, which is my hometown. He is a bookkeeper, and we thought that since he is a veteran and hasn't taken advantage of his rights to study (Bill of Rights), he could go to Spain to pursue medicine if they accept the pre-med exam he took here. The problem is that our income is very small and we don't know about the cost of living over there. Do you think I would be able to find work in a library there? How much do they pay? I would work in a store or a factory if I had to, but then I would have to hire someone to take care of the children. Are servants very expensive? Are apartment rents very high or not? I've heard that the cost of living is going up over there, is that true? Do you think they'll give Manolo credit for his previous studies? When do classes start? Is tuition high? Forgive me for bothering you, but would you do me the favor of going by the university and picking up an application form? While you're there you could find out about the requirements, etc., and if I could work in the library and how much they pay, if I have to take out a work permit, etc. If at the same time you find out that there is an apartment building near the university that isn't expensive and is comfortable for a large family, try and find out the rent. Do you have to pay two months' rent in advance and sign a lease? How long are the leases for? If after three months we decide we don't like living there, can we move? Do they have a Post Exchange or a library in the American sector of the base at Torrejón? I could work in either of the two and since they pay well we probably wouldn't have any economic difficulties. Bear in mind that there are seven of us in the family because Manolo's children also live with us. If I were a secretary I would apply at the Embassy, but I was foolish and made the mistake of studying a profession with practically no future, studying library science in a country where there aren't any libraries! Manolo says it's like starting a refrigerator repair business at the North Pole. According to Wanda your husband is working as a translator; I could translate from English to Spanish but not vice versa. How much do they pay per page? Will they give credit for the studies the children have done over here? Do you have to pay a lot for the schools? Do the children wear uniforms or not? Are uniforms very expensive? Are books expensive? Is it mandatory to go to mass on Sundays? Can you get used to the food over there? Are doctors reliable? Is transportation good? Is it very cold in winter? Should we buy coats here or there? Are they very expensive? What kind of coats? Should we take our electrical appliances or buy them there? Are there Woolworth's and Sears stores there? We have accounts at both of them, so if they do have them we could buy whatever we needed on credit. Is it true that the gypsies steal children? Could my husband work part-time in a business as an accountant? Are cars very expensive? And are the milk, eggs, tap water, and meat of good quality? Is there Alka Seltzer, Coca Cola, Vicks Vapo Rub, Camay and Palmolive soaps, Listerine, Cold Cream, Revlon, Maidenform bras, Red Seal U.S. Number 1 rice, Brookfield butter, Chesterfield, Libby's juices, Kotex, Vanity Fair, Lasser suppositories, Parker pens, Kellogg's Corn Flakes, Kraft cheeses, Hellmann's mayonnaise, Fruit of the Loom underwear, Campbell's soup, Jason shirts, Avon products, Gillette Blue Blades? Am I asking too much? Please do answer me as soon as possible, so we can go ahead and make our plans. Will you answer right away?

Best wishes from your friend
Olga Vázquez

P.S. Regards to your husband. Do they have Foremost ice cream?

FOUND IN THE MAILBOX

Last March 4th the campus of the University of Puerto Rico became a veritable battleground between students fighting for the independence of the homeland and an ominous group of neofascist students who propose to annex the island to the United States.

At about eleven a.m. a protest group of Puerto Rican youths paraded through the campus of UPR, followed by a pro-independence group, to demonstrate against the presence of an ROTC unit within the university area. The ROTC (Reserve Officers Training Corps), an agency of the U.S. Army beachheaded on University territory, has as its purpose the recruiting of Puerto Rican youths into the U.S. Armed Forces. Gathered in front of the building of the Yankee agency, they shouted in favor of Puerto Rican independence. Immediately, Flavia Rivera, one of the leaders of the Pro-Independence Student Federation, made a speech condemning the ROTC presence on the University campus and Compulsory Military Service for Puerto Rican youths in the Yankee Army.

While Miss Rivera was speaking, the ROTC cadets, who were inside the building, began firing their shotguns and throwing rocks at the protestors. The pro-independence youths responded at once to the aggression by throwing Molotov cocktails, rocks and bottles. Answering the call of the President of UPR, Jaime Benítez, the shock force (a special squadron of the riot police) invaded the campus and brutally attacked the students of the PISF, seriously injuring 50 of them and killing 19-year-old Antonia Martínez with a bullet which struck her in the temple.

This is not the first time pro-independence youths and ROTC cadets have had a confrontation. Repeatedly the university student body has condemned the presence of a Pentagon agency at the UPR. About a year ago, on April 23, 1969, 3,000 university students gathered in the UPR theatre to loudly voice their protests over the presence of American military personnel in the principal Puerto Rican center of learning. Last November a crowd of students demonstrated in an impressive march which culminated in the partial burning of the ROTC building on campus. A few months earlier a group of university students had participated in a hunger strike demanding the eradication of ROTC from the campus and independence for Puerto Rico. Simultaneously, various demonstrations took place in favor of these demands and against the war in Vietnam.

In addition to all these university activities, a wave of aggression and assaults by pro-statehood supporters (Puerto Ricans in favor of annexation to the U.S.) and Cuban exiles has been unleashed, with the intention of repressing the growing struggle of the independence movements and counteracting the achievements of the urban guerrillas, known as ACL (Armed Commandos for Liberation). One of the acts of vandalism perpetrated last February by those anti-independence groups was the burning of the newspaper *Claridad,* an organ of the Pro-Independence Movement of Puerto Rico. According to statements by members of the political Commission of the PIM, this criminal act was intended to silence the constant accusations this pro-independence publication has levelled for months against mineral exploitation and the drafting of young Puerto Ricans into the American Army. The existing situation in the country is, therefore, critical, and as political confrontations and official repression increase, the struggle for the independence of Puerto Rico is achieving, in ever-growing measure, support and definitive strength.

My Dear Children:

God grant that you're well upon receiving this letter we're all well thank God. At least we've had some news from you after so long thanks to you Yolanda my child who takes time to think about writing. I know that Eddy can't, that he's busy with his stuff and he's always been like that a little on the lazy side. I hope he isn't offended by what I say but he doesn't even add 2 words to say we're fine mother and father thank God, here everything is the same nothing ever happens but the other day Fermín's 15-year old daughter disappeared and they called the police and it was in the newspaper and everything, there was also a picture of Fermín and he turned out so well with his mouth open and his hat pushed back and he was saying that his daughter had disappeared from home and the paper said in big letters Mr. Fermín Mercado asks anyone who sees his little girl to get in touch with him the newspaper said, his house was full of people because we're so humanitarian around here. The mayor also showed up and said that he could help in the search and he was going to give all city employees half a day off so they could go look for the girl in the fields, well it wasn't anything serious what happened was that Martita had gone away with a boy with a lot of hair and a beard and necklaces and barefooted who came I think from San Juan and lived out in the open on the beach, and they told Fermín yesterday that they had seen her around Fajardo with chains around her neck and barefooted and flowers in her hair but all dirty and kind of faded and with a skirt that swept the ground it was so long and like an old lady who was disgusting to look at, that's the way things go my children and they say that it's God's punishment since Fermín likes to wag his tongue so much and has discredited so many innocent girls with his gossip if you don't like soup they dish out three bowlsful for you as they say.

Your father Sebastián my son no longer has pains in his back and he's happy working and thinking that maybe we'll take a trip your way and he says that when he retires he'd like to go live over there since 2 friends of his are retired and live in Spain and they say it's great for people who retire and they're happy and asked for your address but your father didn't give them anything because he says you don't want that, that's what Sebastián your father says my son, he now spends his evenings watching the soap opera on the television and he enjoys it a lot and sometimes I'm in bed thinking about you and Sebastián makes me get up to watch the nine o'clock show and he tells me it's interesting it's called the something of the Apernines or something like that it's called, I'm, telling you he doesn't miss one installment and one of the actors sent him an autographed picture and everything and he was so delighted he put it in the store where everybody can see it. The business is coming along well altho he says he's tired but he just likes to talk because he's always up and ready at six in the morning straight as a palm and he leaves at nine at night only on account of the Apernine soap opera and when the show isn't on he goes to the pentecostal temple and sits in the last row to hear what they say and what they sing and he says they have a right to believe whatever they want to believe and that their youth learn to have respect and turn away from sin; and it's true what they say about young people being in bad shape in this country because the other day Pedro Caraballo's son had to be taken to the hospital hardly breathing and purple like a crabapple because he put that poison that is worrying everybody so much right into his vein and in the school there was a twelve year old boy smoking marihuana as if it were nothing and Pedro Caraballo's son is twelve years old and shooting himself with a syringe full of the worst there is that even kills people and takes their breath away and then they steal to pay for their vice and they even assault and kill and Sebastián says that in the church they don't.

Yolanda I'm really sorry that you're not going to have your little girl, but don't worry my child God is merciful and if you don't have her it's because God our Father doesn't want you to but continue praying a lot and go to confession and make Eddy go to mass and pray a lot and have faith because things have a way of resolving themselves and one mustn't despair and have hope and faith in God who never forgets his creatures, remember how the same thing happened to Cambucha's Camilita and she wore a habit and made a long prayer to Saint Jude Thaddaeus who is a very strong saint and nothing happened, but she made one to Saint Anthony, who as you know when we are young girls we offer him a bouquet of flowers and everything on the eve of Saint John we put an egg white in a glass to see what it tells us is going to happen, and Cambucha's Camilita after so many prayers got pregnant and had no less than duplicates and it's for sure that it was because

123

she had two saints she prayed to at the same time; a little boy and a girl, a pair to start with God never forgets his faithful my children don't despair and take communion if you want I don't say anything to Eddy because you know how he is but I will to you Yolanda my child because you're so good and know so much and you're so understanding. Camilita's little children are pretty and blond and look like little Americans they're so fat and white and beautiful God bless them.

Ay my children forgive the bother but one always has to tell one's sorrows because it's a comfort, well the other day Elisa the wife of Pablo the school bus driver came into the backroom of Sebastián your father's store and sat on the floor behind a barrel of cod and said that she was hot and lifted her skirt and your father was selling potatos and lard and didn't pay attention to her because he's changed a lot and after 2 hours of lying there she went straight to Pablo her husband the school bus driver and told him that Sebastián had taken undue liberties with her and even the police had to come because Pablo the school bus driver took out the crank to the school bus and wanted to hit your father Sebastián who wasn't guilty of a blessed thing, that's how women are so evil can you imagine, and the people gathered in your father's store and when Pablo left they laughed and said that Sebastián wasn't to blame for the fact that Elisa Pablo the school bus driver's wife doesn't set foot in her house and they say she's one of those sick people who is always after you know what. And Sebastián was furious and told me that she comes up with those things now that he's behaving himself, but that she wouldn't have done that to him ten years back because then he would have, but not now, those times are over when he was strong enough for anyone you know how Sebastián is my children.

Well Yoli don't worry about the little girl pray constantly and offer flowers to the best saints and to the Spanish virgin who'll surely favor you with a girl and we'll all be very happy because God doesn't forget his creatures no matter where they're from and thank you for writing to me my child and tell Eddy that Eustaquio's Cuito sends him regards and wrote down his address because that one really is intelligent and he's going to study over there, so now you know don't be surprised if he shows up over there some day I gave him the address and I just couldn't not even if Eddy doesn't like it. Have faith and pray a lot my children because God never forgets good people.

Kisses and love and hugs from

Mamá and also from papá

Guaynabo, P.R.

Dear Yolanda:

First of all forgive my lengthy delay in writing you, it's just that after a trip you get back so tired at first and when I got back I was like on air and would get terribly sleepy very early, and Rafael tells me that's due to the time change. Rafael knows about everything, my dear, you know he used to play the violin, then he went crazy about chess, after that it was photography, on which he spent a fortune to set up a darkroom, another time he wanted to become a deep-sea diver and his helmet is still around, I turned it upside down, filled it with dirt and put a plant in it. He's curious about everything, and when we were in Salamanca he wanted to bring back as a souvenir a key from the harmonium played by a well-known man to whom a certain poem was dedicated. Well, thank God everything is back to normal in my schedule and with my meals. Let me tell you that in the 24 days I was away from home and eating like a pig from the moment I set foot on the ship, I only gained two pounds, and Rafael likewise. I'm glad it was so little because that means that we know how to eat, I especially controlled my jaws a little.

Getting back to the ship, I was really sorry that the Fluvia burned, but I thank God that it didn't happen while we were on it or all the souvenirs and the clothes I bought for Evy's wedding would have been burned and they cost over $300, so you can imagine. We have very pleasant memories of Toledo and Madrid, the Eiffel tower and the one in Pizza, memories which will never be erased from our hearts.

I've talked so much (I mean written) and we still haven't thanked you for all your kindnesses and for Mayte who took us to Avila in her little car. So thanks a million for everything. Tell Eddy that he really looks great, a little on the thin side, that's all.

To tell the truth we can't complain about our trip: we had a marvelous time on the ship as well as in Barcelona and Madrid; first because we didn't get sick, and then I was so happy over this new experience for us. Secondly because I'd no sooner gotten there than I received a letter at the hotel, from Evy, saying that she had decided to get married, and for her fondest dreams to come true makes me very happy. So any moment now I'll be a grandmother, how time flies!

You know, when we went to your house I told you that you looked a little plump and you didn't say anything, but I found out over here that you're expecting, congratulations, Eddy must be delighted poor thing. How do you feel? Drink a lot of malt and chicken soup, Yoli, lots of nourishment, don't forget this is your first baby. I'm enclosing a copy of the picture we took at your house, look how well it turned out. Eddy looks like he was asleep but Rafael claims that's not so, he's always like that. One just lets oneself he carried away by the good taste of the wine and then suddenly the bomb goes off. Thank you too for the recipe for paella, you're an expert.

Evy and Tony are both fine. She's finishing her studies this summer and will get married in October. He graduated last year in Business Administration and his father gave him a sporty Chevrolet. His parents are very fond of Evy, you know how lovable she is with everyone. Tony's parents have a little yacht and sometimes we go sailing on Sundays, and Rafael has two or three shots of whiskey as he looks at the sea and the island scenery, which I can only tell you is beautiful, Yoli, with all those hotels and the green lawns that look like a movie of Río de Janeiro, honest. I swear that from the time I set foot on the yacht I have my life jacket on, but Rafael says for me not to worry, that it won't sink, that the shark who wants to eat him will have to come out of the showerhead at home. I laugh nervously. Sometimes we go quite a distance from the shore, so much so that you can hardly see our pretty island, and since Tony's father has businesses all over the island he says he's going to buy one of those little Piper airplanes and he said he would take us up in it, but I really won't set foot in it even if they tie me down. And he also has a ham radio station, and Rafael who is so curious goes with him to communicate with countries all over the world. One day they even got Russia, my God, and I asked them if they weren't scared. Evy says that when they buy the plane she's going to learn to fly, she's not afraid of anything and is so sure of herself, poor thing. You can't even tell anymore about her leg; I was afraid she'd limp after her car accident. But she's healed neat as a pin.

Yoli, you take good care of yourself now and don't fall, that's how I lost my first child.

Let me know how everything is coming along. Maybe we'll show up over there because we're thinking about going to North Africa: Granada and all those places.

God bless you and don't do like we did and take so long to write.

Love from Mary

Barcelona, Spain

Señor Don Eduardo Leiseca:

We have read your manuscript of *Unsuspected Nights*, which you sent us for consideration.

Your work, which is well written, deals with modern themes and has some well-developed points. But it seemed monotonous and somewhat daring to us and we fear it wouldn't be widely accepted by the general public.

For these reasons we have decided not to publish it and we are returning the original.

With our good wishes.

Juan F. Lora, Editor
Star Publishers

* * *

No one revealed this to me, but a huge aunthill has spread beneath the cathedral of San Juan, Puerto Rico. Thousands of millions of aunts for each human being. Nevertheless, my maternal ant is an old maid who lives in Río Piedras surrounded by cats and vitamins and scapulars and strange slaves that smell of almonds murdered in summer. Bilingual pseudo patience while my neighbor looks at me with her beautiful blue ice sipping at her glass of Coca-Cola over eyes. Ais and aaiss, evidently pederastic expressions, I think to myself, knowing down deep that I have felt very week this weak, güic undf güic, the devil. Write insufferable Akiro? Deer friend, God be willing that upon receipt. Have you heard about the distinguished dramaturge who studied at Jail University? And then

> the interminable professors of incomparative
> literature
> grammarians disguised as
> Saussurian linguists
> assault us from their thrones
> ferociously unwinding their theories
> on the noble linguage of Shakespeare and the
> noble language of Cervantes
> (pronounced Selbanteh) and one you might say
> ass to debait
> Bituincurrents (Prof.)
> without bin shure of pozessin
> the du nolege of th' fourminshuned.

It's a cruel yoke, a joke that weighs heavily on our colonized necks, and all due to disadvantageously phonetic reasons in many cases, as I was able to verify that summer when I amused myself by having the gall to go into Macy's to buy a sheet and said

> miss would you be so kind and if it's not any trouble
> and you aren't busy and it's handy
> as to sell me a shit,
> that's approximately what I said very proud of my
> clear Anglosaxon diction

129

approved by Archibald the Park Avenue
intellectual
and the girl turned red because she hadn't expected
that I
with my correct tone of voice
my outrageous bearing and my sense of honor
(evident in my Spanish-speaking complexion)
would address a young lady in such an
indecorous and improper fashion and much less
—she said blushingly—
a university student from Cambridge
Massachusetts who only works there
summers, and no shit, she told me, very bad shit
she said while she began to understand my
thirdworldspeaking complexion and my mustache,
you must mean shiit, she said,
oh forgive me, I answered with that unassailable oh
of all the ants of the Bronx
oh right you being right I said,

she might have been the same girl who, on a New York beach, I
had spoken with about the breathtaking beaches of my country
(which was hers congressionally), and I asked her if she would
like to live near our beautiful bitches, a word which then meant
beaches, and the girl answered with an incongruous, inexplicable
profanity in which she mentioned the innocent feminine founders
of my family, and Yolanda, who had been professionally spying
on me, began writhing under the umbrella, laughing uproariously
at what I had said, bitch, she said, you have invited her to live with
our tropical whores, she said, and I acknowledged that it was evil
to have invented that *t* clouding the *i* until it was turned into a
slightly colorless *e*, perhaps I had told her that with the unconscious
intention of insulting her, Yoli concluded, incubating a new
pocketbook analysis for my personal use, you have just called
her a whore dog or at least that's what she understood, she said.
But aside from the momentary discomfort I recognized Yolanda's
admirable ability to laugh wholeheartedly while being consumed
by the most ferocious anger, her nerves completely lax or, if you
prefer, relaz, Yoli, a polished artificial blonde in a swimsuit or in
melodramatic black underwear with the day of the week written
on the dizzying edge of her panties, dedicated as always to destroying my castles with a single lightningword.

* * *

WORMS DO NOT ENTER INTO IT

There is a certaine gum on this islande of Sanct Johan which I had never before hearde of, and inform'd by Johan Ponce de León and other honourable persones who could very well knowe of this matter, they saie that near the mines called Loquillo, there is a certaine gum which comes from the trees, which is white as larde, but very bitter and it is excellente for tarring ships, mixing it with oil without further combination. And it is so excellente because it is bitter, shipworms do not enter into it, as they do into tar pitch. The Indyans and yet the Christyans on that islande call this substance *tabonuco*, and it is very excellente for what I have alleged, when it can be had in such vaste quantities.

G. Fernández de Oviedo, 1552

GOLDE IS NOT AVAYLABLE

Pastures are narrowe from the many guayabos growing along them, grazed upon repeatedly by the cows who eat the fruits therefrom.

There be Holy Rod, balsam, oaks, cedars, laurels, mint, magueys, oranges and all the trees from the other islandes, drumstick trees and cotton plants, all the fruites of the earth and those taken from spain. . .

The principale farming endeavours thereine now are cattle, tanning and principally sugar which grows abundantly on this islande, on which there be a dozen or more sugar mills, the population of Spaniards is decreasing, because as golde is not avaylable, merchandise is lacking and thus noe other endeavours are undertaken.

J. López de Velasco, 1571

THERE IS NOE MAN WHO WITHE A BALLE

. . .this river comes from afar, e're fourteen leagues from this
city, from a mountain called Guabate, and on its banke there is a
tree known as seyba in the language of the indians, which is so
large that the shade it provides at midday, there is noe man who
withe a balle not more sizable than an orange, can traverse it
at that point, albeit the base of the tree is nearly one hundred
and twenty paces from the river, and there was a carpenter named
Pantaleón who had made and began in a hole of the tree, by
boring, a chapel and put into it an altar for saying mass; its width
at its lower base is so great in circumference that fifteen men
could not encompass it and there are creditable men of good faith
who swore on oathe, that they had measur'd it in the presense
of another and found that its contour measur'd seven arms'
lenthe. . .

AND THEY WERE NEVER AT PEACE

From the citie of Puertorrico to the southeast of it there is
a verie large mountain range with three valleyes and it is verie high
being called altogether the Sierra de Loquillo, albeit it be dismem-
bered by the three elevations composing it; the highest is called
the Sierra de Furudi, so named by the Negroes, which in their
language means a place alwayes covered by cloudes; the next is
Espíritu-Santo, and the other Loquillo, it is at ten leagues from
the citie of Puertorrico; it is called Loquillo because the Spaniards
named it thus, in relation to an indian chief living thereine who
often rose against the Christyans and they were never at peace;
from this lande rises a mountain chayne which divides the islande
in half from east to west and it comes to the sea, and the province
of Nueva Salamanca.

Juan Troche y Ponce de León, 1582

ALL OF WHICH ARE WILDE

. . .what they call *piña* because it looks like the pineapple of Spain is excellent but it does not grow all year like the plantains, but only three or four months, its flesh is like a sweet lemon with a few sour spots that look like the flesh of a very ripe peach, but the inside from which the slices are taken is fleshier and firmer; what the fields are filled with is oranges and lemons and limes and citrons, all of which are wilde, but as regards the sweet oranges, they are larger and better than the ones from over there. . .

TO THE MODESTY OF THE CRIOLLAS

. . .the community or environs does not surpass 200 dwellings but some say that only in women, counting blacks and mulattas, there are more than 4,000 and they are cloistered to the point of not even going out to Mass, which albeit this may be attributed in great measure to the modesty of the criollas, more likely it is due to the misery and poverty of the land, as most of them haven't enough for shawls and dresses and they are so proud, that even should a Bishop give them clothing as charity so that they might attend Mass, many do not want to accept it and some who did accept did not make use of the offering as it was made of the clothe used in religious habits.

Fray Damián López de Haro, 1644

SHE WILL NOT BE ABLE
TO ENJOY SUCH LENGTHY EXPOSURE

All things considered, she wasn't described with the detail I could now go into, where she would be shown more beautiful than the ordinary and commonplace due to the charm of her valleys and forests, were it not for the succinctness demanded by history where she will not be able to enjoy such lengthy exposure.

FOR THERE IS ONLY ONE LINEAGE
WITH A SMALL ONE

The women are the most beautiful of all the indians, honest, virtuous and hard workers and of such lovely discernment that the governors, Don Enrique and Don Iñigo said that all prudent men should come to Puerto Rico to marry and it was commonplace to hear them say "for marriage, Puerto Rico."

The natives are usually of large stature, for there is only one lineage with a small one; of quick wit and away from their homeland they are very active and valorous, although from ancient times there is no information, save that of a captain from Flanders, Juan de Avila, a native of this city, who for his deeds deserved that they be recorded in the 3rd part of the *Pontifical* written by Doctor Babia and another gentleman, Don Antonio Pimentel, who was a member of the order of San Juan.

Diego de Torres Vargas, 1647

THEY NOURISH AND SUPPORT THEM WILLINGLY

They give the name of *criollo* to anyone born on the Island no matter what caste or mixture he comes from. They call Europeans whites, or using their own expression "men from the other side". . . They are deliberate, taciturn; they are always observant, but with a quick imagination for discussing and imitating whatever they see; they love freedom, are generous, hospitable towards strangers, but are vain and fickle in their tastes.

They are inclined towards spectacular and honourable acts; they have demonstrated daring in war and they are without a doubt good soldiers for expeditions and short campaigns, for accustomed as they are to sedentary life, they resent leaving it for long periods of time. . .

They look critically upon Europeans; they find bothersome the excessive zeal and energy the latter put into their undertakings and they are dominated by emulation; but they receive them warmly in their homes, they nourish and support them willingly and they feel exulted at having descended from them. The women prefer Spaniards over the *criollos*; they are of a pleasant disposition; but the salt water of the sea rots their teeth and deprives them of that warm, attractive colouring prominent in ladies from other countries; the heat makes them indolent and untidy; they marry very early, are fertile, very fond of dancing and horseback riding, both of which they execute with dexterity and extraordinary ease.

The mulattos who make up a majority of the population of this Island, are the children of whites and negroes. Their colouring is dark, unattractive, their eyes are clouded, they are tall and well built, stronger and better suited for work than the whites, who treat them with contempt. Among this class of people there are many who are quick and free in their speech and deeds; they have always distinguished themselves for their actions and they are ambitious for honour.

INTERESTING FAILING
IN THEIR CONDUCT

An equivocal and intricate character results from this variety and mixture of peoples, but some circumstances are attributable to all of them which we can consider characteristic of the inhabitants of Puerto Rico; the fertility of the land which facilitates their gathering of food causes them to be generous and hospitable towards strangers; the solitude of their rural dwellings accustoms them to silence and contemplation; the delicate nature of their bodies aids the liveliness of their imagination, which carries them to extremes; the delicacy of their organs which makes them shy, also makes them confront danger and even death with contempt; the different social classes existing among them instills vanity and pride in some, depression and emulation in others.

They are generally frugal, light sleepers and shrewd; but they are ambitious for glory, an interesting failing in their conduct.

INVITATION TO A LADY

In order to begin the ball, the guests stand at the foot of the stairs with tambourines, gourds, *maracas* and guitars; accompanied by these instruments they sing a tale in honour of the hosts...

The master of the house appears at the head of the stairs, welcomes the guests and their accompanists and invites them to enter: then they embrace and greet one another as if it had been years since their last encounter.

Each gentleman invites a lady to dance, who, if she has no slippers, as is most frequently the case, borrows them from

135

another, and wearing her hat she begins twirling around the ballroom at such a rapid pace that she seems like a shooting star. The gentleman dances on the opposite side with his hat tilted to one side, his sabre across his back, holding it with both hands; he doesn't change places or make any other motion other than raising and lowering his feet with great speed and force; if he is on a loose board, he gives it his all which consists of making as much noise as possible so that the music and singing can be heard as well as his bare feet. When the gentleman who is dancing or one of those observing wishes to show his appreciation for the lady dancer, he takes off his hat and places it upon her head, sometimes so many are thus placed that, not being able to balance them, she holds them in her hands and beneath her arms; when she tires of dancing, she retires with a curtsy, returns the hats to those who gave them to her and each of them gives her half a crown; this is called *dar la gala*.

Iñigo Abbad y Lasierra, 18th century

THE HOSTILITIES OF CORSAIRS

My name is Alonso Ramírez and my country the city of San Juan of Puerto Rico, capital of the island which is nowadays known by this name, and with that of Borinquén in olden times; between the Mexican gulf and the Atlantic sea it divides itself. It is made famous by the refreshment offered by its delightful waters to those who sail eagerly for New Spain; the beauty of its harbour, the incomparable Morro which defends it, the curtains and bastions crowned with artillery which make it secure. Serving not so much this, as it is also found in other parts of the Indies, but the spirit freely allotted to its children by the character of that land to keep it safe from the hostilities of corsairs.

This is a commitment placed upon the natives by their integrity and loyalty with no other motive, as it is true that the riches which gave rise to its name due to the veins of gold found in it, nowadays due to the absence of its original inhabitants to work them and the vehemence with which the tempestuous hurricanes stripped the cocoa trees which for lack of gold provided whatever was necessary to those trading in it, and as a result the rest of the islanders, became transformed into poverty.

AS BEST I COULD

Prepared to defend as best I could, with my two muskets and four pikes, bullets rained down from the guns of the enemy, but without broaching us; and I answered with the muskets, one taking aim and the other lighting the powder; and all the while we were splitting the bullets with a knife so that having doubled our ammunition to have more shots, our ridiculous defense might be more lasting.

Alonso Ramírez, 1690

A LAMB WITH A STANDARD

On this illustrious promenade, his lordship (the Governor) noticed that among the crowd of men and women following him there was a negro woman very close to his horse and fearing that the latter might run her down as he was very high strung, he warned her to stay away, and she answered in these words: "I have been following Your Grace from the square to see if I might have a coin of our lord to wear upon my breast and I have only acquired a tattered shirt occasioned by this mob; give me the coin and I will go to commend you to God;" This love and sincerity moved his lordship to give her a portion of coins and some pesos to pay for a new shirt.

In front of the convent where the third inspection was made, was a three or four-year-old girl along with many other men and women; and having watched the aforementioned coins being tossed away she said: "Sir governor, I have not received any and I too have said Long live the King"; so pleased was his Lordship with this clever remark that drawing close to the child he gave her many, as she chorused "Long live the King" and "Long live the Governor who gives away coins."

His lordship (the Governor) was carrying a magnificent cane of mother of pearl whose encrustations of gold and silver formed different terrestrial and flying animals.

Four negroes accompanied him at the stirrups of his horse dressed in silver necklaces and livery embellished with shiny braids of the same metal; his lordship had with him two pages with extravagant overskirts; and their hats were adorned in front with his coat of arms in solid gold. In front of the entourage was a negro in the same livery, who heralded the joy of the republic with the happy sound of a trumpet, another was on horseback with two sacks of coins which had been minted in gold and silver for this occasion, which bore on one side the image of His Majesty with his name along the edges, and on the other a lamb with a standard lying against a rock, which is the coat of arms of the city. . .

Anonymous, 18th century

MAY WELL BE CONGRATULATED

The United States may well be congratulated on the acquisition of the island of Puerto Rico.

Henry K. Carroll, 1898

*   *   *

Ptas. 719.00

Building located at	144 Romasáns, Building "D"
Floor	4. No. 3 - right stairwell
We have received from	Don E. Leiseca
the amount of	719.00 pesetas
in payment of	the heat for the current month

Madrid, March 15   1970

GENERAL ESTATE ADMINISTRATION, INC.

Who was Cristeto Aguayo? Why remember him? Why did he choose to live in Nebraska Heights, particularly in the little cream-colored house across the street from where we were living?

At this very hour, would he be mowing the lawn? Would he be classifying his innumerable trophies again? Were the gentlemen from the press paying him a visit? Was he illegally displaying a degree from the University of Río Piedras? Some of these questions would infiltrate villages in order to take charge of suspicious that Yolanda had been preparing with infinite patience, assisted by one or two nosy neighbors as well as her research in several libraries. Naturally, she had also resorted to direct interviews whenever possible.

Cristeto Aguayo was born the 15th of November of 1936 on the beaches of the city of Ponce.[1] Of an unknown father, his mother, Catalina Aguayo, had to work long hours to support her son. From a most tender age Cristeto displayed an admirable capability for carrying out certain tasks. When he was barely four years old he amazed four professional slaughterers by catching an enormous hog with his little right arm and finishing him off with a single knife thrust.

His mother, who at that time devoted herself to slaughtering porcine and bovine livestock, gratefully accepted the professional help her youngster provided her. When he was seven years old a journalist from the capital wrote a lengthy article on him called "A Mozart of the Knife and Blood." His academic life was quite extended, although he never went beyond the third grade, a fully understandable fact in light of the complete dedication the boy had for his precocious occupation.[2] After a long period

---

[1] Army biographers place his birth on July 4, 1931, a date which Yolanda categorically rejects.

[2] The teachers who took part in his education later declared before the television cameras that the boy was quite adept at drawing large knives, scimitars, machetes, daggers, swords, and that he had designed a certain type of guillotine which had a thick needle in place of a blade, a modification which would avoid separating the head from the body thus lessening the loss of blood, a very precious liquid in the preparation of sausage.

during which little Cristeto was profusely interviewed by both local and foreign journalists, his name slowly began disappearing from the pages of the newspapers. These were anonymous years during which the boy never stopped devoting himself to his profession, perfecting it to incredible extremes. He was nothing more than a well paid, but unknown, worker when the Korean War broke out. Cristeto, who was then fourteen years old, realized that he had been secretly waiting for just this sort of favorable circumstance. Since he was not old enough to enlist, he falsified his birth certificate and a short time later, among tears of joy and sadness, the boy bid farewell to his mother and clothed himself in the uniform of the United States Armed Forces. At the sunny training camps the recruit showed such ferocity and cleverness during hand-to-hand combat practice sessions, such dexterity in the use of a bayonet, that the officers could do no less but congratulate themselves on the bellicose nature of their acquisition.[3] On the battlefield, since the enemy had turned out to be a better fighter than Military Intelligence had indicated, uniformed high command, knowing of the existence of the outstanding recruit, and following a quick meeting, agreed to send him to the front. His career there, as might be expected, was meteoric. After three weeks, following numerous combat missions (for which he had volunteered enthusiastically), Cristeto was rewarded with sergeant's stripes. During the most heated battles he could be seen crawling through the bushes with a knife in his teeth, fording rivers or climbing trees. Secrecy was one of his better qualities. He had an amazing ability for penetrating enemy lines and, taking advantage of the shadows, systematically and without loosing his calm, slitting the throats of all the men in a detachment, one by one. He became so zealous in his devotion to duty that he would infiltrate villages in order to take charge of suspicious civilians.[4] On the other hand, what most impressed the officers was his lack of self-interest. When he was informed that due to his proven anti-communist militancy he was being considered for promotion, his humbleness made tears come to the eyes of the

[3] Yolanda insisted that the subterfuge of document falsification was known by all the officers, who chose to overlook it since after all that particular war was considered a mere police cleanup operation. Being that Korea was a country of Orientals who didn't speak English, the cleanup could be carried out by any race on the planet. Cristeto's dexterity in the handling of the white man's weapons was a decisive factor in his enlistment.

[4] In the recent case of My Lai, Vietnam, Cristeto was mentioned as a possible inspiration for the methods employed there.

most hardened sergeants with thirty years of service behind them. Cristeto quickly whispered, without false modesty, that duty and obligation should not be rewarded, as they were qualities that should be expected from every soldier, and that he simply had a mission to accomplish which he carried out selflessly, like an apostle. Nevertheless, in spite of his protests, after four months of duty Sergeant Aguayo Cristeto U.S. 50 50 was granted two more stripes, thus reaching the highest rank a non-commissioned officer can aspire to. During his nights off he could be seen strolling around the perimeters with an air of deep sadness; a cook who had been a reporter even insinuated that, because of his temperament, Sergeant Aguayo Cristeto U.S. 50 50 seemed to have a great gift for poetry. The young sergeant confessed that it was true and blushingly explained that on moonlit nights, following monotonous days of brutalizing inactivity, he would engage in mystical meditation, taking pleasure in revelations such as the aparition of a torrential river of blood, dense clouds of mutilated arms and legs, trees of fresh viscera beneath a sky of dead eyes that sparkled, in his words, like beautiful tropical skies, and all of that against the background music of wails, children's cries, a rustling of bodies thudding to earth, screams and murmurs. Those moments of communication with his innermost being didn't last long, because in the interim Cristeto had taken the necessary steps to put into practice his fighting instinct and was always the first to join any mission of the regiment. His youthful enthusiasm was contagious to those around him who made inhuman efforts to emulate him.[5] All the units in the Army fought over him and he was to be loaned many times to some decimated company whose morale was dragging on the ground. His arrival in these companies meant an immediate restitution of hope. For this reason it came as no surprise when, after five months of being at the front, he was promoted to first lieutenant in spite of his dogged opposition during which he shed anguished tears, explaining that he felt his new status would take him away from the troops, in other words, from his people. In light of this promotion, a group of captains who had graduated from Officer School at the University of Puerto Rico filed a complaint with the regimental colonel alleging that it was a clear violation of army regulations to have waived the rank

---

[5] High officials happily verified that Cristeto's countrymen, smiling, calm, obedient and sentimental, showed an innate capability for decapitating, disemboweling and roasting any kind of living being without losing their serenity nor their habitual smile.

of second lieutenant, an indispensable step for any officer. But the colonel stated affably that such formulas were nothing more than simple bureaucratic measures and since Cristeto was an exceptional soldier, he had to be exceptionally treated. The officers kept silent thereafter not only out of discipline but because basically they realized, with a certain amount of envy, that Cristeto had found his way into the heart of the regiment. Confronted with his new responsibility, Cristeto carried his dedication to new extremes, taking into his own hands tasks which were normally carried out by subordinates. Concerned with the proper instruction of his troops, Cristeto would gather them in a forest clearing, order that a prisoner be brought to him, carefully describe his anatomy, pointing out the weak spots where a blade of steel would find no resistance and, amidst the general expectation, with a movement "as quick as lightning" (his own words when Congress decorated him with the Distinguished Service medal) he would cleanly cut him down, with no spilling of blood, subsequently explaining that his system had the advantage of silencing screams, moans, cries and other bothersome noises that might attract the enemy to the executioner. He explained that this silent labor in the middle of a forest, while it didn't entail the drum rolls and cymbals of witnessed deeds nonetheless filled the spirit with the joy of a job well done. During these talks he would address, with his usual selflessness and impartiality, vast praise to the anonymous heroes who worked without ever seeing the product of their labors, as was the case with aviators who, at a great distance from their target, would hurl live phosphorous, napalm, fragmentation bombs, and delayed action bombs, yet never seeing the result of their efforts in terms of the "human factor." He spoke in the same manner about artillerymen, who had to fire indirectly without even being able to see the place where the shell exploded, and he maintained that in every artilleryman's chest beat the heart of a marine, a simple compensatory phenomenon. Dynamiters couldn't be left off this list; loaded with the most modern means of healthy destruction, they went out under the cover of shadows to the very edge of enemy lines, demolishing grass huts filled with saber-toothed creatures, compelled to return after having placed the charges without any hope of ever seeing their dreams realized. Conscious that the army was a huge monolith composed of the most diverse branches, he would speak admiringly of the jobs that were overlooked simply because they lacked the brilliance and drama of more war-like acts. Among them the office workers, who in their apparently comfortable positions had to type up the lists of wounded, dead and missing long into the night, take inventory of machine guns, automatic rifles, hand grenades, bazookas, mortars, asphyxiating gas bombs, defoliating liquids, flame-throwers, bayonets, pocket knives, and bullets, and who delivered letters from home to the troops, also seeing to it that not a single mosquito net was missing, because if there was anything dangerous in this world it was the bite of a mosquito. He never failed to mention the medics who, in the heat of ferocious enemy attacks, risked their lives caring for the well-being of their own with maternal love, applying compresses, tourniquets, bandages, and giving enemas. Possessor of that gift of oratory which postpones the quintessence of a speech for the end of the act, Cristeto would then slowly begin, without showing his deep emotion and while the troops held their breath and were transported to regions of religious rapture, his homily about the remarkable participation of Catholic, Protestant and Jewish chaplains, priests, ministers and rabbis who had left their quiet parishes in smiling little towns in order to render direct homage to the Holy Spirit on the battlefield. A practicing Catholic, Aguayo Cristeto U.S. 50 50, barely able to hold back his heartfelt tears, told of the actions of these servants of God, who while they were giving extreme unction to the dying were also able to heroically curse enemy deities (Buddha, etc.); he then recounted in great detail how Father Bob Sullivan, from Kentucky, had set aside his breviary a thousand times to take up a machine gun. The tall figure of Father Bob could be seen against the halo of exploding grenades and bazookas, praying with his hands clasped, his blue eyes turned toward the heavens or throwing grenades, engaged in hand-to-hand combat and displaying his virtuous control of the bayonet with ecumenical skill. And Cristeto would bring his lecture to a close by telling an amusing anecdote. He told of a particular occasion when he was confessing with Father Bob in a tent that was being used as a church and mentioned that he was jealous of the reputation he (Bob) was making for himself in the regiment as a knife handler. Father Bob answered that in order to save the white souls of the world it was necessary to know how to handle white weapons, smiling with well-known tenderness and adding that soon he would set aside his use of the knife as he was leaning more and more toward flamethrowers, since fire had been a basic element in the joyous centuries of the Inquisition and was therefore more in line with his priestly vocation. Facing the troops who were anxiously awaiting the punch line, Cristeto would explain that he had to look up the word Inquisition in the dictionary and when he had learned its meaning he had laughed "uproariously" (term he used when he spoke to the San Juan Lion's Club). The troops would applaud approvingly. And the regimental colonel had been known to comment with paternal pride, "It's amazing that in spite of his almost non-existent English and the doubtful color of his skin, he acts as if he were one of us."

But, as Cristeto said before the members of the Inter-American Press Society, good fortune is usually brief and there is no such thing as complete happiness. One morning, while he and a young recruit were delivering seven enemy prisoners, the recruit got nervous and threw a grenade into the group. Cristeto recognized that the manner in which the device was thrown was not totally lacking in interest, and although he lay wounded in the underbrush, he had the professional integrity to inquire who had taught him such techniques. Crawling with half his intestine trailing behind him, Cristeto proceeded to chastise the recruit for two specific weaknesses. First, it was stupid to throw a grenade in an area so near enemy lines, as it could draw attention, thus gravely endangering their lives. Second, it was an inconceivable waste to ruin such exemplary young men, ideal as they were for a live demonstration of bayonet tactics. And while the members of the Press Society voraciously gobbled down their dinners, tremendously excited, Cristeto serenely narrated how on that very spot, motivated by his deepest pedagogical responsibility, while his own blood was fertilizing enemy ground, he proceeded to explain to the stunned recruit the proper way to throw a grenade so that it would reach the greatest number of objectives and so priceless ammunition would not be wasted. Then, standing up, binding his intestine to him with his belt and gathering his own blood in a canteen, he went to each of the prisoners, pointing out the place where each shell fragment had penetrated and, in passing, giving a quick stab in the chest to those who were still agonizing. Then "he fell peacefully to his knees upon the cool grass of spring."[6]

Naturally, lieutenant Aguayo Cristeto U.S. 50 50 was discharged from the army with full honors. The grenade fragment had imbedded itself in his jejunum, an unknown term until that time and one which the retired veteran ruminated on with relentless fury. Out of a job, Cristeto would languidly watch the days and nights go by from his terrace on the beach, consuming more than

[6] Joseph Lamb, *Cristeto Aguayo, A Modern-Day Crusader*, p. 560. Pentagon Publications, 1955

the recommended amount of whiskey. Nevertheless, he was not alone. He had brought his dear mother to live with him. Cristeto had literally covered the walls with photographs in which he appeared being decorated by members of Congress, smiling among a group of journalists, placing the first stone for the construction of a school, participating in the inaugural ceremony of a hospital, taking communion in the cathedral of San Juan, acting as godfather to the tiny daughter of a labor leader, being carried on the shoulders of members of the Medical Association. He jealously treasured countless souvenirs of the war: a pistol seized from a dangerous woman, fragments taken from all types of automatic rifles, bullets of various calibers, his first oriental love's underwear, a cross he had had made from two tibias and which was, along with the first fingernail torn from a remiss prisoner, his most prized treasure. "I had the cross made because I am a Christian," he had declared before a heavily attended meeting of the Ladies' Civic Association. According to news reports of the event, carefully collected by a tireless Yolanda, the ladies shed grateful tears for such a lovely speech, inviting him to join them in the reception room for tea.

When he became of age, five years had gone by since he had left the service. A popular lecturer throughout the country, Cristeto felt the weight of boredom. How could he limit himself to words, to inactivity? It's true that some Latin American countries had requested him to advise their armies (Guatemala, Brazil, Paraguay, Santo Domingo, Uruguay, etc.), but, as he would explain to his friends, that type of work lacked excitement, it wasn't like real action in the trenches. In addition, for him all economic concerns had been fully resolved. But, what about love? He had rejected the best girls from hotels in the capital, repulsed by their gross demands for money. Couldn't they abandon themselves to love, the most sublime of human passions? Isn't that what peace was for? But Cupid had been waiting for him in the town of Canóvanas on the afternoon he was a speaker at the high school graduation ceremony. "The arrow wounded him right in the middle of his heart like a bullet shot by a Garand M1. The sharpshooter was seated in the last row, overcome with love. The wedding took place according to the technique for overrunning a trench: quickly and by surprise."[7] Happiness had finally returned, although two years after the wedding, after a prolonged, voluntary

---

[7] Joseph Lamb, *op. cit.*, p. 942.

fast, his mother died, gnawed away by jealousy. Following such an unfortunate incident, Cristeto had declined to continue his lectures. Once again his name fell into anonymity. Only the little old men of the American Legion remembered him with deep emotion, and they had begun a campaign to collect funds to build a statue of him. They commissioned a sculptor from Arkansas to create the design which showed Cristeto with a flaming sword held high and his feet crushing a seven-headed hydra. Customs, Post Office, and Immigration employees as well as numerous Cuban exiles joined in the campaign with remarkable enthusiasm. But there was one moment which sparkled like a diamond in the life of the veteran. In the height of the tourist season the colonel who had made recruit Cristeto Aguayo a first lieutenant showed up, motivated by sentimental longings. Interviewed by the press (always attentive to great national figures), the colonel urged that the address of his old friend be found for him immediately ("He could have given me lessons in many aspects of the art of warfare," he confessed smilingly). The meeting took place before the television cameras in a hotel in the Condado section of town, under the auspices of a detergent manufacturer. After the cocktails and formal toasts, both were photographed in bathing suits on the beach, with the colonel's finger pointing to the wide scar on the Puerto Rican's abdomen. Those were joy-filled days, but of an ever fleeting happiness, because his friend had to leave after two weeks' vacation to take charge of a tie factory whose trademark ("Gun Ho!") caused Cristeto to evoke many nostalgic experiences. Then, silence, anonymity, interrupted now and then by the loyal persistence of the little old men of the American Legion.

How did Cristeto end up living in our development? Was he attracted by the name of Nebraska Heights? Did the English name remind him of delicious wartime experiences? Yoli's investigation came to a halt at that point. All that can be said is that one afternoon a truck pulled up and emptied a heavy load of furniture across the street from us. We saw the little man with his blond fuzz, with such blond eyelashes that they looked like those of an albino and with a timid, green look and a jaundiced complexion, moving around over there, hunched over and hesitant, arranging everything with the help of his wife, a little mulatta named Millicent Barbosa. Putting aside her pseudo-social worker objectivity, Yolanda immediately developed strong prejudices against the character. "He won't even look you in the face," she would say when we fell into gossiping about the neighbors, "and that humbleness doesn't seem one bit like genuine humbleness but more like hypocrisy; I can't stand that, Eddy, it's a real slap in the face. Can't you see him, sort of hiding, smiling like a sanctimonious friar, and always yes sir of course ma'am and looking down and hiding. And soft, honey, and such carefully manicured nails; he also wears a scapular; he's like a worm or a reptile, that weak, slimy creature." I did what I could to not be infected by Yolanda's disease. I would say to her: "You have to wait until you get to know him, Yoli, then we'll be able to know who we're dealing with."

Thanks to the continuous visits to Cristeto's house by the neighbors (Yolanda suspected that it was mainly due to Millicent's attractions), the Aguayo-Barbosa couple managed to become a part of the community. During their nocturnal get-togethers I could hear them argue amicably while thumping the table with the domino pieces. Yoli found out, through an accomplice neighbor, that under the effects of a few drinks, Cristeto had dared to make a joke about a man who had lost his four sons in the war. That joke seemed to Yoli to be the epitome of the grotesque, and it served to cement her prejudices.

During an unsuspecting outing, I was introduced to Cristeto. He squeezed my hand in his, sticky and damp like certain mushrooms that grow in cemeteries (Yoli laughed at such a macabre comparison).

Upon learning of Cristeto's history, the neighbors adopted an attitude of reverent taciturnity, which grew upon seeing the innumerable battlefield treasures and the many newspaper clippings and photographs of the veteran with great personages. In addition, with his well-known humility, and with certain ceremony, Cristeto had proposed founding a Boy Scout troop in Nebraska Heights, which he himself would train for free in how to use a mountain knife. The idea was gleefully adopted, and it developed beautifully. His neighbors couldn't help but reflect (with certain mathematical coldness) on the fact that the presence of such a personality in the area might bring as a consequence an increase in property value.

At Christmas, and in accord with the solemnity of the festivity, Cristeto Aguayo was invited by means of a charming card signed by all his neighbors to sacrifice the pig that would be roasted on one of the cement patios. The invitation said in part: "You won't deny us the opportunity of watching first hand your artistry with a knife." At Easter, Cristeto openly expressed his ideas on the war that at that very moment was taking place in Indochina. The neighbors were all in agreement with his thoughts.

Inconceivably, Yolanda had forgotten to make note of a detail that seemed to me to bear the greatest importance and significance: Cristeto had a fourteen-year-old son who was capable of demolishing a bull with a single sword thrust.

*   *   *

YOLANDA READS *SEMANA*

BRIGITTE BARDOT PLUCKS
A DAISY OF LOVE

Since B.B. emerged as a beautiful legend under the guidance of Roger Vadim, well-known creator of starlets, the life of this French beauty, symbol of sex and of avant-garde filmmaking, has revolved around the movie industry and love. Both have emblazoned her in the minds of all her admirers as a lovely example of the weaker sex by showing her constant vulnerability to men in the most saucy and varied ways. Someone once said that her heart was like a luxury hotel, and she herself recently stated that she is in no way guilty of capriciousness, as she has truly loved all the men who have occupied a place in her heart, at least that's what she thought until discovering it wasn't true because she loved someone else more.

QUEEN FABIOLA ATTENDS HER NEPHEW'S
WEDDING AS GUEST OF HONOR

The sovereign greeted all the guests with the utmost graciousness throughout the dazzling nuptial events.

JACQUELINE ONASSIS APPEARS UNPERTURBED BY HER
HUSBAND'S CONTINUED INTEREST IN MARIA CALLAS

After spending a few days on the "Christina" with her sister, Princess Radziwill, she flew to Paris to meet Ari.

"MY COUNTRY, MY HUSBAND, MY CHILDREN"
by Her Majesty the Empress Farah of Persia

"The new matrimonial law does not impose monogamy, which would be contrary to the precepts of the Koran."
"We are considering birth control because we do not want to

have an overpopulated country and we want to protect the family unit against its own extinction."

THE OTHER SIDE OF A FILM HERO

Anthony Quinn relaxes in the company of his wife and children at his Italian villa. In the near future he is expected in Spain, where he may star in a film directed by Bardem.

A husband devoted to his wife and a father who is crazy about his children: that is the sentimental profile of a man who has portrayed many tormented characters (*Notre Dame de Paris* with its Quasimodo) and bohemians (*La Strada*) on the silver screen, all of whom have nothing in common with his own reality.

PRINCE ALFONSO OF HOHENLOHE, HARD-WORKING ENTREPRENEUR OF THE COSTA DEL SOL

Owner of a tourist complex, four restaurants, two hotels, four recreation halls, a construction firm. . . He sleeps only four hours per day and personally oversees his business empire.

A SPANIARD ON THE THRONE OF FRANCE: EMPRESS EUGENIE

"The Prince first spoke to me of love in Compiègne."

CANDICE BERGEN: ARISTOCRAT OF FILM

The star of "Live for Life" just finished filming a western in Spain. "I am a melancholy and shy person."

ENRICO MACIAS IN A QUANDRY BECAUSE OF HIS WIFE'S JEALOUSY

Suzy gave him a choice between herself and films. Enrico Macías has chosen love. He awaits Suzy's return.

ROBERT WAGNER . . . MADLY IN LOVE?

He is in a psychiatric hospital for treatment of artistic jealousy over the success of his wife, Natalie Wood.

As the song goes: "Neither with you nor without you can an end come to my sighs. / Not with you because you kill me / not without you because I die."

CARLO PONTI DENIES HIS WIFE IS EXPECTING A SECOND CHILD

Sophia Loren will star in *Anna Karenina* in Russia.

ETHEL KENNEDY, A COURAGEOUS, STRONG WOMAN, FAITHFUL TO THE MEMORY OF HER HUSBAND

The Barnstable judge sentenced her son Bobby to "one year of domestic surveillance" on a narcotics charge.

Her relations with Jackie are almost non-existant.

It seems that obstacles have been put in her way, one after another, by diabolic fate to see if it is possible to make this extraordinary woman crumble.

A MORE SETTLED GUNTHER SACHS

Under the influence of his lovely wife, the popular "playboy" has settled down. He has developed a fondness for the peaceful life of Deauville, accompanied by his wife, and past stormy episodes are long forgotten.

"The years go by. . ." he commented during the ball.

ASTROLOGICAL COURIER

Born under the sign of aquarius with ascendant in Sagittarius. Very perceptive and sensitive, with a great fondness for the arts, especially one of them, which she cultivates with great success.

Born under the sign of Libra with ascendant in Virgo. Very devoted to justice and truth, she always tries to remain calm, but when her will occasionally fails her, she loses control and is unpredictable.

Born under the sign of Cancer with ascendant in Cancer. Very much a homebody, devoted to her family and capable of the greatest sacrifices for loved ones, to whom she consecrates most of her time. Her life will be quiet and without major upheavals, in spite of deciding to emigrate to a far-away country.

Born under the sign of Sagittarius with ascendant in Aquarius. Daring, beautiful, intelligent, with many charms and a deep sense of justice and truth. Through her own efforts and those of well-placed sponsors, she will attain great heights in her career.

Born under the sign of Pisces with ascendant in Gemini. Charitable, she is also a romantic and a dreamer, very devoted to the fine arts, traveling, and dealing with distinguished people. She suffers a minor visual defect such as myopia.

Born under the sign of Pisces with ascendant in Leo. Charitable, humanitarian, reliable, beautiful, intelligent, honest, and displaying great nobility and charm. She will marry an exceptional, very intelligent man, perhaps a rich and famous artist, with whom she will travel a great deal and be very happy.

Born under the sign of Sagittarius with ascendant in Scorpio. Daring, beautiful, determined, intelligent, and full of charm, she is also spiteful and doesn't forgive any discomfort inflicted on her nor any offenses to her person. She'll earn fame and money in a profession of agility and dexterity.

Born under the sign of Scorpio with ascendant in Capricorn. Good appearance, intelligent, but spiteful, he doesn't forgive any wrongdoing or affronts aimed at him, and he is reserved and not a party to harboring secrets. He will earn fame and fortune cultivating an art which he will pair with the exercise of a bureaucratic or commercial profession, and he will marry a beautiful and very artistic woman.

Born under the sign of Aquarius with ascendant in Aquarius. Perceptive and sensitive, with a great fondness for the arts, particularly one, which she cultivates successfully. She will also marry another well-known artist, and between the two of them they will build a home into which several children will be born and abundance will reign through their own efforts.

Born under the sign of Virgo with ascendant in Cancer. Discreet, modest, prudent, very affectionate and very much a homebody, her greatest pleasure is to consecrate herself completely to her family. She will earn money and prestige devoting herself to a commercial undertaking related to far-away countries, in which her name will be highly regarded.

Born under the sign of Pisces with ascendant in Sagittarius. Humanitarian, charitable, reliable, he is at the same time daring and determined, very good-looking, intelligent, and very attractive. He will make considerable money in a profession which will oblige him to travel a great deal and he will marry a very feminine woman who will present him with several children and make him very happy.

Born under the sign of Sagittarius with ascendant in Aquarius. Daring, beautiful, intelligent, with great charm and sensitivity, which prompt her to be very devoted to the arts and to all that is good and beautiful. She will achieve genuine fame and fortune at the head of a perfume or cosmetic industry, and she will marry a fighting man or someone in a military profession, with whom she will be very happy.

GRAPHOLOGY OF LOVE

1) According to the text you have written, it can be said that when the day arrives that you are man and wife, your happiness will know no end. There are many points which indicate an easy achievement of mutual respect during your life together in order to better understand one another, love one another, and go forth hand in hand, with faith in your future. Your feelings, your creativeness, reveal mutual intuition and thoughtfulness which will draw you closer and make your love stronger.

2) As you can see, not only have we not tossed your letter aside, but we have given it a little "boost." The fact that you went out with a boy for eight months and then he left you with no explanation shouldn't be taken too seriously. You must understand that nowadays young men don't want to get involved, and we have to admit that life, in its present context—satisfactions on the one hand and difficulties on the other—doesn't encourage being inclined toward a traditional engagement and marriage. You are unaffected, bent on kindness, generosity. The boy who would suit you best is one who is intelligent, demonstrative, of strong will but with a certain restlessness, deep vitality and total self-assurance.

3) Your impatience was answered this time. Ana is firm, endowed with aplomb and assurance. She is most strongly motivated by her own feelings toward what surrounds her. She appreciates friendship and warmth and is very pleasant overall. Pepe is more complicated. He isn't as open a person. More materialistic, his instinctive dominance is better defined. Although both are independent, Ana is so in a more altruistic manner, she

has better taste. The solution is simply a matter of putting love before all else and beginning to draw closer to one another, patiently and with a desire for understanding, with relish.

4) In no way do we disdain the power of physical attraction and age, and their consequence in amorous relations. What in fact happens is that people are rarely aware of these very important factors. Nevertheless, by dealing with personality and vital strength, temperament and morality, we can establish some fairly valid conclusions. As for you, I won't go so far as to say that your relations are inopportune, but I will say that you are going to encounter the pitfall that you are very much alike: you both strive for practical ideals, in such a way that, at some point, the lack of contrast will bore you. At that juncture, it will become apparent that love has lessened and is no longer what it seems to be now.

HOW TO RESOLVE THE DIFFICULT PROBLEM OF GIFTS FOR RELATIVES AND FRIENDS ON SPECIAL DAYS SUCH AS BIRTHDAYS, CHRISTMAS, THE FIRST OF MAY, FOURTH OF JULY, SECOND OF NOVEMBER, WEDDINGS, BAPTISMS, DEATHS, WEDDING AND DIVORCE ANNIVERSARIES, CORONATIONS, ETC.

Give scapulars; no one can reject or be disappointed with a scapular without feeling profoundly convinced that he will end up in hell.

* * *

The perfect reliability of the heating system was useless. Useless to wrap up in two shirts, two sweaters over the wool pajamas acquired on sale at El Hombre Elegante, useless to curl up under a thick blanket: he shook with ferocious chills piercing into his bone marrow, his forehead smeared with ointments, covered with a mixture of sweat and ointments (but his forehead wasn't a melting pot: the ointments affixed themselves like sticky islands, minute oily lakes, and the torrents of sweat ran between them and fell upon his eyes, upon his chin, upon his chest). He moaned quietly, thinking darkly of the two alternatives before him: alerting Yolanda of his discomfort and listening with his usual masochism to the voices of his sickness. He heard to wind rattling the window, the inconceivable, fickle wind. He was terrified, not so much by the cold as by its possible sequel: long days spent in bed, in pain and without the strength to make the slightest movement. Actually that inertia did not necessarily have to be preceded by a cold. Sometimes he would just stay in bed for days on end, overtaken by an inexplicable drowsiness during which he was barely able to put together a coherent thought, quiet, as if in a cataleptic state, a blind body mutely suffering an anguish which still hadn't totally revealed itself, on the edge of doom for the thousandth time, suffering like a beast that doesn't know on which barbed-wire fence he has ripped open his side, perplexed by that ever more blind dark opening into which he plunged without moving a single muscle until penetrating the intolerable, barely breathing his internal arrhythmia, without a past or a future, vaguely existing in that moment of equal days without any point of reference, perishing in a uniformly static day-week-month, distantly inwardly encouraged by a weak reflection of a thought, a slight awakening of ideas which only served to amaze him without the amazement changing his breathing, likewise truly amazed by that unbounded quiet. It was useless for Yolanda to scream at him that he was lazy, reminding him that he had spent five days in perfect hyber-nation, because he would escape into long, dark hallways and he couldn't put up any defense because he simply didn't have any, he was a pulsating corpse waiting for what. At some point he had ripped open an internal rib cage. Yes but where? yes but when?

yes but why? without rest along the familiar descending labyrinth. Five days can be a thick drop peering into the breach of time. And he suspected an atavistic circulatory anguish, the unexpected reflection of his biological state, perhaps a dark return to the cave, to the glands that made possible the first climb up a tree, perhaps the first brain that appeared over the gills attempting to become lungs was retreating amazingly back in time to finally emerge at that opening without light, a pure vacuum, hardly uncontaminated, a threat to existence. But, wasn't he fooling himself? Oh. Because this time there was a real illness, designated by an ordinary name, a malaise that was easily identifiable by means of a patented product spotlessly awaiting use (because the season gave him no respite) in the showcase of a drugstore: simply stay in bed, a spoonful, a tablet, it's the only way. And of course, vitamin C. His moans rose freely, gaining strength, and his burning, reddened throat offered no resistance. He knew, or rather he suspected, that Yolanda wasn't sleeping, yet remained silent the entire sleepless night. Would she be listening sadistically, gloatingly, to his laments? She had to get up early to meet Mayte at the office; is that why she did nothing to help him? Afraid that if she gave any signs of awareness, he would unleash a whole string of requests: fix me some tea, give me an aspirin, put some salve on me, I can't stand it any longer, Yoli, am I going to die? He would have promised her that this time it wasn't a matter of the gas knobs, of an open window, or of bodies without eyes wandering through the house looking for him in order to subject him to indescribable pain, perpetual visions of panic, closed creations germinated in his childhood; huge monkeys, the pristine "monkey?" This time it wasn't "something" watching him day and night, everpresent beings spying on him from the depths of mirrors, warnings that crept along the corners of his eyes, grotesque masses that would hurl themselves at him, nor was it tremors that would crack the walls and cause the roof to come crashing down and open a gaping hole in the floor, nor the violent firing of a machine gun aimed at him with strange, unexplained hate, nor the words "We've come to settle accounts with you." It had nothing to do with those daily terrors, but rather was a result of the chilled air, of his indiscretion in going out without considering the threat of the weather (he was able to insist that it wasn't the nightmare with a thousand heads, sleep weighing on him like a tombstone, a realm crossed by undefinable premonitions; in that case maybe a pill would have been enough). The fever, the cough that still didn't choose to manifest itself, the chills, could they kill a man?

Total peace, eternal peace, in other words, puff. Not Yolanda, in spite of his groans for the past four hours, not Yochaste this time, surrounded by the penetrating odors of the ointments, the alcohol, the stagnant sweat, while he pedaled his bicycle sweating happily, letting go of the handlebars so that Mirta could see me from her balcony and then I didn't waste any more time: my father was waiting for me, so I leaned the bicycle against the wall and went in. In the small concrete room, cold milk ran through the copper serpentines and collected in a pool; the man with Indian features greeted me as he did every afternoon, tan and powerful and kind, as unaffected as the blade of a hoe and understanding that a boy must be spoken to in the language of fantasy, telling me stories of apparitions while he filled the bottles with the white juice, and I pedaled between the two rows of flamboyants; the dizzying fragrance of the cane fields beneath a pleasantly merciless sun could be sensed from here and sometimes that ecstatic scene would be crossed by the shiny, dark form of a locomotive dragging cars filled with cane behind it and oh miracle I would pedal my war machine with a rifle strapped across my back, following the sap and the resin, injured by the tumors of termites inside the trunks of old, almost meditative flamboyants, but at school they taught me about survival of the fittest and of corollas that resemble that thing women have, it was truly marvelous while coming out of the shadows of the flamboyants and the quarry shook next to me, pierced by the insistent compressed-air jackhammers while the compressors snorted, became silent, filled their lungs and snorted again with greater force and the openings were filled with charges of dynamite and ready everyone take shelter and baroom fireworks and behind a tree I could see enormous boulders blown into the air and dust and stones covering the earth, rocks striking the roofs of the village, the concussion cracking sidewalks and walls, and men drank in the bars as if it were a holiday or stood challengingly in the middle of the street, looking up, furious, and some filed a claim against the U.S. Navy, which was the leaser of the quarry, and then I turned into the gravel path that crunched under the wheels of my tank and father put his hand on my head and introduced his blond, ruddy boss to me, father had given up his store back then because the Navy paid well, and he spoke English with his blond, ruddy boss, this is my son, he would say proudly, but I would lose myself in the motionless breeze of the canefields, standing next to the tracks where the cane crushed by the train wheels would draw armies of ants, intoxicated by the smell beneath the sun and walking in the shade of the almond trees, I would stop next to unbearably fragrant flowerbeds with the murmur of the slow river behind the cane, excited, looking feverishly for what, overcome by the secret fury of the earth, by the roots of my blood, by the oven-like heat where all thought is roasted, softened, survival, Mirta next to me in the canefield on a bed of straw beneath the golden perfume of the predictable honey, I would have crowed like a rooster accepting the challenge of the afternoon filled with strange internalized needles, a deaf roar in my viens, mama and papa snoring afterwards. They're allowed to savor everything. I would have launched my young cock's clarion for the ears of the foliage, for the bees who are allowed to savor everything, for the mongeese chasing one another and emitting sharp cries, my Lord what deep tremors lay within the earth, oh God if Mirta, if I, if the corollas, if the pistils, if the pollen, if the maddening hum, the strangled panting, oh God if I. But I didn't crow (I swear it), he crowed. He was on a branch, singing among the leaves, half hidden, his little chest puffed up, but I didn't crow, I swear it, he crowed crowing and I raised my rifle he crowed was crowing crowing warbling and I listened to the harsh heaving of the compressors at the quarry and a silence charged with fatigue and the air lost all its oxygen: one by one the trees were dying, the jackhammers made no sound but the panting of the compressors overpowered my ears, everything was panting, everything heaved, gasping for air with lungs as tight as the skins on drums and filled with hard air, it was raining stones against the wardrobe, and my sweaters and pajamas fell to the floor in shreds without the tiniest drop of air penetrating me to fill that crack that was clamoring for it with deaf screams of blood and violent heartbeats, Yolanda pale under the sudden lightbulb looked at me wide-eyed without yet understanding why I was flopping around like a fish out of water, why I was lifting my face to the heavens still filled with particles of dust and putrid smoke and why I was opening my mouth and eyes searching for suddenly insufficient oxygen while my lung compressors were becoming paralyzed and what's wrong with you Eddy you said to me and I shook, oh God my crazy head and you said it could be pneumonia Eddy my God and I began breathing brusquely and said I hope its pneumonia.

* * *

Mmmmhjrk dacum derec spatins dec onc subalumm terpet
incin ten olcoren olfer pssp lan curain jrk mmm tuc teken elpon
dcum tur um bana mmf tarac len ten unk unff unfff ftsss ommm
ummmj
grug
grukj
grueslep
grueslepsi
tarc tacrac ster linsfe ond untu struguen ulmer tzaquer
oron
oronsí
ronsic
oronskaram
oronskaramku
tok tok tiki barum barumpa pakbaro umjk
kok koro
kok bak
kolkarak bacum pa
xorilpe xilen pzret sparelke xialer puls xilen xilen xactei lum
dulxrem siranaxpilen ulki ton kilisen lrsent lukiererrel
uh
uhr
uhnmmjrrk
uhnnffrrkj nnnffft
unhh un hulmmmj uhhs fsssjk
an serian psultincarept psuttnlincleirmenten tzuri ujj uggg
ugggk urkgghhjrkjjj

*   *   *

As it was it couldn't continue being but not him, without him, precisely etched as if he had said the word. Only four floors above the broken mirror in the basement, the worn-out curtains, the names of the nicest dogs known (or yet to be known, he would have sworn, bemoaning)? The elevator wasn't so near, but they would have gone up the steps to the depths of the rock most closely resembling the loss of a keychain or the caper of fireflies. And assuredly there were well over four streets, preferably sixteen and a half, where the joke stuck to the walls, it climbed by digging in with its fierce carnation teeth: it climbed because it was impossible to keep going up without stopping under the living room carpet or on top of a snowy sheet of asphalt always as significant as a seal chattering from the heat inside an iceberg, an Eskimo slamming the insufferably pleasant ice door of his delicate igloo, navigator for a highly undetermined system of whales, but in any case it was clearly the cold, with all the doubts that thunderous word implies in this language (it already seemed the only tongue chillingly remembered). But could you climb aboard a firefly, ride on its thin back, assaulted by the nearest hurricane, to the Caribbean? Even when they talked: their mouths would open and provoke a landslide, horses' tails, apples bitten into in September, buckets of hemlock, newspapers as thick as the weeping of a stork, rooms with windows in the ceiling and staircases along the most unexpected walls. Oh but it was ominous, wasn't it then, being something to itself? He would have asked the thick buckle on his belt, the kernel of corn found in front of the Empire State Building, the flag peering with three eyes over a twisted glass ledge, wouldn't he have frankly asked beneath all shadow of a doubt? The three legs of a stool wouldn't have sufficed to chair a less than unforgettable example, even if only tangible at the moment of Yom Kippur or the charming beret caught barely twenty centuries ago. Was he definitely the master of the stairs, of the curtains turned into fans at the decisive hour of the Metropolis? He would have to think, slightly deceased, about the other guy. Whose words sounded like. Three dozen pockets without any ink stains, the keyboard of a sinister Underwood typewriter pierced by an arrow, also his cloak, his so unheavenly cap much like the precisely red morning star or evening star or weekly star (not to mention the word *alcántara* or its ally the fly at every wake). Who would have believed it disbelieving it until the last drop of sand? The drawing coming off the wall making audible its two tongues? The shoe that came off the mute taxicab driver or the T-shirt with four thorns over a yellow bat looking like a cup of tar on it? It was always possible on the asphalt that, naturally, backing into the streets, spreading over the avenues as wide as pistils, as noisily open as the lizard turned into a ballpoint pen. For him (for me?) a simple signal would have been enough: the edge of a sidewalk, beckoning him with its penetrating fingers, spilled champagne on a window, caviar lovingly spread on the eighteen hands of a clock, but it wouldn't have been enough if he thought about it with all the perceptible joy of a funeral, it wouldn't have been enough because it was infinitely shorter than the tail of an armchair (in the basement, of course), infinitely less powerful than the central muscle of an amoeba, a dreamer like an astrolabe in the hands of an Amazonian fisherman, in spite of all the accumulated proof it was evident that they weren't worth more, as much as the dirt forgotten on a hoe or next to the glove of a mermaid he would have said singing without ears. Would she have known it or didn't she go up to the less important words engraved above the stairs? Comfortably perhaps, right there, planted like a palm that bears cups every year, that gives birth to tablecloths and chicken feathers, merely a palm but a palm adjusted to the root of fire and the noisiest silence known by any human being, strange as it might seem. For this they had spent three and a half hours upset inside an orange slice, opening its yellow mouth, going unanswered into the air, mounting the first rifle coming by at this outlandish time of the month? For this, for it, for him or her? Neither in the living room nor in the slipper? Was it four floors or four waterfalls? What was being dragged through there, a street or the skin of a snake, furious on account of the chill sun? Was there flour, ground salt, a melted star, a formerly noisy number? There not being any, he was able to think unconsciously, having it not existing, nevertheless yes, radiant Candlemas in an unbearably spring-like October, extinguished thread of a tiger's mustache, salty bottle *ave maría*. Could he, with a dying artistic pencil or wasn't it so, quite up to it, solemnly miserable, hypothetically archaic, with the whistling presence of a Cro-Magnon bone, oh God four times four on the scratched mirror in the basement, on the fissure as damp as a bolt of lightning at the July hour, oh damn so much without anything that might look like a colloquium, a voice rising out of the hail or the reflection that impregnates a pan singing on the fire. When then? Ask that mutely of the superintendent.

*   *   *

It was like filling your ears with a noiseless hum, a low, persistent, dizzying hum, like grasping a salty ledge without fingers or skin, like breathing a hollow breeze without nostrils, like advancing along an inexistent path without feet. Finally catching sight of a white stain in the damp room, then bending forward and coughing hoarsely, opening his eyes with distant, baseless surprise at the spot he described as red, red on a white background, a red spider with pale lymphatic legs that fell away from the body reaching tensely for the dark hole in the center. His hand hit the faucet clumsily, he turned the knob, and the sound of running water blocked out the deaf hum, soundless in its dizzying, persistent noise. Water surrounded the stain, drawing it out, robbing it of its circular shape, lessening the shock of its red color, moving it toward the rattling drain, the water running among the boulders forming almost imperceptible currents on the quiet surface where he floated on his back, the palms of his hands turned upwards, his eyes open, fixed without fixedness on the irregular surface of the ceiling of the cave. A leaf stuck timidly to his side, a fish ripped at one of his fingers and tore out his nail. Piranhas, especially voracious fish, microscopic hooves, elytrons, ants. Buoyed with slow tranquility, the water turns him in a silent dance, takes him to the thundering depths of the water that gushes and boils. In spite of the darkness, or precisely because of the darkness of the nearby chasm, the water is red. Furiouslyredasblood.

* * *

Most Powerful Sir:

In whatever capacitie, my ambytion and custom has been to serve the Royale Crowne in these parts, by order of the Catholic Monarch and, in order to increase Your revenues and dominion, I now, although steeped in poverty, have wanted to continue serving Your Majestie, awaiting Your favours, as indeed I do awaite them. Among the aforementioned services, I discovered at my owne expense and initiative the Islande of La Florida and otheres in its area which are not given further mentyon for being small and useless.

And I now return to that islande, God willing, to colonize, being able to set sail with an abundance of people with which to accomplish this, so that the name of Christ might therein be praised, and Your Majestie be served with the fruite gathered in that lande. And also I intend to discover more than the said islande, as well as ascertain if I can find, or if it adjoins, the land where Diego Velásquez is or any othere, and I will try to discover as much as I can.

I am to leave here and continue my voyage five to six days hence. Of what I do and see in those parts where I may wander, I will give full accounte to Your Majestie upon my return and request your munificent rewards. And as of now I beg you to grant them because I would not dare to embark on such great undertakings or of such cost, nor could I carry them out, without the favors and considerations of Your August Majestie. And if hithertofore I have withheld asking them, it was due to seeing Your Majestie with great travails and little rest, which I truly feel as though I were undergoing them myself.

May our Lord watch over and bless your Most Royale Person with long life as well as many new kingdoms and honours as may be wished by Your Majestie. From this islande of Sanct Juan and Citie of Puerto Rico, which lie in the Indies of the Ocean, ten days into the month of February, 1521.

Juan Ponce de León

Copto m. Coptic, the language of the Copts.

Copudo, da a. Tufted, bushy, thick-topped.

Cópula f. 1. Joining or coupling two things together. 2. Copulation, carnal union. 3. (Arch.) V. *Cúpula.* 4. (Log.) Copula, the word which unites the predicate with the subject.

Copular va. (Obs.) To connect, to join or unite. —vr. (Obs.) To copulate, to come together.

Copulativamente adv. Jointly.

Copulativo, va a. 1. (Gram.) Copulative. 2. Joining or uniting together.

Coqueluche f. whooping-cough. (F.)

Coqueta f. 1. (Prov.) Feruling or blow with a ferule on the hand by schoolmasters. 2. (Prov.) A small loaf. 3. Coquette, flirt.

Coquetear vn. To coquet, to flirt.

Coquetería f. Coquetry, flirtation.

Coquetismo m. = *Coquetería.*

Coquetón m. A male flirt, lady-killer.

Coquillo m. 1. Vinefretter, an insect which destroys vines. Curculio Bacchus, L. V. *Convólvulo* 2. Jean, a twilled fabric.

Coquina f. 1. (Prov.) Shellfish in general. 2. Cockle. Cardium rusticum, L.

Coquinario, ria a. (Obs.) Culinary.

Coquinero m. (Prov.) Fishmonger, one who deals in shellfish.

Coquito m. 1. (Dim.) A small coconut. 2. Grimace to amuse children. 3. A Mexican turtle-dove.

Cor m. (Obs.) 1. V. *Corazón* 2. V. *Coro. De cor,* By heart.

Coráceo, cea a. V. *Coriáceo.*

Coracera f. (Acad.) V. *Coráscora.*

Coracero m. 1. Cuirassier. 2. (Coll.) a poor cigar.

Coracilla f.dim. A small coat of mail.

Coracina f. A small breast-plate anciently worn by soldiers.

Coracha f. A leather bag, used to bring cocoa, tobacco, etc., from America.

Corachín m.dim. A little leather bag.

Corada, Coradela f. V. *Asadura.*

Coraje m. 1. Courage, bravery, fortitude, mettle. 2. Anger, passion. 3. *Eso me da tanto coraje,* (Met.) That puts me in such a rage.

Corajudo, da a. Angry, passionate, easily irritated.

Coral m. 1. Coral, a marine calcareous production. *Corales*, Strings of corals. 2. The polyp which produces the substance known as coral. 3. (Naut.) A large knee which fastens the stern-post to the keel.

Coral a. Choral, belonging to the choir.

Coralero m. A worker or dealer in corals.

Coralífero, ra a. Coral-bearing.

Coralillo m. A coral-colored snake which is extremely venomous.

Coralina f. 1. Sea-coralline or white worm-seed. Sertularia. 2. (Naut.) A coral fishing-boat. 3. Every sea-animal resembling coral.

Coralino, na a. (Littl. us.) Coralline.

Corambre f. All hides and skins of animals, dressed or undressed; pelts.

Corambrero m. Dealer in hides and skins.

Coramvobis m. (Coll.) A corpulent person, strutting about with affected gravity.

Corán m. Koran, the sacred book of the Mohammedans. V. *Alcorán*.

Coráscora f. (Naut.) Corascora, a coasting vessel in India.

Coraza f. 1. Cuirass, an ancient breast-plate. 2. *Coraza* or *caballo coraza*, Cuirassier. 3. A plate of armour, iron or steel, for men-of-war. 4. Shell or carapace of a turtle, or other defensive armour of some reptiles. *Tentar a uno las corazas*, (Met.) To try one's mettle or courage.

Coraznada f. 1. Pith of a pine-tree. 2. Fricassée of the hearts of animals.

Corazón m. 1. Heart, core. 2. Heart, benevolence, affection. 3. Heart, spirit. 4. Will, mind. 5. Heart, the middle or centre of anything. 6. In a loom, cam. 7. Pith of a tree. 8. *Corazón de un cabo*, (Naut.) Heart-strand. *Llevar* or *tener el corazón en las manos*, To be sincere and candid; to wear one's heart on one's sleeve. *De corazón*, adv. 1. Heartily, sincerely. 2. (Obs.) From memory. *Anunciarle el corazón*, To have a presentiment. *A dónde el corazón se inclina, el pie camina*, Where there is the will, there is a way. *Clavarle (a uno) en el corazón*, To cause or to suffer great affliction. *Helársele (a uno) el corazón*, To be paralyzed by fright.

Corazonada f. 1. Courage, an impulse of the heart to encounter dangers. 2. Presentiment, foreboding. 3. Entrails.

Corazonazo m.aug. A great heart.

Corazoncico, illo, ito m.dim. A little heart; a pitiful or faint-hearted person.

Corazoncillo m. (Bot.) Perforated St. John's wort. Hypericum perforatum.

Corbachada f. A stroke or lash given with a *corbacho*.

Corbacho m. The tendon or aponeurosis of an ox or a bull, with which the boatswain of a galley punished the convicts.

Corbas f.pl. (Falc.) The four largest feathers of a hawk.

Corbata f. 1. Cravat, a neck-cloth, neck-handkerchief. 2. A sash or ribbon ornamented with a gold or silver fringe tied to banners. 3. Ribbon, insignia of an order. —m. Magistrate not brought up to the law; also a layman who has studied neither civil nor common law.

Corbatín m. 1. Cravat. V. *Corbata*. 2. Stock, a close neck-cloth.

Corbato m. Cooler, a vat filed with water, in which the worm of a still is placed to cool.

Corbatón m. (Naut.) A small knee used in different parts of a ship.

Corbe m. An ancient measure for baskets.

Corbeta f. 1. Corvette, a light vessel with three masts and square-sails. 2. *Corbeta de guerra,* A sloop of war.

Corcel m. A steady horse, a charger.

Corcesca f. (Obs.) Ancient pike or spear.

Corcillo, illa m. & f.dim. A small deer or little fawn.

Corcino m. A small deer.

Corcova f. 1. Hump, a crooked back, hunch. 2. Convexity, protuberance, curvature, gibbosity.

Corcovado, da a. Hump-backed, gibbous, crooked. —pp. of *Corcovar*.

Corcovar va. (Obs.) To crook.

Corcovear vn. To curvet, to cut capers.

Corcoveta com. A crook-backed person.

Corcovilla, ita f.dim. Little hump or crooked back.

Córcovo m. 1. Spring, or curvet, made by a horse on the point of leaping. 2. A wrong step, unfair proceeding.

Córculo m. Heart-shell, an aquatic insect.

Corcusido, da a. Clumsily mended or sewed on. —pp. of *Corcusir*.

Corcusir va. (Coll.) To darn holes in cloth or stuff, to patch.

Corcha f. V. *Corcho* and *Corchera*.

Corche m. A sort of sandal or shoe, open at the top, and tied with latchets.

Corchea f. (Mus.) Crochet, a half minim.

Corchear va. Among curriers, to grain leather with a cork.

Corchera f. Vessel of pitched cork or staves, in which a bottle or flask is put with ice or snow, to cool liquor.

Corcheta f. Eye of a hook or clasp.

Corchete m. 1. Clasp, a hook and eye: commonly used in the plural. *Corchetes*, Hooks and eyes. 2. Locket, a small lock; crotch. 3. (Coll.) An arresting officer. 4. An iron instrument for flattening tin plates. 5. Brace used to connect lines in writing or printing. 6. Bench-hook of a carpenter's bench.

Corcho m. 1. Cork, the bark of the cork-tree. 2. Ice-vessel. V. *Corchera*. 3. Bee-hive. V. *Colmena*. 4. Cork, the stopple of a bottle, flask, or jar. 5. Box made of cork, for carrying eatables. 6. Cork-board, put before beds and tables to serve as a shelter. *Nadar sin corcho*, (Met.) Not to need leading strings, or other people's advice; literally, to swim without cork. *No tener muelas de corcho*, (Met.) Not to be easily imposed upon. *Tener cara de corcho*, (Met.) To have a brazen face, to be impudent. —pl. 1. Clogs, a sort of pattens used by women to keep their shoes clean and dry. 2. (Mil.) Gun-tompions, plugs to stop the mouths of guns and other pieces of ordnance.

Corchoro m. (Bot.) Corchorus, a genus of plants. Corchorus.

Corchoso, sa a. Like cork in appearance or condition.

Corda f. *Estar el navío a la corda*, (Naut.) To be close-hauled, or lying to: applied to a ship.

Cordaje m. (Naut.) Cordage, all sorts of rope used in the rigging of ships.

Cordal m. Double tooth. *Cordales*, Grinders.

Cordato, ta a. Wise, prudent, discreet, judicious, considerate.

Cordel m. 1. Cord, a rope of several strands. 2. (Naut.) A thin rope or line used on board a ship; a line. *Cordel alquitranado*, A tarred line. *Cordel blanco*, An untarred line. *Cordel de corredera*, Log-line. *Mozo de cordel*, Porter, one who carried burdens for hire. *Apretar los cordeles*, To oblige one to say or do a thing by violence. *Echar el cordel*, 1. To mark with a line or cord. 2. (Met.) To administer justice impartially. 3. (Met.) To draw lines in order to consider the manner of executing a thing. *Estar a cordel*, To be in a right line.

Cordelado, da a. Twisted for ribbons or garters: applied to silk.

Cordelazo m. Stroke or lash with a rope.

Cordelejo m. 1. A small rope. 2. Fun, jest, joke. 3. *Dar cordelejo*, (Met.) Artfully to pump out a secret.

Cordelería f. 1. Cordage, all sorts of ropes. 2. Rope-walk. 3. (Naut.) Rigging.

Cordelero m. Rope-maker, cord-maker.

Cordelito m.dim. A small rope, cord or line.

Cordellate m. Grogram, a sort of stuff.

Cordera f. 1. Ewe lamb. 2. Meek, gentle or mild woman.

Cordería f. 1. Cordage. 2. Place where cordage is kept.

Corderica, illa, ita f.dim. Little ewe lamb.

Corderico, illo, ito m.dim. A young or little lamb.

Corderillo m. Lambskin dressed with the fleece.

Corderina f. Lambskin.

Corderino, na a. Of the lamb kind, belonging to lambs.

Cordero m. 1. Lamb. 2. A dressed lambskin. 3. Meek, gentle, or mild man. *Cordero ciclán,* A lamb that never lets down the testicles. *Cordero rencoso,* Lamb with one testicle down and the other concealed. *Cordero de socesto* or *lechal,* House-lamb. *Cordero mueso,* Small-eared lamb. *Cordero de Escitia* (Bot.) Polipody of Tartary. Polipodium.

Corderuna f. Lambskin.

Cordeta f. (Prov.) A small rope made of the platted strands of bass-weed.

Cordezuela f.dim. A small rope.

Cordíaco, ca a. V. *Cardíaco.*

Cordial a. 1. Cordial, affectionate, sincere. 2. Cordial, invigorating, reviving.

Cordial m. Cordial, a strengthening medicine.

Cordialidad f. Cordiality, intimacy.

Cordialmente adv. Cordially, sincerely, affectionately, heartily.

* * *

Far, distant cold inside, halted in joints that allow slow movements (rusty hinges) beneath the hot skin, cold with sweat, without being able to stand the weight of my weight on my haunches. The fish squirmed among the boulders. There was slime on the rocks and certain ashen substances, thick and cold, admirably terrifying because they resembled the plush inside a coffin floating beneath the sun, shiny craft. Ashen plush, I said, in a marinade, in other words, very simply enough to set your hair on end.

But then a silent blast of light shone suddenly, digging its claws into the slits of my eyes. I can't say fingers as is usually the case, I must say claws, as is also common, painfully digging into the depths of my half-closed eyes because the blast of light had finally come to pass. And ants all over a mutilated hand (did Buñuel linger to that extent in some remote place?). Perhaps because my left eye was cut by the blade of the sun. Yolanda was leaning over my left shoulder and lowered my lid and anxiously peered inside allowing the razor of the sun, in the drone of thousands of cars in motion all around us, making an island out of us (island, my God, what a crushingly beautiful word attacked by the perpetual sun!), allowing the shiny blade to make its infamous slice into the celluloid. The breeze was coming in through the window raised three quarters of the way, icy cold as often happens in a spring rendered cruel by gusts from the Sierra. The breeze was cold and I expected it, I wasn't dreaming, and it penetrated my lungs, the two painful little sacks, wrung out like small cellophane bags, threatening and hostile. We'll give you a clue so you can win at the next drawing. All you have to do is fill in the coupons as I'm about to explain. A trip to the Canary Islands for three. That would make you happy, Yoli, that would, wouldn't it? There you'd really be happy.

Waves of cars under the long-disgraced sun. Ibiza, forbidden Paradise for those who scribble hundreds of pages worth of nonsense without success. Ashen plush floating among fishes distinguished for their voracity, crocodile, the most exciting night of the year, she said. Alas, the stream of water precipitating down from the concave sky of the cavern, is that what it's like?

Ophelia of Millais, with flowers falling from her crazed hands? Bones stripped purpley. Horizontally visiting the watery ships of the sunken cathedral during a walk. What an extraordinary, plethoric dream of scatological poetry, with deep violas in the background, heard without ears, violas and cellos directly perceived, I mean without bothersome, unnecessary ears, pure perception: they would fade, vibrating without vibrations from the evasive transmitter and would come back vibrating without vibrations to the evasive receiver! From place to place without friction, without any troublesome contacts, without scabs or filth as is found on the collars of shirts, for example. From music to music, among inexistent fish and nevertheless fish with round, steady eyes. Aquarium lights, a phrase as worn out as my two respiratory bags which I hate cautiously because it's stupid to be stuffed with so many things: cords, untold parts and an inflammable fluid as if one were a vile Citroën, a General Electric television set with a suspicious screen, my God and even with lazy hinges and electrical discharges and short circuits, too. It's a well-known fact: if the radiator breaks down, stop, cool down, careful with the diaphragm; its defective functioning could cause irreparable damage to the carburator. But my God we have to accept it, that's the way it is. Nevertheless, looking out of the corner of my eye at Mayte driving recklessly, raising her chubby knee too far to put on the brake, twisting grotesquely to turn the steering wheel, nevertheless, I say, it embarrassed me to not have any unique thoughts, thinking that it couldn't be, a man isn't a machine with fuses and stripped wires that zap! could cause a short circuit. No, what Humanism. It was better to have emerged from the waters on a clear spring morning, with rigid gills that hid their insistent lung design, a trembling fish that blindly fulfilled the obscure requirement of dragging himself dangerously among thundering saurians, imagining legs for himself, climbing the first tree, what a reptilineal beginning. We'll give you a clue so you can win at the next drawing. Coming down the tree and grabbing something as yet unnamed, something hard that sprung from the fury of volcanos, which was over there, among the brambles, named many centuries later with a deaf, guttural sound (because it was necessary to distinguish it with a different roar from the one with which the near proximity of a harmonious brontosaurus, for example, was announced), an already named rock to sharpen it and as they say hone it to build the first ax with which the first house would be built and which would crack open the head of the first neighbor. No. How could you not hate Darwin every day, thoroughly? Let there be light. That's how it's really worth it, Yoli! I understand, clay, but clay doesn't have scales. Fill in the coupons as I'm going to indicate directly. And He created us in His image. How beautiful, Yoli, that's really how! The side from which you were torn still hurts, you are my rib in every sense of the word. Enough, Darwin, go home. Remember your ancestry, honey, you descend from reptiles. What to say, what to answer? Gulp. In those early days thunder baroom thrashed the terrorized nomad tribes mercilessly. Panic-striken they watched the lightning, zap! turn trees to dust beneath the first non-radioactive rain of humanity. Oh but the apple, and the reptile, go on and eat it my friend, you're all alone, grab it. You too would lick Eve's new body, old man, I mean you'd lick yourself, primitive narcissist. The first precariously human intercourse; the first ants probably came to the warm call of pristine semen where my ruined little cellophane bags were already incubating as well as the brain cells of for example Jan Hus, Tupac Amaru, Hitler, Christine Jorgensen, John Lennon, Boulez, Theresa of Avila, Lautréamont, Cristeto Aguayo, Averröes, Jorge Luis Borges, Juan de la Cierva, Plekhanov, Trujillo Molina, Rockefeller, Durkheim, Sade, Thomas Aquinas, Duns Scotus, Bergman, Falla, René Clair, Lenin, García Morato, Godoy, Phillip II, Agüeybana, Galileo, Orozco, Chagall, Renata Tebaldi, Arguedas, Lorenzo Homar, Marañón, Mola, Juan Mari, Dostoevski, Aristotle, Quisling, García Lorca, Zoltán Kodály, Sartre, Lefèbvre, Raskolnikov, Plato, Vasco da Gama, Aguinaldo, Hirohito, Albéniz, Theodorakis, Goya, Bakunin, Victor Hugo, Caligula, U Thant, Che Guevara, Nasser, Polanski, Joyce, Hostos, Proust, Corrado Alvaro, Góngora, Pavese, Neruda, Stalin, Ernest Lihn, Ho Chi Minh, Ghandi, Papini, Albizu Campos, Cárdenas, Tolstoi, Borodin, Liz Taylor, Resnais, Lucien Goldmann, Nebrija, Aristarchus, Einstein, Ongania, Toshiro Mifune, Mao, P. L. Quintero, Nefertiti, Solomon, Maiakovski, Stockhausen, Aureliano Buendía, Rojas Pinilla, M. Delly, Malcolm X, Graham Greene, Papillon, Kant, and even including L.B.J.

Far-off internal chill. It wouldn't suffer the slightest setback in economic policy. Two million pesetas, equivalent to a hundred and twenty-five years. That's how things stand a few days after the encounter with Willy Stoph. Gas station attendants decide not to go to work for the next few days. The work stoppage was decided upon as a result of not being able to come to an agreement with the companies. Now from Paris. Three holidays throughout most of Europe. Switchmen will continue their strike until Saturday night. Eleven p.m. is when Orly airport normally closes. It could become a real madhouse. Various disorders also took place in Rosario, the police intervened with tear gas. Dialogue is open, said Emilio Fermín Michone, but these rebellious groups refuse to participate in the negotiations and they don't have the support of the majority. Two years of prison for Manuel Rodríguez. The population of Santo Domingo abandons the city searching for calmer surroundings during today's elections. There is absolutely no interest in the current voting exercises, Juan Bosch states. Lora, Balaguer, Pérez y Pérez will challenge the will of the people. The United States sells Sky Hawks to Argentina. The international contest of ham-radio operators promoted by Brazil begins today throughout the world. The goal is to establish the greatest number of contacts. Meeting in Krakow: sixth regular session on fishing. The situation in Indochina may be summed up on two fronts. Meeting in Djakarta. The Communist bloc has decided not to appear. Few major issues will be discussed. Reaffirm the neutrality of Cambodia, arrange the departure of foreign troops fighting in that country. Vietcong and North Vietnamese have launched a new offensive. The situation has worsened since the latest battles. Lon Nol. The weather. During the night there was precipitation over Galicia and the Cantabrian area. Variable cloudiness in La Mancha, Canary Islands and Málaga. You have just heard the 2:30 report of the Spanish National Broadcasting system. Temperature in Madrid, 13° Celsius on Huerta Street. Casera for me, I like Casera best. Sports antenna presents. . .

"Change the station, Mayte. Eddy doesn't like that."
On your table, for cocktails, everywh
ampionship contenders, who will be the win
tisfactory and good
arter finals where Valencia
ti and El Cordobes in the bul
use that refreshes
ntested in the League
eal Madr
but there are people who are still not very
darling Coretty brothers, the
riving schoo
beat the Canaries at Bern
of awakening at any momen
Casera for me, Casera for
agreements between the International Monetary Fund and

at five point percent in France
a greater freezing power and magnetic sea, the Ru
I'll create a furor this year
approved in Eu
the brave voice of a daring and persistent repor
iss Paquita has a few words for us, go ahead
ppolytus and Sons Enterpr

"There's nothing on that's worth anything," Mayte says, turning off the radio. "But if you like sports. . . . They even interrupt concerts to stuff soccer or rugby down your throat. Did you watch the series of movies by what's the guy's name? A German, I think; they interrupted it. On channel 2."

"Strojrkeim," I say with a reluctant, negative voice.

"I really don't know. Anyway." Pie-faced, long-haired, Mayte shrugs her shoulders, looks at me a second with big green eyes with little gold specks floating in them. "That's probably who it was. I can never remember those perverse foreign names."

"He was a great director, right Eddy?" Yoli said to show off her sophisticated knowledge.

"Unjrk," I answer.

"Roll up the window, Eddy, the cold air isn't good for you. Look at the Church of Saint Francis, honey, when are you going to visit it? Isn't there a draft on you with the window like that?"

I shook my head from side to side it's not bothering me, because the practical Seat 600 was stopped in the middle of a metallic tide.

"We saw two," Yoli says. "They were very good."

"Well, I don't know," Mayte assures us, shrugging her shoulders, barely opening her mouth, obscuring the sounds in a Castilian way. "But one evening about 9:30 I wanted to watch the film and when I turned on the television set, they were showing something about handball. I mean, turn on the T.V. and psst. What the hell, I climbed into bed and read *The Spaniard and the Seven Capital Sins*. Have you seen anything by Paso?"

"Eddy doesn't like him."

"You haven't missed much. He writes even about the moon. And *The Maids* at the Figaro?"

I shook my head yes: Nuria Espert and Genet, excellently approving. I looked at her and agreed dizzily approving yes.

"Ummm. Jrrk," I concluded.

"Roll up the window, baby. Can you say 'raise your window'? I guess not. You can raise a flag or even a piano, but that's something else. Look over there. The park is probably empty in this weather. But there are enough people for everything in this city. The Viaduct. I had vertigo the first time I crossed it on foot. And those rooftops, my God, the Moorish part of town, it's so beautiful. Sort of mysterious, right Eddy? The Church of Almudena, another treasure. Why do they call them the Sabatini Gardens? The designer? What difference does it make! The main thing is that it's there. Eddy, you must come here more often, love. The Oriente Palace and the Royal Theater. We have time to take a look at them, don't we Mayte? With all this traffic. Eddy, when you get well, we'll have to go spend an afternoon in those gardens. Does your chest hurt a lot?"

"Jrk."

"It could be a touch of pneumonia," Mayte says, looking at me gravely. "What have you been taking?"

"Nothjrrking. Jrrk, uh."

"Ay, I swear I was so scared. His eyes were popping out of his head. I didn't know what was happening to him. What could I do? I wouldn't even have been able to call an ambulance. I just stood there like a klutz and his eyes were popping right out of his head, tearing at his clothes on top of it. Dear God, you can just imagine how scared I was!"

Mayte looked me over from head to toe in a quick, conscientious study and objective appraisal of my possibilities for the grave, aggressively changed gears and mumbled something about something. Might she have discovered a dark brown spot on my chin? She turned on the radio.

carpet department at Rodríguez Department Stores
point that would mean a proced
Bilbao against the

"Just what I was saying," Mayte says. "Nothing like a little class. How are you feeling?"

"Bekjter," I say sincerely because the sun is shining and the practical metal is warming up acceptably, and I am in a delicious Seat incubator, a million experiences on Spanish highways.

"The doctor will see you and decide. You look a little pale and kind of transparent. Go on, you'll soon be over it. Cheer up."

"He was tearing his clothes off, Mayte, he was asphyxiating. He ripped two new sweaters I had bought him at Sears. It even made me forget the emergency number for ambulances. I didn't know anything, couldn't do anything, his eyes were popping out so."

"Jeez," Mayte lets slip out.

"He went to bed dressed warmly, normally, like he usually does when he has a cold. And at four a.m., I don't even want to think about it. And then I had to go to work and leave him alone. But since he was sleeping well I thought he was better. Baby, I called you at ten, you didn't answer. I called at noon, still nothing. I knew you hadn't gone out in the shape you were in. I thought you might be in the bathroom. I called later, nothing. Then I was going to take a taxi when Mayte offered to bring me."

"Hey, now," Mayte says, "a sick husband and she's going to take a taxi that will certainly cost her a few coins. What are friends for anyway? As long as I'm around, don't hesitate to call on me whenever you need me, because if you don't, I'll be angry. Don't think you're alone in this country, don't even let that cross your minds. Listen, I know you're from America where a couple of Spanish guys did whatever they wanted. Who hasn't heard about the black legend?"

My cheeks went crack in a canine smile, alasblessedmothercountryofallsaints, crack.

"Thanks a million," Yoli says with typical tropical sweetness, genuinely appreciative to the marrow of her bones, with that ancient, most appreciative appreciativeness of all of us over there, those of us there whose existence is tolerated because it's a sweet Christian act to let all God's creatures live. "Thanks, you can't imagine how we appreciate this," Yoli concluded while the sound of seraphic violins filled the Seat, a Lament in A minor for sweet Mayte, the savior, a tender heart from Burgos.

"Think nothing of it," says Mayte vigorously. "Don't even mention it, it's the least I could do, you know what I mean. What was my car going to do sitting in the parking lot all day?"

"But the office," Yoli whispers with onion juice in her eyes. "I wouldn't want you to miss on our account."

"Hey, now, what are you talking about?" Mayte bends her elbow and swings it out a couple of times, from her shoulder, accenting her words. "How important is your health? What about your husband's health? Is it worth killing yourself so that a couple of guys with apartments on the Boulevard and a little chalet in the mountains can get richer? If you have to miss work, you miss, that's all. It doesn't seem to me that you're thinking very clearly on this matter."

"I'm thinking, of course, I'm thinking."

"No, you can't tell me that. I know what the story is. Listen, who would hesitate to ask permission to leave in an emergency? Would you like to go to the Royal Theater on Sunday? There's a concert by some Russian. I can get you tickets half-price. Eddy, what do you say?"

I nod my head agreeing energetically, but disagreeing dubiously inside. The street was a refrigerator where ferocious fishes flew around incited by Mancio's mocking smile. Was it an aquarium where Mancio Picapiedras' mocking smile flew around? Dragging his viper along with him in the afternoon, therefore they weren't fish fishes, but piranha piranhas. He would take his viper out to urinate and would walk it poetically among the bushes, harping on his five-year old manuscripts viperly. I wouldn't be able to go to the theater on Sunday. Thanato's agents ruled the streets.

"Depending," says Yoli. "If this one is better we could go."

"Doctor Ibaurilarrazagainchausti is from Bilbao," says Mayte, "but he's good. He'll see you as soon as we get there, Eddy. He's really good, honest."

I shake my head insistently, looking with my wounded eyes at Mayte, patron saint of the downtrodden, in my state of neomute.

"Eddy," says Yolanda, pensively soft, "what did you do?"

"Umjrk?"

"You were lying on the bathroom floor."

"Washjrng my facjrk."

"The faucet was on," says Mayte. "You were practically swimming in the water on the floor."

"Eddy, how are you feeling, love?"

"Throajrt. Lungjs. Painjk."

Yoli was silent and Mayte looked at her in the rearview mirror. The horns were honking. Yoli said slowly:

"Eddy, why did you turn on the gas?"

"Jrrk on?" I looked at her surprised. "Unjrrk?"

"Yes, it was on."

I shook my head, not me.

"The oven, too, Eddy. We smelled it right away. My God, and you were lying there on the floor!"

"It was probably a mistake," says Mayte without looking at anyone, without even looking ahead because she felt she had to look at her knees raised in unison. "Things like that happen."

"A mistake to turn on all the gas knobs? A mistake to turn on the oven full-blast? Do you remember being in the kitchen, baby?"

"Noj. Leavk mej alonjrk."

"You were there but you don't remember it. Dear God!"

"Enough to kill a whole family," says Mayte.

"Oh for God's sake, hush, woman!"

"It might have been a touch of pneumonia," says Mayte. "Ibaurilarrazagainchausti is very good. Christ was so humble that having been able to be born in Bilbao, he chose Bethlehem."

I laugh with false complacency, jrk.

"Are you cold, baby?"

I shake my head no, surrounded by glowing fishes who swim into my sliced eye one by one. The ants scurry along my hands, the windshield, they cover cars, buses, the pavement, the sky that until recently was shining clearly, they climb up Mayte's thick ankles full speed.

"Cover yourself well, baby," Yoli recommends without paying any attention to the ants running along her neck, her forehead, swarming around her lips, jumping on her eyes without even making her blink.

"Leave mej alonjrk! Uh, krj."

"I would have stayed with you. But I couldn't miss a day at the office."

"You should have stayed, girl," says Mayte. "A call saying you couldn't make it would have been enough. With your husband in the shape he's in."

"I didn't think it was that serious. When I got up he was fast asleep and breathing normally and didn't have any fever. He was pale, that's true,"

"Of course."

"Good Lord, honey, you have to take care of yourself. If the cold weather keeps making you sick we'll have to go back to Puerto Rico."

I say no shaking my head wildly, no to Cristeto, no to Mancio, no to the American Legion, no to Nebraska Heights, no to the Immigration Department, no to *El Mundo*, no no no. My hands drop and the ants fall wiggling on my knees covered with those insects. The Seat was crushing them by the millions, you could hear them crackling under the tires.

"We'll have to find out why you lost consciousness."

"Jrrk."

"If it's because you were so weak or the gas. My God, Eddy, it's inconceivable."

"The doctor will know," answers Mayte.

"Eddy, Mayte says she knows a very good psychiatrist who used to go out with her cousin. So there already is a connection."

"No. Uhrk."

"He's not exorbitant, and he's young and understanding, right, Mayte?"

"Well, of course."

"Nn Jrk."

"It's hard to believe that you won't accept what science can do for you, Eddy. Would you prefer to go to a witch doctor?"

"He's a good psychiatric doctor. He studied in Bern and Paris and wrote a book about something. My cousin showed it to me."

With my head I said yes, that he was probably an excellent doctor, but no, while Mayte's face disappeared beneath a shiny, brown mask of ants. I grabbed for the door handle, fearing an accident; nevertheless she drove with utmost calm and stoicism. On my left I recognized the Royal Place vibrating under a thick scab of ants, as well as the trees, the plaza and the Royal Theater and the statues and the fountains. You couldn't see the grass or the earth in the fields, covered as they were, and Carabanchel had turned into an angry brown sea, over which the mahogany-colored shadow of a suddenly dismal Madrid sky was cast. Now an implacable, torrential rain of ants had been unleashed, they fell by the millions everywhere, they came in the vents of the Seat, and I was wondering why Mayte wasn't hastening to turn on the windshield wipers. They made palpitating mounds along the sidewalks, on the curbs and the streets, they covered the posts, the traffic lights, brilliant brown lava that didn't stop, a ferocious deluge that was to last forty days and forty nights. I was listening to the crackling of millions and millions of ants that covered the happy, trusting Castilian city; the monument to Cervantes on the Plaza de España had become a rumbling hill, perfectly conical, and Mayte had become a shapeless, unrecognizable bulk; my feet were disappearing in the uncontainable flood that rose up to my knees, receded a bit and then rose again, reaching the level of my waist; I avoided turning my head so as not to see Yolanda disappear into the dark tide. The Moncloa Plaza was a boiling lake and thick braids of ants threw themselves from the top of the Arch, now completely covered, attached to one another. My God, I thought, and said nothing, amazed that Mayte could continue driving so calmly in spite of having her eyes totally covered.

"So you didn't even have any coffee, honey?"

"Ujrk."

"Roll up the window, honey, it's cold. Eddy, love, promise me you're going to be good."

"Jrrk."

"That you're going to do what the doctor tells you, and you're not going to lean out the window without a shirt on, and that you're going to start eating meat again, that business with the Argentinian professor was a long time ago. And that you're not going to turn on the gas again."

"Itj wajnrt mej!" I turned and pointed with my finger covered with ants. "U. Itj wajr u."

"What are you trying to say?"

I pointed my finger at her while I imitated the gesture of turning on the gas with the other hand.

"He says you did it," Mayte clarified.

"Me! I did it?"

I nodded violently, turning the gas knobs.

"Are you accusing me of. . .?"

I nodded.

"Oh my God, Mayte, did you hear that?"

"You're not kidding I heard it."

"Eddy, honey, the psychiatrist Mayte knows about is very good. Don't worry about the money. Why don't you go see him one of these days? A good talk wouldn't hurt you. Things were coming along fine with Olmo, in spite of the resistence you set up. Or maybe that's why. Try him, love. You have nothing to lose. Listen, he even wrote a book so he's not just a businessman like you said Olmo was. Will you do it even if only to please me? Just once. Try and if you don't like him, well at least make the effort. You need help, you really do. What can a fifty-five minute chat do to you? It's for your own good, baby."

"He studied in Bern and Paris. Why don't you go see him, Eddy?"

"Noj."

"Self-destruction," says Yoli. "I've been watching it happen for a long time. Drinking, locking himself up, he hardly eats. Eddy, enough of mortifying yourself because of things that already happened and that when evaluated carefully and coldly are not the slightest bit important. Ordinary things that everybody sends to hell without paying any attention to them and then on to other things, to live fully. You know what's wrong with him, Mayte? He dreams he's murdering his father and then he can't stand the guilt feelings."

"Good Lord. But a dream is only a dream."

"He has strong emotional ties. Oedipus, you know. It's the most cruel disease in the world, you have to go through it to be able to really understand it. Cruel, cruel. To begin with, you're your own enemy, so you can imagine the rest. Free yourself, Eddy, my love. I'll go with you to Mayte's doctor this week, okay? In Puerto Rico he improved with Olmo. But then he came up with the idea that he was a police informant. Some sort of paranoia, even a baby can see that."

The ants opened a path for the Seat, they fell back in huge waves, they disappeared into the crevices of the earth, into the sewers, large clear spots were becoming visible, bricks, portions of empty wall, and the sky and the pavement showed large, sparkling lagoons.

"It's a good thing the sun has come out," says Mayte. "I thought it was going to rain."

I looked at her very suspiciously for having said that, for pretending she didn't know about the ants. I could see one of her cheeks, a corner of her mouth, a naked arm; the ants were fleeing madly, disappearing, freeing my legs. I tried to crush the ones still under my shoes and Mayte smiled at me.

"Don't brake for me," she said. "I drive quite well."

The blast of light. Drive the noiseless, persistently dizzying hum from my ears.

"Here we are," said Mayte.

Wearing a Basque beret, his chest emblazoned with the emblem of the Athletic Club of Bilbao, a Scandinavian blond who swayed to and fro like a sailor just off a ship, Dr. José María Ibaurilarrazagainchausti exchanged friendly greetings with Mayte who in turn exchanged friendly words of introduction with us.

"Eddy and Yolanda, two good friends from America."

"Spanish-America," Yoli interjected.

Yes, but.

At the very moment when my knees were disappearing and the wall next to me was toppling over—I had to put out my arms to stop it—charming Mayte forced her way through several invisible doors establishing the necessary contacts to avoid our having to wait our turn. As I had lost three fourths of my blood, I was not able to blush effectively at being the subject of the recommendation, a typical Celtiberian procedure, although I did blush without showing any color gulp. And Yoli, who heard me protest with my rasping jrrk, said it wasn't a matter of favoritism, but rather an emergency, and we only had to sit in the waiting room for eight or nine minutes, with me plucking little fish from my mouth with the tips of my fingers; later it was enough for me to open my mouth wide and the fish would jump out, tracing parabolas like swimmers in a diving competition, and the floor was covered with those shiny silver creatures gasping for air since in our atmosphere their gills are nothing more than premature lungs; some traveled farther than expected, wiggling through the door and setting out on a long, desperate journey through the halls, and Yoli begged me to stop littering the floor with that vermin, that's just what she said, it was specifically forbidden to spit porgies and flounder on the floor; the nurses were laughing because the tails and gills of my creatures were tickling their ankles, much amused because the floor covered with my novel decor looked a thousand times better than the bare vulgar parquet.

"That's it. Put your hands on your waist, throw your elbows back and lay your shoulders flat. It's cold, but don't worry, it'll only take a moment. Maricarmen, ready with the special gentleman."

184

And of course, in spite of the ironic turn of phrase, those internal photographs are really marvelous.

"Please wait to see if they turned out well," the girl said.

They solemnly handed Yoli a long, wide negative, the backbone of a fish found on a mountain peak, a diligent fish going about the business of evolution within a petrified cosmic bureaucracy, when he was abruptly interrupted by the appearance of a continent. Does the History of Fishes record that earth-shaking event? Will it record it as a sort of flood in reverse, fully characterized by sudden drought? And me with all those billions of years behind me, so many and yet so few that they hardly seemed to go by at all, so many centuries and I had simply begun to spit blood: I would cough and leave a scarlet stain on my handkerchief. So many millenia of effort to end up with this, irreverently photographed in my most secret zones. So millions and millions of fish fought boldly for millions and millions of years so that some well-evolved fish could come along and photograph with impunity my well-evolved gills. Of course. And to then display the photograph inserted in a machine on the wall.

José María Ibaurilarrazagainchausti, leaning back in his chair, looked at the picture critically, as if it had been entered in a Kodak Instamatic contest, as if he were carefully studying an expressionist abstraction, going hmmm, mmm mmm, pointing out a few spots mmm, and then he looked at Yoli cautiously mmm. Little spots such as might be found in the caves of Altamira near bleeding bisons, old spots, rupestrian of course, products of a certain mineral deposit. Little spots that had not been forseen by the magic artists. My God, little clouds capable of unleashing a storm of cold sweat. I frankly wanted to die. My God, me there, a survivor of the appearance of the continents, me there, apparently calm. My God! Ibauri deigned to look me in the face.

"Have you ever suffered a pulmonary infection?"

"No jrk sir."

"No," Yolanda put in viciously, looking at the stormy sky on the wall.

Larrazaga was looking again, utterly pensive, with the professionalism of a cartographer, at the map on the wall, the dusty roads, the intersections, the railroad crossings, the train tracks, the ditches and gutters, would he discover tiny, arbitrarily dug tunnels?

"Are you sure of that?" he asked threateningly.

"Certain jrk. A cold."

Inchausti shook his beret, it wasn't what he wanted, hot or

cold. He said, truly hopeful:

"Haven't you ever had tuberculosis?"

"No Jrk. Never. Not that."

Yolanda could see lightning on the wall, a kind of doubtful, thick rain. The sky was torn. Inchausti went up to mmm the snap shot of the flowering tree, examining its central branches, its smaller branches, its highest point, its slim, flexible trunk, its innumerable leaves, its abundance of foliage; were little mites carefully sucking its juices? He sat down with a frown, there was something, something, but what, what, lifting his hundred percent Euzkadi beret, scrutinizing me with his Cantabrian eyes. There was something, but what.

"During your childhood, were you ever in contact with someone who had tuberculosis?"

"No jrk sir."

He came closer.

"A neighbor?" he said. "A relative?"

"No jrk sir."

My mother lifted me in her arms and held me so I could see the coffin where my aunt was resting from the worries of life (that's what they lyrically called it). My aunt Rosaura's brown hair was parted in the middle and combed with vaseline, but the hair they had arranged over her forehead outlining her face didn't hide her salient transparent ears; her eyelids and the tip of her nose were also translucid, the eyelids closed in two purple caverns. Her hands were clasped around the stem of a carnation on her chest, she was in a white dress with lilies at her sides. But on her shoulder there was a tobacco-colored stain they weren't able to get rid of, so they had put some white paste on it and powdered it with talc, yet you could see it: a small, antique-red spot which had turned up at the last minute. The waxy color, the sharp profile, the transparency of the skin, I had seen all of them this morning in the endless mirrors at home.

"No friend who had tuberculosis?" Ibauri threatened.

"No."

"Go on, Eddy, kiss your pretty aunt who is leaving us."

"No." Yolanda said.

"It's very strange mmm," Larrazaga answered.

"Kiss her on the forehead, Eddy. Way up, on her forehead."

"Perhaps you had an infection," Inchausti concluded.

"I can't recall jrk. No jrksir. Not me."

"Go on, baby. Your pretty aunty is going to go live with Papa God."

"Perhaps you were sick and your system resisted the illness. You cured yourself without knowing it. The organism's resistance to disease."

"Your aunty who loved you so much and used to buy you candies. That's it, son. Come, I'll wash you with a disinfectant without them noticing it. Poor Rosaura."

Doctor José María Ibaurilarrazagainchausti moved behind the desk making hieroglyphics with his pencil where a prescription should go.

"What were the symptoms?"

"He was suffocating," Yoli said without taking her eyes off the hurricane.

"I was suffocating jrk. I couldn't get any jrkair."

"Any fever?"

"Yes sir. Jjjk."

"High?"

"Burning."

"Cough?"

"Jjjr. No."

"What do you mean no?" Yolanda jumped. "He coughed a lot and was hoarse."

"Asleep. Ktsj. I couldn't telljk."

"And when you woke up, did you cough?" Ibauri asked, looking for a score.

"Yes. But not very much. Jrk. I can't remember much, jrk, I was almost unkrjonscious."

"And when you coughed, was there sputum?"

"Yes."

"A little or a lot?"

"I would cough and my saliva would come out, jjj."

"Aha!" Larrazaga was satisfied; I had performed well for the first two acts and now the moment of truth was drawing near. "And what was that saliva like? Thick?"

"Pretty much."

"What color?"

"It was too dark, I jkouldn't see."

"Wasn't the light on?"

"I think it was brown. And in the morning jrk I coughed in the sink and there was blood," I said surrendering. I held out my wrists so they could handcuff me. I was getting to like Inchausti just because he was Basque and I was a Puerto Rican. I added to make him happy: "Blood, blood, jrk, there wasn't any doubt about it."

"Blood?"

"Of course. Pure blood, doctor."

My God and I was acting as if it were nothing! Ibauri mmm was puzzled, studying the embroidery on the wall, the cross stitches, the threads, the intricate design which would look very nice as a centerpiece on a table; were some of the threads broken?

"It would be advisable to take another X-ray," said Larrazaga, letting the ball heading for the goalpost slip away from him. "It's preferable. This one isn't very clear mmm."

"When doctor?" Yoli said.

"Well mmm, let's see. It would be best for him to rest a few days, wouldn't it? Monday seems all right. Is that agreeable?"

"That's fine," Yochaste answered. "He's never had any lung diseases, doctor. I don't think that X-ray is any good. It's not clear."

"So there won't be any doubt come back on Monday. Directly to my office."

"Fine," Yoli said sharply.

"Do you feel any pain in your chest?" Inchausti wasn't giving up.

"Yes sir."

"When you breathe?"

"Yes."

"When you breathe deeply, here between your ribs?"

"Yes sir. Jrk. What do I have, doctor?"

"You spit quite a bit of blood, eh?"

I began to bite my nails, one by one, with complete devotion, until I got to the flesh.

"Yes," Yolanda said. "And he coughed something fierce. I was so worried, doctor, he couldn't breathe. He hadn't eaten well for days."

"He had lost his appetite," Inchausti agreed, sure of his banderillas. "Mmm. Fever, cough, bloody sputum. Weight loss?"

"Yes sir," I said shyly. "About six kilos."

Banderillero Ibauri ran a few agile steps and placed himself gallantly on the tips of his toes with his hands high in the air and zip he placed the banderillas to the thundering applause of the fans. He was sweating, but his performance had been magnificent. Satisfied, he stood up and said:

"Take this prescription. Some medications, dosage and recommendations that you must follow exactly. Dress warmly, my friend. Do you like Spain?"

"Yes sir," Yoli and I said in a duet.

"I'll bet so. It's a warm country, isn't it? They told me you were from Puerto Rico?"

"Yes sir."

"Ah," he nodded thoughtfully. "It's a pretty country isn't it?"

"Lovely," sensitive Yolanda immediately became emotional.

"Yes, I know it is pretty." Dr. José María Ibaurilarrazaga-inchausti responded. Was there a ringing in his words? Because no one knew better than he that you can be handsome and elegant and lusty and overwhelming and still have your lungs perforated with disease, wasn't that so?

"Well, doctor, thank you very much." Yoli outstretched her hand, and then generously gave him mine. "See you on Monday, then."

"At ten," he said.

"God willing," I said hypocritically, inconceivably.

But Dr. José María Ibaurietcetera didn't seem moved by the extraterrestrial allusion.

I ran to the bathroom, sat on the toilet seat, took off my shoes and began to devour my toenails.

Looking at the old, parched earth created to harbor olive orchards, now flooded by the sun of an irrefutable spring. People talked about what they always talk about: the climate, the high cost of living, the intolerable traffic jams. People talked because that's what words are for, Yoli, they could strike up a conversation with the greatest imaginable ease, completely relaxed and happy over the spring that had finally begun to manifest itself uninhibitedly, without false appearances and the tricks of a small-time magician. The sun wasn't coming out of a top hat or the sleeve of a prestidigitator, it was coming out from behind fleeing, remorseful clouds, it was shining on the metal, on the huge, empty Royal Palace, on the stone of the statues, on the gardens along the avenues with their obsessive red and yellow colors, an extended national flag. God, how could I return to the cold of my room now that? Between sheets smelling of disease ("Think nothing of it, ma'am," I said smiling to the woman who had just stepped on my foot). My God I was nothing more than a stranger, a foreigner, a voluntary exile who was afraid to cough because for the first time red, my most intimate color, terrified me. Oh God, better to be dead. Could anyone assure me that in two hours the cold of the heavens wouldn't complement the dose I already had within my bones? But it was a different cold, more penetrating, disaster, disaster. A vacuum? Where? How to fill it? All vacuums tend to be filled. Irrepressibly. Air in the lungs. A cylindrical phallus for a cylindrical sheath. Recognizable, measurable vacuums, but what about the other inexistent existent vacuums? My God, me riding on the bus in a white shirt, a green tie, a brown jacket bought on Park Avenue under Archibald's persuasive look, covered with a trenchcoat that cost $30 at Macy's, shoes that Yoli had carefully shined, me there, my God, like a well-dressed, well-groomed young dandy, very straight in my seat, smiling stupidly at the panorama of flowers and grass blossoming among the remnants of snow (six ignoble winter months, obliterated by the tourist agencies). My God, me there among beloved foreign accents, with the pockets of my pants full of bloody handkerchiefs, a Spanish-American dude almost six feet tall, slightly less husky now, prematurely grey (sticky handkerchiefs in his pockets), helplessly vulnerable now more than ever before because not even Yoli could get near my deepest inner self, attacked mercilessly at the innermost trenches of my being, my God. Simple, motionless flesh for worms where a fly could come to rest, confident that no movement would frighten it. Oh God the darkness amidst the reigning light outside, inside me Death opened her mouth, vain fires surged from my soul, oh God, free me from this howling of funereal dogs, life had been rudely shattered within my heart.

* * *

San Juan, P.R.

Dear Cousin:

I'm taking a few moments to at least write you a short note. I told you that Rolando, my new boss, is very handsome, didn't I? Well, he's turned out to be a tyrant and a skirt-chaser. He's married with three children and runs after every woman he sees; it may sound funny but the other day he even wanted to have one of the girls sit in his lap just like you see in the comic strips. I don't even want to talk about it; it turns my stomach.

A few days ago I saw Wanda at the Drive-In in shorts and a smocked blouse and she asked me what was wrong with you, that she wrote you once a week and you didn't even have one rotten word to say in return, she said. She told me to tell you to write and not be such a bum.

Víctor is really behaving great and he's stopped drinking and I'm deliriously happy. I always emphasize to him that if we're going to get married and be happy he's going to have to get rid of some of those friends of his who may seem to be his good buddies now but if he were in trouble or sick in bed they wouldn't be so quick to lend a hand. Everything may be dandy now, what pedestal can I put you on and all, but they wouldn't be so quick if he were in bed. You can't fool me. Well anyway, Víctor is studying accounting at night and on Sundays he takes me and mother for rides along Luquillo beach and el Yunque and he's a doll not only with me, since after all I'm his fiancée and it's only natural, but with the whole family (even with Obdulio, can you imagine, as ill-bred as Obdulio is). But Víctor says he understands him, that a person who has spent his life choking with asthma can't be expected to be very cheerful, that's what Víctor says, he's so open-minded. The last time we went to the movies we laughed a lot because the star found out that her husband had a lover and I told him "if I ever catch you with someone else I'll kill you" and he started laughing because he said the way I had said that and put my hands on my hips, I looked just like Libertad Lamarque or maybe Emilia Guiu who starred with Jorge Negrete many years ago. We really did laugh a lot. Now that he's stopped drinking it's easier to visualize a future together because after all, I'm already twenty-seven years old and one begins to worry (I don't mind telling you my age because we're only a few months apart and I wouldn't want to hide it from my cousin anyway. You're about twenty-six, aren't you?).

Wanda told me you're expecting a baby, is that true? If it is, congratulations and keep me in mind for a godmother, Yoli. After all, the family should have priority and if I were the godmother of your baby it would strengthen our fraternal family ties even more. I'm not suggesting that Víctor be the godfather because that would be asking a lot and besides I know you've always had a certain dislike for him even if you never told me so. But if you could see him now, you'd change your mind. As I say, he behaves *muy* nice with me and with the whole family.

The other day I ran into Dr. Winston Olmo at a Condado cafeteria and he asked me how Eddy was doing over there and I told him, you know, that everything was fine and all and he told me that Eddy was a very bright boy, but those things that take place in your childhood are hard to overcome but with the proper direction everything can have positive results, those were his very words, I mean what's bad can turn out to be good and vice versa, God willing. I gave him your address because he said that he wanted to write Eddy a letter personally and I gave it to him and then I remembered that Eddy doesn't want anyone to have your address. I hope he'll forgive me if I stuck my foot in my mouth, I didn't mean any harm. I always talk to Víctor about you two because you really are a very special couple, believe me. Has Eddy also stopped drinking? I die laughing when I think about the time when he was your boyfriend and didn't have a red cent to his name and he went to serenade you with a transistor radio, do you remember that? Víctor also dies laughing and says Eddy sounds like a neat guy. A serenade with the news and sportswear ads on top of it, what a goon!

Well, Yoli, enough for now because rotten Rolando the boss just walked in. I saw him holding hands with a certain co-worker a couple of Sundays ago in the park, but that's another story I'll go into some other time. If you're expecting a baby, let me know Yoli to see what I can make for you. My regards to everyone there and tell Eddy I congratulate him.

Your cousin,
Marisel

P.S. Things are really explosive around here and I'm almost glad that Eddy is over there because he has all those ideas of his.

Río Piedras, P.R.

My Dearest Yolanda and Eduardo:

Thank you so much for your affectionate letter, Yolanda. I was very touched by its contents. I do appreciate your having taken the time to write me such a lovely missive. I didn't answer you right away because I haven't had time. Please forgive the delay. You are always on my mind.

I'm writing you today, but not in the ebullient tone of my previous letter. Much to my regret I had to leave Iglesias' office. Between the manager (a man by the name of Pacheco) and the bookkeeper (a psychotic Cuban woman), my work was becoming impossible. Although I had noticed a certain hypocritical attitude on their part, I was trying to ignore it and continue my work enthusiastically, but this Mr. Pacheco was heaping too many res-ponsibilities on me, intentionally trying to make the job too difficult for me. The Cuban was always very curious about what I was or wasn't doing. Previously she had been very cooperative, relieving me of some of my work (taking care of phone calls when I had to work on the ditto or Xerox machine). She stopped helping me, and I found myself having to race from the telephone to the ditto machine, etc. All of this with the approval of that man. Once I asked a girl they had hired part-time to take over for me in the receptionist's office while I went to the ladies' room (I had eaten fish with cole slaw and it hadn't agreed with me), but she didn't dare leave the filing room where she was working and of course the telephones couldn't be heard there (in the filing room). Another time I asked her to take my place a moment and that time she did come to the office. You know why? Because Iglesias was there. In other words, cooperation with me was limited to when the director was present. On top of that I overheard some gossipy chatter between the Cuban and Pacheco; this guy really thrives on badmouthing some employees to other employees. He tried it with me several times, but couldn't get any response. He sure got a response from the Cuban. I could tell their friendship became a lot more solid and my situation worsened. The Cuban couldn't stand me because I had taken over the position she occupied when Iglesias' secretary was away. She was always trying to belittle me. And the day Iglesias told me right in front of her that he wanted to find someone to take over the receptionist's desk so I could be his personal secretary, she almost destroyed me with the look she gave me. I tried to make a joke out of her stupidity but I realized I had made a real enemy out of that Cuban. I know she was right to be cross with me. This is what happened. When Iglesias bought the photostatic copier, she would spend the day copying personal documents for friends and for herself whenever he was absent. When I suggested that he put tighter controls on it, he authorized me to have the key to it and keep track of its use. This greatly displeased the woman, especially because she knew I was aware of everything that went on. She'd spend her time snitching stamps to send letters to Miami, and snooping and digging in Iglesias' desk. She was always listening for the phone and would fly off to pick it up whenever it rang. Every time someone would come in and ask for Iglesias, she would butt in saying where he was, what he was doing and when he'd be back. It was getting to be a real nightmare for me. She was always asking me tricky questions about Iglesias' comings and goings. I had previously attributed this to an excess of curiosity and had exercised discretion, trying to be cordial with her nevertheless. When, in my judgment, things were going too far and were harming the office as well as Mr. Iglesias, I immediately came to his defense without caring whether or not I gained her animosity in the process. Naturally, when Mr. Pacheco arrived she took advantage of the situation; since she knew he was for annexation, one of that group from Ponce, and I am for independence (I neither hide nor advertise this fact, but somehow it comes out or people can tell, which makes me proud because I don't feel badly about being loyal to my Country), it seems that she used this to hurt me.

I'm just skimming over the events because I don't want to go into details. I never told Iglesias about this nor will I ever do so because I don't want him to feel cornered at any time. Pacheco enjoys the friendship and confidence of Iglesias. He is also an excellent organizer and a person like that is needed in every office. The Cuban woman has been employed there longer than I have; it's difficult to find bookkeepers and the girl (she's young and very cute, married, with two darling children) is very efficient and is used to her salary. Naturally I thought about all this quite a bit. In light of these facts, I tried to ignore all the pressure that was being put on me. But the cup ran over and I couldn't tolerate it any longer. So that Iglesias wouldn't be upset by my departure, I did all I could to make my presence there unpleasant. That is to say, I no longer hid my dislike for Pacheco or the Cuban. I think I accomplished what I intended. Iglesias accepted my resignation and I could tell he was relieved. I certainly felt better; furthermore, when I was cleaning out my desk I was lucky enough to find the name and phone number of a girl who had come looking for a job like mine. So I gave it to Mr. Pacheco and they called her. They interviewed her and I imagine she's already working there. I hope to God that's the case and that Iglesias will have a good, efficient secretary in her! Tears came to my eyes, Yolanda, because the truth of the matter is that I was very fond of Mr. Iglesias, he's so noble and fine and such a patriot.

So now I've told you why I left my job. In any case, thank you, Yoli, as you were the one who gave me the address of that office. I'm not looking for your approval, nor do I pretend to be forgiven (but I do feel obligated to say something to you, Yoli, since you gave me the list of names and offices for me to find work).

I wish you could see what the Woolworth at Stop 18 looks like. That was a real explosion. They've bombed other American stores, too. The University is all caught up in the events. According to the latest news, the "big shots" in the Administration are going to meet to discuss the presence of an American military training center at the University (R.O.T.C.). There haven't been any classes at the University for several days. I think the students have hit the target this time. During one of the marches of the Youth Against Yankee Military Service a young man asked me about Eddy (he knew I was acquainted with you). There are still some Puerto Ricans in Puerto Rico. I'm not taking my flag off my lapel!

I'm happy Eddy has finished the book. When it's published I'll look for it at the Spanish-American bookstore.

Marisel was at the house last night and the poor thing is a mess, all tied up in a nervous knot, because Víctor has a knife and is out to kill her. She misses you a great deal, Yoli, and she says that if you were here it would be a different story. She's lost a lot of weight, and I've advised her to take things easy, because if she keeps on like this she's going to come down with tuberculosis.

The news was just on and they've arrested some leaders from our group and found an arms cache. There is obvious persecution. Things are really getting hot around here, really hot! Well, so long, until next time.

Love from Graciela

Dear Friend:

I know it would never occur to you in your whole life to write me even a postcard. Not to me nor to anyone else. Since I have formidable intestinal fortitude, I'm writing you one more time anyway. There aren't a lot of people for me to talk with so by writing you I imagine that I'm carrying on a conversation with someone. In the afternoons I've been working on a painting that would scandalize you with its verism. I've found a good model, so good that she has shown the patience to wait a good length of time before being paid. The exposition I did several months ago was a total failure, I hardly made enough to pay for the hole I'm living in. My wife is furious and begs me to straighten out, in other words, to find a regular job "like everybody else." I sometimes wonder if I shouldn't have become an accountant or something like that. I ask myself that question when things are at their worst in this vacuum we're living in, but as you can imagine, I'll never stop painting because this is my life and I need the smell of turpentine as much as I need oxygen. I've given up on those halfway experimental things you liked and I've gone back to what I like: realism, although some people's tongues may wear out talking about the hackneyed influence of the great Mexicans (Diego, Orozco, Siqueiros). I think our world should be expressed directly, each work should denounce the absurd society we're living in, I believe in art as a fighting tool. I know this tune is repugnant to you and you'll keep on believing that you can fight just as well with abstract paintings and Op and those fads imposed by certain gentlemen who are only interested in silence and pure decoration, but I can't help that. I have no interest at all in renewing those arguments where we both ended up drunk and more confused than ever. We're just not qualified to theorize, although we are able to work concretely. We are artists of underdevelopment, and we are underdeveloped ourselves.

Some inconsiderate character who spends the day sawing away mercilessly at a violin has moved in next door. You can see the battered eighth notes fall painfully to the floor; I have to get the broom and sweep up hundreds of destroyed eighth notes from the balcony. Some of them, mortally wounded, drag themselves and escape under the door, into the cracks in the walls, behind the furniture, they hide between the pages of books. The same thing happens to the thirty-second notes but they're even more pathetic, they hop along on their thin little legs, squeal, hanging on to the lower bar of the staff, then they somer- sault off and even while they suffer you notice in them a certain tendency towards clowning around and melodrama; the white notes roll along the floor, stumble, bounce, and explode under your heels like monstruous fleas, leaving a sticky liquid on the floor, a slime that is very difficult to clean up; then there are the black notes, they hide fearfully and pile up in corners waiting to be shaken out of rugs; it breaks my heart to see them looking at me with their characteristic humility, not daring to jump or slip away, waiting for God knows what strange musical civil rights, not yet manifesting themselves in favor of their unassailable black power; I approach them furiously and supportively, I explain to them that I'm a painter and therefore do not discriminate in matters of pigmentation, and they look at my mahogany-colored skin and obey and I sweep them up, what other alternative do I have! As far as the semiquavers are concerned, they suffer the same way as any other semi, and I'm convinced that if any mu- sical symbol could adequately represent our countrymen, that symbol would be a semiquaver; they're almost nonexistent, they just lie there, unconscious of everything around them, drowsy, they laugh when the violinist attacks and insults them, they enjoy punishment, they don't smell like anything, they don't weigh anything, they are part of the composition because they haven't any other choice, they don't have the slightest idea that they belong to a determined context, they don't seem to recognize any particular parentage with other symbols; in sum, semiquavers are totally confused entities. Hemidemisemiquavers, on the other hand, in spite of their hateful prefix, are quite another matter: they are fully aware that they belong to the Third World of music and there have been countless instances of guerrillas in their midst; Herbert von Marcuse, composer and author of numerous symphonies, speaks of this lyrical miracle. Well, on a certain afternoon, after trying stubbornly for many months, my neighbor managed to create the explosion of a chord. Something was torn out, like you tear off a sheet of aluminum, and fell solidly on the floor, rolled and came to a stop on my balcony. Do you know what it was? It was the key of G, dented, useless; it moved, agonized, crying with a hair-raising moan; I went to the kitchen and fixed myself a huge drink because I couldn't stand this much suffering. My wife took care of throwing it into the street. That night the pipes in my house echoed like a harmonium. You may laugh at me, Eddy, but those noises you hear at night, the bassoons and the oboes, certain chords of an Aragonese jig mixed with chords from the Star Spangled Banner on the English horn are the quavers and semiquavers and all that staved population that has escaped and gone into hiding in those unmusical or unpoetic corners, and there they stay, fearful that some criminal hand might crucify them on the bars of a staff. It terrifies me at night when I hear those poor beings sing in the shadows, howling in disorder, free from the pillories of harmony, anarchic, trembling at the mere thought that a hand may come along and imprison them in the dungeons of a staff. Semiquavers, nevertheless, adore bars and fear independent life, that's why they're always servile to certain blues, a truly shameful occurrence which has been carefully studied in a lovely little book titled *Fear of Freedom*; its author is a musical researcher named Fromm, who, by the way, has nothing to do with the author of *Fromm Here to Eternity*. It is a known fact that once hemidemisemiquavers are behind bars, they harbor the hope that such an outrageously bad musician might come along that he'll be able to dynamite the walls of the prison. Although it is also evident that none of them will escape injury when such a disaster takes place. Knowledge of that truth is what terrifies semiquavers. In any case, you know I'm sympathetic to the former and I consider their cause an admirable one. Don't you agree?

My regards to the sacrificing Yolanda.

Akiro

San Juan P.R.

Mr. Leiseca:

If you are trying to arouse me with your silence, you have achieved your goal. My notices have been useless, you have simply tossed them into the garbage. Is this how you repay my medical concern for you, the long months of treatment which no doubt did you a tremendous amount of good, to the extent of making you give up drinking, which was consuming you like a cancer? I use the word cancer because it is a specific sickness that relentlessly destroys those who suffer from it (due to the fact that you couldn't specifically point out the location of your illness, you didn't trust my words). Of course it's not a cancer in the literal sense, nor can it be operated on with a scalpel, but in many cases, in order to cure mental or emotional problems such as yours, certain tools are used (they seem to like that) such as electroshock equipment, etc. You already know all about that, but I take the liberty of reminding you of it. I don't know if you might have forgotten that I studied at Yale and that, thanks to my intervention, the girl who killed her father was acquitted because my diagnosis proved we were dealing with a case of manic depressive psychosis caused by the lack of morals in her environment, the promiscuity and the perverse carnal demands of her father. Today the girl is living in our local mental institution and I myself have taken charge of her therapy because, quite frankly, the case has touched me deeply.

But what bothers me most is your silence. What is happening with you? Do you lack the economic resources to pay your bill? Well, that could be taken care of in time. Don't worry too much about that. For now it would suffice for you to give me a brief report on the state of your mental health, without going into detail. How do you feel about your father? And the problems you were having with your sexual identity, have those been success-fully resolved? Are you still skeptical about the validity of my treatment? The rapport established between the two of us, is it perhaps over? Do you hate me? Do you still feel that I'm a useless individual who lives off the insanity of my fellow man, as you told me on that one occasion? Do you remember the time during your

201

childhood when your father wanted to take you to visit some friends and you refused to go because you didn't have your pants on? Do you remember the conversation between the two of you? You said you didn't want to go out because you didn't have any pants on, do you remember that? You were about five years old and your father laughed and said it didn't matter, that you didn't have anything there anyway, in other words, the size of your phallus was so insignificant that no one would notice it. Or worse still, that you didn't have anything. Now then, who lacks that protuberance, who "doesn't have anything" there? "Woman." Do you think your father's statement affected you or not? Did you later compare the size of your penis with your father's? What conclusions did you draw from that comparison, which, by the way, is completely normal? You admired your father, naturally, he was the all-powerful being, a real man with a gender no one questioned. You, on the other hand, were you as asexual as an angel? You didn't have a thing there, God's very image on earth had told you so. Do you see my point? That was no doubt the beginning of a far-from-simple neurosis. To be or not to be. I'll never forget the marvelous way you solved that problem during your adolescence, proving you were indeed a boy, a man, a real male. Do you remember? Of course you do. Don't feel embarrassed. You would masturbate in front of the neighbor. As good a way to solve anonymity as any other. Nevertheless, what I have never been able to understand very well is why you chose that particular neighbor, since she was blind.

Naturally, the wound was there and it was bleeding. You imagined you father disliked you for not being much of a man. You grew up watching him work, earn his living, and you even knew that he had concubines, something which gave him a certain social "prestige" as being "a real macho." That's why you were so submissive to his words, I mean abnormally submissive, a submission which is traditionally expected from a girl. Now then the "yoke" (a word you yourself used) became intolerable once you passed adolescence, when your personality sought desperately to assert itself, to the extent that you took your father's phrase literally in the sense that "there's not room for two roosters in one hen house" (unless one is submissive to the other, but in that case he would seem more like a hen, right?). So your status in the paternal home became emotionally unsatisfactory. You wanted to crow like a young cock, but down deep you were afraid your father would accept the challenge. As is to be expected in such cases, your feelings were completely ambivalent: a mixture of love and hate. You would build up courage, rehearse a few phrases to hurl at him, but when you stood before him you'd begin to stutter; then your father would look at you strangely and typically end up calling you an idiot. In any case, what affected you most wasn't the violence of his words, but rather the indifference, the fact that you were treated like an invisible or nonexistent being. In other words, that you weren't dealt with at all. A human being can be the object of hate, tenderness, love, repugnance, simply because he's there, solidly, and is therefore capable of provoking a whole range of feelings. But a "thing," an unqualified being that isn't even sexually identifiable ("it doesn't have a thing there," but it's not a girl nor an angel), doesn't arouse any kind of feeling at all. Therefore, what could you do to attract your father's attention? Since you were considered by all the world to be a patient little pet who rarely made his presence known, perhaps you would balance out that submission to paternal authority by behaving terribly in school. When your teachers complained to your progenitors, you felt that at least they were being "made aware" that you existed. Besides, you wanted to make them angry, you understand? That was your apparently incongruous way of saying here I am, alive, I'm not a chair, a thing, a rug to be walked on. Your resentment of all established authority was a result of that. That's the root of your rejection of rules that were accepted by everyone else, of "imperialism, generals and priests and bourgeoisie," in other words, of everything that implies moral, political or economic domination. Is that why you affiliated yourself with the country's revolutionary movement for a time? Do you not identify and project your much sought-after personal independence with the independence of your country? You probably disagree with me on this point also, but aside from the fact that I don't happen to share your political ideas (I think we're fine just the way we are), there is nothing reproachable in an emotional conflict being efficiently directed toward some specific activity. Do we care that Napoleon suffered a similar type of conflict due to his small stature? Did that complex perhaps help him reach the stature he occupies in history? Fantastic! Did Galileo have any complexes? Even under threat, he continued with that business of "but it moves." So, properly treated, any neurosis can become a formidable impetus. But when it's not controlled, the person becomes stagnant, incapable of producing the best that's in him. You, as a writer and a person who has dealt with psychotherapy, should know this better than most. Aside from this digression (I have time to write you, because a patient—a paranoid—missed his appointment), remember the defeatist attitude you adopted with regard to your father when you were about twenty years old. You refused to help him with his work at the store, etc. A few years later you began to seriously think about murdering him, and you even began to formulate a plan whereby a barrel of lard would fall on his head. Or you simply wished a truck would run over him. But as usually happens in cases such as yours, you also admired him and loved him deeply; and you felt guilty for even thinking about his death. The contradiction seemed unreconcilable to you, so you turned to drinking: you felt that it was your only avenue of escape from the torture you were bringing upon yourself, of escaping from yourself. But now you know that was no solution; you were merely getting yourself in deeper and deeper. That was when you came to see me, a totally positive step; it showed that you weren't satisfied to just lie back and let things happen, you were taking the first step towards solving the problem. Of course treatment is long and difficult: extracting things that are disagreeable from a person's subconscious is not an easy task. Things that have already begun to rot—do you follow me?—and which disgust us when they finally come to light. One has to be immensely careful at times like that, there are people who cannot confront those truths that have remained hidden for so long, that's why we use chemotherapy to make those difficult steps more bearable. You, however, showed a tremendous strength of character (I'm not joking; you must learn that there are many positive sides to yourself), and recognized that there were certain roots that had to be torn from the subconscious, or rather you realized that those rotten roots were the source of the illness, you analyzed them and recognized in them the basis for your anxiety. That is, of course, a tremendous step in the right direction. But that takes a lot of work and a lot of suffering on the part of the patient and also of the physician (it's not uncommon for a psychiatrist to have a nervous breakdown when confronted with the numerous horrible secrets with which his patients entrust him; isn't that perhaps the reason why we are portrayed in comic strips as insane people?). You then took the necessary steps, but it wasn't long before you bolted. That's something a psychiatrist can expect and predict in ninety percent of the cases, but you were coming along very nicely when suddenly, breaking all the rules (which is just a figure of speech), you disappeared. I was very pleased with the progress you were making, I must confess partially due to professional pride and also out of fondness (you must believe me, Eduardo, you can also awaken affection among those who surround you and not only contempt and repugnance, as you believed before treatment; I mention the fondness without holding anything back, rapport is or should be a mutual feeling, not just one way). I say rapport because it is a perfectly acceptable word, much more expressive than identification, and says so much more in the specific case of psychotherapy.

Are you still working on your book of short stories? Literature can be a great remedy. But I fear for your impatience: you must persevere, otherwise little can be expected. I think Kafka had many experiences similar to yours, but of course, in different circumstances and surroundings. In any case, the comparison is valid.

I am confident that the birth of your child will do you a great deal of good. You will have performed a very important function of every human being and that is procreation, and this alone could give you great strength to confront the problems which arise from all physical or intellectual activity. Don't be surprised if your political involvement becomes less violent, for then you will have responsibilities and satisfactions which didn't exist before. This is perfectly normal and does not in any way mean that you are abandoning your principles, but rather that you have become more moderate, in other words, less excitable. Marriage should have already had this effect on you to some extent; if this is not the case, it will very probably occur with the birth of your child due to all the emotional gratification this experience entails. Also remember that it will please your father to become a grandfather, because he will see in his grandson a projection of you and he will, in a manner of speaking, feel he is a father again and will revive those stimulating feelings of his youth. I predict that relations between the two of you will improve considerably. And I would be pleased to have this verified. Will you take the time to write me a short note about it? I propose this not only as a professional, but as a friend (and because it disgusts me that patients just take off and never give you another thought). You have to believe me; I have feelings too.

What are you planning on naming the child? If it's a boy, don't hesitate to name him after yourself if you feel like it. Eduardo isn't an ugly name, you simply came to hate it just as you came to hate everything that was yours. Don't worry if he happens to be born under an ill-reputed astrological sign, that's all a bunch of superstition (you know: that mania you had that your father had been born under the sign of Cancer, etc.). To tell you the truth, I was born under the sign of Scorpio and as far as I know I'm no monster.

Will you answer this letter? We can take care of the other matter later.

Cordial greetings from
Dr. Winston Olmo, Psychiatrist

Río Piedras, P.R.

Dear Comrade:

I have been needing to get in touch with you for some time now, and Mancio, who is one of the few people who knows your address, didn't want to give it to me. Thanks to a friend who is a neighbor of someone by the name of Wanda Rivera, I was able, purely by chance, to come up with your address.

Before going into anything else, you should know that our comrades have been very concerned over your behavior, which most of them find rather strange. I have had to come to your defense more than once. The matter arose out of a question one of our comrades posed before the Political Committee of the Organization. These are the noteworthy points he brought up, if my memory doesn't fail me:

1. How can you be living like a king in Madrid without having a steady job?

2. If it's true that you're living off translations, where are they? In what magazine, book or newspaper do they appear? What companies are you working for?

3. We know your father isn't helping you out and that you even returned a check for $100 he sent you for your birthday about six months ago.

4. Is it possible that comrade Yolanda found work over in that country as soon as she arrived? It's a well-known fact that an official permit is required and that jobs are scarce.

5. One of our comrades who was on a trip over there saw you leave the American Embassy at 9:00 a.m. last January 10th, carrying a package. Then you got into a car that was obviously waiting for you with its engine running.

As you can see, this matter is dangerous to your reputation. We have tried to have the comrade who raised these allegations against you submit his complaints formally, but he says he will do so when the time is right and once he has gathered all the necessary evidence. The worst of it is that, up to a certain point, the damage has already been done. The truth is that your behavior for the past two years has in fact been strange, but still, that's no excuse for allowing every thought that might cross our minds to come bursting out as an accusation. There have already been confrontations among several comrades because, unfortunately, this whole affair has become a very vicious rumor, quickly spread by word of mouth. So I had to have one of our comrades silenced, as he was insinuating that you're taking money from the C.I.A. and that the business of comrade Yolanda working is just a cover-up.

I advise you to write the Political Committee as soon as possible regarding your activities in Spain. That way things will be set straight and there will be no further thought given to the matter. This is a personal recommendation offered to you as a friend and comrade.

Receive a fraternal embrace from
Miguel

P.S. The comrade making the allegations also commented that the fact you're allowing yourself the luxury of increasing your family proves that you're living in complete financial security. In addition, it has come to our attention that a certain Nicanor Ríos, a young teacher from Ciales, was able to get your address. Be extremely careful with him! Everyone knows him as a well-to-do stuffed shirt and a reactionary, and we're all wondering where his eagerness to write poetry about "the homeland" came from. He has been seen in questionable company lately, and he's so clever he managed to extricate your address from Mancio. That, too, is being held against you because many of our associates feel he sought your address because he considers you to be "on his side." Write soon. Ciao. Regards to comrade Yolanda.

* * *

He could have kept on looking at the walls or the ceiling or the shiny parquet or looking inwardly for the thousandth time without saying a word to anyone because to whom, to whom, walking from the heating apparatus through the frigid lakes (the house had been built so that it would retain the polar chill in winter and the stifling equatorial heat in summer), watching the street through the blinds, the hunched-over people hurrying by, carrying the weight of the cold on their shoulders. Hadn't he memorized the lines on the floor, the spots and ghosts of stains on the walls, the secret interstices through which a low wail of air seeped in, the corners and surfaces where dust—his mortal enemy—had established its headquarters? Large posters distastefully decorating the walls. Mirrors were forbidden, but they ran after him full speed, surprising him anywhere in the house, by turning around he could confront his own sunken eyes, his tight, waxy face, his transparent ears similar to those of Aunt Rosaura, R.I.P. But actually no, not in the past thirty-six hours. In his lethargy he could see a woman moving through the house rubbing things with a cloth; he opened his eyes as much as he could (it was Carmen, who came once a week to do the cleaning), and then he closed them until when, perhaps for twelve straight hours. Sometimes the phone rang and he couldn't even reach out or think clearly about taking the receiver in his hand, it was ringing ringing. He sank into a cold nightmare of heat, his bones stabbed by chills, covered with blankets beyond reason. Distant voices nearby, and the redundant howl of needles in his hip. Nothing smelled like anything. But some afternoons his mother would take him out for a walk around the plaza where children's shouts leapt like crickets, oh but what a hot spicy piquant sun, and the clumps of dirt falling on the strange gray plush box, surrounded by a sea of white crosses, good-bye Rosaura dear sister, mother why are they burying her, mother why. There was a strong connection between mother's hands combing his hair before sending him to school and the sun striking the back of the almond tree in the patio, inseparable things, the little bed next to the starry window and mother's hands scrubbing his ears with a washcloth, oh what a faraway nearness the stew on the stove, and the sea (God, what a sea) beating against the cliffs. But then after a while people had to stay underground. Not only Rosaura, he came to understand, but also Samuel, for example. In spite of the fact that he was tall, had a mustache and hair combed with enough pomade so that the wind created by his speedy rides on horseback through the town wouldn't mess it up. And when he was only twelve years old he stood in front of the house, watching in admiration as the fireball raced by. It was usually on Saturday afternoons. The pony pranced, reared, and Samuel, waving his arm, saluted his youthful audience. Then the rider would tie his horse in front of a bar like in the cowboy movies, go in for a drink, come back out messing up the kids' hair as he went by, and with jingling spurs go to visit Trini. A most notorious romance. In the afternoons, sitting on the benches, holding hands. The boys would watch them enviously. Because Samuel would buy good suits in San Juan, they even shone in the shade (sharkskin, a fad), he was a real man, a model, a hero who, while smiling warmly, managed to keep an unfathomable aura of mystery about him. Why would he disappear? Long days without anyone seeing him. And suddenly in the middle of the night the hooves would clatter by, disturbing the peace of the village. (He was positive all the boys would jump out of bed. Every one of them.) Undoubtedly drunk, he would trot endlessly back and forth in front of Trini's balcony; dawn would find him drinking on a bench in the plaza, his tie hanging undone across his shoulder, Trini fearfully locked up in her room. He could drink for two days straight without falling over, and when father would invite him to the house to eat a comforting stew, he would look at him closely, observe the now ragged geometry of his mustache, his inebriated eyes, but his voice would sound strong, with a masculine timbre, a man isn't born to become stone, Sebastián, he would say seized by an irrational fury, I'm not afraid of death. Several days later the kids would gather under the flamboyant tree in the plaza to watch Samuel and Trini walking by, smiling, greeting their admirers, his heels with taps on them clicking on the cement sidewalks, his light shiny suit gleaming in the sun if it was a Sunday, or shining even if it was a weeknight. But one day rumors traveled through the town. It was true that Samuel had lost a lot of weight, had circles under his eyes, someone saw a little spot of blood on his handkerchief, father didn't invite him to dinner anymore unless the dishes were washed afterwards in boiling water. Then the boys began seeing him in pajamas behind his house, listless, smiling at them palely. Later they took him to a hospital; he came back a year later, all flabby, flashing his eternal smile at the kids, once again he walked around the plaza with Trini. Parents ordered their children to of course say hello from afar, but not to go too close, pay attention to what I'm telling you, and to be careful not to play with their hero's brothers and sisters. They had to be careful. But Samuel was well now, wasn't he? Even though he weighed too much. Everything was going along smoothly, and the people had begun to forget about his trip to the sanatorium. Once in a while he would take a short drink, under Trini's austere, watchful eyes, and he went to dances they held in the village. During the feast days for the town's patron saint he'd show off his dancing prowess, learned in the whorehouses of San Juan, to the envy of the young boys who were already pretending to be men. During the intermissions he would take out his clean white handkerchief with the embroidered initials, dry his face, open his jacket so people could catch a glimpse of his shiny watch chain. Hours later he might get involved in a scuffle (someone had looked at Trini once too often) and his shoes could be heard in the crowd, scraping on the floor, while the old women yelled that Samuel was at it again, fighting with Manolo or Eustaquio. Hard punches from both participants frightened the watchful kids. Everyone was afraid he had gone back to his old ways, they talked about it when they saw him lose weight again and his voice began sounding shrill, without its former deepness. When he smiled, his teeth looked too big. No one would have expected that after his medical treatment, he would again gallop his horse into the wee hours of the morning, dead drunk; people turned on their lights and came out to their balconies, yelling advice at him, warnings, cursing him. Some would even grab hold of the reins, but finally, with a bottle held high, roughly spurring the animal forward, he would manage to get loose. One morning they found him on the outskirts of town in a puddle of blood, his horse grazing peacefully nearby. The blood came from inside, from his lungs, the whole town knew about it. After the funeral, his closed house, which gave off a penetrating odor of cresol, was a source of mystery for all the kids. Those enemies adults always talked about were there: germs, microbes; there death stalked, ferociously, coldly.

He would spend long hours dozing on the sofa; when he would open his eyes everything would go into a wild dance or slip away. On the second day he tried to get up among the words uttered around him here, there, without making any sense, movements of bodies, sounds of footsteps and dim lighting, get on his feet to close all the doors, to cover all the orifices where the miasma of the external world might creep in, blind all the mirrors, in one simple movement forget the pain that wracked his whole body, the nameless plague inexorably puncturing his lungs, the voices that howled premonitons in his brain. But he wasn't able to; lethargically he understood that the new ghosts were quarrelling among themselves to overpower his body.

He desisted from the idea of trying to open his eyes when he verified that the walls were beginning to sweat profusely and the mirrors were rapidly becoming covered with resplendent vegetation.

*   *   *

Was it possible that the Escudero elevator had brought up a surprise right under my nose? That the surprise had knocked on the door twice, oh and me dragging myself to open it and bump right into. Drunkenly him. Had he been drinking? Those eyes reminded me of the turbulent Manchegan roads, the vanes of historic windmills, the dry underbrush, the wheat and the vineyards and the inns were all there. Him too? How? Looking at me and shaking his head from side to side because I was growling or what? A good red wine from, well, Ciudad Real, Valdepeñas, the best wine in the world you know. Could I open the door without being terrified that the cold air?

"But my good man," he said, "come now, my good man!"

And me come in yes sir come in *Don.*

"No, Mr. Eduardo, I'm not a *Don.*"

"Mr. Juan Manuel."

"Listen, not mister. Just Juan Manuel, you know what I mean?"

But me yes of course in my country you call all older people Mr. and Mrs. without exception that's it, tradition, but my tired throat what a visitor I don't dare throw him out. That's it exactly.

"Listen, have you been sick? Because you've got a mug on you that looks like you've spent the last thirty years in a cave. Let me get a good look at you."

"A cold."

"Listen, you know what's good for those colds? You can't beat a bottle of fine cognac. But that's today's youth; my God, they go to pieces over a simple cold. Back in my days we had real men. Look at all my children and my grandchildren. None of them turned out like me. During the war I fought without giving it a second thought. My children were all little. Hey, what's the matter with you? You have an awfully strange expression on your face. And boy are you green. What are you going to do? You're almost knocked out from a cold. Listen, what about your wife, why doesn't she stay home to take care of you? Maybe it's different in your country, but here a woman's place is in the home. What a companion, away while her husband is dying even if its only from a cold. It would never cross Encarna's mind. Suffice it for me to say: Encarna I want the soup on at two, not a minute later, and Encarna knows her place. You understand what I'm trying to say? But then your wife works. Whew, how times change. And might I know where she works? Is it far from here? Not that it's any of my business, but those of us living at the Lérida Estates are like a big family, you see. Hey, are you sweating? As cold as it is? Sweating, my God. Man, what you need is a good bottle of cognac or DYC whiskey, then you just sweat it out, I don't know how you do it locked up inside these four walls, and the other doormen, not that I want to talk behind their backs, but they ask me what you do for a living, that it's strange that you live here without ever going out to work, and I tell them go on it's none of your business, but just in case I tell them Mr. Eduardo is a writer, isn't that what it is?"

"Transjrklatorj."

"You're a writer. Do you know where I'm from? From La Mancha, so put two and two together. The windmills are still there, and you ought to see the parade of German and French and English tourists in that land. Encarna argues that there's no place like Córdoba, where no less than Manolete was from and that other guy I don't like at all. You can buy a certain kind of pastry in Córdoba that they call Manolete in his honor. It's true that girls from Córdoba are good-looking with their long black hair and that rump that makes you wish you were their rider, you know what I mean. And with those little hairs on their arms and their legs that geez. They're hard workers, you know, good housekeepers, with a very clever wit, you understand what I mean, and full of life, they're just as ready to mend a shirt as to embroider a work of art or burst into song if the mood strikes them. That's a God-given charm. A lot of Moorish blood, you probably already know that because you're a man who reads a lot. I bet you can't tell me when ol' "Mangled Arm of Lepanto" died. See there? In 1616, this old man knows a thing or two, don't let anyone kid you. And what do you write? Ah. In Spanish? Of course you people, yes, of course. Listen, the best thing for you is to come here and learn Castilian, because we speak correctly here, differently, you know what I mean, and you sort of talk another way, why your neighbor in the next building, the Cuban, well, José María the doorman, who's from Toledo, can't understand him because of the way he talks, and a side-burned Mexican who came by said that we talk in staccato but what the heck, everyone talks the way he wants in his own tongue, it was even difficult for me to understand Encarna the first few months I knew her back in the times of Primo, can you believe it, how time flies, then she caught on to my way, and me to hers, you know what I mean. Hey, damn, what in the devil is wrong with you?! Are you sleepy? You look like you're about to die. When your wife comes home I'm going to tell her a thing or two, it really ticks me off, what's this business of leaving you alone when you're so sick! Last year around this time you got sick too, didn't you? A cold, and I saw you take up a bottle of cognac; but that was in March, Monday, the 18th of March, you had on a heavy coat, and I remember that your wife came down with a sour look on her face, wearing a yellow coat, because she looked like she had had an argument with you on account of the bottle. Three days later, Thursday the 21st, you both went out very happily at three in the afternoon because your wife had the afternoon off, and you went to the zoo; you came back with a photo you had taken near the Puerta de Alcalá; you were wearing a brown suit and your coat, which was very heavy for that time of year, or for the weather that day because it was a very pleasant afternoon, and when you got to the door you told your wife that a hyena is a truly repugnant animal, that's what you said and Encarna is a witness, because she was fixing me a Pamplona sausage sandwich right at the door of my cubicle."

"Ahhhh."

"Encarna could fix you some broth if you'd like and are feeling so terrible. Encarna spends her whole life in the kitchen, where she belongs, you know what I mean, like a good soldier. Are you comfortable on that sofa? Why are you shaking? You want me to get you a blanket?"

"No, thankjrk youj."

"It really is funny the way you people talk. There's a lot of prosperity in America, isn't there? Big buildings. Listen, those pictures of Brasilia are really something, but there are still a lot of mestizos, Indians, you see? When we got there we married the Indian women, we made them Christians, and also the blacks, but those murdering Englishmen, those Englishmen have never set too well with me, you know what I mean. That's over, of course, and now it turns out that the children are stronger and more powerful than their parents, and perhaps they forget about us what with the United States being so close and all, you know what I mean, they are so powerful. But the language, the tongue, all that, we did it. A lot of people went from Extremadura, and Galicians and Andalusians and even gypsies. Are there gypsies in America? Charm, what you really can call charm, they have a lot of that. They have their own world, you know, their traditions, and those of us who aren't their kind they call "payos," you probably already know that if you're a writer. Can you believe it, in the newspaper there was an article about a working gypsy, geez. Because they won't work and if they do work at all they just shine shoes, things like that. But in the South there are a lot of villages where they tend cattle, which they sell and trade at the fairs, they're good at that. But that gypsy I'm telling you about drives a taxi, and people were wondering how come he was working so hard to the point that they wrote an article about him in the newspaper with photographs and all. You probably saw it. On Sundays and even days that aren't Sundays he drives by, the taxi full of his children and his wife and buddies, singing and clapping to their hearts' content, because they really do have charm, yes sir. Three of them get together and they end up with a party in their own lingo, geez, you've probably heard about la Chunga, they say she's a dark angel, that's just what they say, fallen from the sky but in Barcelona, not Andalusia. Encarna used to sing some and she knew some gypsies in Córdoba that were honest-to-God flamenco singers, yes sir. There was that Pastora Pabón who, geez, *saetas*, you know, singing *saetas* she can't be beat. And those drums, boom, boom, during Holy Week, and she would start out with one plaintive note that was enough to make your hair stand on end, because tell me just what is flamenco, try and explain it. Do you know? No one knows, it can't be explained, you have to feel it in your bones, it has to run in your blood; of course there are people, professors or what have you, who write books (they may know, but it seems to me that it just can't be explained, you know what I mean). Hey, listen, I'm talking to you and you aren't listening! If you want I'll call Encarna. Wouldn't you like some broth? Encarna used to sing a lot too, of course only in her house, just a little *seguiriya*, you know. Flamenco music is good in Córdoba, it's like that all over the south, because you've never heard a person from Galicia sing flamenco or an Asturian or a Basque; I mean unless they're gypsies, but then that's another matter, you know what I mean. Does your wife like flamenco, Mr. Eduardo? You hardly hear that in America, do you?

"Uhhh."

"And where does she work, your wife, if it might be known?"

"Office."

"Hey, there are millions of offices! Then I guess it can't be known."

I say yes, of course it can be known, in a business office

whose name I can't remember. Imported products and there he is, in the middle of the living room, with his eyes clouded by the dusty Manchegan roads and the Valdepeñas wine how I envy him oh small square tower firmly there adding curse after curse because there, here, anywhere in La Mancha it is a well-known fact that curses, curses, dirty words. Him there talking and me wagging my tail like a happy puppy, grateful for the interest he's taking in me, in Yoli, in my country, me grateful but in cold sweats, him there like a windmill flailing his arms energetically while the walls were being covered with gray, black, violet scales, scales that had begun falling off and dropping silently, ash scales that were already covering the floor and were coming up to the knees of the good-looking Manchegan with his clean, threadbare uniform, young hair with no gray, with a yellow part like a path of sweat, oh there he was my God and I couldn't attend to him humanely talking to me of the sweet, self-sacrificing, typically Cordoban and charming Encarna, an exemplary woman, typically Spanish in her kitchen and her chores, and oh rude Yoli, un-womanly, anti-Cordoban, anti-Spanishly dedicated to other labors befitting a man, olé. Oh what a beautiful couch tradition is, how comfortable to lie back on it, oh dear mother olé jrk and the most aroused of penisular doormen gyrates his windmillish vanes and the ashes begin to stir, the scales come off the walls, large fragments, small, tiny ash-dust particles fill the room until the man in uniform disappears in that gray, turbulent air, the Manchegan can't be seen, but his thready voice, accustomed to the central plateau and the thistles and the cracks in the harsh earth reaches me malignantly reaching my mortal ears that will be devoured by what land, this one or that one over there.

"I can see that you haven't followed the instructions," sounded the voice deadened by the ashes. "Haven't you been told to line your garbage can to avoid wetting the floor? You're slipping. Pisses the hell out of me. And the ashes and the cigarette butts should be put into a separate bag, because when the can is emptied those butts all over the floor and those ashes make a whole mess."

I tried to locate him with my usual perceptiveness when he said ashes. It was evident that he too was aware of them in the air, the ones now coming down from the ceiling, the ones becoming a furious whirlwind that made me close my eyes. I couldn't see him, the storm made him disappear. But his voice continued from the ceiling, from the doors, from the heater:

"Of course it's a simple oversight. You're very considerate.

Geez, if you could see the things some of your neighbors leave in the garbage pails, you'd have to work with a gas mask."

I tired to locate him once again when he said those last words, but it was impossible.

"On top of that they don't pay me for the garbage pickup," the doorman born some place in La Mancha continued. "They just simply forget, but you should see the bills they get from the furniture stores, appliance stores, car dealers, they can't forget them, because they're powerful and have a system. It's not that they forget, it's that they don't have one red cent left over; you see the way they live like kings, it's all for appearances, that's the way we are, you know what I mean, pure façade, but sometimes we have to be satisfied with a Spanish sausage, with a mere potato omelette; there's always enough dough for other things, expensive clothes and bracelets, for the big-spender there are always enough smackers. And the furniture which certainly must cost a bundle, don't doubt it for a minute. Figure it out for yourself, all the cars there are in Madrid, almost a million of them, can you believe it? And it seems like everyone is in debt, but as long as appearances can be kept up we live like someone with a rich uncle in the palace, you know what I mean? Hey, can't you say anything, for the love of Pete? Are you dozing? Come on now, try to wake up. What you need is a good dose of cognac and to go out for a walk. I saw you going out the other day, you came back and didn't look too good. I was standing with the other doormen and you ran in and didn't even hear me when I greeted you. You weren't very bundled up; you had on a blue shirt and a very light sweater. Well, okay, if you're sleepy I'm going to leave, see you later. Let me know if you need anything. Encarna would be happy to fix you a good nourishing broth. Just give us a call. Okay, I hope you feel better. But don't think I'm a doorman because I like it. I'm a different kind of man, but since the war, you know what I mean? My family has class, you hear, and my nephew José Miguel is a pilot for Iberia, you know what Iberia is, right? Not just anyone can be one. Yes sir. José Miguel is a pilot for Iberia and when he goes to his village you ought to see all the fine ladies devouring him with their eyes; tall, elegant, a gentleman, bearing, what you call real class. I couldn't tell you the thousands of pesetas my nephew who is a pilot for Iberia earns, pal. But he doesn't even think about it; he has a German girlfriend who says kraus kraus when he brings her to visit his parents. He's a marvelous boy, with no faults, you know what I mean, and his father, my brother, would look his daughter-in-law up and down and would scratch his head trying to figure out how to ask her if she wanted to take back some cheese for her parents in Germany. The girl, as white as show, would laugh and say kraus kraus. Well, pal, good health, see you later, if you need anything, let me know right away. Listen, now, wake up!"

The ashes were stirred up, a path opened, a trail appeared to the door. Did a cold breeze come in and clear the room, whipping up the ashes, sweeping away the ghosts of the wheatfields and the vineyards, dissolving the stumps, making the vanes of the windmills, which had suddenly settled on the floor, begin to revolve again? I would have hoped so. But the door opened, the air came in, it closed loudly, the air stagnated, smelling of smoke, the ashes were drifting down oh drifting, basely covering the words unrolled from the spool carried in the Manchegan soul of Juan Manuel, frayed image of the plateau, heart of the arid plain, endless bore, geez.

* * *

FORECAST FOR THE MONTH OF MARCH

This will be a busy month in which your work will require more effort and much more attention, whether you are a businessman or an employee.

Business affairs will be more active and you will have to put forth more physical effort even as a supervisor. There will be times when your employees will be difficult, so you will also have to pay more attention to personnel matters. But all your affairs will improve through all the people working for you. Use creative ideas to improve conditions in your place of work. Employees born under the sign of Libra will be much busier than usual and you will have to watch them closely to avoid mistakes. It is a propitious time to show your knowledge and abilities, since this period will afford you more opportunities for recognition in all your undertakings.

Perhaps your superiors will occasionally seem difficult and you will have to avoid appearing overly independent and try at the same time to not change jobs hastily. Actually this is a month that may bring changes in your affairs, and unforeseen situations may arise when least expected which will be beneficial to you although they may not appear so at first.

Always try to use new ideas in your work, since it will be much easier for you to resort to originality. Without a doubt a little luck will come your way. The first half of the month will be most favorable for your new ideas.

Further along, especially on the 21st and the 22nd, don't try any new experiments, as you will probably not achieve anything other than setbacks with them and may even provoke antagonism which will be more difficult to combat later.

Perhaps during this month your health will require more attention from you. You may find yourself more interested in matters of physical well-being and the means of improving your health and increasing your stamina. It is advisable to be more careful with trips, tools and machinery. Perhaps you feel more nervous then usual and will be off balance during these days. Therefore, try to sleep more and pay attention to your diet. Don't allow your impulses to lead you to abandon your physical well-being.

Although from now on, or for the next six or seven months,

short trips will be more numerous and you will want to take advantage of them more, it is almost certain that they will not be satisfactory this month. The 8th and the 9th may be useful with regard to marital affairs or business enterprises, but after that you will need to take special precautions.

Be especially careful with trips on the 18th, 21st and 22nd. The 2nd and the 4th may be helpful in personal matters through relatives or new contacts you establish.

This month initiates a period of seven months during which monetary matters will be more tied to close relatives, to your daily undertakings and to the people connected with the latter. It isn't exactly a period of unfavorable times, but you will have to be more careful with expenses, since perhaps you'll be quite liberal with your money.

Creative people will have more occasion to augment their incomes, and all lines of mental work will afford opportunities of producing earnings. The 12th is a day that may see sudden earnings or unexpected losses, so on that date don't take any risks in any direction. The 21st is also a dangerous day for any financial operation. The 4th and the 19th are fairly good days, but the month is not favorable for important transactions.

It is quite possible that the health of your spouse or a relative will become a problem for you, or there may be an elderly person close to you who will affect your affairs. This will be much more damaging to you during the last ten days, a period in which there will be interference in your personal projects. This afore-mentioned period will produce obstacles and delays in your affairs due to marital problems or problems with your associates. A period is beginning during which you will be more greatly influenced by your associates and you will probably have to cooperate with them more fully.

Love may not be a very important factor for you during this month, especially after the 19th, since your emotions will be more controlled and you will be able to turn your attention to more material matters. And this circumstance should be well received since the month is not especially favorable for emotional matters. Loved ones may seem indifferent or perhaps you will be more independent in your relationships with them. The 4th may bring disappointments or some unfortunate happening. The 27th is also a day when an interlude may be disheartening. Your loved ones may be difficult to please or perhaps there will be interference from outsiders. The 9th will be a happier day and is favorable for short trips and visits.

GOOD: 2, 5, 8, 9, 15, 28, 29.
FAVORABLE: 19.
QUIET: 7, 20, 30.
VARIABLE: 4, 11, 16, 17, 22, 24.
DIFFICULT: 6, 18, 21, 25.
UNCOMFORTABLE: 3, 10, 14, 23, 26.
TROUBLED: 1, 12, 13, 31.

(Bruguera Publishers, Inc.)

*　*　*

It's a square or round plane, perhaps triangular, oblong probably. Nevertheless the walls rise and are fused with the ceiling here on my back, ay! If there are windows, then what? Would I fly, yes or but rather? In any case, how can you just hang there like that, a spider spinning its web, how can you but rather. But it turns, a gust of air whistling from the useless radiator makes it turn, naturally. Could it be seen any other way, not a rectangle, not even a square. Are you there? Who isn't? Geez, I ought to say. Why not on the lawn near the window, growing green locks of hair on the ceiling? Or from the window next to the dirt, among the eggplants with their multiple purple breasts, why shouldn't it be so? Neither was the determined plum tree, with its branches multiplied inside potential roots, banana trees planted on top of the broom handle, under the rose bush, similar to a snail ripened with thirst. Also, or perhaps not either. Let's take the example of the fence opening its mouths near the stems, behind them, a little this way of despair, cabbages, how can you? Some round, others square, planted within all possibilities, leaning like a button placed on a baby. Not even to mention the bougainvillea laughing boisterously on the kitchen lamp, not exactly like him in the living room. Or you just can't get by on stupidity hanging that way from a juicy eucalyptus leaf, they might call it an alveolus, with an unpronounceable accent this once, in the same way that it was necessary to die on any given afternoon in August nevertheless, surrounded by crabs or placed in a crib of aborted possibilities. Would there be any way to observe it hurriedly? Naively? There are voices,

> they come from all the heavens,
> from all the afternoons,
> from all the secrets
> of all the half-closed doors,
> from all the ashtrays,
> from the sleeves without shirts,
> they come from the nails,
> from the thorns and needles,
> from the name Chesterfield,

they come barely arriving, as indisputable
as a battling grasshopper.

The light switches watch me smiling, the parquet blushing
on account of the shadow of a green mountain, yellow, mangled
black. And aren't there any terrified hinges? Of coursing there
aregumentation. The handles are watching you calling out from
summer,

from the last petal murdered on the lawn,
atop the showerhead,
on the quadrangle,
over a doubt,
over an unfinished greeting for a blushingly
silent wait, what could happen?
Doors also cry
for pleasures carried away by the rains
on their backs as dry as statues
under a downpour (or in it),
noisily like a moan from a lip peeled
by the noonday dew,
it might not be, it is known in that place.

Even before the smoke managed to approach fear, hysteria,
all that is obviously Orphic, before the smoke managed to engulf
his naked loneliness and penetrate the shameful little tube of a
cigarette, even before the latter could escape and come to rest,
flapping its wings (they're like that), on his upper lip turning its
back on a tooth, long sleeplessness caused by a secret rage. It's
simply a matter of an ethereal example, we know that with the
utmost unawareness. What an image that of a match falling from
on high, dropping from her hand onto the parquet, from the word
"where" onto the checkered tablecloth, from a profuse tassel
to an orthographically disqualified accent if it might be known?
Much worse, I would say. To depart from a fatally unsuspected
rocking toward a draft riddled with nightmares, pass through the
first rough, rose-colored wave, allow the lapis lazuli to polish
the first sailor's tooth

or the second gagged cowbell
or the third extraterrestrial sexton
or the quarters of a divorced man as old
as the most recent rock

and less lasting R.I.P.
You could say no to the ashes, of course,
looking at them head on,
consubstantiating them precariously,
to gaze at them overcome by the urgency of an
easily indispensable, imprecise metamorphosis,
unregainable even myself
from on high and gyrating.

Or cry from ten thousand kilometers away to arrive at the less imperative necessity, more rather, salubriously, rocking you with me, precisely yesterday or at the beginning of never, imponderable because that's what you say, not from another category, still less, in the depths of venerable silk, still more yet than less, but less, less, revolving alas when.

And the window level with the ground,
level with the dust and desire,
level with oblivion,
the window leaning over sound
like a Sunday lashed by light,
there, over there, over the tide, in the shadow
of a perplexed mushroom in damp solitude,
maybe, where, traversing the lemon tree,
the castrated orange tree.
the iconoclast light of a Saturday at 3400 hours,
the glass divided between two equations without nails,
the ice mushy like a macerated lightbulb,
like the white of an egg,
the clocks crosseyed with resentment,

chaos is preferable only if it doesn't come at the determination of a late and unforeseeable minute. While much less, so much the worse for him, for us established here revolving around, because this time it's up to the breeze to depart from the invisible heating element, fervently unpremeditated. Could the triangles ignore this in their endless travels to four points? The fly beating its chilled wings together? Let's conclude that yesno. Not even from up here at this height, with fingers around the long nail, a hanging pendulum like all of them, not then either, sighing eternal lamp. Oh but what are you doing there? I could refer to never as a knee that escapes bearing me in mind nevertheless, furious cauliflower, shy sprout awakened by the pinch of four dark hours like the lesser leaf of an evocation and the window next to the earth, oh the grass my God that came up to my breathing, the irregular segments of the most decided shadow known to formerly human eyes, oh my God those plants not from there, from over there, scarlet with pleasure, courageously protocolar in their desire for the nonapparent, concretized in a procession of magnificently exemplary chlorophyll year after year, oh God how long does it take silence to travel from a mouth to a rotund ear, what is the real name for the accompanied solitude of a death lily, of a healthy root like the romantic finger of the heart, what petrified autumn doesn't come to its feet to reprimand the best leaves of a new spring, what vegetable dentures will clatter with lost, dark eyes, above all when, what yellow highway leads to the word fidelity, where does a recently ravaged cloud hide, empty, disjointedly absent? Indubitably a listless fury could predict it, if not, how else to call him, how else, might it be known?

> There would still be the alternative of inventing an afternoon
> as dusty as an old shield,
> the recourse of becoming mute from screaming,
> of crying in response to consolations and alien

crowds (he has seen it and I have too, she hasn't been able to overcome the decreasing panic of inarticulated sounds either, of the five vicious points of a circle, of a dry arithmetic for the deaf). Seated in the light of a memory without shores or palm trees, how could I? Above all, why? What lamentable aerial significance could I have attributed to it? The square eyes of the parquet perhaps? Or is it simply a matter of the rain not coming, not offering its lamentable melted shoulder? From a hole in the wall of the kitchen that could be moved to the wall of the bedroom? Fill the pipe with a blend of silence, light it with a doubly snow-covered flame, inhale deafly, exhale robust clouds of steel? He would have been reduced to a logical zero, shining like an eyelash, he would have simply evaded it with the same happiness of certain butterflies, stifled by the pain of a summery winter, like a countless gathering under an umbrella held in the fist of a deaf-mute, similar to a card game inside the oven of my house without being able to consult the radio or say good morning to the first particle of scapular dust, greet last week energetically, get rid of the pawn-broker's first clock with a quick kick, what to call it then, of course with the adulterated breathing of the roof settling blushingly over the edges of his ears? He would have had a single explanation:

simplify it to delirium
concretely sunken in its center,
impersonal as a panther;
lurching tripod of an Etruscan rolleiflex
mounted on a teetering word like on
the back of a narrowly escaped disaster,
sleeping traffic light that lost its teeth on Monday,
radically inhuman or quite the contrary:
hopelessly superficial
(never retold legend),
as somber and unbalanced as the last blow
that a mountain aims at twilight,
exactly identical to itself or, worse yet,
to that other one,
exultant for recognizing it as such and no other way,
biting the tears he hurried to count
one by one:

> Monday
> chair
> power
> understood
> yesterday
> suicide
> hand
> pencil
> key
> chance
> coincidence
> then
> later
> never

He repeated the number "never" spitting out the seed of a tear (a salty olive pit) and sat back rocking calmly. Yours is a frightening lot, he thought, looking at his profile in the mirror of a nail, rash wisdom, fluttering unrecognizable signal, watching from there, coming closer to the streak of solidified air, ravaged cold desire, palpitating like a sheet of frost, reducing the cipher one to a hundred, shrinking his elastic finger giving it the size of an elephant or a giraffe sobbing desperately over the absence of macadam, inflating a dream as incorporeal as the best leaf of spring, making it grow to the point of converting it into the septentrional wing of a grasshopper, the lower eye of a fly, the happy hoof of a rhinoceros growing among the daisies. Could he have known it, deciphered it without having to resort to the design of a calendar, for example? The numbers were round, similar to a bottle of wine from which the glass and the cork have been taken, but sober and conscious of themselves, bragging inexactitudes through all the pores of his bent back next to the sunny window, the worm that walks up with its umbrella in the middle of a green tide of stairs, forcefully declappered like a bell seduced by a band of white swallows or the blue lizard of a dead person's little finger. So there was no other choice but to look deeply into the very heart of a spider web? Should it be considered an overlapped, accelerated death? Would there be an efficient way to predict it? Where? Why, above all. Next to the roof? How would it happen? Alertly or without violence? Perhaps yellowing slowly accompanied by the song of a cicada? If it were to be like that, could he? There were the metal veins with their hooves, beneath, behind, next to the words drawn in charcoal among the exalted exclamation points recommending the word danger, a word excessively similar to the last unfound number of the alphabet:

> screaming as usual but admirable
> in his predictable armored silence,
> opposed to the appearance of a Sunday afternoon
> without recognizable shores or beaches,
> convinced that a glass could end up
> a kite made of red paper,
> a suddenly renounced discipline,
> a hiccough without a throat:
> worse would have been the happy consistency
> of hate, or the stringent certainty
> of zero hour on all the magnetic clocks
> of the planet Fear;
> he would have considered deplorable all efforts
> to gather dreams perforated by the needles of the
> eight days of the week,
> of the seventy-four weeks of leapmonth
> par excellence,
> frightful would have been the resignation of a century
> exceptionally endowed with statutes of loneliness,
> and even unpronounceable under the steaming rooftops
> of a word thirsting for unearthed geography.

But, precisely now? And her? Would she
remain there unhooking minutes as long as centuries
with her small navel painted green?
Acid rancor, sweet corolla of gathered belfries
in the midst of a decisive minute, virtuous window
next to the grass.

Any possibility of advancing along an interminable, striped hallway with no end to it, with a shadow triply advancing towards an inexistent door? In what immutably disclosed direction? Towards what unmentionable geography? Where, where? Oh but where? Could his exit coincide with his entrance, embrace both trees? Scatter himself on the branches, solidly airborne? Up to what point was blood an abominable, doubly incomprehensible anchor? Reasons stumbled along in all directions like whips of foam, as sharp as the heart of a mistaken dream: ships attacked by vertigo in the treetops. There he was, in the window on the roof, clinging to his chain, a sleepwalker stripped of his feet? Was the color of language round, the slowly swallowed taste of words hermetic, the censorship of hate green? Were they blows with a rock or blows with a threat, or suspicious hairy determinations? Were they leaves, could he determine it with the speed of a blink? Was he looking out the window, or through the hole of a roof crushing a word filled with pollen? Was a jail, a crack, the blade of a helicopter, or a radiant urgency being formulated among the leaves? It wasn't a matter then of simple spurs of tears, designed by a long-incubated renunciation, by a renouncement of the miraculously alive mirror of a stem? Did it forecast panic staggeringly parallel to the former reasons for failure? Born also with him, precisely fixed on the tiny reasoning of a mite, a dragonfly, of a fatally detached elytron, an artifice as concrete as a dream surprised by the voices of a denial? Who was he, revolving, held up by the numberless devotion of at least twenty-seven fingers? It was probable that the air would rise creating platforms, a stable tide that would trap him against the ceiling, outlining him, making of his wings, his leaves, his blood a disconcerting premise for the man of the future. Imprinted like an address on a silver envelope, an obscure dispatcher shipwrecked in the stone age, vegetably airborne on his favorite undertaking? Useless as a truck, as practical and invulnerable as the tail of a kitten, as accurate as a blind man shooting a crossbow, oh pragmatic poppy thread! Would he have the courage, would he? Even from before the first opening, the first landing among the sheets of October?

From inside, from his steamy, comfortably established prison, from the original caterpillar, and perhaps before that? (He couldn't ignore that since never, of course.) In his present state of mind, would he have been capable of calmly considering the lethargy of a fox's hair, the distantly turbulent placidity of a mermaid lying dead on the banks of a lake, of an insomniac flute among the foliage of the Amazon for example? The mad roar of a reckless violin in a wine-colored waterfall? The thirsty bitterness of a clarinet attacked by a hive of wasps or of a shiny oboe buried in an anthill? The swift flight of a contrabass over the infallible tassels of wheat? Would she have been able to nurse a tuba efficiently in an armchair preferred by a paralytic?

> Put the gong to sleep with an African lullaby?
> Greet the most imposing drum
> with tender tears?
> Listen to the vegetable heart of a viola or the
> mineral lung of a second trumpet
> snore next to the lazy sleep of a baritone
> saxophone?
> That being the case, could he continue living?
> Would he die warmly, with his eyes filled
> with bees, his hair covered with vines, his mouth
> stuffed with perennials, his toes
> turned into violets?
> Would he die that way inside the
> earth's most reputable channels, violently
> secret, somewhat like an embarrassing request?
> Once inside the earth would he be able to listen peacefully
> to his fifteen-legged neighbor mumble a
> vulgarly planetary hour?
> Would he breathe without lungs the secret of a
> vaguely insoluble root?
> Would his blood be his blood or a rampage
> driven crazy by fear? Would he be able to examine
> the gaze of the dew, penetrate the veins of the
> air in a millennial fashion? Could he always do that or not?

Or at least sit in a bed of telephones waiting for the curse of a spider, the grass appearing at the window, the fence disturbing his eyes before any wild presence, sharpened terror, lunar barking, dispersed terrace, disenchanted leopard on the edges of his cuff. He would not be able to, actually, occupied with counting Death's stares, one by one, its cardboard steps, its definitive cotton amazement.

*　*　*

Appel, Abel	747-8320
Appel, Ichabod	564-8093
Appel, Annie	992-5467
Apple, Billy	866-8567
Apple, Joy	576-3243
Apple, Mac I.	416-4554
Applebaum, Nathan	332-5665
Applegate, LaRue	567-1133
Appleman, Maude	339-8765
Ho, Andrew	245-7349
Ho, Bo Yok	436-5462
Ho, Byron	221-3546
Ho, Charlie	376-8402
Ho, Chee	544-9832
Ho,Ho,	332-2232
Ho, Hum	466-5768
Love, Lucretia	225-6459
Love, Job	387-8756
Lovee, Lot	549-3030
Lovely, Adelaide	435-1177
Loveworth, Celestine	276-5946
Lovmore, Antoinette	654-7698
Low, Enoch Q.	243-1781
Patter, Peter	547-8329
Patter, Ada S.	344-7100
Peace, Olive	422-5076
Peach, Lily	566-8934
Peach, Alberta	592-4672
Peach, Ambrose	678-8776
Peacock, Bartholomew	431-7819
Agree, Phillip	275-8323
Agree, Ernest T.	845-4352
Agress, Di	633-7112
Agress, Winifred	229-9230
Ainso, Justin	755-9400
Angel, Jesus	430-7390
Angel, Klaus	583-8672

Angele, Herman	334-6723
Cain Abel	847-1560
Cain, Candy	285-9340
Cain, Michael	432-9438
Cain, Lana	285-9021
Cello, Archibald	598-6739
Cello, Cesar	329-5644
Cello, Polly	967-0764
Cello, Viola	834-2348
Freelove, Brigitte	348-6219
Freelove, Sylvester	455-7241
Freelove, Fidelia	936-7485
Fu, Ah	546-7322
Fucile, Henrietta	432-8456
Fudge, Mabel	692-8564
Fuehrer, Adolph	432-9110
Fuehrer, Valentine	439-0982
Fukov, Mia	259-4593
Knight, Arthur	722-1891
Knight, Chastity	635-8320
Knight, Dawn	321-9482
Ding, Ah Fatt	782-2882
Ding, Don	462-9553
Ding, Ho	567-9021
Dingle, Napoleon B.	669-0007
Dingle, Napoleon B., Jr.	269-7001
Pear, Claribel	533-0776
Pear, Paul	243-7566
Pearl, Homer	549-1073
Pearl, Cherry	349-9062
Pearl, Pearl	458-6143
Peck, Sylvanus	322-8740
Pecker, Penny	546-8235
Simple, Simon	241-7954
Simple, Salome	495-7231
Simpleton, Uri	592-3197
Blinder, Bertha	336-7845
Blinder, Clarence	769-4131
Blinker, Lucy	469-7450
Bliss, Bruno	782-9345
Bliss, Minnie	442-4583
Bliss, Gay	557-9023
Bliss, Roderick	345-1242

```
Bloom, Leopold   ..............................   865-4295
Bloom, Rose      ..............................   542-9785
Bloom, Sylvanus  ..............................   346-6196
Blunt, Pius      ..............................   780-7670
```

*   *   *

Akiro told me the story of Inmaculado Echagüe, the romantic railroad engineer who made the run from San Juan to Mayagüez, pulling along twenty cars of passengers and merchandise. One time while driving the locomotive next to the Aguadilla tunnel, Inmaculado discovered a little house surrounded with poppies; there was a slightly withered woman at the window who, like Europa, still had some attractive aspects. Inmaculado was immediately overcome with passion (Akiro's words). The outcome of that love at first sight was soon evident. Each time Inmaculado Echagüe went by the little house, he would display a whole system of signals with handkerchiefs, hats, caps, facial contortions, shouts of admiration and lop-sided winks. The object of his efforts would in turn offer wide smiles and go up to the fence around the house waving a small handkerchief. On the fifth day of his find, Inmaculado stopped the engine, got off and took her a letter he had managed to compose amidst the puffs of smoke of the locomotive, a properly disconsolate letter in which he expressed his great loneliness as he traveled along the tracks that crossed the Islande of Floweres. After that, once having gotten through the tunnel, Inmaculado used to back up to blow the whistle with four sharp toots, as agreed. In the early mornings, Inmaculado would stop the engine and offer her mournful serenades, accompanied on the maracas by Onofre, the stoker. But passion overcame him to such a point that in one instance it took him sixty-eight days to cover a distance of fifty kilometers with his twenty cars. For such an insignificant reason, Inmaculado Echagüe was dismissed from his job.

* * *

RESIDENCE NO. 144 ROMASANS STREET

APARTMENT D-3, No. 4

Mr. Eduardo Leiseca

Occupant of the above-mentioned apartment

has paid the amount of three thousand

(3,000) pesetas to be applied to the rent due

for the current month (the balance

is three thousand pesetas).

José María Romero

Total: 6,000 pesetas.

Dear Son:

I didn't know your mother had a piggy bank where she kept the money she was stealing from the cash register in the store or from my pockets. I know those things happen in the movies and in cartoons and also with newlyweds, but that it should happen at home, at our age, was something that just didn't enter my head. For the past several months it had worried me that when I tallied the books, I always came out short, but I finally decided I was just getting tired and I should start taking things easy and stop killing myself so much. I thought my brain was beginning to fail me. And now you see what it was all about. She had more than a hundred dollars in a tomato sauce can. Do you know what she wants the money for? Well, she's planning a trip to Spain. I was dying laughing, but I was angry too, because she didn't have to go around stealing from me (I tell her that and she gets mad), she could have just asked me for the money. Well, anyway, she convinced me. So we might go over there in June. She's beside herself thinking about when we'll all be together again. I've thought about going over there to live when I retire; I have a few friends in Madrid and they write me saying it's really good for retired people. I haven't told them anything about your being there.

You say nothing ever happens around here, but we have had a lot of funny things going on. Although your mother says there's nothing funny about what I'm going to tell you and that it may be a sin to talk about it. It's about two men who died in New York last week, and their bodies were sent to their families here on the island. One was from Jayuya and the other from Naranjito, but the caskets got mixed up during the trip and the one from Jayuya landed in Naranjito and vice versa. They had been very well sealed, so the respective immediate families decided to leave things the way they were and not complicate matters. Naturally the people at both wakes cried and groaned appropriately. The people from Naranjito cried the most, until almost four in the morning when some curious individual figured out how to open the casket. When they realized it wasn't their dearly departed one, all the relatives shut up immediately and didn't shed one more tear, and they began to protest and swear that they wanted their body and not anyone else's, that they had stupidly cried in vain, that they would sue the airline and the funeral home to rid them of that damned foreigner, because they weren't going to waste another moan on some intruder who in no way resembled their loved one. The curious guy, who was a very practical fellow, suggested they close the lid and keep on mourning as if nothing had happened, that there was no cloud without a silver lining, and he said they should bury the guy as if he were one of their own and that should be the end of it, that that's the way they should handle it after having cried so much and they could pretend they had buried the real Zenobio which is the name of the deceased. But the relatives wouldn't have any part of that and they said Zenobio had such a cute little mustache and was so blond that not even the angels could be compared to him, and the guy that had been sent to them was clean-shaven and very dark and had a wart on his nose, that if he had been better looking they might have been able to settle for him, but not under such unfavorable circumstances. So they put an ad in the paper that said "Wanted, a man of about 40, blond mustache and striped tie, who answers to the name of Zenobio Aparicio." Zenobio finally appeared in his tomb in Jayuya, but the family there refused to exchange the bodies alleging that they had already mourned him as one of their own, had become fond of him, had adopted the blond enthusiastically and had buried him in the family plot. The family in Naranjito sued the other one for misrepresentation and breach of trust.

Have I told you that a guy named Olmo was by here? He spent quite a while at the store pumping me for information about you, and when I asked him if he was from the police he explained his profession to me. I was suprised you had had any dealings with one of those head shrinkers, because you've never had any of those kinds of problems. Besides, those people always blame everything on the parents, especially on the father, and they end up thinking that we fathers eat our children alive. If the son is a thief, a murderer, or a queer: it's the father's fault. I don't know how the world could get along without us. But those people screw everything up. Who knows what nonsense he might have put into your head and that's why you won't even write us. In order to keep a healthy mind all a man needs to do is work hard and all those crazy ideas go away. Nothing can take the place of good, hard work. Idleness corrupts and diseases the mind, and then you start in with what your mother calls evil thoughts. The great, free men of France talked about that a lot, that guy Proudhon who was really something and knew more than a dog has fleas. I don't think this guy Wilson has read them. It doesn't seem you should have any reason to complain about me; I've been a good father, with the faults we all have as human beings. You never lacked anything, we sent you to school, bought you toys, and if I never talked with you much or was very affectionate it's because I don't think boys should be fondled and petted too much or they'll turn out wrong. Besides, I didn't have much time to spend at home, you know that, because I had to take care of the business by myself from six in the morning until late at night. And besides, that's the way I am, if I'm a little harsh it's because I wasn't raised on any bed of roses either. My life was very hard, and you know I was a good student but my parents died and I had to manage on my own not to starve to death. I finished elementary school at night with tremendous hardships; during the day I worked as a laborer on highway construction, etc. I've done all kinds of work, I was even foreman of the town quarry. And I like to remember those times, because you would take me my meals every afternoon on your bicycle and I would introduce you to Mr. Sykes, who was in charge of the whole project. And I would take the time, between explosions, to read my books by the great, free Frenchmen from before Proudhon himself and from the times of Marie Antoinette and that gang of immoral aristocrats. Some of them, if not all, were Freemasons and even atheists; I was a Freemason and a Rosicrucian. But I was talking about Olmo. The first time he told me he was a friend of yours, but the second visit, not even a week ago, the guy claimed to be a psychiatrist and told me he had treated you for quite some time and then he hit me with this: you owed him some money and didn't want to pay him. Since I know you very well, I told him that was your business (you wouldn't have liked for me to pay him the money). When I told him that he got furious because he had been sweet-talking me for too long to have failed in his mission. I told him I couldn't pay him, that I was me and you were you (just to see what he would do) and then something happened I would never have expected from a man like him. He took off his glasses and started cleaning them and I realized he was crying real tears, crying, I'm telling you, inconsolably and all! He turned away very humbly with his face in his hands, crying and crying like a little kid you won't buy candy for. I asked him what's wrong with you, sir, and if he didn't feel well, and through all of this I couldn't understand a word. And then he started stamping on the floor and screaming that you and I were identical, that's just what he said, that you and I looked like we had been cut from the same pattern, screaming pitifully all the while. And he told me I could eat my money, that he didn't need it, that he would go to his lawyer at the proper time. The gossips, who had heard what was going on like always in any little town, gathered around and he began saying he was a doctor with a degree from I don't know where, that his work was just as hard as anyone else's, that it wasn't fair that no one gave him any consideration and laughed at it (at his profession). Then a fat woman with yellow hair walked in and gave him a pill to take and he left, drying his tears. I saw when they left town; she was driving with a real sour expression on her face, so muscular she looked like a man, and he had his head bent down, the saddest thing I've ever seen in my life. Well, if you want I can send him a check in your name. Or pay him from over there. If you don't have money, I can send you some. Don't be offended, after all, I am your father. Otherwise the poor guy is going to have another breakdown.

What other news can I tell you about from around here? We're still having all those political problems. The Navy wants the people on Culebra Island to get out of there so they can use the whole island for a target range. And Congress approved a resolution so that all Culebrans will have to leave their island; they say that's the best way to protect them, and that Culebra is necessary for National Defense. It's pretty hard because those people have lived there all their lives and they're not going to like being taken somewhere else. Meanwhile, the Navy continues target practice and the bombs keep falling on the town. There are a lot of invalids already; they destroy their fishing nets, they kill and scare away the fish. The pro-independence people started a campaign and went to the beach where they'd set up the targets and stayed there to see if they'd dare shoot their cannons at them. They had to stop shooting. It's turned into a real mess and I'm glad you're not here. They say Culebra is for the Culebrans and not for the American Navy to shoot their guns at. I don't think we're far from having a revolution. They've already burned a lot of American businesses and bombs keep going off. At the university a student from Arecibo, Antonia Martínez, was killed when the police tried to stop the student demonstrations against the university military school. The students burned that school and have gone on protest marches and have had confrontations with the police. Your mother is very nervous because she says it's the Communists, you know that's the usual bogeyman. Also the young men who refuse to go into the Army are on trial, but up to now no one has been sent to jail. So you don't have to worry. They say they don't want to serve with an invading army and that the "good" Vietnamese are their brothers. They also have Vietcong flags. There is another campaign on to keep American companies from exploiting the copper mines, and they say that if they try it they are going to have to walk over lots of dead bodies. When these things happen, it makes me realize that Puerto Rico isn't what it was just a few years back. There are strikes and the workers at a lot of places have flown the Puerto Rican flag, a thing they rarely did in the past because all they were interested in was a wage increase. There is another very powerful campaign on to give the beaches back to the people, and already the people are beginning to go to the beaches of the big hotels like they owned the place; poor, humble people who had never been able to enjoy those beautiful beaches are now going to them in droves without hesitating and they're ready to fight if anyone tries to forbid it. I'm not political although you know I've always felt that we're fine the way we are without the help of the United States, but now I think things are going too far and there is a time when men have to consider certain sacrifices to maintain their dignity. Your mother Moncha gets worried when I talk like this and tells me to be careful how I talk because I'm changing. But damn, I'm too old to keep swallowing all these stories and sometimes I think you may have been right, although not entirely. I have worked honestly all my life to keep this little store and for you and your mother, but now, who can keep them from putting in one of those huge American stores and making us little local merchants go bankrupt and have to work as clerks or laborers in the canefields? Who can avoid it? Besides being so powerful, they are tax-exempt for ten years, while us small local merchants have to pay even for the air we breathe. I realize all this perfectly well and I've already had run-ins with some people. They tell me I talk like this because I'm afraid they're going to build a supermarket or a Woolworth's on the vacant lot on the corner. It's true. That's why I'm protesting. A person protests for something, for some reason. Just like the people on Culebra protest or the young men who don't want to serve in the Army. And it seems to me that those who don't protest are a bunch of chickens or ignoramuses. I haven't had a lot of schooling but I have read the great free men of France. And I tell Moncha that your ideas are a little like Proudhon's, but just a little.

The truth is that one really gets fed up with all this garbage.

We've chosen to have the government we have and we do everything possible to help and to understand the American government, but they don't give us any consideration, they break their promises, they do whatever they please with us without consulting us and they're squeezing us too hard. It's one thing for us to be American citizens and another for them to pretend we're slaves and make fun of us. I think we've had enough humiliation and even those in favor of annexation are disappointed, and they're more American than Washington. Here everything is being done to "protect" the United States from the Communists, but love affairs like this can kill you. We're afraid of the lion ten miles away and we don't realize that a panther is devouring us. And you know the man we have representing the people of Puerto Rico in Congress carries no weight at all and can't even vote, so they can make any decisions they want without his even being able to open his mouth. What a nice role they've given us when even little islands like Curaçao and other ones in the Caribbean, even tinier than we are, are already independent and in the United Nations and all, while we have to wait for a clown who doesn't even have a vote to "represent" us up there in the name of the American government! In my youth I was an admirer of Mr. Pedro Albizu, but later I was a founder of the Popular Democratic Party and I stayed with it because I believed my ideas would become reality in time, little by little and without violence. But now, after thirty years, the annexationists have won the elections and they want to turn this place into a state of the American Union. Well, that's as far as we go. Better to be a republic than an American state. Don Pedro knew what he was talking about and now a lot of people are beginning to realize that; what I didn't like was the violence, but I realize that it was the police who were provoking violence, and like the independence people say, violence was brought here by the Americans from the time they shot their way into the country and they sent our youth to die in their wars. I had my reasons for staying in the ranks of the Popular Party, and I wasn't any reactionary like you shouted at me once in the middle of the street. It's just that I had been a founder of that party in this town and it was difficult to leave it to join some other party that didn't even have good leadership. After so many years I couldn't just abandon ship and jump into the ocean. But now everything is changing too quickly. Things aren't like they were ten years ago. I have been to three funerals in this town for boys killed in Vietnam and I couldn't help but think that one of them could have been you. They bury them with military honors, next to the American flag, and the truth is that it's a hard thing to understand. It's also hard to understand that Gregorio's son, who came back from the war crazy, tried to kill his mother with a knife. And that throughout the country there's a new crop of mental and physical invalids, like happened with Korea. I know that many other young men from Puerto Rico could die in other places, maybe in the Middle East if things don't settle down there. The United States is already getting ready. I think it's time for us to start wearing long pants, we're ready because we're democratic by nature and we won't allow a Trujillo here or any other dictator. And if the United States cares about us so much, why doesn't it give us our independence and help us to become a republic like the one the great men of France wanted? Then all these problems would be over with. And damn, enough of all these lies and fairy tales. Some Peruvian was going around the other day saying on the radio that we were very well off being partners with the United States and all, that independence could bring us a Communist regime and all that drivel. It turns out that the government of his country expropriated some of his land and the guy had started his own little campaign. The story about the Cuban exiles is still going strong. Those are the guys the government uses to scare the wits out of any country looking for independence. I think the Cubans are getting stronger in this country than we are. I wonder what will happen when there are other revolutions in Latin America. Because a lot of the exiles end up here, the United States opens its doors to them, you know how it goes. Here where there's not even enough work for the natives, and those guys come and climb aboard, helped by the Americans.

As you know, I'm opposed to violence, but they've stepped on my corns too many times. Big, foreign businesses are my enemies for a very clear reason: they can make me and all the other small local businessmen go bankrupt. So I'm really not opposed to people like the A.C.L. (Armed Commandos for Liberation), who burn down those big businesses that hurt us so badly. What's more, just between the two of us, if I knew who they were, I would like to help them financially, as long as no one found out, of course. If they help us, it seems logical that we should help them. Every time there's one of those big fires, I feel like celebrating, and I know a lot of other people in my position feel the same way, only they don't show it and even say they're opposed to those tactics. Only from their mouths on out are they opposed! The best thing any businessman opposed to them can do is shut his mouth. Because we shouldn't be so ungrateful and condemn publicly people who sacrifice themselves for us, because if they're caught they could spend the rest of their lives in jail. But there's something else, in general people aren't very bothered by those fires—after all, they're rich men's businesses, and down deep there's always a certain amount of resentment of millionaires, you know how it is. The best part of all is that now insurance companies are refusing to insure those businesses, because the losses have already been too great. I know you're going to say that capitalism is immoral and that they devour one another like tigers, but my answer is what it has always been: controlled capitalism still has its advantages. What we need is a strong government, something like the one in Peru, but that won't go to the extreme of Communism.

You're probably wondering why I'm writing you this testament. It isn't a testament because I hope to live for quite a few more years. It's that there's no one to talk to around here, and your mother doesn't even want me to mention the subject and now she spends all her time with a rosary in her hands and she's very nervous. Every week I spend a little time talking with the boy who brings around *Claridad* (the little newspaper you used to write in, and he says he knows you and asks me how you're doing), that's all. I'm not fully in agreement with the things in that paper, but damn, I'm not fully in agreement with the other newspapers either. Your mother doesn't like the fact that I have a subscription, and she has so many bugs in her head that I don't know why she's not crazy. She can't get rid of her nervousness, and I know it's something she's had since you went to Spain. She sees ghosts everywhere, and she just doesn't understand very well what's happening in this country. Not counting the nosy people who spend their time asking why you're over there; your mother answers with a lot of nonsense, that you're studying and things like that. I tell them you just feel like it, period.

Well, regards to Yoli, and you two take care of yourselves. In spite of everything, your mother is well. She'll get over these indispositions.

Papá

P.S. If you want me to pay Olmo, just let me know, so he won't come around crying his eyes out again.

Río Piedras, P.R.

Dimwit:

Come into the ring and face the bull.

Mancio

* * *

If the great honor you do me to imbite me for the speaker of the afternoon haden conflictioned with my proberbial humbleness, then what about my carreer of a pohet, this humble an sacrificial bale of tears that sings a chanson to the espirit an to life, if the great onor, gentlemens. Is it my duty ipso facto to olganize al my thots an all that estuff that rrombles inside my bery being? To just say them like that in cold blod, so to speak? You want just a sonet, das al? Enrecasilabel? Enefasilabel? Like dat? With rryme o just howeber it comes out? Consolinating I coud ressite one of myself by me, dat is. I must, as a pohet drowned in the most indispensibel tides of our islan curture, I mean, must I raice my boice in front of dis distinguish mitin of the gentlemens of the American Legion, the dream of our sossiety? Asseptin with pleshure, feelin this deeply in the inner souls of the profoun and deep of my hart, oh yes, motu propio. Anyway, dat I shud be chossen to take part in this fecundiated encounter, you see? We don eben need to talk about how we are the beri britch, right? between two curtures. The one dat start with the arribal of de espanich to our dear soils, you follow me? then it was assolupely nessessity the liquidashun of all the primitib habitants, you know, the indiens with so dancherous liders like for essample A Güey Ba Na that they say he was the beri debil hinself, no him but hiss nefew Güey Ban for who the rifel was a kids toy in his hands. Anigüey from there the race of the conquerators gave us this biutiful languach in wich you can hear us, dear frens, in the espich of the cottremporary poltoricanese pohetri and wich we all enchoi at the same time. And ass a poltorican pohet from New York, am I myself a boice and essample of the curture that actulmently is rissin on our litel island? Well sí, of course yes. The funcshun of the great languaches in one is the same gol dat aspireted our most illustratious mens. Two great curtures plugged in one with the other, biutiful dream of humanities filfulled today in the realities of the modern pohets of the great Orbus, and wich will no estop there, dat will overpass the borders! Illustratious gentlemens dat are listenin to me, in dis rroom in wich we find ourselb, what is the funcshun of pohetry? Redundlessly for teachin the World the flourescing of the polimanedic concression that we hab learned

246

with the amalgancy of the two great currents that dominate soutamerica and nortamerica: no eben the crow of a rrooster coud rring more clearer. But now I feel dis introducshon is bicoming essexially long, so I want to pass to the queshum: in this sitiashun, what be the rrole of pohetry? A beri difícil queshun to responce, but I hasten to suchest that the job of the pohet is to reflecshun asskiturately the realité of hiss most profoundest being. Diden the great Hale alrredy say it crazy? An what were his words for prostemity? Rremember dem gentlemens: to bi o no to bi, that is el hassle. But enuff with reflectating an lets go now directionately to pohetry wich is what we come together aquí for. Wich factores will hab to be inclushioned in the art of bersificating rite now todays? Secondarily, no? One clear essample is enuff: usse all the purely colored native asspets of the island and the evolushuned teknick of our fello sitissens of the nort. Dosent our litel island hab a hole world of pohetrical suchestions? Its trees and its banana bushes, for essample? Hab you eber thot profoundingly in the cute litel tamarind fruit, yes o no? What a bitter an at the same time so essweet a creashure, how pretorically full of enchantressing pohetry, mot juste and all! Do you know the pohetry of the ofishial pohet? So fruitishusly colorful and llenita of tamarindous! Recalling his infamous berses when he was nameated Ofishial Pohet of Pororico? I know it from hart, because I liked in bunshes his pohem to the fruitions of the lovetable land. It goes like this:

> Ob what fashon hasst thee God-dios made
> the bitterswit sussubtrance of thainest
> flech, oh litel tamarind ass tasty ass
> the birgen bride who gibes hersef to us
> a fresh mornin an sunk into a pothole
> ob Sprintine dew?
> Diden Amiral Colombo taste
> ob your flabor in our lande insside
> hiss disscoberer teeth an all?
> Suite-bitter tamarind, lend me
> your formula secreta, let me dreme dat
> on lassy abternoons you annession nest
> to my iland hart an promossion
> my insspirashon like a cargo wagon
> dat drags pohetri alon the rrod
> ob the inessorabel futuro.

Ass you hab seen, dat is an emossional song to the moss

pretorical of pohetry ob our biutiful iland. Arent we mobed by dat total sumerssion to the natib soil? But firss I woud like to ressite dos o tree berses more by the same ofissial bart. Por essample, here otra biutiful esspirashon dat you wil al enchoy with no daut and dat be the moss happies ob his iland inspirassions:

The see, her wabes grey like the wisse
hare ob dat great Zenica who, born in
Missuri, took the firss boat to
fiss up tings what was goin bat in de
Groman empire!
Oh, the see, the bitches dat I in
my happi childrenhood I wauked on wit so mush
childrens, almoss babi,
oh, the Morro, bigilating the bay
the great folteress bilt by dose
great, stron an hanssom mens, from whoms blood
surched dis fare land of tamarindos criollos,
an from whoms grace dis languach ebolbed
so to sing our praisses and our own cuplets
like a cargo chip an the tucks wissling
insside the arbor,
can you reconice the song ob its thine hapinece?
Our tender nortern compañion?
Your womens are suite, oh my land,
like the mangó pluck by my hans,
like the raip banana, like the mamey,
like dis citi the Kin of Espane lobed
ass mush ass nowtoday the Pressiden
lobes hiss Wite Hauss, like a jung girl
withau sin, all the nobel fruss, Lor,
an with wissdom we choss the rroad
to hapinece?
What woud Piter Martir of Ingelrran
say now, illustrus man, in hiss cronikels an hiss
hystoricale recountins?
An Abbad an Lasierra, what more thins
coud he do in hiss tesstimoni ob our
orichens an our land?
All dose ellustrish lors, repolters ob
hisstori an ob the firss esteps we taiked,
in hour times an sircunstanshials
would dey dedicait thersselbes ful-tine to dere

laborss like a repolter ob the
Daily Esspress, por essample?
An how com der ar croniclists ob indies
but no ob indiens?
Oh, if dese crisstians croniclists
waked up in dere grabes in faraway Iberia,
watt tings day wouden tell about now,
what moss amassing sorprisses wouden
dey carri in the filfulled sadelbacks
of dere salebots?
Woud dey perhass be detain by our custons?
Woud dey convers in a less snobitch languach?
Woud dey brin dere bisas in order an
woud dey bicom sitissens ob the great land to the nort?
Would dey lern dere new languach by hart
by a crach corse of englich
languach?

An here iss the big cueshioning preocupashionance: if dey
had bicom sitissens, woud dose great tigers of isstori be our
countrimens rite now? Another essample dat pohetry can also
solb such haili discuss cueshions. Becose pohetri is a wepon we
usse to take esspirashions to dere limiss, wich is the same ass
seyin we be possess by the moss elebated espirit non by any
mortel dependin if no a cueshion ob de brabe mens dat rose an
rose so mush dat dey eben named dem asstronauss.

* * *

Then she was talking without my. Jrk. The radio too of course except only music. Monotonous Berlioz trombones. And her saying if such and such, knitting a baby's shirt, putting her hand on her waist sometimes. Oh that shocking. Low notes, they displace the speaker out. Baaaaa. Deeply. The needle lovingly sticks its little head in here, reappears there, perplexed, with its long snake-like tail. And that choir? Did they say Arteaga? No, some other unknown name. They start out with a very low note. Tragedies. Slow contrabasses, many violins, perhaps a loud shattering of cymbals and even its gong. They have just discovered they're original. The world is theirs. *Rings*, by one of the Halffters. Also, Esplá. And the curious combinations of Montsalvatge. The Russian of *The Factory*, very rotund. Prácata, so there. Nothing spiritual, of course. Production, etc. A symphonic five-year plan. Literary language is a dialect. I keep a special place in my heart for my beloved Albéniz. Those prefabricated festivals they have in my country. Casals. Bach and Mozart. They may even go so far as Beethoven. Nothing past that. A Stravinsky has worked in vain throughout a century, *non capisco*. Too revolutionary for sweet, sleepy colonial peacefulness. I imagine Pau buries his head in the sand when he hears an electronic composition. Inconceivable. Let's import antiquities, darling. Chinese poetry from the eighth century. A song of the earth. Displaced Puerto Rican musicians. Starvation salaries. But any old violinist, with a German accent, for example, yes, very good, sir. And me a frustrated musician. A voice student. Good voice. Low baritone. To sing in the shower, how does one open one's mouth in front of an audience in formal attire? Snobs. They horrified me. So I escaped into the choir. I didn't have a diva mentality. Curious that the same thing happened to me in lit. Poor stupid dreamer. Transported to Heaven when I went into a theater. I knew all the famous arias for baritones. A buried dream and keep on truckin'. When I was a child I used to try to get sounds out of the tables, the spoons, the fifth hour, a fly. I used to wander around, living in a constant jungle of sounds. Tormented by what I was unable to express. My deaf and blind parents, couldn't they understand my longing? Ten years old, already. How to say everything I had locked in up here? How to show it? Yes but. Incapable of submitting to the discipline of learning. Impossible like that. When my aunt began teaching me solfeggio I was about fourteen. In other words, I preferred to spend my time with calisthenics. Improve my muscles.

"Did you know I was a voice student?"

"Mm hmm."

"My teacher said I had a good voice, jrk."

"Mm hmm."

"He was a famous tenor, but he suffered from asthma. When he came for my lessons his chest sounded like a bellows. Air leaked out like from a poorly played saxophone. Typically, he had sung for the King of the Balkans."

"Mm hmm."

"I liked that atmosphere. Art, you know. He used to make me sing 'The Volga Boatman.' A rower or something like that. I wasn't too bad, you know? Every once in a while, with my usual anarchy, I would deviate toward things like 'Heavenly Aida.'"

"Mm hmm. I bet it's for a soprano."

"Mm hmm. A tenor."

"Mm hmm."

"I had a thunderous voice, honey. I had learned to vocalize and the notes vibrated in my forehead. At first I was uneasy. Then I would tremble with pleasure, jrk. It was inconceivable that I could produce all that. A rich sound. But as soon as I was becoming successful, I quit. I probably invented that case of stage fright in order to fail."

The needle would take a dive, come up to the surface, and then plunge in again holding its breath. Yes but.

"Mm hmm."

"There were graduation exercises and everything. I remember one girl hitting a high note. Her voice opened up, shattering everything. If that had happened to me I would have locked myself up for at least two years. I couldn't stand the pressure when they would get close to the dangerous part. I would sweat. The piano teacher obediently hitting the keys, and a classmate who looked like an orangutan all puffed up, attacking 'Che gelida manina.' But it seemed kind of ridiculous to me, too. Yelling all those things in Italian. I liked listening to Marina. Jrk. If God had made the sea out of wine, I'd become a duck to swim in it. Delicious. Marina, I'm leaving for faraway places. 'I'm leaving.' Somehow it all had to be fitted in. Many of the sopranos ended up as respectable housewives, surrounded by children, washing out the most recent baby's crap, with fat businessmen husbands. While they fornicate wearily, do you imagine they utter a deep-throated *do*? Several tenors ended up as policemen, detectives, taxi drivers, pilots. What a lack of harmony! One honorable bass we used to call the native Baccaloni ended up in jail for peddling drugs. I'm leaving for faraway places. Others lost their voice but persevered. They're still around singing in radio contests or commercial jingles. Jrk. They're the musical rejects. They take pills, they don't smoke, don't drink, they take care of themselves like little girls because they don't want to lose their voices, or what little is left of them. What an amazing crew! Some of them found a more or less reasonable substitute. One tenor became a painter; since he didn't know how to draw he went into abstract art. Then he began soldering together pieces of pipe, fenders, car doors, screws, in other words, a sculptor using everything under the sun. Jrk. He calls his creations by iron-clad poetic names such as 'The Dream of the Minotaur,' 'Icarus Before Dawn,' etc. I saw some of his works. But I was always disappointed by the thick soldering that looked like horrible scabs. He should have at least learned to use an acetylene torch first; he didn't know anything about soldering, just like he knew nothing about drawing. I began writing. I had to confront the public with the other. Writing was good because you could hide, they couldn't see you sweat. And while they're reading your stuff it's good to stay in hiding. Jrk."

"Mm hmm."

mm hmm

mm hmm

mm hmm

mm hmm mm hmm mm hmm

mm hmm mm hmm mm hmm

mm hmm mm hmm mm hmm

mm hmm

mm hmm

mm hmm

mm hmm

mm hmm

mm hmm

mm hmm

mm hmm

mm hmm

mm hmm

"Just between you and me, you could answer something else."

"Mm hmm. Look how it's coming along, honey. I'll have it all finished in a couple of days."

"You're sewing while I can't stop spitting blood."

"I'm following a pattern someone at work lent me. It has little sleeves and everything. It's pretty warm. I don't know how those seamstresses can make a living working by hand, honey. They lose their eyesight on it. And they're so poorly paid."

"And my throat. I can't stand it any longer."

"I know several nuns who do simply divine work. They knit, embroider."

"And my chest, my chest."

"One is called sister Angélica. I asked her to make some curtains for me. Inexpensive ones, don't think. . ."

"Blood, nothing but blood."

"And a nightgown. That's all they do. And they make beautiful things. Traditionally. . . . It's only your throat, you've been coughing a lot."

"All that blood? It must be something else."

The late Alfred Newman. Today the theme from *Airport* comes to you in high fidelity. The late Newman. Those spectral voices. Violins, the steady beat of a drum. Oh, tropical delight. She said. Muted trumpets. After lunch. What's that? Oh, bossa nova, cosa nostra. Astrud Gilberto. Soft, sophisticated melodies. A flute and the burning steps of a hobbled rhythm. Stan Getz, right? Herbie Mann. Laurindo Laurindus. That too. Hit those cymbals hard like Monsieur Tito, marquis of the Palladium at 50th and Broadway. Drinks are forbidden. But you can take a bottle in your pocket and ask for just a plain soda. Nobody smokes Chesterfield when you can have grass. Leave the butts in the bathroom as if they were Camels, deliciously blended tobacco. Raindrops keep falling on my head, *Gotas de lluvia caen sobre mi cabeza*, what a terrible translation. You can ask for a nearbeer. The epitome of hypocrisy. Puerto Ricans and Black Americans. Sweat it out with a mambo, man, get rid of that ghetto hostility through your pores. To celebrate the last performance of Hello Dolly. My Fair Lady, an authentic Broadway monument. Honeysweet. Those yankees are unique for that. Delicate businessmen. Let us now consume beautiful musical scales, excellent for the health of Wall youknowwhat.

"Besides, that's curable these days," Yoli said behind the restless needle.

"Mm hmm. Hmm?"

"Right at home. A proper diet, rest, medication. The bedspread I had made will be ready next week. The curtains will take a little longer."

They were called rejects. They were more or less cured and walked around arrogantly chubby, limp, without letting themselves get worked up too much. They had friends and children and led a normal life, but a secret finger kept pointing them out. People politely refused to drink from their glasses or eat off their plates. Parents would tell their children that so and so was a wonderful person but. Stay away from him. Oh, for no particular reason. Besides, you had to be very careful with Greeks bearing gifts. The fat, jovial man who had never manifested the disease but who carried it around with him like a cigarette salesman who doesn't smoke. His four wives had departed this world with their lungs carefully perforated. A relapsing widower, he was already courting his fifth victim, like a vampire or a wolf-man. A healthy Dracula. A distinguished proponent of Koch.

"From now on I'll have my dishes and you'll have yours, Yoli. I don't want."

"Mm hmm."

I look at the perforating needle, I look at Yoli's face. I say:
"Also the soap and towels."

"Mm hmm."

The needle pierces the weak membrane, millions of microscopic holes.

"Keep my things separate, you know."

"Mm hmm."

"You're quick to agree. You're as convinced as I am, aren't you?"

"Since you're so determined."

"You didn't want to drink from my glass today."

"I wasn't thirsty."

"Your thirst disappeared when I offered you the glass. Our problems are already beginning. It can't be helped."

"The curtains are really cute. Flowered material, the kind you like. You say I have no taste for color? Well this time you're going to like it, Eddy. It's true that I have a tendency toward gray, dark colors, but what do you want? It reflects my personality."

In spite of his youth he's a great veteran of popular music. A combination of piano and vibraphone. Carl Djaeger? Hmm. Not bad. Latin American music invading the big city. A blond boy descending from the purest Scottish race beating equatorially on a bell. The *Manhattan Transfer* would be quite another thing

254

nowadays. A million Puerto Ricans. For your pleasure, honey. Rice and beans and Spanish in every building.

"You were thirsty but you didn't want my glass. You're afraid I'll contaminate you. It's only normal."

"The nuns told me if I wanted they could make me a tablecloth, Eddy. Not very expensive, but a good one. I wasn't thirsty."

"You said you wanted something cold to drink."

"Something hot. And I had some cocoa. What to you drink cocoa in? A cup. But you really have the attitude of a consumptive. An evil-minded consumptive. If you think you're sick, why did you want me to use your glass? So I'd catch it too?"

"To see if you're as convinced as I am."

Angel Alvarez presented High Fidelity. Peter Something performs the following Sonata by Mozart on the piano. The violin in the background. We do the best we can. Stitching like Yoli's needle, a tireless perforator. Larara, larara.

"We'll have to wait for the next test," Yoli said. "You saw the X-ray was very poor."

"And what do you have to say about all that blood? What can you say to me about that?"

"If you are sick then we're just going to have to give you the proper treatment. What else do you expect us to do?"

"Reject."

"I swear, some of your ideas! That was a long time ago. If you're sick, you have to be treated and that's all there is to it. It's not doing you any good to start hunting up names and nonsense. Do you like the way my knitting is coming along? I'll get to be an expert, don't worry. If you keep up with your hard-headed ideas, we're really in trouble."

"And then what, Yoli. What will I do afterwards?"

"What do you mean?"

"Would we go back there? Jrk."

"Well, of course!"

They are now performing sonata number by the same composer. Heard occasionally in my childhood. Someone was running by outside. A cackling mother working in the kitchen. Saturday afternoon? School books tossed in a corner, hooray for freedom. The same old sun, striking a piece of furniture, spreading a yellow spot on a checkered tablecloth. Flying flies. A certain perfume, a certain tune unleashes something inside. A complete slice of life. Yolanda as if nothing were happening, calm, her awkward fingers moving the tiny steel lance. An elephant could go through the eye of a K bacillus easier than I would go back there. But I had to answer rationally.

"And where would I work?" I said.

"Oh, anywhere."

"They would be stuffing vitamins into every one of my pores. I wouldn't be able to have a drink or even get a little bit of exercise."

"You couldn't work hard. The other nun's name is Sister Carmelita. She was in Cuba until the revolution. She got out in a hurry."

"How many times would they allow us to fornicate a month, Yoli? Will they prescribe that, too?"

"She picked up that Cuban accent and it's really funny. What are you saying? You're getting awfully tiresome, Eddy."

Accompanied by the orchestra and chorus of French Radio and Television, she performs. Villalobos directing. I could think about Portinari, for example. And the guy from Ecuador, what's his name? Music by José de la Cuadra. The ones gone by. The ones yet to come, damn. Inconsolably I look back at the thirties. A man or the man kicked to death? Yunga, Gil dragging along his long, endless crocodile skin. Icaza, now a bookseller? Huasipungo. Mansor's Anthology. What ever became of Padrón? Summer candles or something like that? Belaval on the Island, as good as the best of them. But silence: nothing leaves the four fiercely guarded coasts. Lesson: he defends the status quo. Contradictions, sir. Colonialismus de factus, let's legalize the yoke, he said. That chorus. Ravel? Daphnis et Chloé? No. It sounds like pacatúm, pacatúm. And Yolanda as if nothing were happening, without noticing the needles filling the room, transparent rock-crystal lances humming like delicate mastodons. Bjöerling? A perfectly controlled thread of a voice swelled maliciously on the piercing high notes. A pitiful bell, an inveterate drunkard, alcohol wasn't made for bathing horses. Sea and sky, the Gioconda. The schooner Meneses docked this afternoon, harbor whores, unite.

"Everyone very polite," I said, "but their children won't come near our house. Will we invite the neighbors in? If we serve them drinks in our glasses one of them will probably begin vomiting halfway through the party. Even Cristeto Aguayo, the lion-hearted. They'd gargle at home with a strong biogermicide. They wouldn't be able to sleep for nights on end, and they'd anticipate the moment of discovery for months. Worm-infested lungs. My God!"

"That's projecting. That's how you'd react, friend, and so you think everyone else would behave the same way. You have to eat a lot. You hardly tasted your food. And no wine. Last night you got drunk and started crying shamefully, Eddy. Wait till you see the curtains."

"Will they admit me into a Spanish rest home? I'll butter up the nurse so she'll keep me properly provided with a good dose of red wine. From the window I'll be able to watch the grapes ripen, readying my wine for me. That would be marvelous, Yoli."

"I think she was in Holguín. There was a convent there. She got out in a hurry. I never talk to her about it because she starts up with her propaganda. That Fidel is a monster, etcetera. I change the topic of conversation because she knits and sews like a dream."

"Mm hmm. Mancio would jump for joy."

"Mayte ordered a tablecloth from her. Why should he jump for joy, can you tell me that?"

"I would cease to be Eddy Leiseca. I would be Sebastián's son, that's the one, the guy with the weak chest. We petit bourgeois have weak chests, you know. Workers are quite frankly tubercular. On top of everything else, they'd recommend I go to mass on Sundays to thank God, who so charmingly blessed me with these little worms."

"You talk as if the doctor had already given his verdict."

"Thank you. It's only logical for you to attempt to keep our matrimonial morale high."

"I'm not surprised that you think you're sick like that when you're spitting blood. You'd find yourself some other disease anyway. You'd invent one. What in the hell were you dreaming about last night? You were bellowing like a stuck pig. And then snoring, for a change. That wine is going to kill you. I'm very patient, but one of these days you're going to see. You are really going too far."

Yoli pricked her finger with one of the needles. I saw the red dot blossom luminously. Yolandracula sucked on her finger conscientiously. Bulletin from the Spanish National Radio System. I said:

"Loss of appetite. Fever. Coughing. Weight loss. Sallow complexion. Bloody saliva. Put two and two together."

"If you could see your face when you start with those lists."

"Those little spots on top of it all. Why was the doctor so insistent?"

"You must be delighted. Your masochism is satisfied."

"Has pocket-book culture come back?"

"The bad part about it is that you make everyone else suffer."

"Hasn't Sigmund told you that sadism and masochism are two sides of the same coin?"

Have you just heard Boccherini's concerto for cello and orchestra. Hourly reports from the Astronomical Observatory of Madrid. The representation, defense, and promotion of the national interest. Administration and union services. The needle peeked out, disappeared, wiggled behind the knitting, reappeared, looked at me wide-eyed, and fled terrified what else. A little red dot winked on the fingertip of Yoli's heart. Buy a thimble, that's what she said. The responsibility of a cabinet member. Precept number 48.

"Let's see what happens Monday," Yoli says. "Nowadays they cure that as if it were a common cold."

"Maybe. I'm worried about people's attitudes. An invalid to be dealt with at a distance."

"You can't cross the bridge until you come to the river."

"What a lovely, patriotic, American phrase. But from the north."

Director general of fortifications and construction. General of the Air Force. General of a cavalry brigade. Yolanda said:

"If you were really sick no one would be able to put up with you. The way things are you're intolerable."

"The way things are and you already can't stand me. If at least I could leave a masterpiece behind me. But to die for nothing. 'La Dame aux camélias' rejected. Bécquer, Chopin. Romantically deceased. I'd just be an ordinary tubercular."

"Now there's a plot for a story."

"You can be so cruel when you want to be, Yoli."

"How do you like the way my knitting is turning out? A few months from now I'll be an expert."

"If I were to go to a rest home, what would you do? Would you go back to Puerto Rico?"

"I would stay here."

"And would you go visit me on weekends?"

"I would find a way to get a job near the home."

· "You've already thought about it?"

"Yes."

"So you were already making plans and everything!"

"Of course."

"Let's not get sentimental now."

"If you don't want to believe me, don't believe me. We'll see."

"You're awfully sure it's going to happen! The way you talk it seems like you're hoping it will happen. That's one way to win an argument, isn't it?"

"Good Lord, I don't know how to try and understand you! The worst of it would be your attitude. You'd be full of hate. Would you try to contaminate everyone else, Eddy?"

The special agricultural committee of the Common Market is meeting today. Imports of canned fish. National quotas will be maintained. The first Russian Consulate in the United States. The Moroccan Foreign Minister. The vice-admiral of the Italian navy.

"It's a real shame when your own wife can't understand you."

"Poor thing," Yoli says sarcastically, forcing the needle to take another dive. "You're such a sophisticated soul that a common, ordinary woman like me can't understand you."

"Don't joke about it. It sounds like the truth. And not because I have such a sophisticated soul."

Yoli stamped twice on the floor. She was livid. She stopped her needle in mid air. Furiously red.

"But you sure do like my money," she screamed horribly. "If not, we'd get pretty hungry on your translations. Go on, stop dreaming and get your feet back on the ground!"

My God so many times, now again, the same old thing. To have to explain. I said coldly, with my brutal throat. Dressed in my pajamas. My God, and three sweaters she had bought me. Better to die obediently once and for all. I said:

"Writing page after page isn't work for you. You have to sweat your shirt off, right? Work is the punishment God gave us when he threw us out of Paradise. Writing stories isn't work either."

"If I had believed that I wouldn't have come with you to Spain so you could work in quieter surroundings."

"Yes, jrk, fine. But you haven't even deigned to finish reading my last story."

"I haven't had time."

"It's only ten pages long!"

"What do you think about going to work, coming back to clean house, take care of you, cook, etc.? Scrub the floors, do the wash, take care of the shopping. Do you think I have any free time left?"

"You have plenty of time to read about the bullfights and royal weddings and Sigmund!"

Yoli looked at me surprised. She also looked at me offended. Almost as if she didn't understand, that's how. The needle was in suspense. Her eyes, reddened around the edges, were looking at me; almost guiltily I was meeting her stare.

"I read what I feel like, Eddy. Where is that story?"

There was no greater insult to my profession. I said:

"It took you two weeks to read two pages! If it's so difficult for you, I'm not going to torture you any more!"

"Dear God, give me patience!"

In moments of anger or anguish her overlay of fine manners dissolved.

"I'm not going to allow you to read it. I swear to God I'm going to burn it. It was the last thing I tried to write, but you know my decision not to scribble one more page. I have no talent, no money, and I'm consumptive to boot. You still have time to catch some guy who's an accountant or something normal. Maybe even a bullfighter or a flamenco dancer. It's time to make a desicion."

Then Yoli got up throwing her knitting down, and went to the kitchen for I don't know what. I stayed where I was, dying of resentment. I had hurt her again. She came with me on this trans-atlantic adventure leaving her wonderful job on the Island and now here I was offending her. Remorse. Fine. I got a bottle of wine, a bitter wine that burned my throat. Then I got up. Staggering. And I burned the story she hadn't been able to read. I wouldn't write another line. I wouldn't translate one more damned word. My dreams were as dead as Charlemagne's steed.

* * *

Dear Cousin:

How are you? I'm glad you're well from what you say in your letter and Eddy too and that Eddy is working a lot and is happy. What you two needed was a change.

Oh my dear, it's been like three feet in one shoe around here. One of the secretaries quit and I've been inundated with work because I have to do everything she hadn't been doing. All the files were in a huge mess, and there were more than fifty letters she hadn't answered. She's the one I told you I'd seen with Rolando holding hands in the park. Her desk looked like a garbage can, that's just what it looked like. The only thing she ever did was put on make-up in the ladies' room and flirt with the boys. She was making the poor messenger-boy dizzy. One time she went out with one of the clients, and I don't know what she said she was going to do for him as an employee of the company, fix up some papers or something, and it turns out that the client spent a pile of money taking her to the best nightclubs and they say even to Miami; the whole thing came to light because one day the client showed up drunk, an older man and all, and insulted her in front of everyone because she had stood him up to go out with someone else. You know the skill that kind of woman has to drive men crazy. She's the one who went around saying that Rolan was a dunce and then tried making cuchicoo with him. Of course a man is a man, and she teased him so much she almost got him to go out with her. Fortunately she quit and left everything thrown all over the place while she was at it. She thought the office was a beauty parlor.

My dear, don't ever ask me about Víctor again. We broke up and I cried my eyes out, I don't even want to think about it. For the past few days I've been really edgy. But I'll tell you about it, you're understanding and who better than you, both my cousin and my friend. Well, since the secretary I was telling you about left I've had to take over her job and work overtime sometimes until eight or nine at night. I haven't even had time to breathe, imagine. I'm a very trustworthy secretary and I couldn't shirk my responsibilities. So Rolan asked me to do the work. Rolan isn't the tyrant everyone said he was, he's just a very conscientious man, in the old style, and he wants things done right. Besides, he's very polite and understanding and even though he is the boss he goes out to get sandwiches and Coca Colas for the office people when we work late. Do you think any other boss would do that? Well one night all the other employees had left and I stayed alone with him, but I swear to you, cousin, that he didn't take advantage of me or say anything wrong or dare to touch even one of my fingernails. Then when I was ready to leave it began raining just like in the movies, that's really what happened, and he offered to take me home in his car, a blue Oldsmobile convertible that was only six months old. I of course said yes because the bus would take a long time and it was raining and he was very polite asking to take me home. He was gentlemanly during the ride and even told me a joke that made me laugh a lot given his voice and his serious face, and he asked if he could put up my window so I wouldn't get wet and he pushed a button and the window went up all by itself, and then he put on the air conditioner and he told me to tune the radio to any station I liked and he asked me if I liked classical music and you know I told him that the waltzes from the Vienna Woods, imagine, because I didn't want to seem too ignorant. I realized he isn't any ogre, it's just that they were all envious and wanted to talk against him, because he's a conscientious, honest man. On the way home he remembered he had to visit a client and drove to the outskirts and asked me to wait there, in a very cute, chic cafeteria. I had a Coke and he had a scotch, a J & B because he says it's very smooth and good, and then he took me home. On the way he opened up with me and told me he was married but his wife didn't understand him and wouldn't iron his shirts or handkerchiefs and hates his ties and never has supper ready for him and he'd have to go to a resturant, so that having a home, he couldn't eat in it and sometimes not even sleep in it. It's all very sad and it made me feel bad that a man like him should suffer because of a woman like that who doesn't even comb her hair to welcome him home when he gets back from work, him being an executive and all. And he took her to a meeting he had with Mr. Hoogs, one of the main partners in the business, because there was an important cocktail party and she got as drunk as a skunk and started dancing and taking her clothes off. Can you imagine what a drag? Just his luck. So you can tell from a mile away that it's a clear case of incompatibility and he told me that he was very sorry but he was going to have to get a divorce because love switches off like a lightbulb does no matter what its wattage. In other words he doesn't love her any more and I can understand that, I know a man like him is very lonely. But he doesn't drink like other men do, he just has his J & B and that's all, suffering in silence and who knows if not bitterly, too. Oh dear, but when I got home Víctor was waiting for me and he fussed and said he didn't want me catching rides with anyone and we had an argument, he seemed so selfish and petty with his whims! And the second time Rolan took me (it wasn't raining but I wasn't going to turn down the chance to be taken home and not have to ride on that rotten bus) Víctor went crazy and called poor Rolan whitey, as gentlemanly as he is. He insulted me and Obdulio too, who had come out to defend me. You know poor Obdulio has always suffered from asthma and he's withdrawn and what not, but since he's so quick-tempered he pulled out a knife and cut off Víctor's finger, dear God I don't even want to remember that. The case is coming up in court because Víctor charged Obdulio with aggravated assault or something like that, and it has to be looked into. It's because Víctor called him a tubercular and Obdulio got sort of crazy because what he has is asthma. And then Víctor has started coming to work to spy on me. He goes around asking the janitor all kinds of questions and he acts like James Bond with all the tricks he keeps inventing. He dressed up and to get them to let him in he told the receptionist he worked for the telephone company and was coming to repair a broken line, he said, and one night he got drunk and came to my window with a bunch of his buddies and they began singing songs like hypocrite and wanton adultress woman and other things like that and we had to tie Obdulio up in a closet and lock it because he said he was going to eat him alive (Obdulio was going to eat Víctor), and he had an asthma attack so we almost had to call a priest in because we didn't think he'd make it, but he did get over it and he's still reading all those war magazines and insisting the world is a bunch of crap and men are bad by nature. Meanwhile Rolan continues being awfully good to me and has offered to take Obdulio to the hospital whenever necessary and he said he had a friend who was a specialist in asthma and there was nothing more to be said. He and Obdulio get along famously, and Obdulio doesn't usually make friends with anyone. But that's just the way Rolan is.

What do you think of all this, Yoli? You have a clear head and know how to solve problems like the situation with Eddy, in spite of the fact that the whole family was opposed to Eddy. The other day Rolan told me I was a captivating woman, just like that. What do you think? I'm really in a very difficult situation, some of my co-workers talk among themselves and when I come in they change the subject or stop talking altogether. Have I acted properly? What should I do if he says he loves me? Not that he's actually made any passes, but just supposing. I feel that if he confided in me by telling me all about his personal life there's a reason for it. Should I put on a sweet face when he offers to take me home or tell him that I'd rather take a bus? Please, Yoli, answer me quickly!

Regards to Eddy, love from your cousin and sister,

Marisel

P.S. It's a real shame you're not going to have a baby. Maybe some other time.

* * *

MORAL RATINGS OF FILMS AND PLAYS

Movies. Agent 3 S 3 (3), There Goes the Fireball! (1), The Following Day (2), Anna Karenina (3-R), Antonio das Mortes (4), Robbery English Style (3), Beneath the Roofs of Paris (3), Not With My Wife, You Don't! (3-R), Bullitt (3), Meet Me in Las Vegas (3), Murder Command (3), Attack on the China Sea (n.r.), How I Love You (2), The Hot, Stifling Wind (3), Who Are Our Daughters Out With? (3-R), Crimes of Darkness (n.r.), Two Gunslingers from Texas (2), The Brain of Frankenstein (3-R), The Engagement (4), The Finger of Fate (3), The Doctor, the Nurse, and the Parrot (3), The Red Balloon (1), The Magus (3), The President (3), The Bridge at Remagen (3), The Taste of Hate (n.r.), The Price of Fear (3), The Secret of Santa Vittoria (3-R), The Third Day (3-R), The Vampire of the Highways (3-R), Erotissimo (3-R), Tonight I Dare (3), That Priest (3), This Property is Condemned (3), Fantasia (1), Mickey Mouse Parade (n.r.), Flipper and the Pirates (1), Françoise and Married Life (n.r.), Funny Girl (3), Giant (n.r.), To the Last Drop of Blood (3-R), Hello, Dolly (2), Holliday (2), Jean-Marc and Married Life (n.r.), Karate Killers (3), Tbe Battle of Whiskey Hills (2), Snow White (1), The Girl (3-R), The Long Night of 43 (4), The Doll and the Beast (n.r.), The Scheming Miss (3-R), The Rebel (3-R), The Residence (4), Rebellious Thieves (n.r.), The Son of Tober (n.r.), The Girlfriends of the Wealthy (3-R), Those Who Serve (2), Las Vegas, 1970 (4), The Mischievous Lass (2), Loneliness in the Back Hall (3-R), The Knights of Hell (3-R), Gangsters Don't Retire (2), The Insatiables (4), The Firecreek Gang (3), Mrs. Blossom's Fish (3-R), The Pickpockets (3-R), The Three Musketeers (2), Outburst (3-R), More Dangerous Still (3-R), Kill Me, I'm Cold (3-R), Not a Moment of Peace (2), We're Not Made of Stone (4), It's Easy to Die (3), Notre Dame of Paris (n.r.), No Western Frontiers (3), Oliver (2), Operation Mogador (n.r.), No Bullets and Still Shooting (3), Paris Seen By. . . (3-R), Sins of Youth (n.r.), Pursuit of Life (2), Why We Sin After Forty (3-R), Roar of the Jungle (1), Mutt and Jeff on Parade, II (1), Ladies and Gentlemen (4), If you Meet up With Sartana. . .Pray For Death (3-R), Without a Farewell (n.r.), Tom and Jerry on Parade (1), A Dream of Kings (n.r.), Even a Sheriff Needs Help (1), Tic, Tic, Tic (3), A Zebra in the Kitchen (1), An Ax For the Honeymoon (n.r.), An F.B.I. Cat (1), The Summer of 70 (3),

Thwarted Lives (2), Hooray for the Bride and Groom (3-R), Waco (2).

Plays. Dying Souls (n.r.), A Flamenco Toast (n.r.), Castanet 70 (3-R), The Bishop (n.r.), The Christ of the Soccer Lottery (n.r.), Better Than Ever (3-R), Games People Play (n.r.), The House of Goats (3-R), A Fixed Idea (3-R), The Mamma (4), A Small Cabin (3-R), Life On A String (n.r.), Don't Wake Your Neighbor's Wife (4), Forget the Drums (3), Carmen Goes to the Army (4), Tango (n.r.), Everything In the Garden (4), Three Witnesses (3).

* * *

"Baby, are you there?"

"This is my ghost talking."

"Ah, don't give me that. I can tell it's you by your voice. You're a little hoarse. But you'll get over that, babes. Listen, do you feel any better"

"Yes."

"Did you heat up the soup?"

"Uh huh."

"It didn't turn out too badly, did it? Do you remember what it's called?"

"Garlic."

"*A la castellana.* You had to put a raw egg in it. We must go to the Country Yokel Inn, have you seen it advertised in the paper?"

"Yes."

"They have a dish called chirrifry or something like that. I wonder if that's where our cuchifry comes from. It's food from Avila, where that Castro woman is from, the writer. But first you have to get well. You haven't sent for wine have you? It's not good for you."

"I haven't drunk anything but medications."

"We'll find out the results of the X-ray when we go on Monday, don't worry. You got pretty cranky. These hard times will pass. In the summer we'll go to Santander, birthplace of so many important people. And the beach is out of this world, Mayte has told me it's marvelous. She showed me some color photographs of a little island. Things will be all right for us in Santander because there's no pollution; the people there don't want any factories built because it makes the city ugly, what do you think about that?"

"Spain is different."

"But it's a good idea, isn't it? The problem is, I think that the port is so expensive that the boats go unload in Gijón. You know how Gijón is, all industrialized. The port is so expensive because they want to keep it in top condition, that's what Pepe says, who's from Oviedo. Pepe's a riot and he says the best part of Spain begins at Despeñaperros and ends in Cádiz. He says he doesn't like the rest of it, and he talks like the people from Seville. I'd like for you to meet him, love. He's the messenger and he's always kidding around; every time he goes out to deliver something to a client he comes back with some new joke. Everybody around here dies laughing with him around. If you could see the way he imitates Raphael, like that, the way he shakes, my knees get weak from laughing, baby. Around here they call him Pepillo, the Kid from Oviedo. Sometimes before lunch he takes out some castanets and if you could only see him. He says not even Lola Flores can match him, but he's just joking. Only there's nothing crippled about him and even Circum, his girlfriend, encourages him to keep it up. They call her Circum because her name is Circumcision. You see, she was born on the first of January. She's the one who cleans the office and if you could see her in this cold on her knees polishing the floor with a rag until the entrance to the building is sparkling. As if unconsciously they wanted women to be on their knees, demands set by the traditional machismo. It's the man who rules, the male, it makes me furious. And after all you know what that probably means down deep. Perhaps a homosexual vein. But Pepe isn't one of those, he says he's Andalusian, ya' know, and "th' whole worl' is goo'," and he told Circum in front of everyone that what was she waiting for to decide to get married, that virginity causes cancer. That was so cute, Pepe is really with it. I told him that in his country they say "Asturias, you're so beautiful" and he didn't like that, he says he has the soul of a southern gypsy. Circum is from Zaragoza, where they celebrate the Fiestas of the Pilar, the patron saint. I'm told they are the best fiestas around; we have to go there. I'm dying to get my vacation. We're going to visit a lot of places. Now that we've crossed the Big Lagoon, we have to take advantage of being over here. Pepe says people from Aragón are the most stubborn in Spain, and she pretends to get furious and it's just like watching The Shoemaker's Prodigious Wife, she's so full of spunk. Casona was inspired."

"Why?"

"When he wrote The Shoemaker's Wife."

"That was García Lorca, love."

"Casona, I studied it in school."

"Have it your way."

"Okay, if you say so. Pepe sings a song. Then he says he's going to America, imitates the noise of an airplane, and settles into a chair and says he's Lola Flores coming back from Argentina, Mexico and Puerto Rico. The plane lands and he jumps up and kisses the Spanish soil like Lola Flores herself and his eyes fill with tears and everything. Pepe is a natural-born actor. Listen could you call the grocery store? I don't have time."

"What do you want?"

"Ask them to bring us some beans, okay? And a small package of frozen sausage, you know, all the ingredients for a *fabada*, will you do that?"

"Fine."

"Okay. You can ask for half a bottle of white wine. I think you've improved some and deserve a little glass, if you know what I mean. Oh, Circum told me we have to go to Chinchón. It has a fabulous bullring, tiny but authentic, and a very good anisette factory. Chinchón Anisette, you've heard about it, we had some at Christmas. There are still unpaved roads there. Circum showed me a fan with a drawing of Chinchón on it, really precious. The inns are a dream. Be good, take your medicine, and you'll see we'll be able to enjoy a lot of things. Do you feel all right?"

"Yes."

"Oh, you're so quiet. Mayte asks me how you're doing, since you thought the world was crashing down on you. Also the boss and the other people in the office send their regards and worry about you. You know, they're really good people. I tell them that's the way you are, you know, with those funny habits all you authors have. They say it's only natural, the author of *Marianela* was the same way. Anyway, everything will turn out okay. Don't forget about the grocery store. Do your shots still hurt? Baby, they've punctured your little ass. That's okay, the worst is over. Don't be fuming around like a chimney, it's not good for you, and then your throat gets so bad you can't stand it. Did you get over your dizziness?"

"A little bit."

"You had another nightmare last night. You have to stop thinking, stop mortifying yourself. Your conscious ego isn't up to your superego. You laugh at my movie magazines, but it would do you a lot of good to read that sort of thing, even if just during these days. That banal kind of reading is refreshing, don't you think? Because if you keep on reading those monstrosities where children murder their grandparents and everything is so philosophical and complicated, you're not going to get well."

"If that were the case, you'd be in an insane asylum. What do you have to say about Sigmund?"

"Freud is necessary, and when you get the gist of him, he's not difficult. Thanks to him I've been able to understand you better and I've been able to understand a lot of people's behavior. It's easy to say a person is gross, but what people don't understand is that that person suffers from some complex, a disorder, you see what I mean? And what are writers like you doing but sublimating certain primary impulses, channeling that subconscious world in a positive way, venting certain things that are painful in the substrata of the mind? Come on, I don't have to explain that to you any more! Mayte has begun reading Freud and she likes him; especially those clinical cases. But she has a problem, Mayte thinks that people are helpless, you know what I mean, and that everything is planned up above, in Heaven, God. What I mean to say is that she understands that people go crazy, but she doesn't believe it can be caused internally, she thinks it's some kind of divine punishment. So she thinks that psychiatrists are kind of like priests who try to free that troubled soul from sin. That's quite a little problem because if then, without free will, without. . . I mean things aren't like that. That's what I've noticed, like they don't take that inward aspect into consideration, don't you think? Everything is external, you know what I mean. Why are you so quiet? Don't make any effort for any reason. Don't let it occur to you to go back to your translations, we can make do with what I earn until you find something better. And don't start in with those reactionary chauvinistic attitudes, that business about the pants and all. You know that women have progressed a great deal in the Soviet Union and that hasn't stopped Nikita or Kosygin from being real men. Later, when you're cured, you'll find a better-paying job that will suit you better, that you'll like, because I know that for you English is like mentioning a noose in a hanged man's house, you know what I mean. I don't doubt that what you have is psychosomatic. Babes, get some rest, how do you feel?"

"Okay."

"Good. If you need anything call me. Will you call me if you need something?"

"Yes."

"Why do you answer me like that, in monosyllables? When you get better we'll go to the Royal Theater Sunday mornings, just like we used to. They have good music, and then we'll go to The My Place to have a snack, and then we'll go for a walk around La Paloma and La Latina, those old streets you like so much. Yes, you love them, but you lock yourself up for months. Okay, no more of that. I have to run. Call the grocery store for the things I said. Did you really eat the soup *a la castellana*?"

"Yes."

"Just so you can see your wife hasn't been wasting her time, babes. I still have a lot to learn. Ciao, see you later."

"Fine, see you later."

* * *

My Dearest Yoli:

May the Almighty grant that this letter find you both well healthwise and in every other way.

Thank God we're all very well.

Please don't think I had forgotten you, but we went to P.R. on vacation and with all the preparations before the trip, then the vacation, and then since we got back I have become so lazy with my correspondence that I don't recognize myself. So forgive the delay and let's just say better late than never.

We finally went to P.R., It had been almost two years since we'd been there and we had a very good time. We only stayed for three weeks since Roberto can't be away from the office for long because of his work and I didn't want to stay any longer because to tell you the truth when you go away for a while you sort of lose touch and also I think once you've had children the best place to be is at home.

The kids have gotten so big and they had a great time; I think they especially enjoyed the change of having more room and being able to be out more.

Finín hardly spoke Spanish anymore and let me tell you it was marvelous how in a week she was talking Spanish again and without the slightest hesitation. Here they only teach her English. She's very lively and comes with me when I go shopping at the market.

Little Roberto learned some Spanish, but not a lot since he's a totally independent person.

Father looks really well and if you could see him, he's become quite a dandy, I even saw him in colored shirts. As you can well imagine, I was very worried about him, but I feel better about him now.

I saw Armanda and Luis and they look very well. Luis is planning on opening a store and leaving the police. The other day he was at a bus stop because his car had broken down and a car came by with some guys who began shooting at him, so Armanda almost became a widow. I didn't see their children since they were in school. I think they had some problems, but they've solved them. I also saw Wanda and she told me she was going to the doctor to lose weight, because if you saw her you wouldn't recognize her she's so fat. She's afraid it might be something to do with her glands and that she's going to get cancer. And the anxiety makes her eat all that much more. I saw Marisel your cousin buying some things in Sears and she introduced me to her new boyfriend Rolando; he's a lot older than she is, I think he's probably around fifty. From what she told me things are pretty serious. She said Obdulio's asthma had gotten a lot better and he's not so hard-headed and angry all the time. I saw Chiqui coming out of church dressed in a religious habit; she's gotten very thin since she found out her boyfriend was married and had children. It's a real shame that such a good, intelligent girl who recites poetry so beautifully should end up dressing saints in the church, because I think she's trying to go into the Discalced Carmelites, the ones they lock up and you never see hide nor hair of them again. I think her father is a lot to blame for her unhappiness, because she is very spiritual and all and he spends all his time with his business buying and selling cattle and he's always smelly and one time when a boy went to see her, her father came in covered with manure and started making off-color jokes and the boy who was very well-bred disappeared never to be heard of again; her poor mother is a slave, she's so pretty and blonde that she looks like the image of the Virgin Mary and it's obvious he's no match for her, all dirty and not thinking about anything but his oxen and he comes into the house getting everything filthy with his cigars and his dirty shoes and she keeps her house sparkling, imagine; well you know Chiqui is the image of her mother, so spiritual and all, and it's a shame she's going to leave the world like she says to go into God's service, it's a real crime for her not to get married and have beautiful children like herself. Do you remember what a good classmate she was? And she used to recite my hands blossom.

I also saw Julita Mayoral with her five children. The older ones are all in school and the littlest girl is really pretty. I felt badly, it seems to me they're having a hard time with all those children, but what can you do? May God be willing that they not keep on having kids because things are really expensive in P.R.

Believe me I know I owe you at least one picture of the children, but now we have slides and one is slow about having pictures made from them.

I want you to tell me when you answer if $20 would be enough for you to buy me four pairs of shoes for the children, two outfits for each of them, a tablecloth for a table that seats six, a fan with a bullfight scene on it, two mantillas, one shawl, and some castanets for my little girl. Roberto says he'd like to meet up with Eddy in Madrid so they could share a good bottle of whisky. That's the way Roberto talks but all he really drinks is Miller High Life beer, which is sold a lot around here. Sometimes, whether it's hot or cold outside, I have to go to the store to get him a dozen beers. But he's fine and he's gotten over that little complex he had about the cloudy eye. Foolishness, you know. Now he works for an advertising agency and studies accounting at night.

In N.Y. Spanish children's clothing is very expensive, so tell me if you can get me those things for $20. I had to pay eleven dollars for a cotton dress for my little girl so you can imagine. I'd like for you to get me a set of little skirts and pants that match, unisex style, if they have that over there.

Give Eddy our best.

Love from Josefina

P.S. Wanda told me you were going to have a baby. Is that true? Congratulations, Yoli.

Río Piedras, P.R.

Dear Yolanda:

I was so happy to receive your letter. Thank you for the information.

My husband has been talking to several people and he's about decided we should go to Valencia. Any other extra information you could give me about that place would be most welcome.

You tell me classes begin September 15th, I hope you mean registration, because we've been led to believe that classes begin in October.

Yolanda, regarding clothing and with our trip being toward the end of December, would I be better off, and of course, would it be cheaper, for me to buy our coats here? What kind of clothes should I take? Would I be better off buying them there? What about for the children?

I have another question for you about the schools; the children are in first, third and fourth grades. What paperwork will I need to complete and what will my husband have to do over there before taking them? This is one of the questions you forgot to answer.

Best wishes to your husband. Greetings from

Olga Vásquez

P.S. You didn't tell me whether they have Kotex either.

La Paz, Bolivia

Dear Mr. Leiseca:

In answer to your recent letter in which you ask for information on a manuscript you sent this publisher a few months back:

I wish to inform you that under a new threat of a coup d'état, the Editor-in-Chief of this company, Dr. Cayetano Diffussa y Rivera, a very reliable and honest gentleman, joined, along with all the personnel of the publishing company, the guerrillas fighting somewhere in the altiplano. Marisita Cántaro, who had blonde hair and eyes that were so gray not even the tin from the national-ized mines could compare with them, left. The girl who worked as copy editor, Elisa Joray, also joined the uprising, and they say she turned out to be so fierce in combat that the miners have begun putting her picture in their homes and they call her the little Indian virgin. Heliodoro Castellano, who was the linotypist, also left and Tancrio Melnade, the messenger, and old Lincoln Chungui, who was superb preparing a manuscript for printing, and they all left and formed not one but two guerrilla fronts and here I am. The thing is I have a bad kidney and I can't even carry a pin without my waist feeling like it's going to break.

That's why I can't tell you about your manuscript, and I don't think they have the time now to address themselves to it. And even if they had. . . Because a colonel came (I won't mention his name because the Editor-in-Chief who is so reliable used to call him a gorilla when he'd see his picture in the paper), the colonel came with four soldiers and they searched everything and went at the presses with hammers and the lead sheets looked like chewed-up chewing gum and then they left with the manuscripts, more than thirty of them, and they stacked them in the middle of the patio, poured gasoline on them (or gas, I'm not sure) and set them on fire. The soldiers sat down to watch the manuscripts burn while the colonel drank a bottle of chicha he had in his pocket. And my poor soul had no one for company but God. And then when the colonel was leaving he grabbed me by the neck and told me that was the way to defend a Christian, Western way of life, that's what he said and left. I didn't say a word on account of my kidney.

The head of the guerrillas is called the Tiger of Rionegro now, but I think it's Don Cayetano Diffussa y Rivera himself.

That's all I have to say.

> Severo Strongheim Juini
> Janitor
> Hopeful Port Publishers

P.S. The only peace we have in this country is in the capital city's name.

*   *   *

FROM ONE OF MANCIO'S MANUALS

How to build a scapular

Take a sheet of steel four feet long by four feet wide and six inches thick. Solder a cable two inches in diameter by six feet long to the upper corners. Place around the neck.

Supper for unexpected guests

1) A deliciously seasoned brick on a bed of lettuce. Salt to taste, a drop of lemon. Serve at room temperature.

2) A tasty fruit tree girder. Shred with a fork. Serve with slices of avocado.

3) A nail produced in Toledo 200 years ago. Serve with pimento. An ideal summer appetizer served with chilled turpentine.

4) Breaded mortar slices. Sauté on both sides until crispy. Sprinkle with lye and put into a moderate oven (350°).

5) Cobblestone filling au gratin. To be served on a grilled sheet of zinc.

6) Ground crystal in a Galician plumbing sauce. To be served with mahogany filets in vinagrette sauce or well done hinges in hydrochloric sauce.

(Any one of the above delicious gourmet dishes can be accompanied with famous French Bruyère or Rochefoucault cheeses.)

* * *

"If I could make a fiddler play on the roofs of a village, if I could put a huge plate of fish in a lonely street of a town, but I can't. A bride can make a groom go into orbit with a kiss, but I'm not even him or you. Would you have to be Hebrew? For example Archibald the Park Avenue intellectual. The woman who gave you her seat on the bus to Vigo? He was going in circles but he got there. The driver stopped and he began shaving, it attracted too much attention and wasn't practical. He put a garland around the steering wheel, lace on the mirror, a tablecloth on the dashboard, a rug, and then the powder and hairdo; a bachelor who took care of his nails and his health; he lived in his mobile room, but the walls were pierced by the stars of the passengers who had invaded his privacy. He had religious prints on the windshield and a crucifix. Doesn't the Escudero elevator get stuck every so often? The walls are peeling, the doors squeak, will the ceiling fall in on us? The fuses blow, the light bulbs burn out, everything is falling apart in this building and going back to the earth, the mud, its original dust. Oh, that's the worldly aspect, the mortal part, what does that matter? It's nothing more than a passing through, a minute on Earth. What's important is the other, the salvation of the soul. Look at the nail they used to put up the crucifix, there hasn't been a catastrophe that could get it out."

"Are you comfortable there?"

"We do the best we can, sister. Very comfortable."

"Some of your ideas," I said, pushing aside the trouser legs, the slips, the sweaters that were piling up over my head. "I see you're never going to change, love."

"I never had a better seat. What's under me?"

"Dirty shirts, sweaters, socks, sheets. The worst of it is the poor light. Shall I open the door a little?"

"Leave it the way it is, honey. You like to contradict me. There's enough light. Can't you see me?"

"Sort of, a shape anyway. I can't see your expression very well."

"Marc Chagall couldn't either. Nor could Theresa of Avila or Akiro Crappanels, the famous muralist. It would be wonderful to have wandered around Zaragoza. Potocki resurrected. And Poe? Anyway it doesn't matter at all. Absolutely not at all, is that what you're supposed to say? The strangest thing is that they had built the whole building on the cracked mirror in the basement, with curtains. Was the doorman Italian or Yugoslav or Japanese?"

"Are you talking about New York?"

"Eight floors without any heating and the words came off the walls. The humidity. I would have died there too."

"Go ahead."

"Don't give me that tolerant face of yours. It doesn't make any difference to me. One morning it snowed. It was the first of December, I'll never forget it. A car burned up right across the street. It bellowed all night long."

"It had an alarm."

"Hair-raising. A car bellowing like a bonze."

A trouser leg moves like a pendulum between us; I move it to see Eddy's face. I say:

"Let me know when you get tired of being here, babes."

"I wonder what's become of our three sexy neighbors. The blondes."

"The Danish girls? One got married to a Hindu with a strange name."

"Masanajanara Mejorana."

I can't stand it, I laugh so hard I almost pee on myself. That's exactly the way it sounded. I say:

"Whatever it was. Would you like to go back there?"

Eddy looks at me intently; he doesn't say anything, he puts his chin on his knees and encircles them with his arms.

"It's a great city in spite of everything," I say. "They have everything; from fabulous Lincoln Center to the Metropolitan Museum. We weren't so bad off when you really think about it."

"The Statue of Liberty is pointing up with her middle finger, a typical Yankee gesture, as if she were saying 'up yours coming-from-behind.' "

I'm laughing so hard I can't stand it, I'm almost peeing on myself, man, what a card. I say:

"It's not a finger, it's a torch."

"What would Marc Chagall think? It was a poor French joke. Baby, do you remember Akiro's terrible stories? Manuel the primitive painter in the Metropolitan Museum of Art. New York City. Manuel doesn't know English. He had stuffed himself, because you know how he eats, and his insides had turned to water. He goes up to a guard and says: 'Sir, where is the toilet?' The man exclaimed: 'Oh, Gainsborough,' and took him to the English painter's work. Manuel was exploding. He yelled: 'The water closet, the water closet!' and the guy took him to Hokusai's paintings. Manuel said: 'Sir, I'm going to crap.' The guy took him to the room dedicated to Chagall. Finally he left a small pyramid behind an Egyptian sarcophagus.

I can't stand it, man, tears are streaming down my face. I say:

"Baby, the view from the Statue is magnificent. Better than from the Empire State."

"Archibald lived right in the middle of a million Puerto Ricans. But he didn't learn a thing from that source. He relied on *West Side Story*."

"Bernstein captured something, didn't he? A certain dignity."

"Don't talk to me about that despicable peddler. He didn't capture one shit. Only the money at the box office."

"Well, it was only a musical."

"Lets change the subject."

"Whatever you want. But it's true that the view from the Statue is amazing. No one can change my mind about that."

"You'll have to go to the top of the Himalayas also. We'll move to Nepal, an earthly paradise. We'll spend our lives in a convent eating hallucinogenic herbs and drinking yak milk. We could interview the abominable snowman for Life magazine since they pay so well. I would have a strict diet of self-flagellation. For example, read three warm chapters of *The Brothers Karamazov* before my herb breakfast; before my lunch of roots devour several chapters of Papini's *Finished Man*; before my supper of leaves take in one of Schnitzler's stories or Sábato's *Report on the Blind* you like so well. On days of total abstention I'd consume books with stimulating titles like *The Agony of Christianity*, *The Twilight of Philosophers*, *The Decadence of the West*. Combine Lautréamont with Vargas Vila, Malaparte and Sade. Archibald used to say that someday he'd travel to those places. Probably via LSD in the comfort of his bachelor pad."

"He was a snob."

"He is, he hasn't died."

"Eddy, babes, are you happy?"

"I said he hasn't died."

"I'm talking about the scare we had. Your illness. I think it was psychosomatic. My God the world was crashing down on us."

"Maybe. Unfathomable is the word. What a mystery."

"You have to follow the doctor's advice."

"Yes," he answered obediently, good boy that he was, a wonderful boy, obedient and all. Yes, he said, nodding his head up and down.

"And you made a big drama out of everything. You could already see yourself in a sanatorium. And you didn't want to believe that I'd stay with you. Couldn't you believe it?"

"No I couldn't, not really."

"Hey, but I'm your wife. Can't you understand that? Saint Paul aside, that's the way I felt. I couldn't leave you alone."

"Everything is cold in the city, the song goes. Listen. I haven't found a better spot in the house than this one."

"You see I want to please you any way I can, honey," I replied. I pushed aside the clothes that fell on my head to be able to look at him. "You didn't trust me anymore. Do you remember how we met? In the park." Eddy looked at me shaking his head, his knees up against his chest.

"It was on the bus," he said

"I was eating an ice cream, do you remember?"

"It was on the bus. The old man with the thread on his lapel."

I move the pants leg that falls over my eyebrow. It's dark but at least I can see the light in his eyes. In any case the door isn't completely shut and some light comes through.

"What are you talking about, baby? The old man. . .?" Eddypus trembles. I can see it clearly. He said:

"A thread on his lapel, a horrible thing."

I realized what was going on. I laughed quietly so as not to disturb him. "Yes, what a lapel," I say. "The woman seated in front of us. She had on a white skirt and a red thread on her thigh. I don't want to think about the commotion. They wanted to put you in jail, luckily Olmo interceded."

Eddy growled, but he was calm. Perhaps a little confused, perplexed.

"Aren't those bastards going to put on the heat?" he says. "We're going to freeze."

"There's nothing wrong with the heat, baby. It's inevitable to be thinking about your own country on days like these. There's no winter there."

"They'll impose it one of these days."

I laugh saying:

"The annexationists?"

"Well, of course, who else?"

"When we get back there you'll be okay."

"I'm okay now."

"I mean those shots for your allergy."

"What irritates the hell out of me is your mania about 'when we get back there.' "

"Some day we'll get tired of this voluntary exile."

"It's not all that voluntary. Pressures. That letter from Mancio. He shouldn't have been so rude."

I stroked his hand that was holding an undershirt or a sweater. I took a shoe out from under me and put it to one side. I said:

"It was a joke."

"Don't defend him so much."

"I'm not defending him. I'm just trying to be objective, that's all."

"Your objectivity always goes against me."

"You don't seem happy, Eddy. When really you should be jumping for joy."

"List the reasons, darling."

"The X-ray."

"Oh."

"Wasn't that our biggest worry? My God, I seemed calm on the surface, but inside. . . And you're not happy. At least that's the way it seems."

Eddy put his chin on his knees. Thinking again, thinking, thinking, my God. I said to him:

"Get rid of all those thoughts. Get rid of them, for God's sake. Stop torturing yourself. You're your own worst enemy. Think about how happy you should be. But when I gave you the news, you didn't say a word. I thought you would hug me, run all through the house like a madman, since you had been so worried that it even created problems between the two of us. Didn't you feel anything?"

"Sort of a void."

"Oh, you're impossible! My God, baby, what did you want, to be consumptive? Were you happy about the disease?"

Eddy didn't look at me; he was playing with a piece of clothing. I said:

"That's the way it is, huh? You felt a void, what a revelation!"

"Baby, before going to Nepal, maybe we could spend some time in Finland."

"That would be interesting. But there it's really cold. To begin with, we don't know the language. And they tell me the people. . . Here people care about their fellow man, babes. It's our own language, our own idiosyncrasy. There was no big adjustment when we moved here."

"Don't insult the Spaniards, honey."

"You can really be hateful. Stop trying to run."

"You know about everything from reading a few little books.

But it's more complicated than that."

"Then don't believe a word I say. Moving to Finland means going farther away from Puerto Rico, but only geographically, you'd better understand that once and for all."

"While we're making our travel plans, at least take care of the post office. Will you do that for me, honey?"

"But it's absurd, Eddy! Don't you realize that? That business of going to the Post Office to say we've changed our address must be a crime, and we'd have to list a false address. It must be forbidden. I don't know how you can think of such a wild idea. Who knows if they might even be able to deport us. I can't hide or burn the letters that come to us like you ask either. They're things we need. I don't plan on breaking off with my friends or my country."

Eddy laughed, cleared his throat and said:

"Which is my country?"

Good Lord! When he got like that, mean, sour, I hated him.

"Not the telephone either," I said. "We need it."

"Not at all."

"I call you every day, don't I?"

"That's true. The bad thing is that you're not the only one who calls."

"Oh, some compatriot every now and then who. . ."

I stopped because Eddy's eyes were glaring at me.

"Fine," he answered. "Isn't that reason enough?"

"Eddy, love, they're not enemies. They want to know you, they're friends, can't you understand that? You shouldn't have done that to. . .What's his name?"

"I don't know what you're talking about."

"You do too. Oh, yes. Ríos, Nicanor Ríos. He had written you and as soon as he got to Madrid you were the first person he called. You should have thought that poor guy was probably lost. You should have helped him."

"I don't know him."

"You were rude, admit it. When he called you on the phone."

"Me, rude?"

"That business about telling him that you weren't Eduardo Leiseca but Hernán Cortés. That was brutal. Well, shall we get out of this cell?"

"It's cold."

"It would be worse in Finland. The bad thing is that we've piled the dirty clothes next to the clean ones. It doesn't smell very good."

"You leave if you want to. I'm perfectly fine here."

284

"I'll stay. A little odor won't hurt me. I wonder what poor Nicanor Ríos thought."

Eddy laughed odiously spiteful. I said:

"He probably thinks you're a snob or you're crazy."

"What do I care what he thinks? Do I care about what that guy who wrote calling me comrade thinks? I could have vomited with the greatest ease. If those are comrades, imagine the rest."

"Miguel? He's a gossip. Everyone knows that. He had invented everything he wrote you. It's incredible that you didn't know that."

"I don't care, you understand, Yoli? Whatever it is, I don't care. I don't want to remember those people. We'll be safe in Helsinki. Then on to Nepal."

"Safe! Everything is taken care of with that word. Hey, look, I think this is the pair of pants you had lost, pure virgin wool. It would be funny for you to answer Mancio's letter like you know how, with just one word. Crush him, babes, but don't insult him. It's only a joke. Let's see who's the more clever."

"I have nothing to say to him."

"You probably have a lot; that you don't want to is something else again."

"He's guilty, guilty."

"Can't you talk less dramatically? You really act like the white knight."

"I aimed, that's the truth," Eddy said. "It was a pellet gun. No. A twenty-two caliber rifle. But I didn't shoot, so I didn't kill him. Mancio pulled the trigger."

Madrid, March–December, 1970